Witness Protection 9
S.N.A.F.U.

Holly Copella

ISBN:
ISBN-13: 978-1-947694-22-4

To Attila Hajnal -
My favorite Szekler Warrior and for
providing inspiration for my beloved Zack
&
To Robert Tyler -
For answering all my "stupid questions" so
the FBI won't question my browser history

ACKNOWLEDGMENTS

Copella Books: First Paperback Edition 2021
Cover Artist: Daniela Owergoor
Dani-owergoor.deviantart.com
Model by Grafvision
Model: Attila Hajnal
Stock Photography by NeoStock www.neo-stock.com
Printed by KDP, an Amazon.com Company

PUBLISHER'S NOTE

Chapter 1

Colorado, eleven o'clock in the morning Mountain Time. The mansion's security office wasn't much larger than a closet with bland walls containing security monitors, a small desk facing them, and no windows. A moderately heavyset guard in his late thirties sat at the desk with his back to the door directly behind the swivel chair. The many monitors revealed different locations around the estate. Since there were more security cameras than there were monitors, the images shifted from location to location every few seconds. The security guard dressed in a dark gray uniform barely scanned the monitors before him. Most rooms within the mansion were empty, and there appeared to be nothing going on anywhere around the estate. The guard drank his second cup of coffee while flipping through a magazine on the desk before him. There was a light knocking on the door directly behind the guard.

"It's open," he called out with little care or concern, having seen his visitor approaching within the corridor before he ever reached the office door.

The door opened, nearly clipping the swivel chair, and the mansion's newest security guard entered. The guard, Bogart, was a tall, well-built man in his late twenties. The charming country boy was 'hunky actor' handsome with flowing golden-brown hair and sideburns that were a shade darker.   Since he was one of the mansion guards, he didn't need to dress in uniform like those who worked in the office.   He dressed casually in jeans, a light blue flannel shirt, and his worn cowboy boots.

"You bored too?" the guard in front of the monitors teased the new guy.

Bogart sat on the edge of the security desk and watched the monitors showing the various locations within the mansion. Although there were none in the bedrooms, cameras were set up in most of the corridors and the common areas.   There were also many outside the mansion, including the front acreage, the back property, the swimming pool, and the detached, eight-car garage.

"That has got to be the best security system I've seen in a long time," Bogart informed the guard seated behind the monitors, "and I've seen my share."

"Not only can I rotate the camera," the guard informed him while grinning, "but I can zoom in as well."

"How close can you get?" Bogart asked and eyed the monitors with a little more than a passing interest.   He seemed to be secretly gauging the camera range around the estate.

The guard chuckled and chose the pool and patio area out back where a beautiful young woman in a bikini was sunning herself on a large, round lounge bed.   The young woman at poolside, Zoey, was possibly in her early twenties, if that.   She was a petite, slender woman with her long dark hair cascading down her bikini-clad chest to her large, firm breasts.   She was a vision to behold.   The guard zoomed in on the young woman's cleavage, getting surprisingly close.   Bogart chuckled at the camera's ability to zoom in and shook his head.

"I'm guessing this job has its perks, huh?" Bogart teased and then indicated the attractive, young woman.   "Better not let the boss catch you sneaking a peek at his daughter.   Reeves will have your head for sure."

"When a man is stuck in this room all day," the guard announced, "he has to find ways to entertain himself."

"No volume, though, huh?"

"No, there's no way to listen in on conversations," the guard replied and frowned. "Some of the things I've seen would have been incredible with dialogue."

Bogart tapped the one screen in the lounge with a gorgeous woman not much older than the boss's daughter. "I'd love to be a fly on the wall with some of *her* more heated conversations with the staff. The boss's new, young wife is quite the spitfire."

"That she is," the guard replied.

The boss's wife, Casandra, seen on the lounge camera, was the classic trophy wife from her perfectly bleached, long blonde hair to her high-quality boob job. She was never seen without perfectly applied makeup, slinky clothes that revealed more than enough of her assets, and stiletto heels. In the six weeks Bogart had been working at the mansion, he'd never seen Casandra in the same clothes or possibly even the same shoes. Whether it was first thing in the morning, relaxing at poolside, or dining with her millionaire husband, she was always dressed to kill.

"Between us," the guard reported and cast a sly look at Bogart. "I'm convinced Casandra is getting it on with the boss's second in command."

Bogart cocked his head and eyed the guard, who now smirked and leaned back in his chair. The guard grinned and nodded, confirming what Bogart was thinking.

"Casandra and Decker?" Bogart asked with surprise, then appeared curious. "Have you said anything to the boss?"

The guard suddenly laughed and sat forward. "Hey, you mind your own business around here," he insisted. "You'll live longer. I cause waves for Decker, and he takes it out on me. You don't mess with these guys. I don't make enough to risk my life."

"I hear you," Bogart announced. He continued to scan the monitors then noticed something interesting. He pointed to the lower screen. "What's that?"

The guard focused on the image and rotated the camera. Once he did, they could easily see a man with a hood over his head. He was tied to a sturdy chair in a bland room with stone walls and a concrete floor. Judging by the walls and floor, the room was located in the basement.

The guard groaned and shook his head. "That's another one of those things we pretend we don't see around here," the guard informed him. "No idea who the poor bastard is, but he won't be there in the morning, that's for sure."

Bogart stared at the screen a moment longer, but he couldn't identify the prisoner with the hood over his head. Bogart then nodded and managed a tiny smirk. "You mean when the 'clean-up' crew arrives tonight."

The guard cast a look at Bogart and grinned. "Well, they certainly have you up to speed for the new guy." The guard then frowned. "Around ten o'clock tonight, the camera will go out. They manually switch it off whenever they 'interrogate' men in that room. When it comes back on around midnight, the room will be empty."

"Well, at least you're not an accessory by being a witness to anything," Bogart assured the man.

"Tell me about it," the guard remarked. "Most things that go on around here, I don't want to know about."

§

A few minutes later, Bogart walked along the basement corridor while keeping close to the left wall. The mansion basement closely resembled a dungeon with its concrete floor and stone walls. There were many corridors, and all seemed to be lined with old, wooden doors. Bogart paused near one of the doorways and glanced at the security camera mounted on the wall's upper corner. Since it wasn't exactly state-of-the-art, he was able to watch the direction it turned. When it rotated left, Bogart crossed to the right and stayed out of its line-of-sight. He continued along the corridor until he reached the detention room. Bogart examined the lock on the door then removed a lock pick from his cowboy boot. He inserted the pick into the lock, hesitated a moment, and then tried the handle. The door wasn't locked. He snorted a soft laugh then looked back at the camera. It was coming back his way. Bogart gently pushed open the door and took a moment to peer into the room.

The room was empty except for the bound man seated and tied within the heavy, wooden chair resembling an old-fashioned electrocution chair. The stone walls and limited lighting gave the windowless room a creepy appeal. The old, concrete floor retained remanences of blood from past prisoners. Bogart slipped into the room, keeping close to the door, and looked at the camera installed just within reach. As he had seen within the security office, the camera rotated across the room and only occasionally caught a view of the doorway. He reached up and flipped the switch, stopping the camera from turning, keeping it angled toward the empty corner. Bogart quietly closed the door behind him and cautiously crossed the room toward the tied man whose hood-covered head hung down.

"Hey," Bogart announced while attempting to keep his voice down despite that the camera angled away from them had no audio.

The hooded head lifted as Bogart approached and paused before the bound man.

"It's okay," Bogart announced. "I'm just going to remove the hood. Just keep quiet. Okay?"

The man muffled a response. Bogart carefully pulled the hood off the man's head, revealing duct tape covering his mouth to keep him from making any sounds. Bogart stared in horror at the prisoner. It was Federal Agent Blake Harris, his brother-in-law's boss at the Colorado Springs Bureau. Blake was an athletically built, distinguished-looking man in his forties with light brown hair peppered with gray. Judging by his condition, his captors had roughed him up a little, leaving bruises on his cheek and jaw.

"Jesus, Harris," Bogart gasped and hurried closer to the man he'd recently befriended while on a case.

Bogart crouched in front of Blake, who stared at him in surprise. He pulled the duct tape from Harris's mouth, revealing his swollen and split lip, covered in dried blood.

"Bogart?" Harris gasped in response then quickly cast a look at the camera by the door as if attempting to warn him of it. "We're being watched."

"I took care of it. I'm going to get you out of here," Bogart insisted with sympathy in his voice, "but I can't do anything just now. There are too many killer types crawling all around this place. I have to come up with a plan, but it could take a few hours. You need to sit tight until I can clear a path to get you out."

"Yeah, I can do that," Harris reported and seemed to breathe easier now and even managed a tiny smile. "Is the rest of the team with you?"

"No, just me," he replied. "I'm flying solo on this one."

"I won't ask," Harris replied.

"Why did they nab you?"

"One of my informants told me there was sensitive information on undercover agents and their families being shopped around," Harris informed Bogart. "My search brought me a little too close to Reeves."

"Yeah, that's kind of what brought me here too, except I came willingly," Bogart remarked, then glanced at his watch. "Give me until six o'clock tonight. I'll have a plan to get you out by then. If I can't get you out safely, I'll call the Bureau and have them raid the place."

"I'm concerned someone at the Bureau may be compromised," Harris informed him. "There's no telling how deep this goes."

"Then I'll get you out myself, even if it means blowing my cover," Bogart replied.

Harris panted and nodded, appearing relieved. "Thanks, Bogart."

Bogart patted Harris on the shoulder. "I won't let Twinkie lose her father, I promise."

Once he returned Harris the way he'd found him and restored the security camera to its original condition, Bogart hurried back upstairs before he'd be missed. Once a conman, Bogart wormed his way into the inner circle of Whiskey Tango Foxtrot, his father's former Navy SEAL team turned independent contractors. It wasn't so long ago that Bogart discovered his father's team and the sister he never knew he had. It was his affiliation with the team that eventually brought him undercover to Reeves's estate. As Bogart made his way to the kitchen to grab some lunch with the others, he saw the boss's second in command, Decker, approaching. Decker always looked as if he was about to kill someone. He was a tall, burly, and intimidating-looking man in his early thirties with short, dark hair and a day's worth of stubble on his face. Women seemed to find him attractive, but all Bogart saw was a merciless killer. In a way, he reminded Bogart of his teammate, Kirk, but without Kirk's charming personality.

"You were supposed to be patrolling the estate grounds," Decker scoffed while giving Bogart a less than pleasant once-over. "Where were you?"

"I was checking in with the security office," Bogart replied being oddly truthful for a change. "Checking last night's activity logs."

"That's not your job," Decker retorted while seemingly staring through Bogart.

Something about Bogart seemed to rub the second in command the wrong way. Maybe it was because Bogart was still relatively new, but there was something about how he reacted to the country boy, seemingly sizing him up, which made it feel personal. Bogart was certain his cover hadn't been blown. If it had, Decker probably would have tortured him by now. Decker maintained eye contact in an intimidating manner, and Bogart *was* intimidated. The man wouldn't think twice about shooting him in the head just for kicks.

"I'm in charge," Decker reminded him. "You do what I tell you to do. Your job is to patrol the grounds." Decker straightened proudly as if attempting to make himself seem taller than Bogart. "Get some lunch to go and check out the back perimeter."

"Yes, sir," Bogart replied.

Bogart was about to leave when he saw the boss's young wife approaching from the front room. Casandra looked stunning as always in her casual, pale blue, form-fitting dress and matching stiletto heels. The familiar sound of her high heels clicking on the areas of uncarpeted floor alerted Decker to her presence. He immediately turned his focus away from Bogart and onto the beautiful, young woman. Casandra smiled through ruby red lips while casting a sly glance at her husband's second in command. She then eyed Bogart while maintaining her smile.

"Being a little hard on the new guy, aren't you?" Casandra teased almost seductively, then looked back at Decker.

The moment her eyes connected with Decker's, Bogart saw the hardened man's reaction to the beautiful woman. Bogart wouldn't have noticed the lust in Decker's eyes if the security guard hadn't drawn his attention to it. Now that he was made aware of a possible affair, Bogart could almost see the fireworks between Casandra and Decker. Decker's eyes were locked on the woman, watching her every move and studying her every feature. Her eyes again shifted to Bogart, and she offered a somewhat wicked smile, one Bogart easily recognized. And there it was! Casandra was checking out Bogart, and Decker was crazed with jealousy. Was it possible it wasn't just an affair? Could Decker actually be in love with Casandra? Somehow, that made him even more dangerous in Bogart's mind. Bogart immediately tensed and avoided looking at Casandra. He didn't need to fuel Decker's jealousy.

"I'll be patrolling the back grounds, if you need me," Bogart informed Decker, then headed for the kitchen.

Casandra seemed slightly surprised by Bogart's sudden and somewhat rude departure. She then offered a sly grin at Decker, seductively walked past him, and entered the library. Decker waited only a moment then followed her, shutting the door behind him.

Chapter 2

Coastal Maine, one o'clock in the afternoon Eastern Standard Time. A massive, three-story hotel sat nestled on the tall, secluded cliff overlooking the ocean. The old hotel had been painstakingly renovated to its original grandeur from decades past and offered a spectacular ocean view that seemed to extend for miles. A commercial, fourteen-passenger Bell helicopter sat in the meticulously manicured lawn between the hotel and the woods. The helicopter's massive rotors thumped loudly as they revved faster, preparing for take-off. The hotel's few occupants stood on the back patio and waved to their departing friends. The helicopter finally lifted off, circled over the ocean, and was soon on its way. The young female pilot, Jackie Falcone, skillfully flew the aircraft and her sole passenger away from the remote hotel.

Jackie was an attractive woman in her mid-twenties. Her long, dark hair was pulled back into a ponytail, indicating she was combat-ready despite being casually dressed. She wore her worn, brown leather bomber jacket over a white tank top, revealing her ample cleavage, and her form-fitting black pants showed off her athletic build. Her soft-soled, calf-high boots completed the ensemble and her mildly dangerous look. Jackie had an innocent beauty about her, which led most to

11

underestimate her ability to kick ass. Not many realized that she was as deadly as she was beautiful. Jackie cast several quick glances at her sole passenger, Zack Kinsley, who seemed to stare out the side window at nothing in particular. He seemed quieter than usual.

Zack was shorter than average, barely making five-foot-eight, but he had a surprisingly athletic build, which would almost certainly go unnoticed beneath his black combat fatigues. The moderately handsome man in his early fifties was easily brushed aside as harmless, which was a mistake made by many. His brown hair, now peppered with gray, was kept short and neat, although moderately spiky on top, lending a look that was somewhere between intimidating and cuddly. After being apart from her teammate for such a long time, Jackie was actually surprised at Zack's silence. When it was just the two of them alone together, he would often talk. He'd talk more than most people ever realized possible for such a quiet man. His relationship with Jackie was a special one. Today seemed different.

"Is everything okay?" Jackie finally asked.

Zack seemed to jolt from his private thoughts and looked back at Jackie. "Yeah, everything is fine," he replied, then shifted in the co-pilot's seat. "Scorpio agreed to turn the hotel into a safe house."

Jackie shot several looks at him and was almost stunned by the announcement. "Really?" She had to think about that a moment. The perceived good news didn't explain his strange mood. "Judging by your silence, I was almost certain she had shot down the idea."

"No, actually, she was surprisingly receptive to it," he replied, then snorted a soft laugh. "Which is pretty astounding, considering Hayden did everything in his power to undermine my efforts."

"Hayden Vandyke," Jackie muttered and felt her stomach tie in knots. She then huffed under her breath. "I can't believe you'd subject your own kids to that man."

"He'd worn out his welcome at the last place," Zack remarked, then casually shrugged. "What was I supposed to do?"

"He's broken and angry," Jackie reported while shooting a quick look at her teammate. "I know what lurks behind that arrogant smile of his, and it's not good."

"That's in his past," Zack corrected, then tensed a moment while sinking into thought. "We all deserve a second chance." He then shifted and returned to reality. "I'm not ready to give up on him just yet. Besides, I think it's a good fit. Scorpio and Kane can handle him. He won't be a problem."

"It sounds as if everything went pretty well then," Jackie remarked almost cheerfully. Her mood quickly dropped, and she again eyed him. "So why do you seem *off?*"

Zack glanced at his watch. "How long until we reach the airport?" he asked.

"Doesn't matter," she replied and let out a long, loud sigh. "I'll do laps around the airport until you decide to tell me what's bugging you."

"Holden's waiting," he reminded her, then eyed her while raising an arrogant brow.

"You weren't worried about him waiting when you insisted we stay for lunch. He can wait a few minutes longer," she announced while casting a sly look at Zack. She knew him too well. "And I know once he's on board, you'll be quiet most of the flight."

"It's a long way back to Colorado," Zack retorted with some arrogance. "Even I can't stay quiet that long."

"Spill it."

"You're almost as bad as Kane," he muttered, then finally groaned while raking his fingers through his short hair. "I'm worried about Scorpio. She may look like her mother, but she takes after her father."

Jackie eyed him but didn't comment. It would be rude to express her concerns with that statement. A female version of Zack was something no one wanted.

"She's a bit cold-hearted, like me," he continued as if reading Jackie's thoughts. "I just don't want her turning into me. I keep hoping her relationship with Rayner puts her on a better path, but I fear she's going to dominate him eventually." He sighed with defeat. "There's nothing I can do for her but sit back and wait for her to implode."

"The guys stole Rayner from her for six weeks," Jackie reminded him. "I'm sure some of what you were seeing was just her missing her boyfriend."

"Maybe," Zack replied, then fidgeted in his seat. "I should probably return in a few weeks after everything is set up for the safe house transformation and see how things are going. I'm sure they could use some additional assistance."

"Is Sal still renting the place for his little get-together?" Jackie asked, then smiled teasingly. "What does Kane call it? The 'mob convention'."

"Last I checked, Sal was still having his little get-together," he remarked and again looked at his watch, swiftly changing the subject. "Sorry I made you stay for lunch. Even if we fly straight through with only fuel stops, you'll still be flying a couple of hours in the dark."

"I took that into consideration," she informed him. Jackie hated flying long distances in the dark. It wouldn't be so bad if everyone else weren't sleeping on those journeys. Sometimes, it was tough staying awake with everyone else sleeping. "I called Holden before we left your kids. He's booking some rooms at that hotel just outside the airport in Michigan."

Zack considered the comment and nodded. "They have a nice lounge there," he remarked.

"You and Holden can enjoy the lounge," she announced matter-of-factly. "I told him to book me a massage, and I'm going to use the sauna."

Zack was quiet a moment, but it was apparent he had some devious thoughts racing through his mind. Jackie didn't comment, but she knew the way his mind worked. He finally cast a look at her and raised a curious brow.

"Co-ed?"

"No," she firmly replied, having been expecting the comment or something similar. "And even if it was, you wouldn't be joining me."

"You really are no fun," he muttered.

"Maybe you can find some overnight company in the lounge," Jackie informed him while offering a sly grin.

"Really, Jackie?" he scoffed and shook his head. "It's like you don't even know me."

She rolled her eyes and groaned. It was always the same conversation with him. "What do you have against spending the entire night with a woman?" Jackie finally asked while shooting a glare at him. "Just once, wouldn't you like to wake up alongside someone in bed?"

"I would, but Holden keeps ruining that for me," Zack remarked.

Jackie sneered at him. "Not funny," she scoffed.

Zack smiled and chuckled. "I thought it was," he teased. His smile immediately faded. "Besides, I've spent weekends with Katya. It's overrated."

"I'm not sure Katya really counts."

"How can she not count?" he demanded while glaring at Jackie and seemed a bit offended. "My guy parts fit into her lady parts. Am I missing something? What sort of requirements are necessary for it to *count*?"

"Maybe someone who doesn't want to kill you afterward would be a good start," she remarked.

"Okay, I know where this conversation is going, and I don't approve," he informed her. "Stop trying to fix what isn't broken."

Fix what wasn't broken? Jackie's mind was racing. Everything about Zack screamed something was broken. She hated inserting her thoughts into his lifestyle, but she couldn't help herself.

"You need a girlfriend," she remarked and instantly regretted saying it the moment the words left her lips.

"I have plenty of girlfriends," he replied.

She saw that one coming. "They aren't girlfriends, Zack," Jackie insisted and raised a cocky brow. "They're fuck buddies."

A sly grin crossed his face. "Best kind of girlfriends," Zack countered.

"Don't you want an intimate relationship?"

"I already have you for that," he replied.

Jackie internally groaned. "I meant one you can have sexual relations with," she countered.

"Again," Zack announced with little emotion. "Holden is preventing that."

Jackie rolled her eyes at his joke in poor taste. He was impossible! "Never mind."

"Maggie was the only woman I wanted," Zack informed her. "She was special. I don't need anyone replacing her. I'm happy with the way things are in my life. All of my needs are currently being met." He then hesitated. "Being a single father isn't easy, you know."

Jackie heard the comment and refrained from lashing out. She cast a look at him and sharply raised her brow. Up until a few months ago, Zack didn't even know his children existed. His 'single father' bullshit didn't float, but Jackie would again let it slide. They flew the rest of the way to the airport in silence. She couldn't force Zack to have a personal conversation with her if he didn't want to.

The helicopter landed not far from the refueling station, which was only a short trek to the private terminal. Jackie's federal agent husband, Holden, waited outside the terminal. Even though Jackie and Holden hadn't been apart for more than a few hours, seeing him waiting for her always gave her a rush. The kind of rush that made her want to handcuff him to a bed and have her way with him. Well, again. Holden Falcone was a ruggedly handsome man in his mid-thirties. Standing just a tick under six-foot, he was built less muscular and more athletic with broad shoulders and a toned chest. His neatly trimmed, black hair matched his excessively dark brown eyes. He had the perfect disposition, making him one of the FBI's finest. Serious and calculating, he was a rational thinker, never allowing his emotions to overtake his demeanor, well, except when it came to his wife.

Holden had been waiting outside from the time he'd seen the helicopter come into view and made his approach as Jackie shut down the aircraft.

Zack removed his headset, nudged Jackie, and indicated the approaching man. "He's like a loyal dog waiting for his master to return," he remarked.

"Yeah, he says the same thing about you," Jackie teased and flashed a cheap smile.

Zack eyed her and didn't appear humored. "I'll tap her off," he remarked. "In case you want to use the little girl's room."

"That's very nice of you," Jackie replied, then raised a brow as if reading into the kind gesture. "Just so we're straight; Holden's riding shotgun until we reach the next stop."

Zack frowned at the comment but didn't seem pleased with his inability to play her. "Fine," he reluctantly muttered. "I'll take a nap in the back."

Jackie climbed out of the helicopter and jumped down just in time to leap into Holden's arms. He kissed her quickly then pulled back just far enough to meet her gaze.

"I booked you a massage for eight tonight," Holden announced cheerfully, then appeared curious. "We should be there before then, right?"

"I'm hoping to be there by six," Jackie replied. "Maybe we can have dinner first."

"Perfect."

"While I'm in the sauna sweating out those margaritas from our vacation, you and Zack can have a few drinks in the lounge together," she announced.

Holden raised a curious and somewhat skeptical brow. "His idea or yours?"

"Definitely his," Jackie replied. She certainly wasn't going to tell Holden the truth that she wanted Zack and Holden to spend more quality time together.

"Liar," Holden muttered, then grinned and kissed her again.

Chapter 3

Colorado, five o'clock in the afternoon Mountain Time. Bogart hurried away from the detached, eight-car garage while fiddling with his watch. He'd soon need to put his plan into effect if he wanted to rescue Harris from the basement detention cell. He just had a few more details to iron out before implementing his plan. Avoiding the big boss, Reeves, and his second in command, Decker, for the next hour was imperative. He couldn't risk either man sending him on some errand that would take him away from the estate or, worse, have him work with someone else, keeping him from slipping away unnoticed. Rescuing Harris was now his first priority, but he wanted to keep his cover intact, if possible. Since it was getting close to dinnertime, the kitchen staff would be bustling about getting dinner together. Slipping through the kitchen would be the best route to the basement entrance.

Decker and Reeves wouldn't be in the kitchen so close to dinner. They'd want to avoid the hustle and bustle of the kitchen staff. Bogart entered through the back kitchen door. He was greeted by the wonderful smell of dinner cooking, reminding him he hadn't had much to eat for lunch. The kitchen staff of four was tending to their duties and barely noticed he was there. Bogart maintained course across the large kitchen and headed for the hallway entrance. He entered the back corridor just off the grand hallway and nearly collided with Reeves's young, attractive daughter, Zoey. She jumped with surprise then laughed at their near collision. Zoey was dressed casually for dinner in jeans and a silk button blouse. She wasn't nearly as high-maintenance as her wealth suggested she should be.

"There you are," Zoey announced with a strange smile on her face.

Bogart seemed a little surprised by the comment. It wasn't as if she'd ever looked for him before. What did she know that he didn't?

"You were looking for me?" he asked while cocking his head and giving her an odd look.

"No, not me," she replied. "Casandra was looking for you."

"Casandra?" he asked with surprise. "Why would she be looking for me?"

"She wanted to run to the city this evening after dinner, but it's the driver's night off," Zoey replied, then shrugged. "I guess Daddy said you would take her."

Bogart eyed Zoey suspiciously. "I thought that was more Decker's thing," he remarked then immediately tensed, suddenly putting the reasoning for *that* together. Now it made more sense. "I mean; I thought Decker was her official escort, you know, in case something happened."

"I'm guessing Daddy needs Decker tonight," Zoey informed him.

Bogart drifted into thought. Playing chauffeur slash bodyguard for Reeves's trophy wife was low on his priority list tonight. That Decker couldn't take her; it suggested Reeves and Decker intended to interrogate Harris this evening before killing him. Dinner was at six, so Bogart had to make sure he got Harris out between six and seven. Reeves almost certainly wouldn't bother with Harris until at least ten that evening. He'd want to make sure his daughter and the staff were tucked away for the night. Even if Bogart didn't have a rescue planned for that evening, escorting Casandra would be the last thing he'd want to do. Decker's jealous nature wouldn't handle that news very well.

"Everything okay?" Zoey asked, apparently noticing Bogart lost in his thoughts.

"Well, not exactly," Bogart reluctantly replied and fidgeted. "I think I should hear it from Decker. I'm not sure he'd approve of me leaving the estate and especially taking over his usual duties."

Zoey raised a curious brow then grinned. "Are you concerned that Casandra will make a pass at you?" she almost teased. "Or are you more worried that Decker will find out and kill you?"

Bogart stared at Zoey with some surprise and a loss for words. "Why would you--?" He couldn't even finish the sentence.

Zoey laughed softly and shook her head. "I know more of what goes on around here than most people think," she informed him, then smirked. "It's like Peyton Place around here."

Bogart fidgeted slightly and seemed to find his silver lining in Zoey. "Then you'll understand that I don't need any more misunderstandings with Decker."

"Yeah," Zoey replied with a tiny, humored grin, then nodded. "He'll kill you without thinking twice."

"And I'd like to avoid that."

Zoey grinned while studying Bogart. "I don't want to see him kill you either," she teased. "You're one of the nicer guys around here." Her grin then increased. "I'll help you out, but you'll owe me one."

"Done," Bogart agreed a little too quickly. "What's the plan?"

"I'll mention Casandra's evening plans to Decker, and he'll squash them," Zoey replied.

"Think that'll work?"

Zoey raised a curious brow while eyeing Bogart. "Have you met Decker?" she asked. "If he tells her she's not going with you, trust me; she's not going."

"If you could do it discreetly and not mention me at all, I'd appreciate it," Bogart remarked.

"Decker may be scary, and he may be smart," Zoey informed him, "but I know how to play him."

"And while you're doing that, I'll be hiding in the security office," Bogart informed her. "If you would be so kind as not to tell anyone you saw me, I'd appreciate it."

Zoey smiled and laughed. "You're nothing like the other guys on Daddy's payroll," she remarked.

"I kind of enjoy breathing," Bogart replied.

"Bogart," a man called from down the grand hall.

Zoey pushed on Bogart's shoulder. "It's Daddy," she announced. "Go. I've got this."

Bogart didn't bother looking and walked along the back hallway as if he didn't hear his boss. His boss continued along the hallway, heading toward his daughter and the direction Bogart had gone. Reeves was a taller, well-built man in his late forties with short, dark brown hair and a clean-shaven face. He wasn't necessarily unattractive, but without money and influence, it was almost a given he hadn't gotten a high-maintenance woman like Casandra based on his looks. Women like Casandra were attracted to wealthy men with power. Reeves was about to call again when Zoey hurried to greet her father.

"Daddy, we need to talk," Zoey announced and raised her brows dramatically. "It's important."

"Can't it wait?" Reeves asked, then nodded toward the connecting hall. "I need to speak to Bogart."

"No, it can't wait," she insisted and clung to his arm, turning him toward his study. "I want to go to college abroad next semester."

"We discussed that, Zoey," Reeves announced while turning somewhat angry. "I'm not leaving you out of my sight. It's a dangerous world out there."

"It's a dangerous world in *here*," she countered.

Reeves groaned and shook his head. "Do we have to do this again?" he demanded and seemed reluctant to get into it with his daughter. "You've already completed your first two years at college here. There's no reason you can't finish them here."

"Yes, we have to discuss this again," she demanded and arrogantly folded her arms across her chest.

Her father finally gave in and directed her toward his study so they could talk in private.

§

An hour later, Bogart slipped back into the basement, being sure to avoid the security cameras, and approached the main power breaker. He opened the box then removed a small bottle from his pocket. It resembled a bottle of clear nail polish, but it obviously wasn't. He liberally applied the gel inside the main control providing power to the basement and security office. He recapped the bottle and returned it to his pocket. Before he even shut the breaker box door, the corrosive was starting to melt away the internal wires' outer coating. Bogart hurried away from the breaker box and paused in the doorway. He impatiently looked at his watch several times then heard footfalls in the corridor. He stepped just out of sight and waited.

As if on cue, a guard walked past. Bogart again looked at his watch. The fumes from the corrosive started lingering in the hallway, and the lights went out. Bogart darted from the room and into the darkened hallway as the guard removed a flashlight from his pocket. He shined the light at the detention room door. As the guard opened the door and stepped inside, Bogart crept up behind him. The guard shined his light toward the prisoner in the chair but then seemed to sense something behind him. As he started to turn, Bogart kicked him in the face with his cowboy boot. The guard dropped to the floor, out cold. Bogart dragged the guard the rest of the way into the room and quickly shut the door. He took a moment to switch off the camera, even though it was currently inoperable, and hurried for the man wearing the hood over his head. He removed Harris's hood and the duct tape covering his mouth.

Harris gasped and appeared relieved when he saw Bogart. Bogart removed a switchblade knife from his boot and cut the duct tape binding Harris's wrists to the chair's arms. He then cut his ankles free from the tape as well.

"You need to undress," Bogart informed him, "and make it fast. We won't have long before they check on you if the camera doesn't come back on."

Harris eyed him skeptically but did what he asked. Bogart undressed the guard and tossed the guard's clothing to Harris. Once Harris had his clothing off, he immediately slipped into the guard's clothes. Bogart hurriedly dressed the guard in Harris's clothes. Harris then helped Bogart move the guard into the chair. Bogart swiftly removed a roll of duct tape from his pocket and bound the man's wrists to the chair. He tossed Harris the roll of tape. Harris did the same to the man's ankles and then placed a piece of tape over the man's mouth. Bogart placed the hood over the man's head, and both headed for the door. Bogart switched the camera back into the 'on' position before leaving, even though the power was still out. They entered the corridor just as the emergency generators came on. Bogart indicated which direction they needed to go and hurried Harris along the corridor.

§

The younger, second shift guard fiddled with the monitors within the security office as the door opened. He looked back at the older guard who entered the room. The older guard seemed frustrated but not riled.

"What happened?" the younger man asked.

"Power went out, but it didn't affect the entire house, just the basement," the older guard replied. "The backup generator already kicked on. How's everything in here?"

The younger guard groaned and again fiddled with the controls. "Only half the cameras came online with the backup generator," he scoffed. "We lost half the cameras."

"I'll check on our V.I.P. guest," the older guard informed him.

"That one's working," the younger guard replied and indicated the screen.

Both saw the bound man within the chair with the hood over his head. It didn't appear as if he had moved.

"We're good," the younger guard informed him. "He's not going anywhere."

"These power outages happen too often," the older guard remarked, seeming disgusted. "The security system in this place sucks. Which cameras did you lose?"

"We still have on the front gate and the main entrances to the mansion," the younger man reported.

"Good enough," the older guard replied. "Contact the power company. Tell them to send someone out here to fix that right away."

§

Bogart hurried Harris, now dressed in the guard's uniform, to the large, detached garage located behind the mansion. Seven of the eight garage bay doors were closed. Only one bay door remained open, revealing a sleek, black sedan within the darkened bay. Since it was after six, it was already starting to get dark outside. Bogart and Harris disappeared inside the garage and paused alongside the expensive car. Bogart handed Harris a semiautomatic pistol, which he slipped down the back of his pants. He then gave him the keys to the sedan.

"You'll find a pair of sunglasses on the passenger seat," Bogart informed him. "There won't be anyone manning the gate this time of day. Anyone sees you, just give a finger salute to the brow and keep driving."

"Maybe you should come along," Harris just about insisted. "You know we're going to raid the place."

"My cover is still intact," Bogart insisted. "I covered my tracks. They won't be able to trace your escape back to me. With a little luck, they won't even know you're gone for a few more hours."

"We won't find anything when we raid the house, will we?" Harris asked, now seeming slightly defeated.

"Nope," Bogart replied. "Follow procedure anyway. Reeves has *influence* on all the right people. He can get them to do anything in exchange for his silence."

"I know. He was a low-life blackmailer who made it to the big league," Harris scoffed then appeared curious. "This doesn't seem like your kind of mission. Why are you working this case?"

"We learned through our sources that not only does he have sensitive information on government officials and military operations, but he also has confidential information on Ross and the guys. Maybe even Jackie. He has enough on the team's secret operations to complicate our lives significantly." Bogart offered a tiny, unsettling smile. "Since I'm the only one without a background to speak of, I was the best option to go undercover."

"How long have you been here?" Harris asked.

"Six weeks," Bogart informed him. "After we discovered Reeves's operation, the guys had Othello beef up security at the lodge just in case our home was compromised."

"Six weeks?" he remarked, then shook his head. "Have you found anything?"

"No, nothing," Bogart informed him, then hesitated. "Well, not finding anything is actually something. I installed a device on Reeves's computer. Othello hacked it and found sections had been whitewashed. I'll need to keep searching for some sort of flash drive."

"Maybe we'll find it when we raid the house," Harris announced, then revealed his concern for the man. "Are you sure you don't want to come along?"

"No, I'll be fine," Bogart informed him. "You need to go, and I need to get back inside and start working on my cover story."

"Thanks, Bogart."

"Tell Monique and Colleen I said 'hey'," he announced while grinning.

"I will."

Bogart watched as Harris got into the sedan and pulled out of the garage. The black, luxury car drove at a steady, slower pace down the long, winding driveway toward the massive front gate. Bogart waited until the car passed through the open gate before hurrying back to the house. He glanced at his watch. It was only six-thirty. He'd made good time. The family and, more importantly, Decker was still having dinner in the dining room. With the power outage being confined to the basement, the rest of the house would be none the wiser. If the security guards believed the power outage was just a fluke, they certainly wouldn't interrupt Decker at dinner to mention it. As far as the guards knew, the prisoner was still tied up in the detention cell.

Chapter 4

Michigan, eight o'clock in the evening Eastern Standard Time. The airport hotel lounge was moderately full that evening despite the early hour. The lounge had a long bar that encompassed most of the back wall with enough seating for twenty patrons. The moderately dark atmosphere was meant to lend a romantic vibe, but it made the room feel somewhat seedy, like some olden day speakeasy. There were booth tables along the walls and smaller tables in the center. Most of the clientele seemed to be middle-aged businessmen traveling alone. The bar's 'days gone by' atmosphere may have kept most of the traveling businesswomen away, particularly since there were nicer hotels just a few miles further away from the airport. Holden and Zack entered the dimly lit lounge and looked around. Holden was about to speak while pointing to a nearby table when Zack headed for two seats at the bar. Holden groaned and followed him. Both men ordered beer on tap and drank in awkward silence. Holden shifted and seemed to be searching for something to say.

"Did Rayner and Scorpio have a happy reunion?" Holden finally asked.

"I suppose," Zack replied without looking at the man seated beside him.

Holden nodded and looked away. Making small talk with Zack wasn't exactly easy. Despite all the time Zack spent at their house, Jackie was always around as sort of a buffer.

"Has Scorpio's shooting improved?" Holden asked, making a second attempt to strike up a conversation.

"No," Zack replied.

Holden rolled his eyes and minded his beer. Second effort attempted and failed. A few minutes of awkward silence passed before an attractive, young woman dressed almost too nice for the lounge approached them. She paused alongside Holden and appeared to be waiting for the bartender, who didn't seem interested in taking her order.

"Service is so slow around here," the attractive woman announced, then turned to face Holden.

Holden cast a look at her out of the corner of his eye but didn't really pay much attention to her. She remained facing his profile and retained her smile.

"Was your flight delayed?" she asked, attempting to start a conversation with Holden.

Holden glanced at her, managed a tiny smile, and returned his attention to his beer. "My wife and I have a flight in the morning."

"Smooth," Zack muttered from his other side, just loud enough for him to hear.

"Buy me a drink?" she pressed while smiling sweetly at Holden.

Holden raised his left hand and wiggled his ring finger without looking at the young woman. "Still married," he announced.

The young woman giggled and moved a little closer to Holden. "That's okay," she remarked. "She doesn't have to know."

Holden reached inside his inner jacket pocket without looking at the woman and flipped open his badge at her. Her eyes widened at the sight of the FBI badge, and she immediately took a step back while managing a tiny, nervous smile.

"Maybe another time," she announced while fidgeting then hurried away.

As Holden returned his badge to his inner jacket pocket, Zack grinned and chuckled.

"You knew she was a hooker the moment she walked up, didn't you?" Zack remarked without looking at him.

"Yeah, I saw her prowling the room when we first entered," Holden replied and sipped his beer.

"See that woman in the corner?" Zack asked and gave a slight nod to their left.

Holden managed to look across the room out of the corner of his eye. A woman in a white dress sat at the corner booth alongside a young man.

"The one in the white dress?" Holden asked and again minded his beer.

"She's giving him a hand job," Zack casually remarked.

Holden turned his head and had to look more closely. He suddenly tensed and again minded his beer. "Christ," he muttered under his breath.

Zack chuckled lowly into his glass of beer. "For a classy place, this lounge is notoriously skanky," he remarked.

Holden eyed Zack and raised a curious brow. "You think this place is classy?" he mocked.

"By my standards," Zack remarked with a casual shrug. "The beer is expensive and watered down, but the floor show never disappoints." He then indicated the mirror behind the bar. "These are the best seats in the house."

Holden glanced at the large mirror behind the bar. They could easily see the entire lounge through the mirror without turning their heads from where they were seated. Holden smirked and chuckled.

"I wondered why you wanted to drink in such an expensive bar with lousy beer," Holden remarked with some humor.

"Entertainment value alone is worth it," Zack replied with a sly grin on his face. "Kirk and I would hang out here during long layovers and play a little game."

"What sort of game?"

Two hours later, Holden and Zack had a pile of dollar bills on the bar. Both men laughed while appearing moderately buzzed.

"Okay, last game of the night," Holden announced, then indicated his cell phone face down on the bar before him. "Jackie should be returning to the room soon."

"Winner takes all," Zack remarked while sitting up straight on his bar stool. He scanned the mirror behind the bar and zeroed in on his next target. "Man in the polka dot tie with the woman in the red skirt."

Holden scanned the mirror for the couple in question. "Okay," he announced.

"They've been arguing the last two hours," Zack informed him.

"Yes, I noticed."

"She's going to either pour beer on him or slap him across the face in the next ten minutes," Zack announced.

Holden suddenly chuckled. "I'll take that bet," he replied. "You've been wrong almost sixty percent of the time."

"Bullshit," Zack scoffed and indicated the pot. "Most of that is your money."

"Whatever," Holden groaned and waved his hand. "There is no way that woman is going to react in that manner. Did you see the size of that diamond ring? She's not risking pissing him off."

"Now, we wait," Zack remarked with a low chuckle.

Both men sat in silence and kept an eye on the mirror, watching the couple at the distant table. The woman in the red skirt suddenly slapped the man across the face then dumped her beer on his lap. Holden groaned loudly and slammed his palms on the bar top.

"Brutal," Holden cried out.

Zack chuckled while collecting the pile of dollar bills. Holden threw his hands in the air while watching the woman storm from the lounge.

"Why?" Holden exploded. "Why'd she do it?" He then glared at Zack. "You saw something. What did you see that I didn't?"

"When he came back from the bathroom, he palmed the waitress's phone number," Zack informed him.

Holden groaned in irritation. "Where the hell was I when that happened?"

"I misdirected you," Zack replied with a tiny shrug as he placed the money in his pocket. "I got you to watch that man on the other side of the bar."

Holden suddenly glared at Zack with a surprised look on his face. "Did you scam me?"

Zack grinned and chuckled, then sipped his beer. "I most certainly did."

Holden groaned and shook his head, then wagged his finger at Zack. "You are an evil man."

"Common knowledge, Holden," Zack casually replied. "You can't seriously be realizing that just now."

"I'm going to the bathroom," he muttered with disgust and walked away from the bar.

Holden was only gone a moment when his phone dinged. Zack picked up Holden's phone, saw a text message from Jackie, and pressed the button. The thumbprint ID screen popped up. Zack removed a latex glove from his pocket, slipped it over his hand, and placed his thumb over the thumb plate. The cell phone unlocked, and the message was revealed. Zack stared at the picture of Jackie up to her chest in the room's whirlpool tub. The message read, "Waiting for you." Zack groaned with desire, frowned, and reluctantly pressed the button to exit the screen. He set the phone back down on the bar. When Holden returned from the bathroom, Zack casually indicated his cellphone.

"You're being paged," Zack announced with little emotion.

Holden checked his phone, grinned at what he saw, and placed a few bills on the bar. "Remember, we're leaving at eight tomorrow morning. Don't stay up too late," he informed Zack. "See you in the morning."

§

Colorado, ten o'clock in the evening, Mountain Time. The back of Reeves's mansion revealed just how isolated the estate actually was. The large, in-ground pool with a swim-up hot tub was nestled on the back patio. Not far from the pool was a fire pit, which contained an outdoor grilling station, a table that seated ten, and outdoor sofas built into the area surrounding the pit. A gorgeous, white gazebo took up a large piece of property not far from the fire pit. The driveway continued past the house and to the massive garage in back.

Bogart walked across the back yard beyond the eight-car garage with his cell phone to his ear.

"I was sort of expecting a lot of activity tonight," Bogart remarked into his phone. "Did Harris make it back?" There was a pause. He sighed with relief. "Yeah, I'm glad to hear. Just waiting for the bomb to drop, that's all. Any minute now, they're going to make the discovery--"

Bogart's attention shifted to the house. Several men were seen running around in a state of panic.

"I think they discovered the switch," Bogart remarked. "I'd better make an appearance." He paused at something said on the phone and again glanced at the house. "No, I'm fine. I don't need an extraction, and I certainly don't need a rescue team. My cover is one hundred percent intact. It'll look like Harris escaped on his own. I made sure I covered my tracks. Gotta go."

Bogart disconnected the call and hurried back to the house while perfecting his clueless, country boy look as he ran into Decker and the guards bustling about.

"What's going on?" Bogart asked.

"Prisoner escaped," Decker announced in a tone that was gruffer than usual.

"Do you think he's still on the grounds?" Bogart asked and looked around. "How much of a head start? Want me to check out the back acreage?"

"No, he's long gone by now," Decker informed him. "We have bigger problems. Feds are going to be crawling up our ass any minute now."

"What do you want me to do?" Bogart asked.

"Greet them when they arrive," Decker informed him. "You don't know anything anyway. Show them around. They won't find anything. The detention cell has been scrubbed."

"Okay, I'm on it," Bogart replied.

As Bogart turned and headed for the house, a tiny smirk crossed his face. The sound of police sirens was heard as they approached the mansion, catching Bogart's attention and wiping the smile from his face.

"Well, Harris," Bogart muttered to himself and cocked his head. "It would seem someone on your payroll gave our friends a little head's up."

§

It was just before midnight as Bogart watched the last of the federal agents drive down the long driveway without finding anything or making a single arrest. Harris hadn't seen the faces of any of the men involved in his abduction and had nothing concrete on any one man. He could show them the room in the basement, which had already been cleaned up for the feds' arrival. Harris had been hoping to find something, but there was nothing to see as Bogart had attested. Being they were still working on the backup generator, they couldn't even show any security footage that would indicate Harris had been in the mansion. Not that it would matter. The mansion guards would have deleted any evidence long before they arrived.

Once the feds were gone, Bogart sat out front on a half wall just far enough from the main entrance that he could talk on his cell phone without being overheard by anyone. Bogart seemed a little out of place at the elegant mansion setting in his faded jeans and worn cowboy boots. Although only two stories, the mansion took up a large area and resembled a fort with tall walls and sturdy doors. Despite being early fall, the landscaping still contained much of its beauty and even some flowers. The fountain in the center of the circular driveway dwarfed most fountains found in parks. It was almost fifteen feet tall with several levels and an angel on top, but Bogart wasn't interested in checking out the scenery. He just needed privacy with his phone call.

"Our friends just left," Bogart announced into his cell phone. "Everything is still running smoothly and on schedule." He then heard voices around the side of the house near the garage area. Bogart kept his cell phone to his ear as he headed for the side of the house. "Wait. Something's happening. Decker sounds pissed."

"Find Bogart," Decker's angry voice demanded. "I want to know where he was between six and seven this evening!"

"Crap," Bogart muttered into his phone. "Maybe I didn't cover my tracks as well as I'd thought." There was a moment's pause as the person on the other end spoke. "No, I've got this. When it comes to running cons, I'm in my element." He hesitated and again listened on the phone. "No, I've got this. I *don't* need extraction."

Bogart disconnected his call, placed his cell phone in his jacket pocket, and headed around back to the gazebo where several men had gathered.

"Someone call for me?" Bogart announced with his best country boy grin.

Decker approached Bogart with a look of rage, pulled his semiautomatic, and aimed it at Bogart's face. "Give me one reason why I shouldn't shoot you where you stand?" he snarled.

Bogart stared at the gun pointed only a foot from his forehead and attempted not to panic. "I didn't touch your imported brandy," he announced. "That was all Marv."

One of the men, apparently Marv, stared at Bogart with astonishment then cast a nervous look at Decker's profile. "I did *not* touch your brandy!"

Decker didn't take his eyes or his gun off Bogart and maintained his sneer. "I'm not talking about my brandy," he demanded. "Bennington said he was jumped by the fed in the detention cell around six o'clock when the security cameras conveniently stopped working. Kicked in the face by a man's booted foot." Decker cocked his head and raised his arrogant brows. "The fed was barefoot when we tied him up. So I'm only going to ask you once before putting a bullet in your skull. Where were you between six and seven this evening? You're the only man whose whereabouts can't be confirmed during that hour."

Zoey appeared near the entrance of the gazebo. Decker immediately lowered his weapon and attempted to conceal it from her view, although she'd obviously seen it when she first arrived. Apparently, it was something she'd seen before, but her father still wanted the men to pretend she knew nothing and that they were all innocent.

"I saw him a little after six when I walked out on dinner this evening," Zoey announced to Decker, then cast a stern look at Bogart. "I can tell you exactly where he was and what he was doing."

She had Decker's full attention now. Zoey seemed tense and nodded, indicating she wanted to speak privately with Decker. Decker holstered his weapon and approached the young woman. As she spoke confidentially with him, Decker suddenly exploded in rage. Bogart immediately tensed. If Zoey had skipped dinner with the family, it was possible she was somewhere unexpected and actually saw him slipping Harris out to the garage. Zoey then said something to Decker, which silenced his outburst but increased his hostility. Bogart flinched at the look of rage on the intimidating man's face. The remaining men positioned their hands on their weapons while casting looks between Decker and Bogart. Bogart knew it was possible he was a dead man.

Chapter 5

Six hours later. It was six o'clock in the morning, Colorado time. A large, muscular man sat quietly in the dimly lit room with a look of disgust on his stern face. Kirk Mandel was a large, muscle-bound man in his mid-thirties and stood an imposing six-foot-four. He had broad shoulders, a large chest, and biceps the size of tree trunks that were barely hidden beneath his tight, black shirt. His buzz cut and thick facial stubble made him look moderately intimidating, although undeniably handsome. His mostly serious look conveyed he wasn't someone to be messed with and that his muscles weren't just for show. Kirk listened as his two comrades lightly argued, which was nothing new for Beck and Monroe.

Beck Larue was a ruggedly handsome man in his mid-thirties with short, light brown hair. He stood over six feet tall and maintained an impressive athletic build. Although his kind, hazel eyes begged to be trusted, he had a somewhat superior air about him. Despite his charming appeal, he was devilishly smart and relied on his intelligence over his charm. The man he argued with, Monroe Dallas, was a tall, lanky man in his mid-thirties with more of an athletic build than muscular. His light brown hair was neatly trimmed, and his handsome face mostly clean-shaven. Monroe seemed the type of man who took pride in his appearance, and he had an innocent sort of appeal, which often allowed most to put their guard down around him. The two men continued their curt exchange, talking over each other, obviously annoyed about something.

"Will the two of you give it a rest?" Kirk finally snarled, lacking any patience with either man.

"You know, it's moments like these where I miss Zack," Beck announced almost casually.

"I know I'd feel a lot better knowing Zack or Jackie were close by," Monroe added.

Kirk turned his head and glared at the two men not far from him. Both men were zip-tied to their respective chairs. "If the two of you don't shut up, when I get free, I'm coming over there and killing you both."

Beck and Monroe eyed the large man zip-tied to his own chair within the mansion's basement detention cell.

"Well, this *is* partially your fault," Beck casually insisted to the large man.

Kirk glared at Beck with a look meant to kill. "My fault?" he demanded. "How the hell is this my fault?"

"I said *partially*," Beck corrected.

"Personally, I blame Ross and Gil," Monroe remarked matter-of-factly. "Ross should know better than to leave us unsupervised, and Gil abandoned us while trying to reconcile with his wife for the one-hundredth time."

"Ex-wife," Beck corrected.

"We don't know that they ever officially divorced after their last 'impromptu' wedding," Monroe reminded him.

"If Bogart is still alive, I'm going to kill him," Kirk muttered under his breath and then made another effort to fight the zip ties binding him to the chair.

They could hear the sounds of men laughing in the corridor. All three fell silent and listened. The door opened. A guard entered the room with Bogart only a step behind him. All three had to be surprised to see Bogart alive and well, but they didn't react to his presence while in the company of the guard.

"Who are they?" Bogart asked the guard while eyeing his bound teammates. "Are they feds?" His mocking grin was enough to enrage all three of his captured friends.

"No idea. They're not carrying any ID," the guard remarked. "The boss wants to keep them alive for now. We may need them as a bargaining chip if the feds return."

"Makes sense," Bogart replied and again eyed all three. He then met Kirk's gaze. "Who do you work for?"

"Fuck off," Kirk snarled.

Bogart kicked Kirk in the chest, mildly stunning him with the move. Jackie had been teaching her brother well, although Kirk's look was even more hostile now. The guard snickered, amused by Bogart's response to the large man.

Bogart then eyed the guard. "Mind if I ask them a few questions? See what I can get out of them?"

"Knock yourself out," the guard replied, then indicated the lifeless camera. "Since we're still running on the backup generator, it's not as if anyone will witness it. Just don't kill any of them."

"Don't worry," Bogart teased and grinned. "I'm going to ask *nicely*."

The guard laughed and left the room, shutting the door behind him. All three men glared at Bogart as his look immediately turned stern.

"What the hell--?" Bogart demanded in a hushed shout. "I told you I was fine."

"Just get us out of here," Beck remarked and indicated the zip-ties.

"I can't do that," Bogart replied.

"You'd better," Kirk snarled in response.

"Things were a little tense here before you guys showed up," Bogart insisted while shaking his head. "Now, they're on high alert. I made some calls, but Gil's about five hours out. You're going to have to sit tight until he gets here. Once he's here, we'll coordinate a rescue."

"We were supposed to rescue you," Monroe scoffed.

"Now that's your own fault, isn't it?" Bogart insisted and shot a glare at Monroe. "I told you I was fine. By the time Gil arrives, I'm hoping to have the flash drive, and we can all leave together. I won't have you guys ruining six weeks' worth of undercover work. Not when I'm so close to getting what I came for."

"We thought your cover was blown with Harris," Beck remarked.

A strange and twisted smile crossed Bogart's face. "Turns out 'daddy's little girl' provided me with an alibi," Bogart announced with some humor. "She told Reeves's second in command that we were together when Harris escaped."

"Why would she lie?" Monroe asked with surprise.

Bogart grinned almost slyly. "What can I say? She's hot for me, and I was more than willing to indulge her fantasy," he teased.

"I thought you were cleaning up your bad-boy reputation," Beck remarked.

Bogart eyed him and considered the comment, then grinned. "I am," he replied, "but she did save my ass." His grin then increased. "And she's *really* hot." Bogart then looked at his watch. "That reminds me. She'll be waking up soon looking for round three." He cocked his head. "And I don't want to disappoint her. So you three just sit tight while I go upstairs and have hot, shower sex."

All three watched Bogart hurry from the room. Kirk then sneered while Monroe and Beck shook their heads.

"We get to sit here and cool our heels for five hours while Bogart gets laid," Monroe muttered. "I swear, I'm doing something wrong."

"Can't exactly blame him," Kirk muttered and received looks from his teammates. He glanced back at them and shrugged without care. "I'd do the same thing if I were in his position."

§

Colorado, noon Mountain Time. Jackie's helicopter landed at the private terminal within the Colorado Springs Airport. The terminal was little more than a small building containing a lounge for private passengers and pilots, restrooms, and vending machines. Other outer buildings housed private planes belonging to locals. Many other small planes were outside the buildings. The helicopter barely touched down when Zack sprang out the side door and started the task of refueling while Jackie finished shutting down. Holden sat in the co-pilot's seat and watched Zack dart for the pumps like the pit crew at Indianapolis Speedway. Holden wearily ran his fingers through his hair and groaned.

"How does he do it?" Holden finally asked. "He has twenty years on me, he's probably hungover, and he still runs circles around me. Five hours in a helicopter, and I'm exhausted."

"Well, you do spend quite a bit of time behind your desk at work," Jackie remarked while slyly eyeing her husband. "And then there are those Sundays on the couch."

"Only during football season," Holden insisted in his own defense. "And I've seen Zack planted on our sofa for an entire weekend with only the occasional bathroom break."

"Speaking of bathroom breaks," Jackie announced and opened her door. "I'm going to the little girls' room."

"I'll get us some drinks from the lounge, but first, I'd better check my voice messages from work," Holden replied while removing his cell phone. He then cast a quick look at her. "Zack's going home tonight, right?"

Jackie withheld her cringe. She hated when Holden asked her that question. She knew it meant he was ready to spend time at home without Zack hanging around.

"I'll contact the guys and see who's around," she replied, then dreaded the words that followed. "If no one can come for him, I may have to fly him to the lodge."

Her husband's reaction was precisely as she had anticipated.

"You're not flying to the lodge and back today after that long trip from Maine," Holden insisted.

Jackie didn't comment as she jumped from the helicopter. She then gave him a look and raised her brows, more or less indicating he should pick his poison. She already knew what his response would be. When he didn't reply, she turned and headed toward the private terminal building.

Holden groaned and shook his head as he watched Jackie enter the terminal. "He's going to end up staying the entire week with us. I just know it," he muttered, then got out on his side.

A few minutes later, Jackie returned from the private terminal with her cell phone in her hand and a puzzled look on her face. Zack was still refueling the helicopter when she approached him. He gave her a curious look.

"Something wrong?" Zack asked.

"I tried calling everyone, and no one's answering," Jackie reported while remaining deep in thought. It wasn't normal to get no response from anyone.

"Did you try the satellite phone at the lodge?" Zack then asked.

It was a silly question. Of course, she tried the lodge. "No one answered there either," she informed him. "I'm going to try Gil on his helicopter radio."

Jackie climbed inside the helicopter, flipped a switch, and placed her headset on.

"Eagle One, this is Reaper, you copy?" she announced as Zack approached the open helicopter door.

Zack casually rested his lower arms across her leg that was dangling from the open door. She was used to physical contact with Zack, even though he wasn't the physical type with others on the team. There was a loud, shrill, piercing sound in her ears over the headset. Jackie yanked off the headset with a startled gasp.

Zack straightened, having heard the sound through the headset as well. "What is it?"

She gave him a slightly baffled look. "Gunfire, I think." Jackie threw another switch, and the radio crackled loudly, allowing both to hear the noise. "Gil, you copy?"

They heard the loud sound again. Gil's voice then came across the radio, although somewhat static-filled.

"Uh, hey, Jackie," Gil announced almost casually. "Can't really talk at the moment. We're taking on some heavy gunfire."

Jackie felt her heart pounding with anxiety. "What's your twenty?" she just about demanded.

"About half a klick west of Bogart's little covert operation at Reeves's mansion," Gil reported.

They heard a loud grinding. Jackie and Zack both made faces at the sound. It wasn't good.

"What was that?" Jackie demanded.

"Ah, nothing," Gil informed her. "Just the rotor catching a stray bullet. What's your twenty?"

"About ten minutes from you, if I put the pedal to the metal," she announced with concern. "Can you hold out that long?"

"Don't really have much choice, do I?" Gil reported over the radio with little emotion.

Jackie was already feeling her concern for her team rising. Zack lunged away from the open pilot's door and stopped fueling the helicopter. As he bolted into the back of the aircraft, Holden approached from the terminal with some bottled water and saw Jackie prepping the craft. He picked up the pace and hurried for them.

"Something happening?" Holden asked, sharing their concern.

Without warning, Zack grabbed Holden's arm and pulled him into the back with him. The bottles of water flew across the back of the helicopter. As Holden crashed into one of the rear seats, Zack shut the side door with added vigor.

Chapter 6

As Jackie's helicopter approached Gil's location, she could see the mansion surrounded by woods and fields in the near distance. The familiar, faint rat-tat-tatting of gunfire could be heard even above the sound of the helicopter. Jackie slowed her approach when she saw another aircraft not far from her emitting smoke and rapidly descending. Concern swept over her. It was Gil's helicopter! Zack removed two automatic rifles from a hidden compartment and handed one to Holden. Holden accepted the weapon with some uncertainty. The team was in trouble, but he had no idea who they were fighting. As a federal agent, he couldn't just blindly jump into a firefight without knowing the whole story. Jackie watched Gil's helicopter successfully land in the nearby clearing. She was grateful he was able to land and didn't crash as she feared he might have.

Jackie flipped a switch enabling her radio. "Eagle One, you copy?" she announced.

"Yeah, I copy, Reaper," Gil replied over her headset. "You're about to enter the war zone. Ross is joining in on foot while I do a quick patch job on my old girl. Team one is pinned down toward the rear of the house. Team two made it out the front and are attempting to draw some of the fire away from team one."

"Bogart really stepped in it this time, huh?" Jackie remarked to Gil.

Jackie knew her brother, Bogart, was a capable and crafty son-of-a-bitch, but he was really good at backing himself into corners, particularly when there were pretty women involved. It was his biggest weakness.

"Actually, your brother needed to rescue his rescue party," Gil responded over the radio.

Jackie could hear Ross in the background, shouting orders above the helicopter engine.

Gil maintained his usual calm demeanor despite the desperate situation. "We're looking at about thirty armed men," he casually announced, revealing far less emotion than Ross in the background. "Naturally, most of them are wanting a piece of your brother. Harris and the fed brigade are about thirty minutes out."

Ross was again heard in the background before coming on the radio. "Jackie, Ross here," he announced. "Please tell me you brought your fed boy toy with you."

Jackie groaned at the comment and then eyed Holden, who was listening in on his own headset. Jackie shook her head. The guys loved Holden, but they also enjoyed picking on him.

"Yes, Holden is with us," she replied.

"Good," Ross responded, then seemed to hesitate. "The guys are reporting in. Hold your position."

Jackie veered the craft and away from the danger zone and hovered a moment while Zack slipped into his nylon harness. Ross returned to the radio.

"Have Holden symbolically flash his badge from your position," Ross informed her over the radio.

Holden paid closer attention to the words coming over his headset and appeared curious about his involvement.

"Harris will back us up. He's given Holden the green light to intervene on behalf of the Bureau," Ross continued over the radio. "We'll finish tenderizing these bastards just enough for the feds' arrival."

Jackie glanced back at Holden, flipped a switch on the main console, and then pointed at him, indicating he was broadcasting live over the loudspeaker.

Holden flinched then straightened, taking his cue. "This is the FBI," he announced loud and bold, which projected from the speakers outside the craft. "We have you surrounded. Ceasefire and lay down your weapons." It wasn't much of a surprise when the firing was still heard. "I repeat. This is the FBI. Ceasefire and lay down your weapons!"

Jackie threw the switch, cutting Holden's microphone. It was a symbolic gesture at best. The bad guys weren't simply going to surrender because of a federal agent's presence, but the team needed to follow protocol in order for Harris to clean up the mess.

Zack fastened his harness, eyed Holden, and grinned slyly. "You certainly showed them," he announced, then handed Holden a nylon harness.

Holden accepted the harness, eyed it, and then looked back at Zack. "I'm *not* jumping from a moving helicopter."

"We're not moving," Zack insisted with little emotion. "We're hovering. You're needed on the ground."

"I won't be properly identified," Holden informed him. "I don't want my own men shooting me by accident."

Zack removed a black, official FBI bulletproof vest from the secret compartment and extended it to Holden. He eyed the vest then glared at Zack.

"Did you steal this from my car?" Holden demanded.

"Not important," Zack replied and removed his headset, tossing it aside. "Gear up!"

Holden cursed at Zack under his breath, removed his headset, and then slipped into the vest. Zack handed him the nylon harness. Holden eyed the harness, groaned, and snatched it from him. Jackie took the helicopter in a wide circle away from the gunfire, then lowered just above the wooded area between Gil's helicopter and the mansion. Zack pulled open the side door, increasing the loudness of the helicopter rotors. He and Holden slung their rifles over their shoulders and attached the cables to their harnesses.

"Ready?" Zack called out above the loud noise of the helicopter as it hovered.

"Not really," Holden muttered while nervously eyeing the open side door and the ground below. It was a long drop, particularly for someone who wasn't used to jumping out of helicopters.

Zack tossed the ends of the cables out the open side door then grinned at Holden. "Last one on the ground buys the first round," Zack announced, then jumped backward out of the helicopter, sliding down his cable.

Holden groaned and eyed Jackie, who now watched him with a tiny, tense smile.

"Good luck," she announced.

Holden managed a smile, blew her a kiss, and then held his breath while stepping backward out the open doorway. Jackie managed a tiny cringe, hoping Holden wasn't just showing off for her benefit. Outside the helicopter, Zack reached the forest floor first and detached the cable from his harness. Holden slid down the cable reasonably fast, not putting enough pressure on the clamp, and didn't slow much while heading for the ground near Zack. Zack watched Holden botch the landing and crash to the ground, landing on his backside.

Holden groaned from where he sat on the ground and rubbed his backside, "That's going to hurt in the morning."

"You could have slowed your descent a little more," Zack informed him while extending his hand to him. "You didn't need to show off on my account."

Holden glared at Zack then grabbed his extended hand, allowing Zack to help him to his feet. Zack unhooked Holden's harness and motioned for Jackie to leave. The helicopter flew away with its trailing cables. Both men slipped out of their harnesses, discarded them, and unslung their weapons. They hurried through the woods toward the sounds of gunfire.

§

Bogart and Monroe ran across the back patio, remaining out of sight, and threw their backs against the wall. Gunfire could still be heard coming from several directions, although the noise had decreased since Gil's helicopter went down. Both men were panting heavily while taking a two-minute break from the action.

"Are you sure about this?" Monroe asked while scanning the area for a possible ambush.

"Not one hundred percent," Bogart remarked as they moved closer to the nearby glass doors. "I saw Reeves accessing a wall safe on the security cameras last night. He put a flash drive in the safe. That has to be the one we're looking for."

"Last night?" Monroe asked while briefly glaring at the man alongside him before resuming his watch of the area around them. "Maybe you should have spent a little less time banging the crime lord's daughter last night and a little more time breaking into his office, then we wouldn't be here trying to break back into the house we just escaped."

Bogart cast a disappointed look at Monroe. "I can't figure out if you're jealous or just cranky," he remarked.

"Both. Not that this hasn't been fun," Monroe announced while keeping his weapon aimed across the grounds, "but I think it's time we get what we came for and amscray before the feds arrive."

"The feds have arrived," Bogart corrected.

"Holden doesn't count," Monroe insisted. "Let's just get the damned flash drive and get out of here."

Bogart moved closer to the French glass doors and glanced through them into the study. Thankfully, the room was unguarded.

"I'm working on it," Bogart informed him as he removed his lock pick kit and began manipulating the lock. "It's not as if I have a key to get inside, you know. That state-of-the-art lock on the study door is pick proof."

Monroe eyed Bogart, who didn't seem to be getting anywhere with the lock. "Just break the glass," he finally groaned.

"It's shatterproof," Bogart snapped back with some irritation. "I've done my homework during the six weeks while I was here."

Someone stepped in front of the glass doors within the study. Bogart looked up with surprise, realizing they'd been spotted. Zoey stood on the other side of the glass within the study and stared at him with a strange look of fear and confusion on her face.

Bogart's expression dropped. "Oh, that's not good," he muttered.

Monroe glanced at the door and saw the young woman as well. He was about to comment when she unlocked the door and took a step back. Bogart and Monroe exchanged quick, bewildered glances. Bogart cautiously opened the door and stepped into the study without taking his eyes off Zoey. He kept the rifle in his hands but didn't aim the weapon at the confused and frightened young woman. Monroe slipped in behind Bogart and kept an eye outside as well as on the unfolding scene within the study.

"Why did you unlock the door?" Bogart asked with some surprise. "You know your father's men are after us."

Zoey stared at him a moment and almost seemed to relax. "My father's a bad man," she informed him, then shook her head. "No matter who or what you are, you have to be the lesser of the two evils."

"I'm sorry, Zoey," Bogart announced, then slipped past her and approached a large painting on the wall behind the desk. "I didn't mean for you to get involved, but we need to get what we came for." He pulled the painting away from the wall to expose the safe and briefly glanced at her. "You shouldn't be down here. It's not safe." Bogart slung his rifle over his shoulder then nodded to the nearby bookcase. "Hide in the study panic room until this is all over."

Zoey didn't take her eyes off him while showing little reaction to his comment. She then indicated the safe. "I can open that."

Bogart and Monroe stared at the young woman with astonishment.

"You'd do that?" Bogart asked with some surprise. "You'd help us?"

"All those gunshots outside," she informed him, "that's the sound of freedom. I'll finally be free from my father and his corruption."

Zoey moved past him and easily opened the digital safe. When the lock beeped, she stood aside. Bogart opened the safe to reveal cash, jewelry, and other valuable papers. Bogart tossed the money and the jewelry from the safe and found the flash drive.

"That's what you came for?" Zoey asked with surprise and eyed the money and jewelry strewn across the floor.

"That's what we came for," Bogart informed her, then placed the device in his pocket. "You need to get inside the panic room. The feds will be storming the place soon. You'll be safe there until they arrive. Ask for Agent Blake Harris. You can trust him."

Zoey nodded, then quickly kissed Bogart. She backed away from him and headed for the nearby bookcase. She pulled on one of the books, and the bookcase popped away from the wall, revealing a doorway. She disappeared inside. A steel door slammed shut, and the bookcase slowly slid back into place, covering the entrance. Monroe looked back outside. A man suddenly appeared with his weapon aimed. Monroe raised his rifle as a gunshot rang out, startling him. The man was suddenly thrown to the ground from the shot. Bogart and Monroe's leader, Ross, stood in the doorway with a rifle in his hand. Ross Madrid was a handsome, distinguished gentleman in his early fifties with a full head of mostly graying hair. His piercing blue eyes and charming smile made him seem approachable and almost refined, but most never knew the calculating genius hidden behind his smile. Despite his age, he was in excellent physical shape with enough hidden muscle mass and stamina behind him to put much younger men to shame.

"Did you get it?" Ross asked.

"Yeah, we got it," Bogart replied as he joined them then handed the flash drive to his boss.

"That just leaves one more minor task," Ross announced.

"Reeves won't be easy to find," Bogart insisted.

"He's around here somewhere," Ross informed him. "Kirk and Beck are out front. No one left the estate grounds. Find him before Harris and his men arrive."

"He's probably in the basement," Bogart informed him. "It's the second safest place in the mansion."

"Where's the first?" Ross asked.

Bogart nodded to the nearby bookcase against the wall.

"Panic room?" Ross asked.

Bogart again nodded. "He's not in there," he remarked. "His daughter accessed it. She was the only one in there."

"You two find Reeves," Ross announced, then indicated the flash drive before stuffing it into his pocket. "I need to get this to Beck. We don't want the FBI having access to all our private information."

"We're on it," Monroe replied.

Ross hurried out the French doors to the back patio while contacting Beck over his ear transmitter.

§

Jackie circled the large clearing just a stone's throw from the action on the estate grounds. She could see Gil's disabled helicopter in the field, but she didn't see any sign of Gil. Although it was possible he was captured, she sort of doubted it. Jackie took her helicopter down and landed not far from Gil's helicopter. She flipped a few switches then swiftly removed her semiautomatic from her hidden shoulder holster. Jackie threw open the helicopter door and aimed her weapon, searching for any signs of armed guards. Her teammate, Gil, appeared from behind his helicopter with a rifle slung over his shoulder and a semiautomatic in his hand.

"Nice of you to have my back," Gil announced, genuinely happy to see her.

Gil Rafferty was on the upper end of thirty, if not in his early forties. His short dark hair was peppered with gray, making his age difficult to tell, and giving the handsome man a moderately distinguished look. He stood almost six-foot-tall with an athletic build. His dark eyes were soft and kind, offsetting his somewhat serious look, making him difficult to read. Gil replaced his gun and returned to his helicopter's already open engine compartment. He quickly began working on fixing the problem created by several bullets. Jackie snatched her rifle from the aircraft and took a lookout position so Gil could repair his helicopter without fear of being shot. A large

German shepherd dog wearing a black bulletproof vest ran from the woods for her.

Jackie saw the dog and appeared relieved. "This is no time to be marking territory, Darth," she reprimanded the dog.

Gil's silver sable German shepherd, Darth, had a mostly black face and a slightly sloped back for that show dog appearance. He weighed close to one-hundred-twenty pounds of mostly muscle. With his tongue hanging partway out, he seemed happy and friendly, which was mostly true, but there was another side to the working dog. The serious former guard dog turned special ops. Despite the dog checking her out, Jackie kept watch on the nearby woods even though Darth would notice someone approaching long before she did.

"Can you fix it?" Jackie asked Gil in concern without taking her eyes off the area surrounding them.

"Yeah," Gil replied. "A little duct tape will do the trick. Well, temporarily."

"Duct tape is the only thing holding that piece of shit together," Jackie announced with a tiny, humored smirk. Taking cheap shots at Gil's old, battle-worn helicopter had become their new *thing*.

Gil cast a stern glare at her profile. "Some of us don't spend every dime on new toys, Jackie," he scoffed, then resumed working with his roll of duct tape, tearing a strip off with his teeth. "Not all of us have sugar daddies to put a roof over our heads."

"In what world is Holden a sugar daddy?" she demanded without looking at him. "But if you really want to play that game, I suppose that makes you Beck's bitch."

Gil hesitated, then glanced at Jackie while raising a cocky brow. "Kind of rude," he remarked then shrugged, "but I'll give you that one."

Jackie smirked and laughed. It was kind of true. Gil spent most of his time at the lodge in the Colorado Mountains with a few of his teammates. Beck and his wife, Pinto, were permanent residents at the lodge, while Kirk, Zack, Bogart, Gil, and Monroe split their time between various houses and the lodge. Ross spent most of his time at his own farm, only a few miles from the lodge, with his wife, brother-in-law, and niece.

Monroe was the only one of the lodge group that owned his own home, although he seemed to spend more and more time at the lodge these days. Zack and Bogart spent almost as much time at Jackie's home now as they did at the lodge, while Gil occasionally split his time between the lodge and his ex-wife's home in Virginia. No one knew for sure how many times Gil and his wife had divorced and remarried. Honestly, they'd stop keeping track.

Chapter 7

Kirk and Beck sought refuge behind an expensive black car parked several yards from the large fountain. Both men took on fire from the four guards at the front of the house. While Kirk clutched his rifle and waited for the opportunity to strike, Beck sat with his back against the car and held his finger to his ear transmitter.

"Copy that, Ross," Beck announced over his transmitter. "We'll hold our position."

Kirk didn't bother looking at Beck. "What's the word?" he asked.

"Ross caught up with Monroe and Bogart," Beck informed him. "They're inside the mansion, and they got their hands on the flash drive. We need to keep these assholes busy for a little while longer."

"Easy enough," Kirk replied with little emotion. "We'll just let them wear themselves out or run out of bullets. Whichever comes first."

"Ross is making his way back to us with the flash drive," Beck reported. "I'll need to see what's on it regarding our team and safe houses."

Holden darted across the driveway from a small wooded area not far from where he and Zack had been dropped off. By the time the men on the porch saw him, Holden was already casting his back against the car, crouching alongside Kirk and Beck.

Kirk eyed Holden and smirked in amusement. "Look," he teased. "Our backup arrived." Kirk then raised a humored brow and mocked Holden. "This is the FBI. Ceasefire and lay down your weapons." Kirk chuckled. "And they didn't do it?" He shook his head while grinning. "I thought for sure that would've worked."

"Good afternoon, Kirk," Holden scoffed. "It's nice to see you too."

"How was your little beach vacation?" Beck asked while seeming moderately cheerful and a little too relaxed.

"Put Jackie in a good mood?" Kirk teased while offering a devious grin.

Beck leaned his head back against the side of the sedan and seemed reflective. "I'm thinking about taking Pinto on a trip somewhere this spring," he casually remarked, then appeared curious. "Is there a lot to do on the beach? I just think we might be bored after a day or two."

"There's plenty to do," Holden casually insisted. "Lots of water sports. I'd think you'd enjoy that sort of thing."

As several bullets shattered the side window of the car, Beck considered the comment then nodded. "Of course, I enjoy water sports," he replied. "SEALs like the water."

Kirk's expression dropped as he turned his head and glared at both men. "If you girls are finished doing each other's nails, we're trying to kill some bad guys here."

Beck eyed Kirk and raised a brow. "No, we're just keeping them busy," he reminded him, then looked back at Holden. "What do you think of those 'all-inclusive' places?"

Kirk rolled his eyes and groaned. "That's it," he scoffed. "I'm done here." Kirk suddenly straightened and fired his weapon with purpose, shooting each man on the porch. He then glared at Holden. "Where's Zack?"

Holden frowned and shrugged. "Have you tried the roof?" he asked.

Kirk looked around then took off across the estate with a mission to find Zack.

§

Jackie and Darth patrolled the area in front of Gil's helicopter while he did a quick patch job using an entire roll of duct tape. Jackie kept her assault rifle in both hands and at the ready while Darth seemed less than serious and scratched at his black, bulletproof vest. Darth suddenly snapped to attention, looked at the woods, and snarled. Jackie reacted, aiming her weapon in the direction the dog indicated and ducked behind the helicopter. Gil stopped working, snatched his nearby rifle, and rolled beneath the aircraft as well, also aiming his rifle into the woods.

"Darth," Gil announced. "Kommen."

Darth responded to the German command and raced beneath the helicopter with Gil. He lay on his belly alongside Gil, almost mimicking his position, and watched the tree line as well. Jackie scanned the area through her riffle scope but didn't see anything. She was about to comment when she heard the sound of four-wheelers approaching.

"Shit," she scoffed and again scanned the area. "They're sending scouts out to find the helicopters."

"Sounds like more than two," Gil informed her. "If they're all riding quads, we're going to need to disable them before they have a chance to surround us. We won't last long exposed like this."

"I don't suppose Zack has a grenade launcher in his fun bag on your bird," Jackie remarked.

"I wish."

The sounds of the four-wheelers were getting closer. All three remained alert and in position. Four quads appeared from the woods, slowed when they saw both helicopters, and then headed both left and right of the woods.

"I see four," Gil announced while following them through his scope. "I have right; you take left."

"Roger that," Jackie replied.

Both opened fire, striking the tires of the four-wheelers. Two more quads appeared from the woods and separated as well.

"Son-of-a-bitch," Jackie cried out and attempted to follow the four-wheeler with her rifle.

Gil fired several shots at the one to his right and missed. Jackie spun around and fired at the quad now circling the field in order to get behind them.

"I have the quads in back," Jackie called out. "You get the stragglers on foot in front."

As Gil fired at the men on foot now seeking cover, the four men fired back. The ground in front of Gil erupted from a close call, but the men couldn't get a clean shot at him. Darth snarled and barked viciously while holding his ground, awaiting the order to attack. Jackie took out one of the two quads that had circled behind them while dodging fire from both men. The men firing at her from the rear couldn't get a clean shot, but she was somewhat exposed to those coming at her from the front. The man from the fallen quad rolled across the ground, leaped behind his destroyed vehicle, and fired at her. Jackie crouched low to the ground, giving him less of a target while simultaneously firing at the remaining man on his quad coming directly at her, also firing his weapon.

Given the difficultly of firing a weapon and steering, it made it harder for them to hit their targets. Jackie returned fire and took out the man's weapon, but that didn't stop him from racing toward her with purpose. Best-case scenario, he'd ram the helicopter and do some serious damage to the craft. Worst case, he'd kill them both. Jackie's rifle was spent, and she didn't have time to reload with the quad racing toward her. She tossed the rifle aside and removed her semiautomatic from her shoulder holster. With a steady hand and careful aim, she shot out the front tire. The quad pulled heavily to the left and veered away from the craft before flipping. The rider was jettisoned through the air and tumbled across the ground. The first man, who had taken cover behind his quad, now ran for Jackie while aiming his weapon. Jackie fired first, but admittedly quick and sloppy, winging the man rather than getting in a kill shot.

When she turned, the man from the wrecked quad was already alongside her with a Bowie knife in his hand. Darth appeared out of nowhere, snarling viciously as he leaped on top of the man, latching onto his forearm. Darth rode the man down to the ground and tore into the arm holding the weapon. The man attempted to wrestle Darth off him, which was more challenging than it sounded, considering the dog's weight, his bite radius, and the pressure of thrust behind his head toss. The man managed to reposition his hand holding the knife and thrust the knife into Darth's side. The tip of the blade just about bounced off the bulletproof vest, successfully pissing off the already pissed off dog.

The man managed to punch Darth in the face, although it didn't deter the dog or loosen his bite. The man became angry and repositioned the knife in his hand, preparing for a jugular thrust. A shot suddenly rang out. The bullet from a semiautomatic struck the man dead center in the forehead. Gil lowered his weapon and yelled a command in German. Darth released the motionless man, leaped off him, and returned to Gil. The man Jackie had earlier winged was now in a crouched position, firing at them. Jackie rolled across the ground and sat up firing. She shot the man twice in the chest. She just barely heard Gil shouting a warning to her while he fired his weapon. A man from the front of the craft jumped on top of Jackie, crouched on the ground. He took her the rest of the way to the ground, landing on top with a knife in his hand, and attempted to stab her in the throat.

Jackie held the knife back with both hands and thrust her knee into his ribs several times before inflicting enough pain to distract him from his mission to kill her. Darth was suddenly in on the pile-up and clamped down on the man's calf with his teeth. The man cried out in agony and attempted to kick the dog off him. Jackie knocked the knife from the man's hand and punched him in the face. Gil kicked the man in the side with enough impact to toss him off Jackie and across the ground. Darth refused to let go of the man's leg and rolled with him. The moment the two stopped rolling, Darth re-established his hold on the man's calf and violently tossed his head while snarling. The man yelled and screamed profanities while kicking Darth with his free leg. Jackie was suddenly standing over the man and kicked him in the face.

Gil whistled for Darth. Darth released the unconscious man and excitedly ran for Gil, wanting praise for being such a good boy. Gil frowned his disapproval but crouched down and gave the dog the praise he deserved. He then looked up at Jackie as she brushed dirt and grass from her pants.

"I don't like what Zack's been teaching him," Gil informed her. "It's nice having Darth watching our backs, but if he keeps going in freestyle, he's eventually going to catch a stray bullet. Maybe even friendly fire."

Jackie frowned and nodded, unable to defend Zack on his quality time with Darth. "I know," she replied with a reluctant sigh. "I lectured him about his use of the phrase 'sic balls' on more than one occasion."

Darth suddenly perked up to the words and tilted his head with interest and possible enthusiasm. Gil noticed the dog's reaction, then groaned and shook his head.

§

Ross hurried across the driveway to the luxury sedan Beck and Holden remained crouched behind while watching the front of the house. They hadn't seen any signs of movement in the last ten minutes. The sound of gunfire was now sporadic, although they had heard multiple gunshots coming from the nearby field. Holden was undoubtedly worried about Jackie falling under fire, but he also knew she was prepared for whatever they threw at her.

Ross handed Beck the flash drive. "See what's on here," he instructed. "Scrub anything relevant to the team before turning it over to the feds."

Holden eyed Ross and raised an arrogant brow. "Fed sitting right here," he announced.

"Flash the badge next time you say that," Ross informed him while slapping his shoulder, then grinned. "Carries more weight."

"Always a pleasure having you visit, Ross," Holden muttered, then looked back at the house from behind the car. "What's going on in there? Should we go in?"

"You should probably wait for Harris," Ross informed him. "I don't have any authority."

"Now you're just messing with me," Holden remarked lowly under his breath.

"A little," Ross teased while smirking.

Beck chuckled in his throat at the conversation while swiftly working on his laptop. His smile then faded as he stared at the computer screen. "What is this?" he demanded, then looked at Ross.

"What?" Ross asked and eyed the screen.

"Hundreds of old family photos," Beck announced with some irritation, then glared at Ross. "This isn't the right flash drive!"

"It was the only one Bogart found in the safe," Ross insisted.

Beck snorted a sarcastic laugh. "Well, it's certainly not the drive filled with super-spy stuff and blackmail worthy secrets," he remarked. "Do we even know where the real flash drive is?"

Ross groaned and rubbed his eyes. "That's the only lead Bogart had," he replied in a defeated tone. "He searched the office, and you ran a scan on Reeves's computer. That's all we have."

"Great," Beck scoffed in disgust and slammed his laptop lid shut. "Somewhere, out there, there could be files upon files of our operations, our families' personal information, and all our safe house locations. I'm already living off-grid, Ross." He met Ross's gaze. "I can't go any further off-grid than I already am. You're in the same boat."

"We'll figure it out," Ross remarked while sinking into thought. "We're still looking for Reeves. When we find him, we'll force him to give up the location of the flash drive."

"Can we not talk about interrogation in front of the federal agent?" Holden asked without looking at them.

"Relax, Holden," Beck announced with a sigh. "We aren't going to waterboard the guy."

"I prefer electroshock therapy," Ross muttered.

Holden's brows knitted as he turned his head, glaring at Ross.

Ross flashed a grin and chuckled. "You're too serious; you know that?" Ross tapped his ear transmitter. "Monroe, you copy?"

"I copy," Monroe replied over Ross's ear transmitter.

"Wrong flash drive," Ross announced to his comrade. "We need Reeves alive if we want to find the one with all the goodies on it."

"Roger that," Monroe replied over Ross's ear transmitter.

Chapter 8

Decker entered the study while holding his MP5K submachine gun in both hands. He scanned the room and saw the wall safe open and empty. When he noticed no one in the room, he shut the door behind him, hurried behind the desk, and saw the contents of the safe scattered on the floor. Decker slung his weapon over his shoulder, grabbed a nearby briefcase, and dumped the papers from it. He grabbed the stacks of cash and jewelry and stuffed them into the soft leather briefcase. When the study door opened, he spun while snatching his weapon hanging on his side and aimed it at the doorway. Reeves aimed his semiautomatic in response, then relaxed when he realized it was his man. Decker again slung his weapon and finished loading the valuables into the bag.

"Did they get it?" Reeves asked with a slight snarl in his tone while remaining by the closed door, guarding the opening from any unwanted visitors.

Decker snatched a decorative cigarette lighter from the desktop, pulled the top off, revealing the flash drive, and flashed it at his boss. "No, they didn't get it," he replied, then replaced the cap. "They took the decoy from the safe." His look turned stern. "Where's Casandra?"

"She's waiting for us by the basement door," Reeves replied. "Where's my daughter?"

"Try the panic room," Decker announced while indicating the nearby bookcase. "If she's in there, she's not opening the door for me."

Reeves hurried to the bookcase, pulled on the book lever, and stood aside as the bookcase popped away from the wall. The steel panic room door was sealed. Reeves pounded on the door so his daughter would be able to hear him through the thick steel.

"Zoey," Reeves announced while standing close to the door. "Come on, honey. We need to go."

On the other side of the panic room door, Zoey stared at the security monitors located along the back wall. The feed was the same as in the security office. In addition to the wall of security monitors, there was a small day bed, shelves of supplies, a wall-mounted phone, and a functioning toilet in what resembled a closet. Zoey looked at the camera feed that revealed her father in the study outside the panic room door. She tensed a moment, then removed the wall-mounted phone and pressed several numbers. The phone only rang twice before a familiar male voice answered.

"Who is this?" Bogart asked from the other end.

"Bogart, it's Zoey," the frightened woman announced in a hushed whisper into the phone, although it was silly to whisper since her father would never hear her through the thick door. "There's no time to explain. Daddy and Decker are in the study. I think they have what you were looking for. It's a gold embossed cigarette lighter concealing a flash drive. I saw Decker put it in his pocket. I'm pretty sure they're heading for the escape hatch in the basement. You can cut them off." She hesitated a moment and held her breath. "Casandra will be with them. Please don't shoot her."

"Thanks, Zoey," Bogart replied. "You stay put. I'll keep Casandra out of the line of fire."

Back in the study, Reeves continued to pound on the panic room door. "Zoey, come on, honey," Reeves insisted. "We need to go."

"Leave her," Decker just about ordered and tossed Reeves the soft leather briefcase. He then unslung his rifle, preparing for a firefight. "They have nothing on her; it's us they want. The feds won't arrest her. She'll be fine. You can send for her later." He then indicated the study door. "We need to get out of here. Now."

Reeves groaned with defeat and allowed the bookcase to close over the sealed panic room door. Decker headed for the study door, opened it, and aimed his weapon into the hallway. When the area was secure, Reeves followed him from the room. Both men hurried down the back hall and reached the basement entrance where Casandra waited. For the first time, she was wearing sensible shoes in anticipation of a hasty getaway. Decker pulled her behind him without explanation.

"Stay between Reeves and me," Decker instructed without emotion. "Move when I move; stop when I stop. If I tell you to get down, you get down."

Without response, Casandra and Reeves quickly followed Decker down the stairs into the basement. While holding his MP5K in both hands, he kept it aimed at each doorway they passed. Reeves kept watch behind them with his semiautomatic in his hand. Decker held his hand up while stopping. Both stopped behind him. He had them wait while he moved forward with his weapon aimed at the last door on the right. Decker moved into the doorway and aimed his gun into the room, but there was no one there. Decker turned just in time to see Bogart move from one of the doors behind Reeves and Casandra.

"That's far enough, Reeves," Bogart shouted.

Decker immediately leaped into the nearby doorway. Reeves aimed his weapon at Bogart and fired, forcing Bogart to fire back in response. In that split second, Reeves pulled Casandra in front of him. She screamed as the bullet struck her in the shoulder, sending her to the floor. Bogart cursed and was forced to duck into the safety of the doorway, giving Reeves enough time to bolt into one of the rooms across the hall from where Decker had taken cover. Decker peered into the hallway and saw Casandra on the floor.

"Casandra!" Decker cried out in something resembling horror.

When Monroe poked his head out of the doorway across from where Bogart was hiding, Decker fired at him in anger and rage. Casandra was left lying on the concrete floor, clutching her bleeding shoulder and crying.

"Let her go!" Decker shouted at them while firing several shots to keep them from shooting the injured woman. "Come on, Casandra. Keep down and come this way. You can make it!"

"We don't want her, Decker," Bogart called back. "I wasn't aiming for her!"

Reeves removed a remote control from his jacket pocket and pressed a button. A large section of the stone wall behind them moved inward, revealing a secret passageway.

"Cover me," Reeves announced to Decker.

"We just want the flash drive," Bogart insisted, hoping to retrieve what they came for.

"You shot her!" Decker shouted back in anger. "What kind of bastard shoots an innocent, unarmed woman?" He again looked at the sobbing, injured woman attempting to crawl her way to him. Decker fired several shots down the hallway, covering Casandra. "Come on, Casandra!"

"I didn't shoot her," Bogart shouted back. "I was aiming for Reeves. He used his wife as a human shield!"

Decker's entire body suddenly stiffened. He then glared at Reeves in the doorway across the hall.

"They're lying. I wouldn't do that," Reeves snarled back then held out his hand. "Give me the flash drive, then go get Casandra. I'll cover you."

Decker shifted his gaze to the sobbing woman now clutching and clawing at the concrete floor, unable to pull herself any further. She feared standing, afraid of being shot again. Decker looked back at Reeves and showed no emotion.

"Did you *ever* love her?" Decker asked while glaring at Reeves and cocking his head.

"What?" Reeves demanded as he stared at Decker with surprise. "Of course I love her!"

"Good," Decker replied, then looked down the hall past the injured, crying woman and sneered at Bogart. "I'll give you the flash drive, and then you let us go. No one else has to die down here, Bogart."

"Give us the flash drive," Bogart replied, "and we won't stop you from leaving. You have my word."

Decker removed the lighter from his pocket. Reeves stared at him in horror.

"Don't do it, Decker," Reeves threatened. "The information on that drive is priceless. Don't give it to them for Casandra. Women like that are a dime a dozen."

Decker glared at Reeves in anger. "I thought you said you loved her," he scoffed in silent rage.

"Decker," Reeves snarled, then aimed his semiautomatic at his second in command. "Don't you even think about--"

Decker turned his weapon on Reeves and pulled the trigger without hesitation. Reeves barely had time to gasp as the bullet exploded in his chest, immediately dropping him to the floor. Decker swiftly returned his attention to Bogart down the hall just past Casandra.

"Show of faith, Bogart," Decker announced. "Step into the hallway and show me your hands. I get the girl; you get the flash drive. I just want the girl."

Bogart drew a deep breath and slung his rifle. Monroe cast a look at Bogart and revealed his horror.

"You aren't actually going to do it, are you?" Monroe demanded.

Bogart frowned and eyed Monroe across the hall from him. "If he shoots me, you shoot him," he announced, then held his breath. "But he's not going to shoot me."

"What makes you so sure?" Monroe demanded while revealing his concern.

"He loves that girl more than he wants me dead," Bogart replied. "He's willing to die for her. Trust me. I know what I'm doing."

Monroe groaned and shook his head. "If Jackie could see you now," he muttered.

Bogart stepped into the corridor with his hands up in front of him. Decker aimed his weapon at Bogart and stepped into the hallway as well. Monroe kept his gun aimed at Decker. Decker cautiously approached the dead man across the hall. He collected the remote control and the soft leather briefcase without taking his weapon off Bogart. He slung the briefcase strap over his neck and shoulder, then made his way closer to them and the injured woman. Casandra kept her eyes locked on Decker while stifling her sobs. As he approached, she slowly moved to her feet, fearing one of the men would shoot her the moment she stood. Decker pivoted her behind him then dropped the lighter on the floor. He forced Casandra to back up down the hall to the opening in the wall while keeping his weapon trained on Bogart. He motioned Casandra into the opening then darted in behind her, sealing the door.

Bogart released his breath and lowered his hands. Monroe stepped out of the doorway while lowering his weapon as Bogart approached the discarded lighter on the floor. He pulled the lid off to reveal the flash drive hidden within the decorative metal casing.

"You're very lucky, Bogart," Monroe informed him.

"Luck had nothing to do with it," Bogart assured him. "Decker never cared about the information on this drive. He only cared about Casandra. We got what we wanted, and he got what he wanted."

§

Beck sat on the floor of Jackie's helicopter with his laptop and frantically tapped on the keyboard. The flash drive disguised as a cigarette lighter stuck out the side port of the computer. Ross and Monroe leaned against either side of the opening from outside the helicopter while Jackie and Gil put the finishing touches of duct tape on Gil's severely injured helicopter.

"For what it's worth--" Gil announced with a slightly defeated sigh. He then looked at Kirk, Zack, and Bogart while grinning. "Who's flying with me?"

All three men raised their brows and took a step back without responding.

Gil eyed them suspiciously. "What?" he demanded and indicated his helicopter. "You don't think she's seaworthy?"

"Seaworthy, perhaps," Kirk remarked with little emotion. "But will she stay in the air--?" He cringed in response and shook his head. "Smart money says no."

"There's more duct tape on that thing than there is metal," Zack informed him. "I've used up most of my nine lives. I'm not wasting my last life flying in that piece of shit."

"Big babies," Gil scoffed at the men. He sighed with defeat and then looked at Darth, who happily panted and wagged his tail where he sat before him. "At least Darth is willing to fly with me."

Zack turned to leave and slapped his thigh. "Darth," he announced with little emotion.

Darth excitedly barked and ran after Zack. Gil folded his arms across his chest while staring after his dog with astonishment.

"I'm feeling a little underappreciated here, guys," Gil remarked.

Kirk and Bogart didn't even comment as they turned and walked away.

Jackie offered a sympathetic smile and patted Gil's broad shoulder. "I have faith in your repair skills," she insisted.

"Take her for a test run with me?" Gil asked while raising a curious brow.

Jackie's eyes widened with surprise and mild horror. "Are you kidding?" she just about gasped. "If we both die, who's going to look after our kids?" She gave a nod to the nearby team.

Gil shook his head as Jackie headed back to her own helicopter to check on the flash drive's status.

Beck straightened and pulled the flash drive from his laptop port. "I removed any mention of us from the thumb drive," he insisted while handing it to Ross. "He had a few juicy tidbits on us, but nothing our enemies don't already know."

Ross accepted the flash drive and appeared curious. "Maybe we should make a copy of the drive for ourselves," he remarked. "You know, just in case. Might be something of use for later down the road."

Beck flashed a grin. "Way ahead of you," he teased. "I already downloaded a copy to my laptop."

"Good job," Ross replied, then handed the cigarette lighter to Bogart. "You're up, Bogart. Take this to Holden and explain that we found a second drive without giving up too much detail."

Bogart stared at Ross with something resembling horror. "If I go back there, Harris and Holden are going to detain me for hours," he lightly whined, attempting to gain some sympathy.

"This was your mission," Ross replied, then grinned. "You're not getting any sympathy from me. Man-up. We'll meet you back at Jackie's house."

Bogart frowned in response. "Fine."

Chapter 9

The following afternoon, a handsome, well-dressed man in his late twenties entered the ritzy art gallery located near the shopping district within Colorado Springs. The gallery currently only had a dozen or more visitors. The massive gallery was a labyrinth of walls containing artwork and many sculptures by local artists. Track lighting, as well as ceiling lights, showcased the artwork to potential buyers. Judging by his expensive clothes and the way he carried himself, the handsome man, Michael Rinaldi, obviously came from money. He barely glanced at any of the expensive paintings and artwork as he made his way through the labyrinth. Michael had a headful of thick, dark hair and perfectly bronzed skin. He was athletically built with just enough muscle mass to make quite an impression on most women. The gallery owner, Dwight Rosenthal, saw the younger man, stopped what he was doing, and approached with a delighted smile on his face.

"Michael," Rosenthal announced cheerfully while greeting the man with his hand extended.

Rosenthal was a moderately handsome, clean-cut man in his mid-forties. He was shorter than average with a classic 'dad bod' and a certain regal appeal. The gallery owner's light brown hair was naturally graying, which added to his distinguished look.

Michael accepted his hand and shook it. "Mr. Rosenthal," he announced. "How's business?"

Rosenthal made a face and shrugged. "Slow, but it'll pick up this evening," he announced and once again grinned. "And, please, call me Dwight." He then laughed. "You've been dating my daughter a month now. There's no need for formalities." Rosenthal then tilted his head and appeared curious. "I didn't think you were going out until later this evening."

"Our dinner reservation isn't until seven," Michael informed him, then offered a tiny smile. "I just couldn't wait that long to see her."

"I was worried you were canceling," Rosenthal remarked then laughed somewhat insecurely. "She would have been devastated."

"No, I'm definitely not canceling," Michael informed him, then reached into his pocket. "In fact, I'm dying to give her an early birthday present."

Michael opened the six-inch-long, black velvet box to reveal a stunning, ten-carat diamond tennis bracelet in white gold. Rosenthal stared at the bracelet with some surprise, then beamed with delight. Michael shut the box and returned it to his jacket pocket.

"Think she'll like it?" Michael asked while grinning.

Rosenthal snorted a laugh. "She's going to love it," he replied.

"Where is she?" Michael asked.

"She's around somewhere," Rosenthal replied while maintaining his grin. "Why don't you wait in the office? I'll find her and send her back there. You can surprise her. She'll be thrilled."

Michael smiled his agreement, then headed across the gallery for the back. He entered the office near the rear of the building and shut the door behind him. Rosenthal's office was larger than most offices and contained many expensive paintings with sold tags on them. The antique desk was barely visible beneath shipping supplies, and a nearby table was cluttered beyond recognition. Rosenthal and his daughter used the office as a staging area to crate the sold artwork and evaluate new work sent by local artists to sell on consignment. The shop had their favorite, best-selling artists, but they always welcomed new talent. Michael walked across the large area and eyed the expensive, sold paintings waiting to be packaged and shipped. Some of the price tags were shocking. He observed a particularly hideous painting and noted the enormous price tag on it. It seemed unfathomable that someone would pay that much for something so dreadful. He heard the office door open and turned while rousing his best smile. His expression suddenly dropped.

"What the--?"

A twelve-inch, silver-sculpted decorative dagger slashed him across the throat, spraying his blood onto the hideous painting. Michael barely had time to cry out as he instinctively clutched his bleeding throat before collapsing.

§

Rosenthal's beautiful, young daughter, Emily, approached the office. Emily was a petite girl in her mid-twenties with her light brown hair pulled back into a messy ponytail. Her dress was smart yet somewhat sexy, showcasing her moderately athletic body. She wore excessively high heels to add height to her otherwise short frame. Emily seemed pre-occupied with the list her father had given her. It was out of character for her father to pull her away from a potential customer to complete such trivial tasks.

"This could have waited," Emily muttered and shook her head.

She opened the office door and entered while studying the list in her hand. Emily took two steps into the room before slipping and nearly falling. She caught her balance and looked down. There was a large pool of blood on the floor. She followed the blood to the spattered painting. Her eyes then dropped to Michael's lifeless body face down on the floor. His eyes were open, and the large, deep gash across his neck was clearly visible. Emily screamed in horror at the gruesome sight of her dead boyfriend.

§

Holden entered the art gallery's backroom while the detectives and the crime scene crew were still conducting their investigation. He took a moment to scan the large office area and flashed his badge at several police officers, who attempted to keep him away with the other lookie-loos. The moment the police officers saw the badge, they backed off. After taking in the entire scene bustling with forensic photographers and investigators, Holden approached the homicide detective he'd dealt with many times in the past. Detective McGrath was only a few years older than Holden and had made quite a name for himself in the homicide division. He was a reasonably handsome, clean-cut man with short dark hair and stood a tick over six-foot. He had just enough muscle to seem impressive, although not necessarily the aggressive, fighting type.

McGrath saw Holden and released a deep sigh. "How did I know they'd send you?" he remarked and shook his head. "Am I being punished?"

"Just not your day, I suppose," Holden remarked, then flashed a tiny smirk.

"How's Jackie?" McGrath asked while offering a tiny, sly smile as his mood lightened, indicating he'd only been kidding with the federal agent. "Come to her senses and leave you yet?"

"She's pretty much the same but with a nicer tan," Holden replied with little emotion. "I'll be sure to tell her you're still dogging her. She'll happily kick your ass."

McGrath grinned and chuckled. Holden glanced at the dead man on the floor. The scene was so fresh; they hadn't even gotten around to the chalk outline yet. Without getting too close, Holden crouched down and studied the dead man. A strange look crossed his face. He then straightened and eyed McGrath.

"You know who he is, don't you?" Holden asked.

McGrath nodded while raising his brows. "I know," he replied. "That's why I called the Bureau. Mafia types have been dropping dead all over the state. I just wasn't expecting to find one this close to home."

"What do you know so far?" Holden asked while studying the crime scene.

"The victim, Michael Rinaldi," McGrath began then raised his brow and eyed Holden, "son of the infamous Sebastian Rinaldi, was dating Emily Rosenthal, the gallery owner's daughter." McGrath consulted his notebook. "Michael arrived about an hour ago. Rosenthal sends him back here, gets his daughter to surprise her, and she finds her boyfriend dead." McGrath shut his notebook. "Michael was killed approximately ten minutes after he arrived at the gallery. No signs of struggle. He either knew his killer, or it happened so fast, he didn't even have time to react. He couldn't have been dead more than ten minutes when the girlfriend found him. If she'd gotten here any sooner, she probably would have run into the killer herself."

"Lucky break for her," Holden muttered and again scanned the room. "She'd probably be dead too."

"I haven't questioned her yet; she was too distraught when I arrived," McGrath informed him. "You'd think someone dating the son of a notorious mob boss would be able to roll with the punches a little better."

"If he had been honest with her, perhaps," Holden remarked, then eyed the blood-spattered painting near the body with a stern, serious look. He then squinted and pointed at it. "Is that the *actual* sticker price for that painting?"

"Quite valuable for something so hideous," McGrath replied, then indicated the room. "Everything in here is worth a small fortune."

"And nothing was stolen?"

"Our victim is wearing a Rolex watch and had a couple hundred dollars in his wallet," McGrath remarked. "Nothing was touched." He then approached a table and picked up a clear evidence bag containing the diamond tennis bracelet within the opened velvet box. "Found this in his pocket."

Holden eyed the bracelet and raised his brow. "Wow," he announced. "How many carats is that?"

"I'm guessing it's about ten carats," McGrath replied. "Worth about twenty thousand dollars. It was a gift for his girlfriend. Definitely *not* a robbery."

"Definitely," Holden replied, then frowned. "This is our guy. The motive fits. All mafia types, throats slit, and nothing stolen." He looked back at the detective. "I suppose the security cameras were mysteriously down as well."

"Just like the others," McGrath replied.

"The killer must have been watching our friend, learning his routine, and studying potential murder locations," Holden remarked. "He always knows when, where, and how to strike. In a twenty-minute window, he disabled the security cameras and killed the guy in a public location all without being seen." Holden sank into thought then eyed the detective. "He did his research on the gallery, which means he was here at some earlier point in time checking out the security system. We'll find him on the security tapes."

"How would we even know where to start?" McGrath asked. "We don't even know what we're looking for. Hundreds of people come to the gallery every day. We could be staring right at the guy and not know it's him."

"We know Michael Rinaldi just started dating Rosenthal's daughter a month ago," Holden replied. "Two weeks ago, our slasher killed DeLuca outside that restaurant a few hours from here. We should review the security tapes starting from two weeks ago."

"That's still a lot of people," McGrath replied. "We don't even know what to look for."

"We know he was here in the office, scoping it out, at some earlier date within the last two weeks," Holden insisted, then pointed to the camera in the corner. "He knew the office had a camera, so he must have been in the office at some point. The traffic in and out of this room can't be that heavy. Facial recognition will help us cross-reference people seen on security footage from street cams around DeLuca's crime scene. We may get lucky and find a match."

"I'll request copies of old footage from security," McGrath announced with a sigh. "Start a list of everyone in and out of this office."

"Where's the girlfriend who found the body?" Holden asked.

§

Holden approached Emily being consoled by her father on the sofa in the employee's lounge. The lounge was a small room, since they had few employees, and only consisted of a couch, two small tables, a set of cubicles doubling as lockers, and a small kitchen. For an otherwise uninspiring room, it had numerous framed paintings on the walls and tasteful decorations. Rosenthal had his arm around his daughter while she attempted to hold back her tears, although she appeared almost sedate now. Holden paused before the father and daughter on the couch.

"Ms. Rosenthal," Holden announced. When she looked up, he flashed his badge. "I'm Special Agent Falcone." He replaced his badge. "I'm sorry for your loss."

"FBI?" her father remarked with some surprise. "Why would the FBI be investigating this?"

"That's an excellent question," Holden replied while studying the distraught father and daughter. "What do you know about Michael Rinaldi?"

Emily stared at Holden, appeared somewhat puzzled, and sniffed. "We'd been dating for a month," she informed him. "I'd say I knew him pretty well. Why do you ask?"

"Do you know who his father is?" Holden then asked.

"Sebastian Rinaldi," her father replied. "We'd both met him a couple of times."

"Okay," Holden continued, then reluctantly sighed, not wanting to come directly out and say it. "Do you know *who* Sebastian Rinaldi is?"

Both stared at him with some confusion. "What does that mean?" her father asked.

"Sebastian Rinaldi is high up on the mafia food chain," Holden informed them. "His son, Michael, was in the *family* business."

Both stared at Holden with a look of reality hitting them in the face.

"What?" Emily gasped with some disbelief.

"I know this is a bit of a shock for you," Holden replied with his own understanding. Michael keeping his family business a secret made a lot of sense. He wouldn't want to scare away the woman he loved.

"Is my daughter in any danger?" Rosenthal asked while clinging to the young woman. "Are they coming after her next?"

"I don't think your daughter is in any danger," Holden informed him. "Whoever did this completed his intended mission. There's no reason to believe they'll be back. I just need to ask a few questions."

"My daughter didn't see anything," Rosenthal insisted and turned stern, realizing Michael's death was potentially a mob hit. "She doesn't know anything, and I don't think you should involve her any further."

"Dad," Emily whispered, practically pleading with her father.

"No," he announced in anger. "You're not getting involved in a mob hit."

"Maybe he lied about who he was," Emily gently informed her father, "but I still loved him." She looked back at Holden, drew a deep breath, and straightened proudly. "What do you want to know?"

"In the last two weeks while you were with Michael, did you notice anyone suspicious hanging around?" Holden asked. "Did Michael seem distracted by anyone?"

"I can't think of any particular incident," Emily replied. "He wasn't looking over his shoulder or anything weird." She then hesitated. "Although--"

"What is it?"

"I'm sure it's nothing."

"That doesn't matter," Holden remarked. "Tell me anyway."

"Well, we were at a restaurant bar having a drink while we waited for our table," Emily announced. "Some man wanted to buy us drinks. The bartender pointed him out. Michael seemed angry and refused the drinks. When our table was ready, Michael excused himself. I can't be sure, but I think he talked to the man."

"What did he look like?"

Emily shook her head. "Honestly, I didn't really take notice," she replied. "One of our local artists was at the bar, and I was talking with him."

"I'll need the name of the restaurant, a description of the bartender, and your artist friend's name."

§

Holden walked through the now empty gallery, which had been closed after discovering the murdered mob boss's son. As he placed his small notebook in his inner jacket pocket, Harris approached him from the front door where a police officer was posted guard. Harris's facial bruises from his brief encounter at Reeves's mansion were still prominent but healing nicely.

"Anything?" Harris asked, meeting Holden halfway within the gallery.

"Pretty much the same as the others," Holden announced with a defeated sigh. "No one saw anything, security cameras were disabled, and no sign of struggle. This guy knows his target, knows his surroundings, and strikes hard and fast. Detective McGrath is going to review the security footage for the past two weeks. Maybe we can collect a few guys for facial recognition and compare them to footage from other crime scenes in the weeks leading up to the killings." Holden straightened and tensed. "How did it go with Sebastian Rinaldi? Is he going to cooperate with our investigation?"

"Oh, yeah," Harris announced with excessive sarcasm. "He's going to cooperate fully." He then rolled his eyes and shook his head. "While he played up the old 'no mafia ties' gambit, his men were skulking around gathering intel and preparing for war."

"So they're blaming whatever family they're feuding with at the moment?"

"I've no doubt the emergency room will be bustling tonight setting broken bones," Harris muttered. "Talking to any of the

77

families won't get us anywhere. They're going to take matters into their own hands and paint the streets with blood if we don't find out who's behind this."

"Offer someone else's head on a platter, huh?"

"Better than letting them wipe out a city block trying to find the killer themselves," Harris replied, then eyed Holden and tensed. "You know what you have to do."

Holden groaned and rubbed his eyes. "I'd rather keep Sal out of this," he remarked. "Trouble finds Sal without taking it to his doorstep."

"Sal may not be an active player in the game, but he's warming the bench," Harris announced. "You need to see what he knows before someone drags him off the sidelines and forces him to play."

"Fine," Holden announced with a sigh. "I'll drop by Sal's and say hello."

"All off the record, of course."

"Always is," Holden replied, lacking enthusiasm.

Chapter 10

Sal Romano's Colorado Springs country mansion was nestled on a large parcel of land beyond tall, stone walls. The professionally landscaped estate didn't have a hedge out of place. Weeping willow trees and faux split rail fencing lined the long driveway. The driveway split off to the left to circle a large fountain outside the front door while the remaining driveway branched off to the kitchen, staff wing, and eventually to the massive, detached, eight-car garage. A new, black, luxury sedan pulled up to the front of the house and parked. A man in his mid-forties got out of the car, removed two grocery bags from the back seat, and headed for the double front doors. The wealthy homeowner was Salvatore Romano. Sal was a robust man with a round cherub face and a youthful appearance. His clothes were casual yet stylish. It was apparent the man took care of himself.

Sal unlocked the front door using a code rather than a key on the state-of-the-art keypad. He entered the foyer and walked past a smaller scale, "Gone with the Wind" staircase and headed down the grand hallway toward the kitchen.

"Rosa," he called out to his house manager as he entered the elegant yet modern kitchen through the swinging door. "They didn't have that black cherry ice cream you love so much, so I got you strawberry instead. I hope that's--"

Sal looked up and saw two muscle-bound men in expensive suits sitting before the marble-top island counter. They were devouring an entire cheesecake that was still in the expensive bakery box. Sal froze and eyed the two moderately familiar men in their late thirties. Both men stood around six-foot-four and were built like professional wrestlers. Between their large, muscular chests and biceps, the additional girth of their hidden shoulder holsters almost kept their arms from touching their sides. Both men, neither looking particularly friendly, stared at Sal without saying a word.

Sal indicated the massacred cheesecake on the island counter. "I was saving that for tonight," he informed the two men.

Neither man took their eyes off Sal, who still didn't move. He was attempting to place the men. It wouldn't be the first time he'd seen enforcers invading his quiet, little home. A man appeared from the pantry doorway. Sal was finally able to breathe when he saw his old friend, Giovanni. Even though his friend was a notorious, former mob boss, Sal was still relieved. It could have been someone much worse. Giovanni was a handsome, moderately athletic-built man in his late forties with dark hair and a classic Italian look about him. Although he was somewhat imposing, standing a little over six feet tall, his reputation as a powerful mob boss was his most intimidating feature.

"Giovanni," Sal announced and managed a relieved smile. "You gave me a bit of a scare. At my age, that isn't exactly healthy."

"Given either of our reputations, it probably wasn't the smartest move, but I didn't want to risk waiting outside for you to come back from your grocery store run," Giovanni teased, then held his arms out to Sal as he approached. "How are you doing, my old friend?"

Sal set his bags down and gave Giovanni a manly hug. Giovanni pulled back, grinned, and lightly slapped Sal's face.

"Look at you," Giovanni proclaimed. "Wasting away to nothing. Curse that maid of yours. She's starving you."

"Down another five pounds," Sal reported proudly while grinning. "Rosa allows me one desert a week." He then indicated the two intimidating men glaring at him while they continued to shovel cheesecake into their mouths. "Your boys seem to be eating it all."

"I don't recommend you attempt to take food from either of them," Giovanni announced. "They're not as friendly as they look." He then shrugged without care. "But at least they're housebroken."

"Good to know," Sal remarked and removed the ice cream from the bag. He approached the freezer and stashed the ice cream before either muscle-bound man made a move for it. "Where's Rosa?"

"I gave her the night off," Giovanni informed him, then added a slightly humored smile. "The old gal was in a bit of a hurry to leave."

"Hmm?" Sal casually reflected while hiding his knowing smile. "I wonder why?"

"She left your dinner in the oven."

Sal eyed his old friend and unpacked the rest of his groceries. "Another surprise visit," he remarked. "I know that can't be good. Are you in trouble?"

"Me?" Giovanni asked, then smirked. "Almost certainly, but that's not what brought me here."

"Marco?"

"Have you heard?"

Sal leaned his back against the main counter facing Giovanni and drew a deep breath. "I've heard things recently," he replied. "Rumors."

"They're all lies," Giovanni firmly insisted, then held his breath. "My son didn't kill those men. I know he's been acting a little out of sorts since his wedding fiasco. Took off before I visited you the last time, and I haven't seen him since. But it's not like him to kill men in cold blood like that. He wouldn't do it."

"Ruffled quite a few feathers," Sal remarked.

"Yeah," Giovanni sighed with defeat. "Now, he's a marked man. Every hitman and bounty hunter in the west is out looking for him. One million dollars with a bonus if he's brought back alive." He drew a deep breath and shook his head. "I'm desperate, Sal. They're going to kill my boy. Even if they bring him in alive, whoever gets him is going to do a thousand times worse."

Sal shut his eyes as if in pain and shook his head. "I can't do it, Giovanni," he muttered, then opened his eyes and looked at his old friend with sympathy. "Marco wants my friends dead. Last time you were here, you said as much."

"I'm sure he's over that by now. Your friends can find him," Giovanni insisted. "They can find him and hide him until we get this all sorted out." There was a moment of silence. "I'm desperate, Sal. I'll give them the million plus the bonus if they just keep my boy alive."

"They wouldn't even know where to start looking for him," Sal remarked. "Marco has to know bounty hunters are looking for him. He'll go into hiding."

"He's already in hiding. I think I know where to find him, but I can't go after him," Giovanni insisted. "The moment anyone sees me poking my head out, they'll be on my tail. You wouldn't believe what I went through just getting here undetected."

"Sal?" a male voice called from the foyer. "Sal, the door was open. Are you here?"

As Holden stepped into the kitchen, both enforcers leaped to their feet and reached for their guns hidden in their shoulder holsters. Holden appeared startled and reached for his weapon as well. Sal quickly moved away from the counter and stepped between the men.

"Let's not do this again," Sal announced while holding his hands out to both parties.

Holden saw Giovanni and groaned loudly. "Oh, not again," he muttered. "I really need to call first."

"Holden," Giovanni announced cheerfully and approached him with his arms out to hug him.

Holden took a quick step back and kept his hand on his weapon in his holster. "That's close enough."

Giovanni chuckled and lowered his arms. "Still nervous, huh?" he teased.

The oven dinged, catching everyone's attention.

Giovanni suddenly grinned. "I believe dinner's ready," he announced cheerfully and reached for some oven mitts. "Who's hungry?"

Holden slowly released the handle of his weapon as Giovanni removed the casserole dish from the oven. He set it on the stove and removed the lid revealing the large, perfectly cooked pot roast with small potatoes surrounding it. The intimidating man deeply inhaled the fantastic aroma and groaned his approval.

"Hmm, pot roast," Giovanni announced. He then glared at his two starving goons, who appeared ready to pounce on the roast with their bare hands. "Don't just stand there. Set the table, you big mooks."

§

After an uncomfortable meal seated across the informal kitchen table from Giovanni and his hired goons, Holden leaned back in his chair and eyed the two large men, who ravaged what was left of the pot roast straight from the casserole dish. He then glanced at Sal and Giovanni.

"Something on your mind, Holden?" Sal asked while offering a tiny smirk. "I know you didn't just stop by for a bite to eat."

"I was anticipating speaking to you in private," Holden informed him.

Giovanni, taking the hint, eyed his two men. "Make yourselves useful and clean up," he gruffly ordered.

Both muscle-bound bodyguards collected the dirty dishes and headed across the kitchen, where they promptly began rinsing the plates. Giovanni looked back at Holden and grinned almost proudly as if he solved the federal agent's dilemma. Holden eyed Giovanni and gently strummed his fingers on the table.

"I'm not sure I should be discussing this in front of you," Holden remarked.

"You think I don't know about the wave of murders among prominent *families* in the Colorado area?" Giovanni asked while raising a skeptical brow.

"That is why you're here, isn't it?" Sal then asked Holden. "You wanted some insight into the killings, correct? From an *insider's* point of view." Sal then managed a tiny, smug smirk. "Of course, I'm not actually an insider. You always did have a little trouble accepting that fact."

"You've made that perfectly clear numerous times, Sal," Holden replied with little emotion. "We can keep playing that game, if you'd like. I'll admit; I'm more comfortable with plausible deniability."

Giovanni chuckled lowly in his throat. "He sounds like one of us," the man teased.

Holden cast a look at the notorious mobster. He obviously wasn't happy with the comparison. Sal drew a deep breath, casually leaned back in his chair, and cast a look at Giovanni.

"Maybe, just this once, you'd like to trust the feds," Sal insisted, then shrugged. "I'll leave that up to you."

Giovanni frowned and appeared uncomfortable. He folded his hands together and leaned on the table, looking a little too "Godfather" for Holden's liking, and met the fed's gaze.

"The other families are blaming my son," Giovanni informed him. "They think Marco's the one killing their men."

"Why?" Holden asked.

"Because of what happened at his wedding on my island," Giovanni replied.

Holden shifted uncomfortably and sat up straight. Apparently, he remembered the aftermath a little too well, despite not having been there, but that was another story.

"Whoever is killing them has working knowledge of each of the families," Giovanni continued. "It's how he gets so close and what put the million-dollar bounty on my boy's head."

"One million dollars?" Holden suddenly stiffened. "That would mean--"

"Yes, every hitman and bounty hunter on the entire West Coast is searching for my son. Dead or alive," he reported.

"I don't understand how they've concluded that it was your son," Holden insisted and shook his head. "The attacks I've seen could easily have been committed by anyone on the streets."

Giovanni groaned softly and shook his head. "Those are the ones that have been reported," he informed him. "I'm talking about the *rest* of them."

"The rest?" Holden asked and appeared interested.

"The hits happening at their homes and private businesses," Giovanni replied without taking his eyes off Holden. "The ones where they don't call the local law in to investigate."

"How--?"

"There are enough people on the take to forge death certificates, Agent Falcone," Giovanni insisted while showing little emotion.

"Why are you telling me this?" Holden then asked while processing the information. "Sounds to me as if this will cost you if your people find out."

"I'm already caught in the crosshairs," Giovanni informed him. "I want my son back alive. I want you to conduct a fair investigation and not just assume my son is responsible. I don't want you building a case around him because you'll find more than enough evidence against him. You need to investigate from a different perspective. Eliminate him as the prime suspect and start looking at who else has motive."

"I'm willing to give him the benefit of the doubt, especially since I haven't even compiled a list of suspects yet," Holden replied. "But I'm going to need a starting point. Who are some of these 'other' deaths that haven't been reported?"

"We both need to tread very lightly, Agent Falcone," Giovanni insisted. "If it's a starting point you want, I can suggest you begin with Vinnie Scartelli."

"Vinnie '*the knife*' Scartelli?" Holden remarked while raising his brow. He snorted a soft laugh and shook his head. "There's a venomous snake."

"Vinnie's about seventy years old. He's been out of the game for over a decade," Giovanni informed him. "His grandson died last week. The grandson that lived with him. Ruled an 'in-home' accident. Happened at his estate. He wanted to call some homicide detectives, but his other grandson *convinced* him they'd handle it 'in-house'." Giovanni leaned back in his chair. "Now that the dust has settled, his remaining grandson is back to disowning the old man again. He might be willing to talk to you, but you'll need to remain discreet and not involve anyone else in the Bureau. Some of your own ranks can't be trusted."

"Does he have a security detail?" Holden asked.

Giovanni suddenly chuckled. "Some very devoted, old dogs who'd do anything for the old man," he reported.

"Sounds as if I'll be shot before I ring the bell," Holden muttered.

"I advise showing up within the next hour. He doesn't like being disturbed after eight," Giovanni informed him. "Tell the guard at the gate that you brought Vinnie his favorite white German chocolate. They're his weakness, and it's also code for a visit from an old acquaintance." Giovanni's brows rose commandingly. "Very important. Make sure you actually have a box of white German chocolate." He chuckled softly. "If you say you have it and don't produce it, he'll probably slit your throat."

"That's pleasant," Holden muttered, then shifted in his chair. "Where do I find this white German chocolate he likes so much?"

"Germany," Giovanni replied while grinning, then cast a look at Sal.

Sal suddenly groaned and glared at Giovanni. "You were snooping in my office, weren't you?"

"Old habits," Giovanni replied.

"I bought that for my daughter's birthday," Sal insisted.

"I'll order you a case of the stuff. He doesn't have a month to wait for that particular order to arrive from overseas," Giovanni remarked then indicated Holden. "Give the fed the chocolates. Help out your old friend."

"Fine," Sal moaned. "First my cheesecake and now my chocolates." He stood. "It's as if you're all secretly working with Rosa to keep me on my diet."

Chapter 11

Vinnie Scartelli's estate was showing signs of neglect. The long, concrete driveway leading up to the old mansion had numerous cracks, the lawn possibly hadn't been mowed since the end of summer, and vines were growing up the side of the building. The mansion itself needed a fresh coat of paint, now looking more like a haunted house. It was possible that the sheer size of the mansion and estate was more than the older man could handle. Perhaps his source of revenue was no longer flowing his way either. By the looks of the outside, it was safe to assume the interior wasn't much better. Within the house, the lounge to the rear of the mansion hadn't seen its glory days in decades. Dark wood throughout the room was in serious need of polishing, cobwebs had formed in the tall corners of the ceiling, and most of the antique furniture hadn't been used or properly cleaned in many months.

A man in his early seventies sat in a plush, antique chair. Despite his age, Vinnie Scartelli remained a force with which to be reckoned. He was tall and lean, but it was an athletic lean. He had a head full of thick, gray hair and his fair share of wrinkles, but there was a lot of fight beyond his tired, blue eyes. To most, he remained a frightening man with an extremely bloody reputation. Vinnie stared at an elegantly framed photo of his son, daughter-in-law, and his two grandsons when they were just teenage boys. While stranded in his thoughts, he heard a commotion that seemed to start in the foyer and carried over into the grand hallway. Vinnie set down the picture, casually leaned back in his plush chair, and removed an impressive .357 Magnum from a cleverly hidden holster built into the arm of the chair. He had just enough time to open his book and lay it across his lap, concealing the weapon beneath it, before the lounge door was thrown open.

Vinnie's grandson, Vincent Scartelli III, entered the room and paused just within the doorway. Vincent was six-foot-one with broad shoulders and an athletic build. Much like his grandfather, the man in his early thirties was somewhat imposing at first sight. He had lush, dark hair with captivating blue eyes, much like his grandfather. He was as handsome as he was villainous. Vincent was accompanied by three intimidating-looking men who worked for him. His own private mercenaries for hire. The first man, Bart, was over six-foot-two and built like a professional wrestler. He had a massive upper body with an incredibly thick neck. The man in his late thirties was not particularly attractive, but his muscle mass seemed to be his selling feature. Since he had been losing his hair, he kept it buzzed short, matching his thick, facial stubble. Although he wasn't the smartest man, he was a skilled fighter, making him the perfect soldier, but certainly not a leader.

The second man, Detrick, had an impressive build, although not nearly as muscular as his counterpart. Detrick was as bald as a cue ball and as thick as a brick house. He stood over six-foot-two with enough muscle mass to back up his tough boy attitude. The man in his mid-thirties had a steely-eyed gaze that conveyed his uncaring attitude. Despite being an attractive man, most women took one look at him and turned and ran the other way. He was frightening at best. Years in the military made him a dangerous mercenary. The third and last man, Carter, had just enough muscle mass behind him to be noticeable without being excessively muscular. Carter was the brains of the operation as well as a skilled fighter. The man in his mid-thirties was as handsome as he was deadly. Standing over six-foot and built athletic leaning toward muscular, he was an impressive sight. His sandy blonde hair was kept short and business-like, and his blue eyes were captivating. Despite his charm and appeal, he was a dangerous man. More dangerous than his pretty-boy looks suggested.

Vinnie stared at his grandson and the smug sneer on his youthful face. The older man raised his brows and didn't seem impressed by his grandson.

"You could have tried knocking," Vinnie remarked with little emotion.

"Would you have let me in?" Vincent asked while maintaining his arrogant look.

"You know, Vinnie--" Vinnie began but was interrupted by the arrogant young man.

"It's Vincent, Grandfather," Vincent insisted with a mildly irritated sneer.

The young, angry man didn't want anyone comparing him to his father or his grandfather. Refusing to go by Vinnie was the first step in securing his own legacy. Vinnie frowned and shook his head at the arrogance of his surviving grandson.

"I was going to make a point on respect and a certain code of ethics," Vinnie remarked then sighed, "but it would only be wasted on your entire whoring generation."

Vincent snorted a laugh and smirked his irritation. "My younger brother was brutally murdered, and you want to preach about how, back in your day, you had honor." His smirk turned into a sneer. "Your generation was no better than mine, except my generation has the guts to do what yours wouldn't. You let some ridiculous code cloud your better judgment. You raised my father to be a weak man, and it got him killed. Then you took my brother in and turned him into another weak man, which also got him killed."

"And your arrogance is what's going to get you killed," Vinnie insisted with a sneer, although he refused to raise his voice. "There was a time that I would have struck you down where you stood. It would have been considered a mercy killing. Obviously, there's no hope for you. You'll never be half the man your father was."

Vincent sneered at his grandfather. "Tread lightly, old man," he snarled and flashed his weapon in his shoulder holster as a shallow attempt at intimidation. "You may be my grandfather, but that doesn't mean I won't kill you."

"If you're going to make those kinds of threats, why don't you just do it?" Vinnie snarled, then reeled in his hostility and again resumed his calm demeanor. "Let's see how that ends for you."

Vinnie's finger tightened on the trigger of his carefully hidden Magnum aimed directly at his grandson across the room. The younger Vincent seemed to think better of it and allowed his jacket to fall back over his shoulder holster. Vinnie's finger loosened on the hidden weapon's trigger.

"You're in no position to make threats, old man," Vincent scoffed back. "Your attack dogs are completely useless. Not sure why you keep a couple of old guys like that around in the first place."

"Of course you wouldn't," Vinnie casually replied. "You don't understand loyalty because your men only respond to money. They'd turn on you and each other in a heartbeat. My men, who you probably should have killed when you had the chance, aren't hired goons like "The Three Stooges" you have there. I keep my men around because they're loyal. They've stood by me for more than just a paycheck." He considered the comment and then shrugged. "Okay, so maybe they're not as young and intimidating as your strike team there, but we've been together a long time. So long, in fact, that they've learned to read my mind." A tiny smile crossed Vinnie's face. "Take now, for instance."

Bart and Detrick were suddenly struck in the back of the heads with the stocks of two rifles. As Carter turned, both of Vinnie's older guards aimed their rifles at his head.

"See," Vinnie announced and seemed pleased with himself. "With anyone else, they would have pulled the trigger, but they know I don't want a war with my only living grandson, no matter how despicable he's become." Vinnie casually removed the Magnum from under his book and laid it across this lap. His humor was short-lived. "What brought you charging into my home uninvited, *Vinnie?*"

"I'm here to collect my brother's belongings," Vincent informed him.

Vinnie shook his head with little reaction. "You aren't entitled to anything that belonged to your brother," the older man announced. "You turned your back on him when he was alive. You don't get to mourn him now that he's dead." He then straightened proudly in his chair. "Of course, we both know what you really came here for."

Vincent turned angry while glaring at his grandfather and took a quick step toward him. Vinnie sneered and aimed the Magnum revolver at his grandson. "If you so much as twitch, I'll put a very large bullet in that very tiny brain of yours."

"I want what is rightfully mine," Vincent snarled despite heeding his grandfather's threat.

"Your brother's insurance policy?" Vinnie just about teased then grinned. "Your brother held onto that to keep you in line. Now that he's dead, I'll just hang onto that. The safety deposit box key is safely hidden." Vinnie then leaned forward without lowering the large weapon. "And if anything should happen to me, it'll be in the hands of the FBI." Vinnie casually sat back in his chair while smirking. "You may want to pray that I don't die before you. There's no statute of limitation on murder."

Vincent's eyes narrowed in anger. "Everything you've done," he snarled, "all the people you've killed. How can you justify holding something like this over me all these years?"

"It goes back to that moral code thing that you don't understand," Vinnie informed him. "You can kill your enemies, but you don't kill their families. As long as I have that insurance policy, you'll never kill another innocent person again." Vinnie then sneered and waved his gun. "Now take your henchmen and get out of my sight."

"We can do this the easy way or the hard way," Vincent insisted.

Vinnie raised a brow and smirked. "We're already doing this the easy way," he replied. "Get out, or I'll forget that you're my own flesh and blood and blow your fucking head off."

Vincent's two henchmen, who had been knocked to the floor, slowly recovered while holding their heads. Bart and

Detrick appeared angry and ready to fight the men who had struck them, but they were at a serious disadvantage without their weapons.

"This isn't over, Grandfather," Vincent insisted.

"Oh, that's where you're wrong," Vinnie replied while showing no emotion. "But, you know where to find me if you ever want to take another swing at me."

Chapter 12

Holden's black blazer pulled up to Scartelli's estate around seven-thirty that evening. The gate was open, and there appeared to be no one manning it. He looked up at the camera aimed squarely at the entrance. It was recently busted. Holden tensed slightly. Giovanni was adamant that Holden go alone without additional agents as back-up, but it was starting to feel a bit like an ambush. Sal seemed to trust Giovanni and would undoubtedly warn Holden if he thought his friend was setting him up. That didn't seem to put Holden at ease any though. Holden cautiously drove through the open gate and proceeded up the long driveway, keeping watch on his surroundings. It was still light enough that he could see the entire grounds. As he pulled up to the estate, despite the large garage in the back, Holden noted several cars parked out front. That in itself seemed odd.

Since his retirement, Vinnie was a refuted recluse. Apart from his grandson, a few guards, and some staff, he didn't entertain. Holden pulled up closer to the front of the mansion and eyed the parked cars, assessing the situation. There was a fine line when dealing with someone like Vinnie. A show of trust was critical, yet that trust, when misplaced, would get a man killed. Holden needed to walk that fine line. After sitting in his vehicle for several minutes scanning the surrounding area, he finally grabbed the box of white German chocolate and got out of his car. He cast several looks around as he approached the steps to the mansion. When he heard a car door shut, Holden spun, instinctively reaching for his weapon, but somehow resisted drawing it despite every fiber of his being telling him that he should. Holden stared with some surprise and allowed his hand to relax on the grip of his holstered weapon. Gil, who was dressed in a freshly pressed black suit and tie, casually approached Holden with a sly sort of smirk on his face.

"You certainly are jumpy tonight," Gil announced, finding humor in Holden's twitchiness.

"Gil? Where did you come from?" Holden just about demanded then eyed the suit he wore. It wasn't often any of the guys dressed up. Explaining blood to the dry cleaners was difficult. "What are you doing here?"

"I was staking out the place for a few minutes before you arrived. Sal called Jackie and told her you were about to do something stupid," Gil replied, then shrugged. "So she sent me to cover your back."

"Considering this isn't exactly Bureau sanctioned," Holden remarked, "I'm happy for the extra pair of eyes."

"Front gate camera has been tampered with as well," Gil reported.

"Tampered with?" Holden remarked. "The thing was smashed beyond recognition."

"Made me hesitate before pulling up too." He then eyed the box of chocolates. "What's with the chocolates? Wining and dining the mob?"

"Long story," Holden muttered and again looked around. He focused his attention back on Gil. "Just let me do the talking, okay?"

"There's a reason Jackie sent me over the other guys, Holden," Gil insisted with little emotion.

Gil had the best disposition of all the guys, having the perfect combination of intimidation and quiet observation. Jackie knew what she was doing when she chose Gil to provide backup for her husband. Both men headed up the steps to the large porch.

"By the looks of the security camera at the gate, it's possible we're not the only ones here," Holden informed Gil. "We need to proceed cautiously."

"You're the boss," Gil announced with little emotion.

Holden paused before the double doors, hesitated only a moment, and then rang the bell. As the elegant bell chimed, Gil stood just behind Holden and kept a watchful eye on the area surrounding them, almost as if expecting an ambush. The door opened, revealing Vinnie's man with an AR-15 in his hands aimed at Holden and Gil. Holden twitched and fought his first instinct to reach for his own weapon.

"What do you want?" the man demanded in a gruff, hostile tone.

Holden, who already had his badge in hand, flipped it open. "I'm Special Agent Holden Falcone here to see Vincent Scartelli."

"If you don't have a warrant, I suggest you call ahead and make an appointment next time," the man snarled. "Vinnie isn't taking any more callers tonight."

The man was about to shut the door when Holden spoke up. "I brought him white German chocolates."

There was a moment's pause as the large man suspiciously eyed Holden. "You did?" he asked with some surprise, then eyed the box of chocolates.

"It's important I talk to Vinnie," Holden insisted.

The guard lowered his weapon, although keeping his finger near the trigger. He then nodded to Gil. "Who's he?" he demanded.

Holden seemed to scramble for a response when Gil smiled and flashed his own FBI badge.

"Special Agent Rafferty," Gil replied.

Holden cast a sideways glance at the badge but only caught a glimpse of it before Gil closed it and slipped it back inside his jacket.

"Fine," the guard huffed and moved out of the doorway. "You can see Vinnie, but keep it brief."

Holden and Gil slipped past the large man and entered the foyer. The guard shut the door behind them. The first thing they noticed was the second guard positioned at the bottom of the stairs with his own intimidating weapon. The first guard took the box of chocolates from Holden's hand and inspected it. Since it was still in its original, untampered wrapper, he seemed convinced it was safe. Rather than return it, he headed past them.

"This way," the guard announced and headed down the grand hallway.

Holden and Gil followed the large, armed man down the hallway to the third door on the right. Holden cast a look at Gil and raised a curious brow.

"That's my suit, isn't it?" Holden muttered.

"I certainly didn't jet back to the lodge to fetch mine," Gil muttered without looking at Holden.

The guard tapped twice on the door, then opened it and entered. Vinnie remained in his plush chair and set his grandson's photo on the end table alongside him.

"Who was at the door?" Vinnie asked, then cast his eyes upon Holden. His expression dropped to disappointment. "You let the feds into my house?" He glared disapprovingly at his man. "What's wrong with you?"

The guard approached his older boss and handed him the box of chocolates. "He brought these for you."

Vinnie eyed the box of chocolates a moment before accepting them. He hesitated, then looked at Holden and offered a somewhat pleasant smile.

"Please, forgive my manners," Vinnie announced, then indicated the nearby sofa. "Have a seat. Would you like a drink?"

Holden and Gil sat on the antique sofa. Gil seemed unusually relaxed, although Holden remained slightly rigid.

"No, we're good, thank you," Holden replied.

"And you gentlemen are--?" Vinnie pressed.

"I'm Special Agent Holden Falcone," he announced, then hesitated and indicated Gil. "And this is my associate, Special Agent Gil Rafferty."

Vinnie unwrapped the plastic from the box of chocolates while eyeing both men. "I've never had federal agents bring me chocolates before," he remarked and raised a somewhat suspicious brow. "I'm not sure what to think."

Holden watched as Vinnie opened the box. The older man eagerly eyed the assorted, white chocolates. He then smiled and extended the box to Holden.

"Have a chocolate," he announced.

Holden was about to decline when Gil suddenly jabbed him and indicated the box the older man held extended toward him. The look Gil shot Holden spoke louder than any words. Holden and Gil each stood and took a chocolate from the box. Vinnie watched as both men savored the expensive chocolate. He then smiled, satisfied that they weren't poisoned. Vinnie removed one of the chocolates for himself and bit into it. He savored the flavor, taking longer to eat one piece of chocolate than most people would. He finally eyed both men while maintaining his smile.

"So what brings the feds to my home," Vinnie asked.

"We heard about the death of your grandson," Holden remarked then hesitated. "We're sorry for your loss."

Vinnie drew a deep breath and seemed to tense for the first time. "Which one of the rat bastards told you?" he snarled with some irritation. "That's why you're here, right? You heard about *what* happened to my grandson."

"Yes, we heard about what happened to your grandson," Holden gently replied, wanting to keep on this man's good side. His age aside, Vinnie had a frightening reputation, and there was no doubt he wouldn't think twice about killing both of them. "We're trying to catch a killer. We're not here because of what you did or didn't tell the police. As far as my associate and I are concerned, we were never here." Holden drew a deep breath. "We just want to find this guy."

Vinnie suddenly sneered. "It was Giovanni, wasn't it?" he scoffed in irritation. "Every hitman in the region is hunting his son, and he wants you to get him off the hook."

"I'm not getting anyone 'off the hook'," Holden insisted. "I just want to stop a killer."

"Well, fortunately for you, I'm possibly the only person other than Giovanni who doesn't think Marco is the killer," Vinnie informed Holden.

"Why's that?" Holden asked while attempting to hide his surprise.

"I have two grandsons, Agent Falcone," Vinnie remarked, then hesitated and sneered. "Well, I *had* two grandsons. When my daughter-in-law died, my younger grandson wanted to live with me, and the other went to live with his father." Vinnie plucked another chocolate from the box and again savored it. He then returned to reality. "Although born a year apart, they were almost identical. Most people had a difficult time telling them apart. Vincent is a reckless boy with a broken moral compass. Anthony, on the other hand, was a wonderful boy." Vinnie managed a tiny smile while sinking into his own thoughts. "He wanted to be an artist." He cast a quick look at Holden. "I had private teachers out to the mansion for his art classes when he was a boy. He even turned the pool house into an art studio. Some artsy people from the city wanted him to do an art show. His life was coming together perfectly." Vinnie then sneered. "His worthless brother, on the other hand, had been following a destructive path since he was a young teenager. My son lost control of Vincent several years back. The kid thought he was invincible. About five years ago, he killed a police detective in front of the woman he was dating at the time."

"I heard about that," Holden remarked, remembering the story. "She was going to testify against your grandson, but she was killed along with a couple of U.S. Marshalls in the safe house where they were keeping her until the trial."

The older man frowned, then nodded. "That's when my son realized he'd lost Vincent. Having that young girl killed was the final nail in his coffin, I'm afraid." Vinnie sank into thought a moment and again met Holden's gaze. "I'm far from a saint, but I'm glad I got out when I did."

"Fifteen years ago," Holden announced. "Around the time you took in your grandson."

"Yes, Anthony was fifteen when his mother died."

There was an unusually long silence as Vinnie seemed to drift out a moment. He shifted uncomfortably in his chair and met Holden's gaze.

"I read about the other killings. They were all bad men." He raised his brows. "The sort of man I was in my youth. Anthony was the reason I retired. When Anthony moved in with me, I knew it was time to get out of that business."

"Why do you think Marco is innocent?" Holden finally asked.

"Yes," Vinnie announced and shifted in his chair. "I sometimes lose my train of thought. You see, Marco knew Anthony and Vincent. He knew them quite well. Your killer has been targeting bad men. Men who were killers themselves. He meant to kill Vincent, not Anthony, and Marco knew Vincent didn't live here. The killer you seek must have followed Anthony thinking he was Vincent. If he knew either of my grandsons, he didn't know them very well. He killed the wrong man."

Holden sank into thought then met Vinnie's gaze. "What happened the night Anthony was killed?"

"Anthony ran out to the art store for some painting supplies," Vinnie replied. "I was already in bed when he got home." He indicated the big man standing just inside the doorway with the weapon aimed down at the floor. "My man found him the next morning in his studio out back." Vinnie suddenly sneered. "His throat had been slit. Just like all the others."

Holden tensed slightly. "I'm sorry you had to go through that," he remarked. "Was there any sign of a struggle?"

Vinnie shook his head in response. "My other grandson, Vincent III, insisted it had to be someone Anthony knew. Someone he trusted betrayed him. He's the one who convinced me not to go to the police."

"None of the victims showed signs of a struggle," Holden informed him. "But we don't think they knew their killer. We think the killer watches his victims; studies them and their surroundings, searching for the perfect time and place to attack."

"I want my grandson's killer to pay," Vinnie informed Holden, "but I'm positive it wasn't Marco."

Chapter 13

Once Giovanni had left Sal's mansion, Sal locked the door and set the alarm for good measure. He didn't need any additional surprises that evening. It was almost eight o'clock, and his maid, Rosa, would be returning soon. Despite what Giovanni said about his son, Sal still wasn't convinced that Marco wasn't responsible for the killings. Not so long ago, when Giovanni last showed up unannounced, he had been concerned about his son's behavior after his wedding massacre. Giovanni claimed his son blamed everyone for what happened, including Whiskey Tango Foxtrot and Sal's daughter, who had been personally responsible for taking down Marco's monster bride. Still, Giovanni was an old friend, and he deserved Sal's best effort. In the morning, he would pay a visit to the guys, who were camping out at Jackie's house for a few days before heading back to their remote mountain lodge.

Sal returned to the kitchen in search of something sweet, being his promised cheesecake had been devoured by Giovanni's ravenous thugs. As he entered the kitchen, he saw a young woman dressed in black casually sitting on the main counter. Sal jumped with surprise then seemed to relax when he recognized the woman.

"Jesus, Nevada," he scoffed. "You scared the crap out of me. You're lucky I don't walk around armed these days."

"You really should," Nevada informed him without cracking a smile.

Nevada was best described as a beautiful temptress of mass destruction. The young, female bounty hunter was possibly in her mid-twenties and stood almost five-foot-eight. Her bronzed, caramel-colored skin was nearly makeup-free yet flawless in complexion. Nevada's wavy, golden-brown hair hung below the shoulders of her extremely athletic body, and her wardrobe consisted of what could best be described as a black stalking outfit, which was both low-cut and form-fitting. Her ensemble was completed with a short, black leather jacket and mid-calf, black leather boots that were functional rather than fashionable. Nevada's piercing, emerald green eyes all but conveyed her total and complete lack of empathy for everyone. There was no denying she was a frightening mix of sexy and malicious.

"Does anyone knock anymore?" Sal finally demanded.

"Considering the company you've been keeping, I'm guessing you know why I'm here," Nevada remarked, ignoring the question.

"I'm not as stupid as I look," Sal informed her. "Unfortunately, I'm not in the mood, Nevada. I don't know anything more than anyone else about Marco."

"Marco's daddy stopping by tells me you do," Nevada replied while raising a cocky brow. "That million-dollar bounty on Marco's head would be life-changing for me, Sal. I can finally afford to get out of Zack's 'my way or the highway' program. Let me have Marco. You know I'll bring him in alive."

"Maybe you should make a deal with Giovanni then," Sal replied with little interest.

Sal approached the pantry, opened one of the doors, and removed a package of cookies. There was a sticky note attached to it. It read, 'eat healthy'. Sal groaned, ripped off the sticky note left by his doting house manager, and opened the package of cookies.

Nevada suddenly let out a humored laugh as her eyes widened. "I actively avoid Giovanni," she informed Sal. "And now that his son has a price on his head, I'm staying well below that man's radar. If he even sees a bounty hunter in his crosshairs, he's firing first and asking questions later."

"That really is your problem, Nevada," Sal informed her while munching on a cookie.

Nevada frowned and jumped off the counter. "You know, I really thought you'd be a little more accommodating," she remarked.

"Oh, I'm sorry," Sal remarked and extended the pack of cookies toward her. "Did you want a cookie?"

She sneered her irritation with him. "Fine, I'll find him without your help," Nevada scoffed, then turned to leave. She suddenly stopped, turned back toward him, and snatched a cookie from the pack. "I skipped dinner."

Nevada bit into the cookie while maintaining her glare, then turned and left through the back door. Sal watched her go and shook his head.

"Girl needs a better hobby," he remarked, then tossed the package of cookies on the island counter.

Sal was about to approach the refrigerator when he seemed to consider something and looked toward the back door. The green 'activate' light wasn't lit on the security system. Nevada certainly hadn't deactivated it between the time he'd set it until the time he'd reached the kitchen, which meant Nevada had already been inside the house when he activated the alarm. Why was it now deactivated? Sal suddenly became alarmed. He hesitated only a moment before rounding the island counter and reached beneath it. He removed a carefully hidden semiautomatic from its concealed compartment and listened to the mostly silent house. A creak was heard just outside the kitchen from the hallway. Sal partially lowered himself behind the island counter, resting the gun on the counter aimed at the doorway.

An armed man stepped through the doorway into the kitchen but saw Sal too late. As the man aimed his weapon, Sal squeezed the trigger and fired a round into the man's shoulder. The intruder flew back against the doorframe.

"Drop the weapon, or the next shot takes away all your pain," Sal announced in an oddly calm voice.

The man, riddled in agonizing pain, dropped his weapon to the floor with a loud clatter.

Sal then indicated the kitchen table. "Have a seat, son."

The young man clutched his bleeding shoulder in agony and approached the table. The shooter was a reasonably good looking man in his mid-twenties with a military buzz cut, suggesting he either just got out of the military or he was a mercenary wannabe. The young man kept a nervous eye on Sal then took a seat. Sal tossed him a dishtowel.

"Put some pressure on that, would you?" Sal remarked. "You're bleeding all over my kitchen floor. My housekeeper hates that."

The intruder placed the towel on his shoulder wound and applied pressure.

"How many friends are with you?" Sal asked.

The man shook his head. "Just me."

"Don't lie to me, son," Sal announced with a deep sigh. "You aren't very good at it."

"I'm new to the game," the young intruder replied.

"Yeah, well, you won't make it very long at the rate you're going," Sal informed him. "You may want to make a life-altering decision while someone pokes around in that wound digging out that bullet." Sal raised an arrogant brow while watching the young man, who almost seemed to be going into shock. "First time being shot?"

The young man nodded.

"Hurts twice as much coming out as it did going in," Sal informed him. "Where's your friend?"

He nodded toward the doorway. "Study," the man replied, now looking a little pale.

"If the sight of a little blood bothers you, you're in the wrong profession," Sal remarked.

There was a loud commotion from the hallway. Sal aimed his weapon at the hallway entrance. A man was launched through the swinging door and struck the island counter. He attempted to straighten, not even paying attention to Sal. Nevada passed through the swinging doorway with her eyes locked on the intruder.

"Care to take another swing?" Nevada asked.

The man lunged for Nevada. She spun into a roundhouse kick, connecting with his chest, and sent him back against the island counter. While he was already halfway to the floor, she kicked him in the face and sent him the rest of the way to the floor. Sal lowered his weapon and eyed Nevada.

"Wasn't exactly expecting to see you back here so soon," Sal remarked.

Nevada eyed him and shrugged. "I don't hold a grudge," she insisted. "I heard the gunshot and felt something a little too much like compassion, so I came back."

"You were a Marine, right?" Sal asked the woman.

Nevada smirked. "Oorah," she replied.

Sal reached beneath the counter and tossed her a medical bag. "Our friend, there, needs a bullet removed," he remarked. "Give him half a dose of the localized pain killer. But only enough to take the edge off. The boy needs to feel just enough to make some tough decisions regarding his life choices."

Nevada suddenly grinned and approached the kitchen table. "Oh, I do enjoy 'tough love'," she announced. "It's kind of like torture but without being entirely frowned upon." Nevada took a seat alongside the young man and met his gaze with a stern look. "Now, don't go passing out. It won't be nearly as much fun for me."

Sal placed the gun down the back of his pants, removed some zip ties from one of the drawers, and approached the unconscious man on the floor before the island counter. He glanced at the young man seated at the table and saw him flinch when Nevada injected his shoulder with the syringe.

"Big baby," Nevada scoffed.

"What's your name, son?" Sal asked the young man while zip-tying his friend.

"Jack," he replied, now sweating profusely as he avoided looking at the wound while Nevada cleaned it.

"Kind of squeamish for a hitman," Nevada muttered.

"He's new," Sal casually informed her.

As Nevada dug in the bloody wound for the bullet, the young man squirmed in his chair. When she finally removed the bullet, the man gasped several times and attempted to relax.

"Wouldn't it be easier on you if you just left me for the police to worry about?" the young man asked.

Sal straightened after zip-tying the unconscious man, then eyed the young man seated at the table. "Who said I was calling the police?" he asked, then raised a cocky brow. "Guys like me don't call the police to handle hitmen. Too many questions."

The young man eyed Sal with some concern.

Nevada suddenly grinned. "Are you going to interrogate them?" she asked with a little too much enthusiasm. "If you are, I am *so* in."

Sal groaned and shook his head. "Not really my style," he informed her. "I think I'll take the guy on the floor for a little joyride. Dump him off in the middle of nowhere. Give him time to think about *his* life choices." He then indicated the young man. "After you patch that one up, we're going to let him go."

The young man stared at Sal and seemed surprised. "Why would you do that?"

"We all make mistakes, son," Sal informed him. "I'm just giving you a chance to learn from yours. Do yourself a favor. Learn a trade. Make something of yourself. You clearly weren't built to last on the path you've chosen."

"I can't believe you'd do that for me," the man remarked. "You don't even know me."

Sal nodded. "I know you," he replied. "I was just like you when I was your age. Only I got to be pretty good at what I did." He shook his head. "Trust me; that's nothing to be proud of."

Chapter 14

It was nearly eight-thirty that evening, and the team was camping out in Jackie's house within the quiet development on the outskirts of Colorado Springs. Jackie and Holden had a large living room, perfect for entertaining, which was good, considering how often they seemed to have visitors and overnight company. An island counter with seating for four divided the living room from the kitchen. In addition to the sofa, love seat, and two plush chairs, the additional seating at the island counter allowed the entire team to hang out together when they weren't having drinks on the back patio. Several stacked, empty boxes of pizza occupied the island counter. They managed to keep Kirk away from the last pizza so Holden and Gil would have dinner when they returned. The coffee table contained several empty bottles of beer, giving the room a frat house sort of appeal.

Jackie sat on the arm of the plush chair Bogart occupied and leaned on the back of the chair near his shoulder. Ross sat on one end of the sofa with Beck and Monroe, who were in yet another heated debate about something trivial. Kirk, Ross, and Bogart shared the same boring looks at the two men who never seemed to give it a rest. Kirk sat forward in his chair on the opposite side of the room from Jackie and Bogart and eyed Beck and Monroe with a serious look.

"Let's play a little game," Kirk announced. "It's called 'which one of you dumb shits will I punch in the mouth first if you don't shut the fuck up'."

"Kirk," Ross lightly scolded.

"Just saying what everyone is thinking," Kirk informed Ross with little emotion.

"Okay, guys," Ross announced while groaning, then leaned forward from his position on the sofa. "We aren't at the lodge. No fighting, arguing, or rough housing. There are too many Ward and June Cleaver types living around here. Let's keep it family-friendly, or we're leaving tonight."

Monroe and Beck shifted in their seats, taking Ross's words seriously. He'd do it too.

Kirk stood and eyed Monroe and Beck with a mildly mocking grin. "In that case, I'll just hold off beating your asses until we're back at the lodge."

Ross shook his head with disapproval but didn't comment as Kirk headed into the kitchen to fetch another beer. He returned with four bottles of beer, handing one to each of the guys and one for himself. Ross didn't need another since he was still nursing his first bottle. Jackie was alerted to the sound of two cars pulling up to the house. She knew the sound of Holden's official Bureau blazer and quickly leaped up from the arm of Bogart's chair. Only a moment passed when the front door opened. When Holden and Gil entered the house, Jackie was quick to greet the two men with a mildly anxious look on her face.

"Is everything okay?" she asked while eyeing each man.

Jackie hated to admit that she was paranoid about her husband's recent meeting with the former, aging mob boss, but she'd heard about Vinnie's kill count and the gruesome manner in which some of the men had been killed. It was enough to unnerve her.

"Yeah," Holden replied while making a face. "Vinnie the knife was an absolute delight."

Jackie again eyed each man and attempted to downplay her concern, although she quite possibly failed. "He didn't try and kill you, did he?"

Gil suddenly chuckled at the question. "It may have sounded like sarcasm, but Holden exaggerates," he reported. "For the former, cut-throat mafia-type, he was actually quite cordial. Even offered us chocolate."

"Because he wanted to see if we had poisoned it," Holden muttered, although it was obvious Gil was aware of Vinnie's reasons.

"Did he offer any leads?" Jackie pressed.

"We'll talk about it when we're alone," Holden informed her.

Jackie glanced at the team scattered about the room, then looked back at Holden and shrugged. "We are alone."

Holden stared at Jackie a moment with a look resembling disapproval, but he seemed to give in. "Vinnie doesn't think Marco killed his grandson. Vinnie's older grandson, on the other hand, seems to think otherwise. He may be the one who put the bounty on Marco's head in the first place."

Ross approached, took a broad stance, and folded his arms across his chest. "So every hitman and bounty hunter is going to be hunting Marco." Ross shook his head. "There's something I wouldn't want to get in the middle of."

Gil then looked around. "Where's Darth?"

"Zack took him for a walk," Bogart reported. "The moment Zack showed up, Darth went insane and practically did cartwheels by the door."

Gil shook his head while making a face. "I think Darth has been spending too much time with Zack," he remarked. "Those two are up to something."

"He's probably pissing on a thousand spots, marking his territory," Kirk muttered from where he leaned against the island counter.

"I think he was referring to Zack," Holden casually informed Kirk.

"Yeah, so was I," Kirk replied, then shook his head. "Darth is a fucking dog. He's not *up to* anything."

"First off," Gil launched in response to Kirk. "Darth is *not* a fucking dog. He's my partner." He then frowned. "I'm more concerned that Zack is teaching Darth *tricks*."

"I'm going to assume you don't mean fetch, rollover, and play dead," Monroe muttered.

"More like kill and sic balls," Gil scoffed.

"Why do you always assume the worst?" Zack demanded from behind Kirk by the kitchen island counter.

Kirk didn't even seem startled that Zack had mysteriously appeared behind him. Darth trotted across the living room, ignoring everyone, and jumped onto the vacant plush chair. He placed his head on the chair arm and shut his eyes. All eyes were on the exhausted dog. Gil eyed his dog and remained somewhat suspicious. Darth seemed fairly tired from what had to be a short walk. Zack approached the sofa, cast himself upon it, and shut his eyes as well. Everyone was curious, but none seemed willing to ask. When the doorbell rang, Darth opened his eyes and woofed under his breath but didn't bother lifting his head. Gil again eyed the dog and his lack of interest in who was at the door.

"Why does Darth look like a hungover sailor on shore leave?" Gil just about demanded but didn't seem surprised when Zack didn't respond.

Holden approached the front door within the foyer and opened it, revealing a police officer. The middle-aged uniformed officer was one of Holden's neighbors who lived at the end of the street. He was a tall, sturdy man with a clean-cut, youthful face.

"Josh," Holden announced while eyeing the man in uniform. "What brings you by at this hour?"

"I'm here about your dog," the officer announced in a stern voice.

Holden tensed but maintained his smile. "We don't own a dog."

The others glanced at the chair. Darth was gone. When they eyed the sofa, Zack was also gone. Something was definitely up.

"Your four-legged, frequent houseguest then," the officer reported, not sounding humored by Holden's response.

Holden groaned and shook his head. "What did he do?" he finally asked.

"He jumped the fence into my yard and humped my police K-9," the officer announced with increasing irritation. "She was only out in the yard for five minutes. I opened the door to call her in, and there he was, defiling Officer Zena."

Holden placed his hand over his eyes and held his breath. It was hard to tell what was going through his head.

"I swear," Josh continued. "It was as if the dog was on some secret, covert mission, waiting for the two seconds I turned my back."

Jackie suddenly cringed and had to look away. It was a covert mission, all right. Orchestrated by Zack and carried out by Darth.

"I am so sorry," Holden finally announced.

"What am I supposed to do?" the officer demanded. "If she's pregnant, she's out of commission until the puppies are weaned. Do you have any idea how bad this is going to look?" He then hesitated and seemed stressed. "Do you have any idea the sort of torment I'm going to receive from the other officers at the precinct?"

"I truly am sorry," Holden informed him, then held his breath. "If it turns out she's pregnant, we'll pay for the vet bill to terminate the pregnancy."

Gil suddenly bolted for the door and glared at Holden. "There is no way in hell you're doing that," Gil suddenly launched, then turned to the police officer in the doorway. "Darth is my dog. He's my responsibility. I'll buy Officer Zena from you. Just tell me how much it'll cost to replace her with another K-9."

The police officer stared at Gil with some surprise. "I have no intention of terminating the pregnancy," he informed Gil. "And she's not just a dog. She's my partner and a member of my family, so there's no way I'd ever sell her. Not to mention my kids would kill me."

"What can I do to make this right?" Gil asked.

The officer held his breath. "I'll deal with the embarrassment at the station, but you need to pay for her vet bills and find homes for the puppies."

"I'll do that," Gil informed him. "Holden has my information."

The police officer nodded but remained mostly irritated by the entire situation. "Try and keep that dog of yours on a leash from now on."

"Yeah, both of them," Holden muttered.

Once the officer left, Gil shut the door. Holden and Jackie exchanged looks but didn't dare speak. What was about to follow wasn't going to be pretty. Gil turned and appeared angry.

"Zack!"

There were several snickers from the other guys. Gil shot looks at them.

"Yeah, it's really funny," Gil snarled, losing his cool for possibly the first time, and sneered at his teammates. "Can you guess what all of you are getting for Christmas this year?"

Gil stormed through the house and finally found Zack sitting on the back patio smoking a cigar while enjoying a glass of whiskey. Darth saw Gil and ran behind Zack's chair, almost as if he knew he did something wrong. Zack didn't even bother looking up as Gil approached.

"What the hell were you thinking?" Gil demanded while standing over Zack. "Did you just wander through the neighborhood, see the neighbor's dog, and think, how can I fuck up Gil's life today?"

Zack glanced up at Gil and showed little emotion. "Of course not," he scoffed.

The rest of the team made their way onto the porch for a front-row seat to Gil's interrogation of Zack. It was a 'once-in-a-lifetime' event.

"Officer Zena came up as Darth's perfect match on Tinder," Zack replied, then shrugged. "So I arranged for a play date."

"Probably hoisted him over the fence into their yard," Monroe muttered under his breath.

Zack glared at Monroe, having heard the comment. "Darth could jump that fence as if it wasn't even there," he remarked, then looked back at Gil. "Darth works hard. He needs to have a little fun, just like the rest of us. So I did what any friend would do. I took Darth out and got him laid. No big deal."

"No big deal?" Gil snarled. "You do realize there's a good chance that police dog is pregnant with Darth's puppies."

Zack stared at Gil with a strange, almost stunned look. "Of course I realize that," he casually replied. "If Darth was going to 'get lucky', the female dog needed to be in heat. I do know how these things work."

"You know I'm stuck with those puppies," Gil snapped back.

Zack suddenly grinned and puffed on his cigar, pleased with himself. "And what amazing puppies they're going to be," he announced. "The best of the best."

Gil stared at Zack a moment, then frowned. "Well, you do have a pretty good point."

Holden rolled his eyes.

"Sal gave me Darth's papers after I 'adopted' him," Gil remarked.

"You mean stole him," Ross countered.

"He has an amazing pedigree," Gil continued while ignoring Ross's comment. "He was imported from Germany as a puppy."

"Officer Zena has some nice bloodlines, too," Zack insisted. "Comes from a long line of police dogs."

"Please don't tell me you broke into a police officer's house to find that information," Holden muttered while shutting his eyes.

Zack eyed Holden and raised a brow. "Of course not," he insisted. "I already told you, they were a perfect match on Tinder."

"I'd take that as a confession," Kirk remarked to Holden while hiding his humor.

Chapter 15

Jackie, Holden, and the team sat on the back patio well past ten o'clock that night. Their house was nestled on a one-acre corner lot with a privacy fence around the back yard. Several large trees inside the fenced area added additional seclusion. The covered patio had enough outdoor furniture to seat the entire team and a few extras. Beyond the concrete patio was an outdoor fire pit with a nice sized fire blazing on the cool fall night. The fire pit provided enough light for them to see the area surrounding them and lent a warm, romantic glow. The guys were nursing their bottles of beer while Zack sipped his whiskey. Beck and Monroe were able to put their irritation with each other aside for the rest of the night, allowing everyone to have a good time while discussing old missions from their Navy SEAL days.

Jackie always loved a good story involving her father, even the ones she had heard many times before. She affectionately clung to Holden's hand while nuzzling her head against his shoulder as she listened to the stories of the team's 'glory days'. Bogart's cell phone dinged, indicating he had a new text message. A text message was strange, considering mostly everyone he knew was on the patio with him. He removed his cell phone from his pocket, eyed the screen, and appeared slightly baffled at what he saw.

"Huh?" Bogart announced while staring at his phone. "Othello sent me a text." He then looked at the guys. "When did Othello start selling car insurance?"

The guys suddenly shifted in their seats and appeared unusually interested. Although Othello was a high-tech kind of guy, the former SEAL team typically avoided things like text messaging and social media. Their interest in Othello's correspondence with Bogart sparked Jackie's curiosity.

"What does it say?" Ross asked almost eagerly.

"He wants to discuss my current insurance needs and see about including a SAR policy," Bogart remarked, then eyed the guys while squinting. "It sounds almost as if he's talking in code."

"Ah, hell," Ross groaned and leaped up from his chair.

Zack was already on his feet and took off across the back yard. The rest of the guys sprang up from their seats and awaited orders. Jackie and Holden remained seated and somewhat puzzled by everyone's reaction. Bogart stood, although he still didn't understand what was happening, and shifted looks at the remaining men.

"Did I miss something?" Bogart asked.

"Sal sent a coded message to Othello," Ross informed Bogart. "You're our point man. Or have you forgotten?"

Bogart maintained his clueless stare. "I've been out of the loop the last six weeks," he reminded them. "Maybe you forgot to include me in on that."

Ross considered the comment then nodded. "I guess you did miss that meeting. The coded message means Sal is on his way over, and he's coming in hot," he replied, then eyed the remaining men. "We need to secure the perimeter and make sure he's not being followed."

Holden stood and groaned. "And on that note, I'm going to bed," he announced.

"You aren't curious?" Jackie asked with some surprise at her husband while jumping to her feet.

Holden snorted a laugh and pulled his wife into his arms. "I'm pretty sure I know why he's on his way over here," he insisted. "And I already know I don't want any 'part in' or 'knowledge of' that conversation."

"Oh," Jackie remarked sympathetically and patted his chest, understanding that it probably had to do with Holden's earlier visit to Sal's house.

"I've had my fill of mob bosses for today." Holden kissed her quickly yet firmly on the lips. "Wake me if the house is under attack."

As Holden headed inside, the rest of the men started to scatter, leaving just Jackie and Ross. She eyed Ross and appeared curious.

"I'm kind of with Bogart on this," she remarked while rubbing her chilled arms. "I don't remember hearing anything about this new set-up."

"We worked on it while you and Holden were on your extended vacation," Ross informed her. "It's part of the new security system we implemented at the lodge."

"Oh, when you abducted Scorpio's boyfriend for six weeks?" Jackie teased.

"Yeah, during that timeframe," Ross replied. "If something happens, we can send a coded message through Othello. He's instructed to send coded messages to Bogart. Your brother is the only one of us who has no traceable past from his conman days." Ross sank into thought and shook his head. "Something must have happened with Sal tonight that he needs to stop by unexpectedly. I wouldn't doubt it has something to do with Giovanni sending Holden to Vinnie Scartelli's house."

Jackie fidgeted uncomfortably and groaned. "No wonder Holden darted out of here so fast," she muttered.

"Insurance policy is code for 'watch my ass, I'm coming in hot'," Ross informed her. "Sal must be concerned someone is watching him and possibly monitoring his phone calls. I'm sure he's been driving around for an hour or more making sure he's not being followed, but, under the circumstances, he'd rather not take any chances."

"If this has to do with Giovanni's son, I can understand his concern," Jackie remarked, then tensed as she eyed Ross. "You know what he's going to ask, right?"

"I have a pretty good idea," Ross replied with a look of disapproval.

They heard a car pull into the driveway. "That must be him," Jackie remarked. She then heard the garage door electronically opening and appeared curious. "I guess one of the guys opened the garage door for him."

Ross nodded Jackie toward the kitchen door. "Let's just keep up our guard for the moment."

Once Jackie and Ross entered the house, Ross positioned himself behind the island counter and removed his semiautomatic from his shoulder holster. Jackie approached the interior garage door and waited for some sort of signal. There was a light, rhythmic tap. She looked back at Ross. He nodded and straightened, appearing to relax. Jackie unlocked and opened the garage door to see Sal in the doorway. He smiled warmly when he saw Jackie.

"Sorry to disturb you at this hour," Sal announced, then stood aside.

A man wearing a sack over his head and his hands zip-tied in front of him was forced into the kitchen. Jackie was almost glad Holden didn't stick around to witness Sal's little abduction. He certainly wouldn't be pleased knowing their favorite mob boss brought a bound and hooded man into his home. The home of a federal agent. Thankfully, the bound man didn't know where he had been taken. Sal entered behind the man with Beck bringing up the rear. He then shut the door behind them.

"This is our new friend," Sal informed Jackie and Ross.

Sal removed the hood to reveal Jack. Jack nervously looked around, then held his hands out. Sal removed a knife from his pocket and cut the zip ties.

"Jack, say hello to my friends," Sal announced.

Jack managed a tiny, nervous smile. "Hey," he replied timidly.

"What's going on?" Ross asked Sal.

"Well, Jack and his friend broke into my house tonight," Sal replied while remaining unusually upbeat. "They were looking for Marco. Long story short, Jack came to the conclusion that he wasn't cut out for the hitman lifestyle, and he wants to share some vital information in exchange for a clean slate."

"Please don't tell me you water-boarded the guy," Ross muttered.

"No, I just shot him," Sal casually replied, then smiled and indicated the blood soaking the man's shirt. "Jack's new. He decided being shot really isn't for him."

"I'm really afraid to ask," Ross remarked while folding his arms across his broad chest.

Sal's look turned serious. "Giovanni asked if you'd find his son and keep him alive until he can clear Marco's name," he reluctantly informed them. "Between the information Giovanni gave me on where you could probably find his son and the information Jack here has on some of his competition, I thought you might be interested in taking the job." Sal hesitated, then raised his brows. "He's willing to pay the bounty on his son's head if you can keep him safe."

"What's the quote being floated around?" Beck asked.

"One million at last count," Sal replied.

Beck groaned at the amount and rubbed his eyes. "If that's what's being offered for Marco," he announced, then looked at Ross, "there's going to be some pretty tough customers coming after him."

"It's dead or alive," Sal added.

"Of course," Jackie moaned while raking her fingers through her hair.

"What happened to Jack's associate?" Ross then asked.

"Nevada is taking him for a little drive," Sal informed him.

"Nevada?" Jackie just about gasped while shooting a look at Sal as her mind suddenly raced. "Nevada, the bounty hunter?"

"You know her?" Sal asked with surprise.

"We met," Jackie muttered while frowning.

"She's the least of our worries," Sal insisted. "The bounty hunters are just a minor annoyance. That's where Jack comes into play. He already told me that Vincent was the one who put the bounty on Marco's head, but he also knows guys who've done work for Vincent in the past. Jack gives you that list, and I'll introduce him to Othello for a new life and a clean slate."

Ross appeared deep in thought. Beck and Jackie eyed their boss as if attempting to read his mind.

"Are you actually considering it?" Beck asked.

Ross looked back at his teammates. "Vinnie Scartelli said Marco didn't kill his grandson," Ross remarked. "Marco may very well be innocent. If not for that little tidbit, I would stay far away from this. There's a bigger picture here. If Marco is killed, it could set off a very bloody mob war. But if we can keep Marco alive and prove he's innocent, it would earn us some well-deserved bonus points with every organized crime family on the West Coast."

"And if we fail, it'll put all of us in a very bad predicament," Beck informed him while shifting uncomfortably at the thought.

"Are you opposed?" Ross then asked Beck.

"I didn't say that," Beck replied a little too quickly.

"Then I assume you're onboard," Ross muttered, then looked at Sal. "My team and I will confer with your man in the garage; then we'll stuff him back in the trunk for his ride to Othello's place." He then indicated Jackie, refusing to address any of his team by name in front of Jack. "You tell her what you know about Marco's location."

Sal nodded and headed across the kitchen to confer with Jackie.

Chapter 16

Despite turning in just before midnight, Jackie was wide-awake in bed alongside her peacefully sleeping husband. It was already four o'clock in the morning. The room was mostly dark, but the sun would be rising in about two hours. Based on information Giovanni provided regarding safe houses he owned, there were three places where Marco might be hiding. The team hastily threw together a plan of attack to find Marco, and they would leave around six-thirty in the morning. Since Giovanni gave three locations where he thought his son could be hiding, that meant the team needed to split up and check each one. To make that work, Gil would need to pull his helicopter from the repair shop. Hopefully, the mechanic already had the repairs completed, or it would be a short trip. Both helicopters would then take their respective teams to the two distant locations in opposite directions, while Kirk would drive the third team to the closest site.

Jackie found it difficult to sleep, burdened with having to tell Holden she'd be gone for an undetermined amount of time. Once they found Marco, she'd be committed to the assignment and forced to stay at the safe house for the duration, which could be anywhere from a few days to several weeks. Returning home would breach the safe house's location, wherever that might be, and they couldn't risk that. Jackie lay in bed staring at the ceiling while occasionally glancing at her sleeping husband. Telling him was always the hardest part about leaving on assignments. He never had a problem with it, but she often felt it was unfair to him because it always came with a two-minute advance warning. Holden rolled over onto his side, facing her, seemed to wake, and glanced at her. His eyes again shut.

"How long will you be gone?" Holden asked in a weary tone, giving her an easy out.

"One day," she replied, then held her breath. "Or possibly three to four weeks. I guess it depends."

Holden rolled onto his back and peered at her, possibly surprised to hear the length of time she'd be gone. "*Possibly* falls under the three-day rule," he informed her.

Jackie managed a smile and laughed softly. "Since when?" she asked coyly.

"Since always," he insisted with a humored grin. "If you're going to be gone three days or longer, I get 'tide-me-over' sex. And anything with less than six hours warning, I get to choose the position." Holden raised a curious brow and smirked almost knowingly. "When are you leaving?"

Jackie playfully frowned. "In about two hours."

Holden again shut his eyes and chuckled. "Oh, rookie mistake. You should have told me when you came to bed last night," he teased, not bothering to hide his amused grin. "Climb aboard."

Jackie hid her smile and practically leaped on top of him. Holden grunted from the surprise attack. He opened his eyes and looked at her as she smiled down at him.

"I could have told you when I came to bed," Jackie replied while affectionately caressing his body, "but that wouldn't be nearly as much fun."

He gave her a strange look and offered a tiny smile. "Why's that?"

"Because I enjoy it when you take charge in the bedroom," she cooed.

Holden suddenly groaned at the comment and flipped her over, reversing their positions. "Brace yourself," he announced. "We're about to wake everyone in the house."

Jackie laughed while caressing his chest. "Give it your best shot, Agent Falcone."

Holden grinned deviously, then kissed his wife passionately and with a sense of urgency. As his hands firmly caressed her body, Jackie's mind seemed to stray. Normally, she'd meet his urgency while doubling down on his rising aggression. For some reason, something seemed off. Her emotions were getting the best of her, and she felt a strange need to slow down. Jackie's heart suddenly felt heavy. She wasn't sure why, but she was worried she'd never see Holden again. Finding and protecting Marco was just another job. There was no reason to believe she wouldn't come home like always. So why did she feel this way? Jackie slipped back into reality as Holden aggressively kissed her neck, his breathing becoming heavier with his increasing desire. He seemed to hesitate, lifted his head, and met her gaze. His look was somewhat concerned.

"Are you okay?" he asked, his mind obviously reeling over her lack of aggressive response.

Jackie roused her best come-hither smile and brushed her concerns aside. She eagerly caressed his shoulder and chest with great affection.

"I'm wonderful," she informed him, then warmly kissed his lips, met his gaze, and placed her arms around his neck. "I don't deserve you; you know that?"

Holden managed a tiny, throaty laugh. "Yeah, sure," he teased, then smirked. "We both know you should be married to some admiral or general. Let's face it; when you married me, you settled."

She smiled and shook her head. "No, not at all," Jackie replied warmly. "You're the only man I've ever loved, Agent Falcone."

Holden stared into her eyes a moment and seemed to tense slightly as if seeing something that now concerned him too. Perhaps he was sensing her worries.

"If you're having second thoughts about this mission, you don't have to do it," Holden boldly announced. "Even if Marco isn't a serial killer, he's still the son of a mob boss and comes with his own tainted past. You don't need to put your life on the line for someone like that."

Jackie smiled then kissed Holden warmly but passionately on the lips. She met his gaze and maintained her smile. "Are you planning on making me scream or not?" she teased.

Holden held his breath a moment, then groaned and kissed her with renewed aggression.

§

Around five o'clock that morning, Jackie walked onto the dimly lit back patio with her cup of tea and a cup of coffee. Zack sat reclined on the oversized, padded wicker chair with his feet propped on the coffee table. When he saw Jackie, he placed his feet on the concrete floor and sat forward. He managed a tiny smile while accepting the cup of coffee. Jackie squeezed into the small, empty spot alongside Zack and casually placed her legs over his lap. She sipped her tea and stared into the mostly dark morning. She loved the early morning, particularly before sunrise. It was always so peaceful. Even the chilly morning air didn't bother her.

"Did you get any sleep?" Jackie asked without looking at Zack.

"Stupid question," he replied with little emotion and sipped his coffee while staring across the yard. "How did Holden take the news about our new assignment? Did he demand plausible deniability?"

"Stupid question," she teased back. "When dealing with mob bosses, the fewer the details, the better." Jackie studied Zack as he stared off at the horizon beyond the neighborhood. "Everything okay?"

"No better; no worse than usual," he replied and placed his filled mug on the coffee table without moving her legs off his lap. Zack then partially turned and nestled his head against Jackie's chest.

"Oh, no," she announced in a firm tone while attempting to stop him from making himself comfortable against her. "We're leaving in an hour or so. You aren't napping against me now."

Zack shut his eyes. "Your thoughts on the subject are irrelevant," he muttered while nestling in as he clung to her with a vice-like grip.

Jackie groaned, gave in, and sipped her tea. "I can't help you if you don't talk to me," she insisted.

"You help me without talking to me," he countered in a weary tone. "Right now, I just need you to be a soft, warm, vanilla-scented pillow."

She drew a deep breath and sighed with defeat. There was no point arguing. "Fine, I'll be your pillow for the next hour," Jackie groaned in response.

There was a lengthy pause.

"I got a text from Kane yesterday," Zack muttered from his relaxed position against Jackie.

Jackie hesitated while attempting to gauge Zack's mood. "Something bad?"

"Depends on perspective," he remarked.

"Meaning?"

Zack sighed with defeat. "Scorpio broke up with Rayner shortly after we left," he informed her.

Jackie tensed with some surprise. "She did?" That was not what she was expecting to hear. She thought for sure his daughter and her boyfriend would be too busy in the bedroom to fight about anything. Jackie shook her head, feeling bad. "I'm sorry to hear."

"I know it makes me a bad person," Zack remarked, "but I'm a bit relieved."

"Spoken like a true father," Jackie muttered.

Zack tensed slightly but didn't lift his head. "Do you think so?"

"Fathers never think any man is good enough for their daughters," she informed him, then groaned while sinking into her own thoughts. "Look at mine."

Zack suddenly chuckled. "If memory serves me, he beat the crap out of Monroe," he teased. "Not that I understood why at the time." He then shifted and nuzzled her almost insecurely. "I shouldn't be happy about her breakup. Rayner was good for her. She needed someone like him to keep her grounded." He held his breath. "To keep her from turning into me."

"You're not as bad as you think you are, Zack," Jackie informed him.

"No, I'm worse."

"The parts of you that you don't like came from your military days," Jackie informed him. "Scorpio may have a few demons rattling around in her head, but she's not going down some dark path."

"She needs a suitable boyfriend to prevent her from walking that dark path," Zack insisted, then seemed to sink into his own thoughts. "Walker will be staying at the hotel a few weeks. He's a regular Boy Scout and pathetically devoted. Sort of like Gil but younger. Maybe Kane and I could--"

"Don't try to set her up," Jackie announced sternly. "She'll meet someone in her own time."

"That thought is a bit unsettling, Jackie," he remarked. "Think about the men who'll be staying at her hotel. A lot of them are seriously damaged. Some almost as bad as me." He then hesitated. "Some even worse."

Jackie snorted a laugh. "Yeah," she muttered and rolled her eyes. "Hayden Vandyke."

"Thankfully, I don't have to worry about Hayden," Zack informed her.

"Why's that?" Jackie asked, then considered everything she knew about the man. "He's a bit of a pervert. An aggressive bastard too."

"I know he puts on a good show," Zack remarked, "but he never got over the death of his wife. It's possible he's impotent too."

"Really?" Jackie practically gasped, then shuttered just thinking about the man. "I wouldn't have guessed that by the way he behaves."

"The man is seriously broken," he replied. "Good thing for him too. If he even thought about touching Scorpio, I'd have to kill him."

"I wouldn't worry about it," Jackie insisted, then laughed at the thought. "He's definitely *not* her type. She's not hooking up with someone like Hayden."

"Thank God for that," Zack muttered. "That chemical mixture would be like dropping a nuke on the East Coast."

Chapter 17

Team one, consisting of Gil, Monroe, and Darth, took off in Gil's mostly fixed helicopter and headed west. One of the three safe houses on Giovanni's list was inside an old, abandoned gold mine that was a decent trek from any town. Once they reached the area, Gil's helicopter flew overhead, checking for any signs of an abandoned vehicle. Just because they didn't see a car, that didn't mean Marco wasn't hiding out within the mine's safe house. They were told that the mine's entrance was pretty well hidden and nearly impossible to see from the air. With Giovanni's coordinates, Gil landed just far enough away from the perceived mine entrance that they could still sneak up on Marco. If he were deep within the underground bunker, it was unlikely he'd hear anything happening outside.

All three disembarked the helicopter and headed in the direction of the mine entrance. Even with exact coordinates, it was still difficult to find the cleverly concealed doorway. Darth sniffed around the area and was finally able to find the hidden entrance for them. A chain-link fence covered in faux shrub had been concealing the doorway. Monroe pulled open the fence and uncovered the fiberglass door that was painted the same color as the surrounding hillside. Monroe and Gil exchanged looks and their approval.

"Giovanni certainly spared no expense with his safe houses," Gil remarked.

Both men removed their semiautomatics from their shoulder holsters.

"Let's hope he's right about Marco heading out to one of them," Monroe replied.

"News travels fast in certain circles," Gil informed him. "If Marco's been paying attention to anything in the last twenty-four hours, he has to know he's in trouble."

"Providing he has been paying attention. If he's in here, I'm guessing he's not getting the greatest cell phone reception so deep underground," Monroe reported, then indicated the door. "You want to knock, or should I?"

Gil shrugged. Monroe tried the door. Not surprisingly, it was locked. He removed a lock pick kit from his pocket and worked on unlocking the door. Despite the great lengths Giovanni went to in order to keep his safe house hidden, he didn't go all out with the lock. Monroe picked the simple door lock in under a minute, reclaimed his weapon, and pushed open the door. Both men aimed their semiautomatics into the dark tunnel.

"Well, this is creepy," Monroe muttered and removed his flashlight.

He shined his light into the mine but didn't see anything. They cautiously proceeded inside. Several lights suddenly came on, brightening the mine corridor. Both hesitated and looked around.

"Motion sensor," Monroe responded.

Darth wandered ahead of them while they remained by the entrance. Gil noticed a secondary door standing open just inside. The thick metal door was similar to that of a bank vault. When the door was closed, and the large spindle was turned, bolts would project into the surrounding metal frame. It would be nearly impossible for any intruder to gain access once the door was sealed.

"Monroe," Gil announced and indicated the door.

Monroe looked back at Gil and the vault door. Nothing short of an explosion would open that door had it been sealed. The fact that it wasn't, in itself, was a pretty good sign of what they'd find, which was almost certainly nothing.

"I don't think he's here," Gil informed him. "If he is, he didn't bother locking himself in."

"Maybe he's not as smart as everyone thinks," Monroe responded and indicated the tunnel. "We're here now. We should check it out."

Gil nodded and followed Monroe along the well-lit, reinforced mine shaft. They walked almost one hundred yards before reaching a steel door where Darth waited and sniffed around the area. Both men approached with their weapons ready. Monroe tried the door. It was unlocked. Despite the door being unlocked, they didn't let down their guard. Once the door opened, Darth entered ahead of them. The safe house was surprisingly luxurious, considering it was more or less a bunker inside a cave. There was a spacious living room and kitchen combination with moderately expensive yet sturdy furniture. In addition to enough seating for eight, the living space contained a large screen television, a fully stocked bar, and an exercise bike. The only table seating was stools in front of the island counter separating the kitchen from the living room. Toward the back, there were two bedrooms, each containing two queen-sized beds and their own bathroom.

Both men looked around the empty bunker. It was a nice set-up, but it didn't appear as if anyone had been there in a long time, judging by the dust and cobwebs.

"One down, two to go," Gil muttered and replaced his weapon to his shoulder holster.

Darth suddenly looked at the open doorway and snarled, alerting them to potential danger. Gil swiftly removed the semiautomatic from his shoulder holster and exchanged looks with Monroe.

"Marco?" Monroe whispered to Gil with a curious look.

"We're about to find out," Gil muttered and positioned himself alongside the door just out of sight. He then signaled to Darth.

Darth immediately silenced and joined Gil, where he remained hidden behind the open door. Monroe bolted for the bedroom doorway and took a lookout position. Both remained silent and motionless while listening for whatever it was in the tunnel that had caught Darth's attention. From his position alongside the door, Gil could hear someone within the tunnel. He signaled to Monroe, hiding within the bedroom doorway. Monroe kept his weapon aimed at the entrance. A man stepped into the bunker holding a gun containing a silencer and glanced around the luxury safe house. When nothing moved, he entered and approached the bedroom doorway while keeping his weapon aimed. Judging by his weapon containing a silencer, he was almost certainly a hitman. Gil had the man's back within his sights.

"That's far enough," Gil announced without giving up the safety of his position.

The man aggressively spun around, preparing to fire. Gil fired first, striking the man in the shoulder, winging him. He clutched his bleeding shoulder without dropping his weapon and seemed even more determined to take down Gil. The man's finger tightened on the trigger. Monroe fired from behind, hitting the man in the leg. He immediately dropped to the floor, his weapon falling from his hand. Gil and Monroe kept their guns trained on the man. Gil kicked the gun away from the injured, bleeding man then aimed his weapon at the open doorway.

"Darth," Gil announced and indicated the tunnel. Darth bolted into the tunnel. "You secure him. I'll sweep the tunnel in case there are others."

§

Team two, consisting of Kirk, Ross, and Beck, headed to the closer location just northeast of Colorado Springs. Kirk drove one of the jeeps they kept in a rented garage not far from the Colorado Springs Airport. They drove almost an hour from Jackie's house to a heavily wooded area. The area was remote and made a perfect location for a safe house. Ross rode shotgun and fiddled with GPS on his cell phone before the signal dropped on him.

"Well, it's up here somewhere," Ross announced with a sigh and looked at Kirk behind the wheel. "Start looking for secluded driveways."

It wasn't long before Kirk indicated a road just up ahead. "Think that's it?"

Ross eyed the barely visible driveway and sighed. "Only one way to find out," he remarked. "We'll need to find a good spot to park the jeep where it won't be spotted and go the rest of the way on foot."

Kirk turned onto the old driveway and pulled into a secluded area within the woods. All three got out of the jeep and followed the driveway while remaining within the woods so they wouldn't be spotted. They walked more than one hundred yards before spotting a log cabin on the lake. Apart from being a little larger and possibly a little nicer than most cabins in the woods, this particular, single-story cabin didn't look to be anything special. Its size suggested it contained at least two bedrooms. There was a large, covered front porch and an equally large, covered back patio. There seemed to be quite a few windows, although little could be seen through the curtains. The cabin was situated within the woods, allowing for plenty of cover. The lake was only about twenty feet from the patio and contained its own dock and a small motorboat.

"That's it," Ross informed them. "A cabin on the lake. We'll need to stake it out."

Kirk groaned and leaned against a nearby tree. "Couldn't we rent a boat, some fishing equipment, and stake it out from the lake instead?"

"Would be a sweet cover," Beck muttered.

Ross eyed both men a moment with surprise, then chuckled. "Look at that," he announced, sounding somewhat pleased. "You two actually agreeing on something for a change. I'm proud of your teamwork efforts." Ross's smile then faded. "No."

Both men groaned then focused their attention on the cabin, attempting to peer into the windows with their small binoculars.

"I see something through one of the windows," Kirk remarked. "There's definitely someone in there."

Ross lifted his own pair of binoculars and scanned the cabin. He nodded in agreement. "Definitely movement," he replied. "We'll stake out the place a little while longer."

"I could go up for a closer look," Kirk informed him.

Ross held up his hand. "Give it a few minutes," he insisted. "Let's see what we see first."

They heard a crash followed by a woman's scream.

Ross groaned and straightened. "We've seen enough," he announced and nodded to the front door. "Kirk, take the front. Beck and I will attack from the rear."

All three men removed their weapons and dashed for the cabin while keeping low to the ground. Kirk headed for the front while Ross and Beck headed to the back. When Ross was sure Kirk was in position at the front door, he nodded to Beck. Beck straightened and kicked in the back door. Ross charged in first with his gun aimed. There was another loud, thunderous crack, which was Kirk taking down the front door. The main room of the cabin contained the living area and the kitchen, making one large room. Three young, lean men dressed in faded, ripped jeans and graphic t-shirts spun in surprise to the unannounced interruption and aimed their semiautomatics at the intruders.

A brief glimpse of the room revealed a dark-haired man, possibly Marco, tied to a chair with his head hanging down while a young woman sobbed on the floor near his feet. The young woman was startled by the men breaking down the doors as well, although she appeared more relieved at the possibility of a rescue. Ross shot the first man in the shoulder, effectively taking him down. The two remaining men seemed panicked when they saw that the men breaking in also had weapons. The first young man ran for the back bedrooms. Before the second man could even aim his gun, Kirk shot him in his leg, dropping him to the floor. The man dropped his weapon, clutched his injured leg, and held up his free hand while screaming like a frightened child.

"Don't shoot," the injured man frantically cried out. "I'm unarmed. I'm unarmed!"

The man's reaction was a bit surprising. Beck cast a strange look at Ross, silently questioning the sobbing man. Kirk had already taken off after the other man, who fled into one of the back bedrooms. Ross approached the man who was clutching his bleeding leg while screaming on the floor.

"Don't shoot," the man continued to scream. "I'm not armed!"

The distraught woman was even surprised by the injured man's wailing. She seemed to return to the reality of her situation and looked up at Ross from her position on the floor near the tied man.

"Are you going to hurt us?" she asked in a frightened tone.

Ross appeared surprised by the question, then managed a smile and shook his head. "No, we're here to help."

"Thank God," she gasped and quickly sprang to her feet to untie the man bound in the chair.

While Beck collected both men's discarded weapons, Ross approached the tied man, who appeared unconscious.

"Marco," Ross announced firmly. "Can you hear me?"

The man slowly lifted his head and looked at Ross. To his surprise, it wasn't Marco! Ross frowned and groaned with disgust.

"It's not him," he announced to Beck.

Beck swiftly tied the man with the leg wound then looked up with surprise. "It's not?" he gasped, then looked at the mildly beaten man. "Then who is it?"

Ross eyed the frightened, young woman. "Who are you?" he asked. "What are you doing here?"

"Our car broke down about a mile from here," she announced, then indicated the man clutching his bleeding shoulder. "That one offered us a ride to a working phone. He brought us here and started beating up my boyfriend." She shuttered slightly and insecurely rubbed her shoulders. "I was terrified to think what they intended to do to me."

Ross sneered and kicked the man with the shoulder wound. He cried out while continuing to hold his bleeding shoulder.

"I'm sorry," the injured man screamed in agony. "I'm sorry!"

"You're only sorry because you were caught," Ross snarled, then indicated for Beck to tie him as well. Ross looked across the cabin. "Kirk!"

There was a loud crash from the back bedroom. The third man, who had attempted to flee, was thrown from the bedroom and across the cabin. Kirk stormed out of the bedroom after the man now trying to escape from the angry, big man. Kirk grabbed him by the back of the neck and slammed him headfirst into the nearby wall.

"Kirk," Ross again called out.

Kirk finally looked at Ross while standing over the disoriented man. "What?" he demanded as if annoyed that he'd been interrupted.

"It's not him," Ross announced and indicated the beaten man, who was now free from his bindings.

"They did try to shoot us," Kirk announced while maintaining his irritation.

"I'm not saying you shouldn't beat them," Ross remarked. "Just, well, don't kill them."

Kirk smirked and gave a firm, pleased nod. He returned for the man who again attempted to bolt for the door. Kirk punched him in the gut and then in the face, knocking him backward into the wall.

Ross returned his attention to the woman, who no longer appeared frightened, and indicated the man on the floor. "If you want to kick him a few times," he announced, "be my guest."

The woman turned angry and kicked the man repeatedly in the midsection. He screamed and cried, now no longer the tough guy who had beat up her boyfriend and threatened her with physical harm. Beck removed a set of car keys from the other man's pocket and tossed them to Ross. Ross handed the keys to the beaten man.

"Here's your ride to town," Ross casually informed him. "We'll leave the men tied here. You can call the police or just leave them here to rot for all I care. Your call."

Kirk punched the man a few more times, seeming to enjoy himself a little too much. Ross glanced at his watch then eyed Kirk.

"Wrap it up, Kirk," Ross firmly announced. "We should go."

Kirk finally punched the man in the groin, dropping him to the floor. Beck shook his head at Kirk's final blow, then approached the writhing man and tied him as well. Ross smiled at the young man and woman.

"You'll understand if we don't stick around," Ross informed them. He then turned for the front door and twirled his finger in the air. "Move it out!"

Beck and Kirk followed Ross from the cabin. The young man and woman exchanged looks then eyed the discarded guns on the nearby coffee table.

Chapter 18

The newer black blazer pulled up to the small, dilapidated motel on the edge of town. The motel, situated on a concrete slab foundation, was just one field away from the parking lot of the massive, newly-built casino. Detrick, Carter, and Bart got out of the vehicle and stared at the creepy, abandoned building with the same expression. The ten cabin motel, fashioned in an "L" shape, had seen better days and had possibly been abandoned for more than a decade. The roof needed work, the old, wooden siding was in dire need of painting, the windows were boarded up, and the weeds were tall and thick around most of what should have been the paved parking lot. Detrick made a face and withheld his somewhat humored laugh.

"Marco wouldn't be caught dead in a rat trap like this," Detrick announced and shook his head. He then looked at Carter, who seemed equally puzzled. "You were given bad intel. Maybe they meant the casino next door."

"No, this is the place," Carter insisted while scanning the rundown row of motel rooms strung together. "The exterior may be just a façade, so no one suspects anything. We should check it out." He cast a look at Bart and nodded to the side of the building. "Bart, you go around back." He then indicated the far cabin to Detrick. "You check that way, and I'll check the office."

While his two muscle-bound friends each went opposite directions, Carter headed for the office on the end. Rather than pick the lock, he firmly shoved his shoulder into the door and easily broke in. The door opened, and thick cobwebs floated downward, indicating no one had been inside the office in years. The motel was a dead end. Carter frowned and turned where he stood on the small, deteriorating porch. His two friends soon returned.

"There's nothing here," Bart announced with annoyance. "We should try the other places on the list."

"Maybe we should check out the casino," Detrick again suggested. "Have a quick look around."

"Marco isn't at the casino," Carter insisted, clearly irritated. "We have a few other safe houses on the list Vincent gave us. We'll just go to the next place on the list. He has to be at one of them."

"Marco has a weakness for the craps tables," Detrick informed Carter. "We're here. We should at least check it out."

"He's *not* in the casino," Carter again announced, this time with a little more insistence. "I'm in charge, remember? We're not going to the casino. We have other places to look, and we've wasted enough time here already."

§

The casino beside the abandoned motel seemed to have a decent crowd despite only being mid-morning. Banks of colorful, noisy slot machines covered most of the casino floor and along the walls. The center contained dozens of table games crowded with people. Some of the tables were noisy, while others contained patrons steadily losing money. The nearby craps table seemed to have the largest crowd and was alive with excitement. Men and women cheered at another lucky roll of the dice. One man, in particular, had a large stack of chips in front of him. That man was Giovanni's son, Marco. Marco stood a little over five-foot-ten with an incredibly athletic build. The man in his late-twenties had dark, nearly black hair that was neatly trimmed to the point of perfection. His dark eyes and dark facial stubble gave him the perfect balance of handsome and rugged, making him just about every woman's dream. He oozed charm and sophistication while his clothes screamed wealth.

The craps dealer placed a large stack of chips in front of Marco after the win. He glanced at the two attractive women on either side of him, who were also excited about his win. Both seemed a little overdressed, considering the time of morning. One was a busty blonde woman with long, wavy hair and a layer of makeup. She wore a red, form-fitting, low-cut dress, revealing a lot of her cleavage and most of her legs. The second woman, a redhead, wore an equally sexy black dress, showcasing her assets as well. Both women seemed compelled to touch Marco's suit jacket after the win as a form of congratulations.

"I'm feeling lucky this morning," Marco announced to the dealer, then laughed, "but I'm not about to press it further." He again eyed both women, seeming to size them up. "How about drinks in my suite? It's after five somewhere."

Both women smiled knowingly and seemed eager to cozy up to him.

Marco grinned, then pushed his chips across the table. "Color up," he announced. He then glanced at both women. "Meet me at the elevators in ten minutes. I'm going to cash out."

Marco collected his fistful of purple chips and crossed the casino to the cashier cage. Several security guards seemed to be watching Marco, but he didn't take notice. He approached the cashier cage and set his stack of purple chips on the counter. The woman smiled and started counting out one-hundred-dollar bills. He collected his wad of cash, shoved it in his front pocket, and then left the cage for the elevators. The casino security guards continued to monitor him. One of the guards, a tall, lean man in his mid-thirties, Sims, approached the pit boss standing near the craps table. Despite his expensive suit, Sims was a mostly average man and easily went unnoticed.

"Who was that high roller?" Sims asked.

"Jerry Maxwell," the pit boss replied. "He's been coming around the last few days. We comped him one of our suites the last two nights. Won close to fifty grand."

Sims nodded, satisfied with the answer. "We'll keep an eye on him," he announced, then left the pit area. Sims continued off the casino floor while removing his cell phone from his jacket pocket. He pressed a button on his phone and waited a moment. "I found your man. He's not exactly hiding." There was a pause. "Don't worry; he's not going anywhere for at least an hour, but I'll keep an eye on him. I want my finder's fee." There was another pause. "See you in an hour." He then disconnected the call.

§

Team three, consisting of Jackie, Zack, and Bogart, headed east of the Colorado Springs airport in Jackie's helicopter. They flew over what would constitute a small city and headed toward the outskirts of town. From the air, they could see the casino taking up a large parcel of land just on the edge of the town. It looked quite busy for that time of morning. Beyond the bustle of the casino was the dilapidated motel that had been abandoned for years. Given its close proximately to the casino, it seemed surprising that the land hadn't been utilized for some profitable business or, at the very least, bought by the casino for additional parking. Jackie set the helicopter down on the other side of some trees, concealing the craft from anyone who might be hole up inside the old motel. Jackie, Zack, and Bogart crossed through the woods and staked out the abandoned building from the rear, and then ventured to the front as well. There wasn't any sign of life coming from the motel.

After watching the place for more than twenty minutes, all three approached the front, remaining out of view of any of the windows. There weren't any security cameras of any kind. Perhaps they were given bad intel on the motel. It didn't look anything like a safe house. They approached the motel office with its boarded windows located at the far left end of the string of motel cabins. Zack tried the door and discovered it wasn't locked. He eyed the door jamb, noted the splintered wood, and then ran his finger along the fresh break. Jackie and Bogart exchanged bewildered looks.

"Okay, this can't be right," Bogart remarked. "It has to be a mistake."

"The door has been recently broken," Zack informed them, then glanced around. "The wood is freshly splintered. Someone else was here not too long ago."

"Marco?" Jackie muttered. "Or worse?"

"Let's find out," Zack replied.

Zack entered the cobweb-infested office with Jackie only a step behind him. He looked around the small, bland office thick with cobwebs. The cheaply-made front desk, covered in a layer of dust, was falling apart from age and shoddy craftsmanship. There were a few chairs alongside a small counter that possibly contained a coffeemaker once upon a time. Most auto mechanic shops had nicer offices. Jackie remained in the doorway while Bogart stood on the rotting porch and scanned the area surrounding the motel for any unwanted visitors.

"Anything?" Bogart muttered from outside while shaking his head. Obviously, he already knew the answer.

"Cobwebs and spiders," Jackie muttered from the doorway as she flicked a large spider off her shoulder.

"This was a waste of time," Bogart remarked. "I think we were played."

Zack stomped on the floor and listened. Several fat spiders were sent scurrying away from the vibration.

Jackie watched him and appeared curious. "What is it?" she asked.

"From the looks of it, the motel appears to be sitting on a cement slab foundation," Zack informed her as he approached her and the door. He moved past her and looked around outside at the foundation beyond the porch. "But the floor isn't solid. It's hollow beneath."

"Could there be a crawl space?" Jackie asked while following Zack off the porch and around the side of the motel office.

Bogart hurried after them.

"No, there wouldn't be a crawl space with a concrete slab foundation," Zack informed them.

Zack continued around the back of the building with Jackie and Bogart following. He paused in the back and pointed at the old-fashioned exterior cellar door.

"There also wouldn't be the need for a cellar door with a concrete slab," Zack announced. "That means the foundation is fake. Probably created to conceal whatever is beneath the motel."

As he approached the cellar door, Jackie and Bogart remained on his heels. Zack opened the doors built mostly into the ground and walked down the concrete steps. He reached an old, wooden door, pulled it open, and revealed a thick, steel door with a state-of-the-art, electronic lock on it.

"I'll be damned," Jackie announced with some surprise as she stared at the digital keypad.

"How do we get in?" Bogart asked.

"Try the last four digits of Giovanni's cell phone number," Jackie insisted. "Sal said we should use Giovanni's cell phone if we ran into any problems."

"What's his number?" Zack asked.

Bogart removed his cell phone and pressed a button. He showed the screen to Zack, who then eyed Bogart.

"Is there a good reason why you have Giovanni's personal number in your cell phone?" Zack asked somewhat skeptically.

"Sal gave the number to us," Bogart insisted while staring at him with a strange look. "Did you think I intended to memorize it?"

"Yes." He then shifted his attention to Jackie. "And this is why I don't give out my cell phone number," Zack muttered while shaking his head with disapproval.

"You have a cell phone?" Bogart asked while cocking his head with a stunned look.

Zack punched in the number without responding to the question. The light on the digital pad turned from red to green. Zack turned the handle and pushed open the door. Jackie and Bogart drew their weapons as Zack peered into the room. He entered without drawing his semiautomatic. The basement bunker was set up much like the cave bunker with a living room and kitchen combination, the same style of furniture, entertainment, and exercise equipment. The motel safe house had two bedrooms next to each other and a shared bathroom. Zack checked the first bedroom while Jackie checked the second bedroom. Bogart looked around the kitchen and living room area. There were take-out boxes, some from the casino restaurant, dirty glasses, and a partially empty bottle of expensive whiskey on the counter between the kitchen and living room. Similar take-out boxes and dirty dishes covered the coffee table as well.

"The bed's been slept in," Zack announced from the first bedroom. "Some dirty clothes on the floor."

"Used towels in the bathroom and a toothbrush," Jackie remarked.

"Judging by the looks of the dirty clothes, whoever has been living here has expensive taste," Zack called out to her while out of view of Bogart in the living area.

Bogart picked up the bottle of whiskey. "Expensive whiskey, too," he replied while eyeing the bottle, then set it back down. "It has to be him."

Jackie appeared from the second bedroom. "The towels in the shared bathroom are dry," she announced. "He hasn't been here for at least a day."

Zack appeared within the bedroom doorway. "His clothes and bag are still here," he announced to Jackie. "It's possible he just stepped out."

"We should notify the others and tell them we found evidence that he was here," Jackie insisted, then looked around. "He may be somewhere nearby."

"We should check the casino," Bogart announced from across the room and indicated the take-out boxes. "A lot of the take-out food came from the casino."

"We should wait here," Zack corrected. "He's coming back."

"Too much ground to cover in the casino," Jackie remarked, then gave her brother and Zack a curious look. "If you have every hitman on the West Coast looking for you, why would you go to a casino?"

"They've only been looking for him for the last twenty-four hours," Zack informed her. "Those take-out cartons could be from days ago."

"If he's at the casino, he may not even be aware anyone's looking for him," Bogart chimed in.

Both eyed Bogart but didn't seem convinced.

"Think about it," Bogart continued. "If he's doing well at the craps table, there aren't exactly a lot of news stations playing on a casino floor."

Zack and Jackie then exchanged looks.

Jackie raised her brows. "He does have a good point," she remarked. Being a former conman himself, her brother had good instincts.

"Then we're going to the casino?" Bogart asked, seeming a little too eager.

"No, we're waiting here," Zack insisted with little emotion. "We'll lay a trap for him. It'd be best if we took him down in here with no witnesses and no collateral damage. Too many eyes in the sky in a casino. We don't need every hitman and bounty hunter knowing the faces of the people who have Marco."

Chapter 19

The bedroom suite within the casino was four-star luxury, from the king-sized bed to the gas fireplace and balcony with a view. The black-out curtains were drawn over the double glass doors to keep out the late morning sun, successfully keeping the bedroom dimly lit. Loud male grunts were matched with female cries of ecstasy and some unladylike profanity. Within the king-sized bed, Marco panted as he collapsed between the two young women. The women immediately moved against him, snuggling the naked man. Both women appeared pleasantly exhausted after their late morning romp.

Marco grinned and managed a tiny laugh. "That was fun," he announced, then eyed each woman.

"Certainly one of my better mornings," the first woman teased.

"Mine too," the second woman added while affectionately running her hand along his chest and abdomen.

"The two of you should come back later tonight," he insisted, then grinned slyly. "We can take a bubble bath together. The tub's certainly big enough."

"You do realize we charge by the hour," the first woman reminded him, then grinned slyly. "No matter how much fun we have."

Marco chuckled and caressed their shoulders while they clung to him. "That's okay," he replied and seemed moderately humored. "I assure you; I can afford it."

The women giggled and cozied up to the wealthy man, allowing their hands to caress his bare chest and shoulders. He then glanced at his watch while clinging to the first woman.

"By my estimate, I have another ten minutes left on the clock," Marco announced, then eyed both women with a moderately devious look. "Do you know what I'd love the two of you to do?"

The second woman chuckled in her throat. "We have a pretty good idea," she cooed.

"A pillow fight," Marco announced.

Both women lifted their heads and eyed him with some surprise.

Marco grinned. "Always been a fantasy of mine."

§

The casino security guard, Sims, stood watch near the elevators and periodically glanced at his watch. It had been almost an hour since Marco and the two women had gone upstairs. He was starting to fidget now, not wanting to lose his finder's fee. Vincent's three hired mercenaries entered the hotel lobby, looked around, and spotted Sims near the elevators. They approached him while attempting to keep a low profile.

"Are you Sims?" Carter asked.

The casino security guard nodded. "Yeah, I'm Sims," he reported.

"Is he still in his suite?" Carter pressed.

"Yes, it's on the sixth floor," Sims replied. "Suite 604 at the end of the hall."

Detrick handed him an envelope. "He better be up there, or we're taking your head instead of his."

"He's still up there," Sims reported while stuffing the envelope inside his inner jacket pocket. "Neither of the girls came down yet. I'm sure they're keeping him busy." His look then turned stern. "Don't hurt either of the girls. They're not involved in any of this."

"As long as they don't do anything stupid, they'll be fine," Bart reported.

When the elevator doors opened, all three men got in the elevator. Sims was in a hurry to leave and returned to the casino adjacent to the hotel lobby. The casino owner, a short, mousey looking man in an expensive suit, saw him and approached with two large, muscular guards in tow.

"Sims," the owner announced in a gruff tone, then stopped before him. "We need to locate one of our guests. Find out which room Jerry Maxwell is staying in and then meet us by the elevators."

Sims tensed slightly at the command then nodded in response. "What's he done?" he asked in an attempt to stall for time.

"There's a substantial bounty on the man's head," his boss informed him. "We need to get to him before anyone else does."

"Uh, yeah," Sims replied and straightened. "Let me check the computer."

Sims fidgeted as he hurried toward the front desk. Allowing his boss to come between Vincent's mercenaries and their bounty wasn't in Sims's best interest, and he needed to slow his boss's pursuit.

§

Once the pillow fight had ended, both women giggled and again cuddled against Marco from either side. He grinned like a schoolboy and held both women in his arms.

"I enjoyed that," he informed them. "Maybe I'll get in on that pillow fight later tonight after our bath." He removed his arms from the women lying on either side of him and sat up. "But, now, the craps table is calling. Feel free to use the shower, but do so on your own dime."

Marco crawled over the first woman and slipped into his boxers, then pulled on his pants. He removed the wad of cash from his pocket, peeled off a few bills, and set them on the nightstand.

"Take as long as you need," he informed them. "Show yourselves out when you're finished."

The women appeared pleased as they collected their money. They placed the cash in their purses and then headed into the bathroom, taking him up on the shower offer. Marco finished dressing, seeming refreshed and cheerful. When he heard the shower start, his mind wandered a moment. He brushed aside any thoughts of remaining in the suite and headed for the door. He no sooner opened the door when he saw the three intimidating-looking men standing in the doorway. Marco gave them odd looks and attempted a smile.

"May I help you?" Marco asked.

Carter pushed Marco into the room and away from the door. Bart crossed the room while looking around then headed for the bathroom. He closed the bathroom door so the women wouldn't hear their interaction. Detrick shut the main suite door behind him and stood in front of it.

"That was easier than I thought," Carter announced with a moderately humored smile as he removed a pair of zip ties from his pants pocket.

"Who are you?" Marco demanded.

"I'm sorry," Carter announced almost pleasantly while smiling. "I'm Carter." He indicated the man by the closed bathroom door. "That's Bart." He then nodded to the man by the door while remaining cheerful. "And that's Detrick. We work for Vincent Scartelli."

Marco's expression suddenly dropped. He vigorously shook his head. "I had nothing to do with his brother's death," he insisted.

"Well, that's for you and Vincent to sort out," Carter replied while maintaining his jovial demeanor and held up the zip ties. "We're just the couriers."

"I feel like I'm missing something," Marco remarked and eyed the three men.

"You mean like the million-dollar bounty on your head?" Detrick asked while grinning.

"Dead or alive," Bart teased.

Marco's expression suddenly dropped as he shot looks at all three men. "You're kidding, right?"

The three men chuckled.

"I think he finally figured out how much trouble he's in," Bart announced with a humored laugh.

"There's an added bonus of another quarter-million if you're brought in alive," Carter informed him. "So we'll do our best to go that route."

"Don't be confusing alive with unblemished," Bart remarked, finding the comment amusing. "Something for you to keep in mind."

The electronic door lock hummed behind Detrick, surprising him. Detrick turned while simultaneously reaching for his weapon. The door was suddenly thrown open, knocking the large man across the room. The casino owner and his two large guards charged into the room with steel batons in their hands. Carter and Bart attempted to aim their weapons, but the casino owner's guards immediately charged for them. Swinging their steel batons, the guards knocked the guns from the mercenaries' hands. The moment Carter and Bart lost their weapons, they came back swinging, punching the large casino security guards. Detrick was back on his feet and tackled the casino owner across the room and into the armoire containing the television. The runt of a man struck the television, smashing the screen, but he still managed to come back swinging. For a smaller man, he didn't go down easily. Detrick punched him several times in the gut and then punched him in the face. Carter and Bart had their hands full with the two guards, blocking punches and landing some of their own.

While the casino owner and two guards fought the three mercenaries, Marco saw his opportunity and bolted from the room. He ran into the sixth floor corridor and saw Sims in the hallway several yards from him. Sims panicked and pulled his own baton. Marco didn't think twice as he charged for Sims, tackling him to the floor. Both men roughly struck the floor with Marco landing on top. Marco punched Sims twice in the face and kneed him in the groin for good measure. He snatched the steel baton from Sims, who now clutched himself in agony.

Loud thumping and crashes could be heard coming from the suite down the hall. Marco sprang to his feet, not waiting around to see who was winning, and ran for the stairs.

§

Bogart sat on the sofa within the safe house apartment beneath the dilapidated motel. He appeared bored while flipping through an old girly magazine. Jackie sat on the arm of the chair closest to the bedroom and watched Bogart as if waiting for him to say something. There was no doubt in her mind that he would soon comment. He finally shifted on the sofa, cast the girly magazine aside, and glanced at his sister.

"So now that Scorpio broke up with Rayner," Bogart announced matter-of-factly, "do you think Zack will be upset if I ask her out?"

Jackie groaned and shook her head. "I knew I shouldn't have told you that," she muttered, then shot a glare at her brother. "Any thoughts you're having about Scorpio, you can put right out of your head."

"Hey, I'm a pretty decent catch, if I don't mind saying so myself," Bogart announced.

"Do you honestly think Zack wants you boinking his daughter?" Jackie asked in turn.

Bogart considered the question, opened his mouth to respond, and then thought better of it. "You're right; he'd probably kill me for just looking at her."

"Exactly," she replied, knowing all too well how Zack would react. "Get it out of your head."

"But she's sexy *and* dangerous," Bogart pouted while allowing his head to fall back against the sofa. "Now that I know she's available, I can't stop thinking about it."

"Heads up," Zack announced through Jackie's ear transmitter. "I have eyes on Marco, and he's coming in hot."

Jackie touched her earpiece while perking up and responded in concern. "Anyone chasing him?"

"Not that I can see," Zack replied from the other end. "I'll keep watch for any additional company outside. You take him down quietly as we discussed, then be prepared for a fast exit."

Jackie darted into the bedroom while motioning Bogart to the main entrance. Bogart leaped over the back of the sofa, moved alongside the door, and hid behind it. They'd get the slip on Marco once he was inside the safe house, taking him down without fear of collateral damage.

"Ah, hell," Zack shouted in something resembling anger through their ear transmitters. "Outside, now!"

Jackie immediately reacted to Zack's words. She ran from the bedroom toward Bogart and the door. Both ran up the concrete steps. Bogart threw open the basement door, and they bolted outside just in time to witness Nevada tackling Marco to the ground. The two landed roughly and rolled several times. Marco lost his steel baton when they hit the ground. He swung his fist without even looking and punched Nevada in the jaw, momentarily stunning her. Marco sprang to his feet, realizing he'd just hit a woman but then soon noticed Jackie and Bogart running for him. Zack then appeared from the woods where he had been hiding and ran for him as well. Marco panicked and ran back for the casino parking lot. Zack angrily motioned for Jackie to take care of Nevada. Jackie ran for Nevada, who was just now returning to her feet. Zack and Bogart continued their pursuit of Marco, who made it into the distant casino parking lot. When Nevada attempted to bolt past Jackie for the casino, Jackie stepped into her path, cutting her off.

"Marco is my bounty," Nevada announced with a hiss in her tone.

"No, you let him get away," Jackie shot back. "Zack and Bogart are going to take him down, and then he'll be under our protection."

"Get out of my way," Nevada snarled while sizing up Jackie. "I don't want to hurt you."

"You can give it your best shot," Jackie announced, refusing to let her pass.

Nevada threw a fast, hard punch for Jackie's face. Jackie deflected the blow and the kick that immediately followed. She then swept Nevada's legs out from under her, sending her crashing to the ground. Although somewhat stunned by the nearly effortless takedown, Nevada swiftly sprang to her feet and again faced Jackie, who wasn't about to let her pass.

"You may be the better fighter," Nevada snarled, "but I fight dirty."

"I train with Zack," Jackie scoffed, refusing to be intimidated. "I know every dirty move ever invented."

Jackie and Nevada heard the faint sound of a car's tires burning out within the casino parking lot. When the two women looked, they saw a black car speed down the road. Nevada cursed and bolted back to the front of the motel for her parked car. She jumped into her car and took off after Marco, despite having a good head start. Jackie cursed under her breath and ran for the woods, not waiting for Zack and Bogart to circle back. Once she reached the other side of the woods, she ran into the clearing where her helicopter waited. Jackie jumped into the pilot's seat and prepped the craft. As the helicopter started up, Zack and Bogart could be seen at the woods' edge. Both men ran for the aircraft and jumped in the back just as she was ready to take-off. Their timing was nearly perfect.

"Go, go!" Zack cried out while shutting the side door with added vigor.

Jackie lifted off, flying the helicopter above the trees and over the casino in the direction the black car had headed. All three noticed the precession of vehicles racing away from the casino, all pursuing Marco.

"We're not the only interested party," Zack muttered and shook his head.

"The casino probably uses facial recognition," Bogart informed them. "I wouldn't doubt word got out about his location. That was probably why he was running when you spotted him."

"You were right, Bogart," Jackie remarked. "He must not have realized he was being hunted."

"Probably been gambling at the casino the entire night," Zack informed them while frowning. "How the hell did Nevada intercept?"

"You know that woman?" Bogart asked Zack with some surprise.

"She's a bounty hunter," Zack replied. "Former Marine and a black belt in karate."

"She's hot," Bogart remarked, although he possibly meant to say it to himself.

"Well, you can get that thought out of your pants," Zack informed him with little emotion. "If you look at her the wrong way, she'll tear you apart. Nevada hates men." He then considered the comment. "Actually, Nevada hates people in general."

"So how *did* she find him?" Bogart then asked and appeared curious.

There was a moment of silence.

Jackie suddenly groaned and cursed under her breath. "The helicopter," she muttered. "She saw my helicopter at the hotel in Maine when I picked up Zack. If she somehow knew we were looking for Marco, it would have been very easy for her to wait at the airport and keep tabs on my helicopter. She probably saw us disperse from there and knew we were going after Marco."

"She couldn't exactly follow us in the helicopter," Bogart informed her.

Zack sneered and shook his head. "She slapped a tracker on the helicopter," he snarled. "We'll need to sweep the bird for bugs the next time we're on the ground."

Jackie nodded to the city below. "I see Nevada's car," she announced, then looked around. "I don't see the black car Marco was driving."

"I saw the plates. It's the vehicle that's actually registered to him," Zack informed her and scanned the area with his binoculars.

"The same car everyone else is looking for," Bogart remarked and shook his head. "That's not going to end well for him."

Zack zeroed in on something and pointed to the left. "On the other side of the city," he announced. "There's a black car driving erratically. I think that's him."

"Nevada's going to be right on our ass the entire way," Jackie announced, then cast a look at Zack in the back. "We're going to lead her right to him."

"We don't have much choice," Zack remarked while hovering over her shoulder. "Just stay on Marco's car, but keep far enough away that the rest of the guys looking for him aren't aware we're looking for him as well." He then looked at Bogart in the back with him. "Contact Kirk and Gil. Let them know we have confirmation and are in pursuit of the suspect. With all the company he's attracted, we're going to need all hands on deck."

Chapter 20

Thirty minutes later, Jackie's helicopter flew overhead far enough away and to the east of the vehicle that they would remain undetected by the fleeing mob boss's son and stay off Nevada's radar as well. The black car was now driving at a normal speed so as not to attract additional attention. Marco had managed to elude the precession of vehicles that had been attempting to follow him, which was nothing short of a miracle. With the other interested parties out of the picture, Marco would soon work on the next phase of his escape plan. An alternate hiding location. Within the helicopter, Zack continued to scan a stretch of isolated road far from the small city.

"Well, there's Nevada," Zack announced while practically looking behind them. "She's heading far to the east of Marco but still following us. We'll be out of her view soon, but she'll still be able to track us."

"Can we put enough distance between her and us so we can double back and intercept Marco before she reaches us?" Bogart asked.

"Not at this speed," Jackie reported. "We don't want to lose Marco." She then hesitated and thought of something she hadn't before. "Although--"

"What is it?" Zack asked while peering over Jackie's shoulder as she looked at the helicopter's navigation.

"Well, judging by the direction he's going, it looks as if Marco is heading for the safe house on the lake," Jackie remarked, then cast a quick look at Zack's face directly over her shoulder. "If he stays on this road, he's going to run right into Ross, Kirk, and Beck."

"They can intervene," Bogart announced.

"Might be best to let him reach the safe house," Zack informed them. "It's pretty much isolated, which means no collateral damage. It would be better if we let the guys ambush him there."

Zack climbed up front with Jackie, having to step over the seat to accomplish it, and disrupted her flying due to the tight quarters. The helicopter teetered as a result. Jackie elbowed his hip several times.

"Don't do that," she cried out. "You're going to make me crash!"

Zack ignored Jackie's concerns, flopped into the co-pilot seat, and snatched the radio from its cradle. "Kirk, you copy?"

"I copy," Kirk replied.

"Our friend is coming to you," Zack announced into the radio. "If you double back, you can greet him at the 'house'. We have our own friend to lose."

"Copy that," Kirk responded.

Zack replaced the handset and glanced at Jackie. "Time to lose Nevada. Get ahead of her tracker due east. Once we're out of range, swing around and head for the lakeside safe house from the north. Nevada will have to take a lot of back roads to catch up to us. Hopefully, Kirk will have Marco by the time we reach them."

"You've got it," Jackie announced while grinning.

"Nevada's going to be so pissed," Zack remarked and seemed almost amused at the thought. He chuckled lowly. "She's amazingly aggressive when she's angry. She may even try to kill me."

Jackie eyed him, finding his joy in that thought rather disturbing. She shook her head, conveying her disapproval. "You need a new hobby."

"Maybe if you sparred with me more often in our relationship, I wouldn't feel the need to sneak out and spar with other women," Zack retorted matter-of-factly.

Jackie cast a glare at Zack, somewhat stunned by the comment. Although he didn't look at her, she could see the tiny smirk of amusement on his face. Truth be told, Jackie actually enjoyed sparring with Zack, but she was aware that, in his warped mind, he considered it to be a bizarre form of foreplay. She knew how his mind worked. On the plus side, she always had that silver bullet in her arsenal if she ever needed to redirect Zack.

§

Ross, Beck, and Kirk approached the cabin by the lake from the woods in the opposite direction of where they had initially parked the first time so their jeep wouldn't be spotted by someone heading down the driveway. All three paused just before the clearing and scouted out the area.

"We need to be careful," Ross informed his men. "We don't know if the local police will show up for the men we left tied in the cabin."

"They should have been here by now," Beck remarked. "I'm guessing they picked up the guys and left already."

"Or they weren't here yet," Kirk announced with some concern. "We don't need some country cop showing up while we're staging our little ambush party."

"Be on the lookout for friendlies. I'm on point," Ross announced. "Watch my six."

Ross headed for the cabin while keeping low. He approached the back door, stood to the side, and waited for Beck and Kirk to join him. Beck remained alongside the cabin while Kirk took a lookout position by the back porch steps. Ross eyed the door and saw the doorjamb had been crudely fixed after their earlier visit. He tried the doorknob. It wasn't locked. Ross looked back at his men and signaled to them. Both joined him on the porch, taking flanking positions on either side of the door. Ross pushed the door open then moved into the doorway while keeping low and aiming his weapon. The cabin was empty. Ross stepped inside and immediately aimed his gun behind the door. There was no one there either. The cabin's layout allowed him a perfect view of the entire interior except for the bedrooms and bathroom. There were several spots of blood on the floor where they had taken down the first two intruders. All three of the men they had tied were gone, indicating the police must have arrived and removed them already.

As Ross moved across the cabin, Beck followed. Kirk remained just inside the doorway and watched the area outside. Ross and Beck checked the bedroom and bathroom then lowered their weapons.

"All clear," Ross announced.

Kirk shut the back door and moved to the side, remaining on lookout. "I guess the police were already here," he remarked.

"Looks that way," Ross agreed. "Let's roll out the welcome mat for our friend."

§

Marco's black sedan pulled off the back road within the heavily wooded area, turned onto the long driveway leading up to the cabin, and parked in the area where Kirk had earlier parked his jeep. Marco got out of the car carefully hidden within the woods, looked around, and listened for any unusual sounds. The area was peaceful. When he was sure he wasn't being followed, he rounded the car for the trunk and popped it with the electronic key. He grabbed his bug-out bag from the trunk, shut the lid, and hurried through the woods toward the cabin. He continued along the path in the woods for ten minutes with his bag slung over his shoulder. When he reached the clearing before the cabin, he took a moment to look around and again listen. When nothing moved, and he heard no sounds, he hurried across the clearing for the back door. He unlocked the door, unaware of the crudely fixed doorjamb that had been busted only an hour or so earlier.

Marco closed the door behind him and took two steps into the cabin before abruptly stopping. His eyes immediately strayed to the blood on the floor. Marco panicked and turned to leave when he saw Kirk standing behind him with a gun aimed at his face.

"What took you so long?" Kirk asked in a somewhat demanding tone.

Marco slowly dropped the bag from his shoulder and put his hands in the air. "This isn't happening," he muttered under his breath.

"Oh, I assure you, it is," Ross announced from across the room.

Marco looked over his shoulder and saw Ross approaching from the nearby bedroom. Beck stood alongside the front door with his weapon in his hand as well.

"We're in a bit of a hurry," Ross informed him.

Kirk picked up Marco's bag and slung it over his shoulder without lowering his weapon. He then motioned Marco across the room toward Ross and Beck. As Marco crossed the room, he stared at the blood on the floor.

"How many people are after me?" Marco asked with concern.

"Dozens of hired killers, I'm sure," Ross casually informed him.

"Are you going to kill me?" Marco asked.

"If we were, you'd already be dead," Kirk muttered, showing little emotion.

"Who are you?" Marco asked while looking at all three as he approached Ross and Beck with Kirk only a few steps behind him. "You look familiar. Did you do work for my father? If you're looking for a bounty, I'm sure he'll pay whatever you want for my safe return."

"Relax, Marco. Your father hired us to keep you alive," Ross informed him. "We'll save introductions for later. Right now, we need to get you out of here before others show up looking for you."

Marco seemed to relax and lowered his hands. "Oh, in that case, I'm glad to see you."

"Let's just say we're the lesser of the evils," Ross informed him, then indicated the front door. "Stick close. We're heading out the door and to the left. Straight into the woods. If we run into any trouble, keep your head down, and stay behind me."

Marco nodded. Beck opened the door partway, scanned the area, and then stepped onto the porch. As he remained on guard, Ross and Marco headed from the house with Kirk behind them. Beck kept watch, while partially turned, and moved with them for the woods. Beck then saw something shimmer within the woods not far from them.

"Down!" Beck cried out while firing his weapon.

Ross tackled Marco to the ground while Kirk and Beck fired at the shooter hiding behind the tree. Several nearly silent shots were fired back at them as they took cover. The sniper had a silencer on his weapon, indicating he was probably a hired killer and not a bounty hunter. Ross hurried Marco to the side of the cabin and safety. Beck remained hidden behind the porch and returned fire, allowing Kirk time to run behind the cabin as well. Kirk rounded the back of the cabin, while Beck held the sniper's attention, and darted across the clearing for the woods some distance behind the gunman. Kirk kept behind several trees while making his way closer to the shooter, who was barely visible to him. The sniper was unaware of his presence as he made his way closer.

Ross indicated that Marco should follow him to the back corner of the cabin while Beck kept the shooter's attention on the front. A shot was suddenly fired at them from the woods near the back corner, splintering the wood siding near Marco's head. Marco leaped for the ground while Ross spun and fired several shots into the woods.

"Back inside," Ross gruffly announced to Marco while practically dragging him alongside him to the back of the cabin and safety.

While Ross returned fire into the woods behind him, Marco darted around the cabin and ran for the nearby dock where a boat was tied.

Ross saw him running for the open and exposed dock and sneered. "I'm going to shoot the bastard myself," he muttered while firing several shots into the woods at the second gunman, providing some cover for Marco.

Marco ran across the dock and swiftly untied the boat. He was about to jump inside before casting off the second line when he suddenly stopped. A tarp covered what appeared to be two bodies, and there was a pool of blood on the bottom of the boat. Marco cried out with alarm, then ran back for the cabin and cast his body against the side of the building near Ross. Ross fired another shot into the woods then looked back at Marco.

"You came back?" he snarled.

"There are dead people in the boat," Marco informed him with a look of horror.

Ross appeared curious and glanced at the boat. "Did you get a look at them?"

Marco shook his head. "Looked like two people," he replied. "They were covered with a tarp."

Ross cursed under his breath, "Son-of-a-bitch." It had to be the man and woman they had earlier saved from the three ruffians.

A helicopter was heard approaching. Marco looked to the sky and scanned the area. Jackie's helicopter suddenly appeared over the lake. Ross looked at the aircraft and signaled both directions, indicating the shooter's locations. The helicopter buzzed over the cabin and barely slowed. There was a loud thump on the cabin roof. Marco looked to the cabin roof above them while listening to the sound of someone thumping around. He panicked and ran for the woods in the direction Kirk had headed.

"Marco," Ross bellowed out in anger. "Get the hell back here!"

It was too late. Marco darted into the woods and was gone. Zack tumbled onto the porch roof from the main tin roof, moved into a crouching position, and aimed his assault rifle into the woods, firing several shots. A man flew out from behind a tree and hit the ground. Ross moved away from the cabin and ran after Marco. Zack ran back onto the main roof despite the sharp pitch, crossed the peak, and slid on his hip down the side to the front porch roof. He remained in a semi-reclined position while scanning the woods through the rifle scope. The sniper fired a shot at Beck, but he was concealed behind the tree. Zack remained still and patiently waited.

Within the woods, Kirk made his way closer to the mostly hidden shooter. He was now only several yards behind the gunman. Kirk remained hidden behind a tree and waited for the sniper to fire at Beck. Kirk kept low and poked his head out from behind the tree. The shooter heard him and spun at the same time. Kirk aimed his weapon and saw the young woman they had earlier rescued from within the cabin. Kirk was momentarily surprised at the turn of events. The woman didn't even hesitate when she saw him and squeezed the trigger. A shot rang out. The woman gasped as Zack's bullet tore through her chest. She stared at Kirk as the gun fell from her hand, and then she dropped to the ground. Kirk stared at the dead woman in stunned disbelief.

"What the fuck--?" he cried out in anger.

It would appear as if the innocent man and woman they thought they rescued earlier hadn't been so innocent after all.

Chapter 21

As the helicopter circled over the woods, Bogart remained in the back and scanned the area with his binoculars. He shook his head with disgust.

"I can't see anything," Bogart announced. "It's too thick down there."

"Communication is down as well. Must be in a dead zone," Jackie informed him. "I thought I saw Ross take off after him, but I can't contact anyone."

"Try the road," Bogart insisted. "Maybe he's heading back to the road. Marco could have his car parked somewhere around here."

Jackie circled around and headed for the back road. Marco appeared from the woods on foot, looked up, and saw the helicopter. He panicked and ran across the road. A pickup truck nearly struck him then squealed to a grinding halt. The male driver waved him into the truck. Marco jumped into the passenger side, and the truck took off down the road.

Within the helicopter, Bogart lowered his binoculars and cried out, "Now who the hell is that?"

"The idiot," Jackie scoffed and followed the truck. "Does he think it's a rescue?"

"For the son of a mob boss, he's not too bright," Bogart scoffed.

Within the pickup truck, Marco turned in the seat and looked back at the helicopter in hot pursuit.

"Are you okay?" the driver asked in a somewhat unrefined tone, making him sound a bit like a redneck.

The driver, Rowen, shifted his small, beady eyes to the rearview mirror several times. Obviously, there was little hope to outrun a helicopter with a pickup truck. Rowen was a tall, well-built man in his late forties. His rugged good looks were attributed to his short, spiky hair and facial stubble attempting to resemble a crude sort of beard. Rowen laughed and shook his head, seeming almost amused by the situation.

"Damn, you never see this much activity in these woods," Rowen announced, then seemed to consider the comment. "Well, except during hunting season."

Marco cast a look at the older country boy, attempted a smile, and nodded.

"Of course, hunting vermin is pretty much all year round." Rowen's grin then increased as he glanced at Marco. "Especially those with a million large on their heads."

Marco nervously looked back at Rowen, who now had a revolver aimed at him.

Rowen grinned slyly. "It's nothing personal, Marco," he announced. "You understand."

"Is everyone out to get me?" Marco just about demanded while recoiling in his seat.

"Yep, pretty much," Rowen replied cheerfully in his unrefined country accent. "Consider yourself lucky. Us bounty hunters are more willing to take you alive. Some of them boys looking for you will sacrifice the extra dough because killing you is easier."

A black SUV suddenly appeared alongside them and rammed the front quarter panel of Rowen's truck. Rowen dropped the gun to grip the steering wheel with both hands, but he was too late. The pickup veered sharply to the right and sideswiped a tree. The truck jolted to a stop, tossing both passengers violently in their seats. Marco quickly recovered, threw open the door, and bolted from the truck. He darted into the woods as the newcomer, who ran them off the road, popped out of his vehicle just behind them and fired at Marco, striking the trees near his head. Hawthorn, the hitman within the black SUV, wasn't a very tall or large man by any means. He was in his late thirties and stood possibly five-foot-nine with light brown hair that was neatly trimmed on the sides and slightly spiky on top. He was meticulously clean-shaven and neatly dressed, giving him an almost gentlemanly sort of appeal, although he was anything but a gentleman. Built only somewhat athletic and not particularly handsome, his killer instincts seemed to be his finest attributes.

Rowen leaped out of his damaged truck with an AK-15 in his arms, hid behind the quarter panel, and fired at Hawthorn behind him. Hawthorn retreated behind his car door and fired back. The helicopter suddenly buzzed overhead. Bogart sat in the open side door and fired at both men. Rowen and Hawthorn both retreated into their vehicles. Hawthorn burned out on the back road and drove away. Rowen attempted to take off, but his flat front tire was stuck in a ditch. He cursed and slammed his hands on the steering wheel.

"Son-of-a-bitch!"

A newer jeep slowed alongside Rowen's truck. The passenger side window lowered, and the driver, a bounty hunter named Quinn, grinned at him. Quinn was about five-foot-ten and built solid with a little, added muscle behind him. Considered a bit of a pretty-boy, the man in his mid-thirties kept thick facial stubble to toughen up his baby-face. His medium brown hair was kept short and moderately stylish, making him physically appealing.

"Better luck next time, Rowen," Quinn announced, then laughed while giving his competition the middle finger.

Rowen sneered and picked up his rifle. Quinn saw the weapon, gasped, and hit the gas. Rowen fired several shots, aiming for the jeep's tires but missed. Jackie's helicopter was then seen flying over the woods in the direction Marco had run. Quinn's jeep attempted to follow, hot on her tail. Kirk's jeep suddenly flew onto the road, struck Quinn's jeep in the front panel, and raced after Jackie's helicopter. Quinn's jeep ran off the road and into a ditch. He attempted to get the jeep out of the ditch but ended up throwing mud everywhere. Rowen could be seen just down the road with a tire jack in his hand, laughing and giving Quinn the middle finger. It seemed obvious the two men's paths had crossed on numerous occasions in the past.

Kirk's jeep flew along the back road, pursuing Jackie's helicopter. When the helicopter hovered over a certain spot, she was announcing to the team that Marco had been spotted in that area. As the jeep slowed, Zack and Kirk jumped out of the back of the moving vehicle with their rifles and ran into the woods. Ross drove Kirk's jeep with Beck riding shotgun. The jeep picked up speed and stayed in pursuit of the helicopter, just in case Zack and Kirk failed to locate Marco. Ross and Beck kept an eye on the road, the woods, and the aircraft in the sky. When Ross looked back at the road, Nevada's car was suddenly in front of him. Ross slammed on the brakes, jolting both men harshly against their seatbelts. Nevada threw her car into park, leaped from the vehicle, and ran to the woods. As if like clockwork, Marco appeared from the woods, saw Nevada, and attempted to veer to the right. Nevada pounced on him with all the grace of a panther.

Nevada and Marco rolled across the dirt road several times. This time, Nevada landed on top. She punched Marco in the face then thrust her knee into his groin for good measures. Zack and Kirk stopped at the edge of the woods just in time to see the knee shot to the groin. Both men cringed and seemed to feel the pain. Nevada flipped the writhing man over onto his belly and zip-tied his hands behind his back. Zack and Kirk closed in from the woods as Ross and Beck approached from their jeep. Nevada moved to one knee and had a semiautomatic in each hand aimed at both sets of men.

"He's mine," she snarled, prepared to shoot. "Back the fuck off!"

All four men kept their distance from the beautiful yet unpredictable woman. There was no telling if she'd shoot or not. Two black blazers suddenly appeared on the road and skidded to a sliding stop. The windows lowered, and men in the front and back opened fire. Nevada gasped with alarm and was barely able to aim her weapon. Zack tackled Nevada to the ground, shielding her from their gunfire, while Kirk, Ross, and Beck fired back at both vehicles. The mercenaries attempted to get out of their trucks, having the number advantage over the three men. Zack rolled off Nevada and fired at the men as well. Nevada grabbed her discarded weapon and also returned fire. Two of the men who had left the vehicle fell to the ground. The remaining men moved to the opposite side and used the car as cover. Marco rolled for the nearby ditch and safety while Zack and Nevada dove for cover behind Nevada's car.

Jackie's helicopter suddenly appeared behind the two blazers. The sound of the massive rotors was almost deafening. Bogart fired from the side of the aircraft at the exposed men, who were unable to hide from the helicopter over top of them. Several men went down. The two remaining men leaped into the first blazer and tore off down the dirt road, being no match for the shooter in the aircraft. Jackie's helicopter lowered and landed on the road not far from the vehicles. Kirk and Zack pulled Marco to his feet and hurried him to the awaiting aircraft.

"I caught him!" Nevada cried out while chasing after them with her gun still in her hand, although she wasn't cocky enough to aim it at any of the men. "He's my bounty!"

"Have at it," Ross shouted back above the loud helicopter rotors. "You want him?" He angrily pointed at the helicopter. "Get your ass in the chopper because that's the only way he's staying alive!"

Nevada sneered and climbed into the helicopter with Zack, Marco, and Kirk. Ross backed away from the aircraft, looked at Jackie, and twirled his finger in the air. The helicopter lifted off and flew away. Ross motioned Beck to Nevada's car.

"Meet me at the rendezvous," Ross announced. "Make sure you're not followed."

Beck nodded and ran for Nevada's abandoned car. Ross jumped into Kirk's jeep, and they drove off in separate directions.

§

Rowen cast his tire iron aside, unable to fix the flat tire with the ruptured tire wedged in the ditch. The sound of a

jeep's tires burning out in mud could be heard not far from
him. Rowen straightened and looked up the road further and
watched Quinn, with his head sticking out of the window,
attempting to rock the jeep in drive and then in reverse out of
the muddy ditch. Rowen sighed and approached the angry man
in the jeep. Quinn cursed, took his foot off the gas pedal, and
looked back at the approaching man.

"If you've come to gloat--"

"No, I didn't come to gloat," Rowen replied with defeat
and indicated his truck. "We're both in a spot here. Why
don't we put our pettiness aside and work together just this
once? We get your jeep out together and go after Marco as a
team. One and a quarter-million split two ways is still a lot of
cash."

Quinn frowned and seemed to consider the idea. He finally
groaned. "Fine," he scoffed. "Just this once, we'll work
together."

Rowen placed several larger rocks in front of the tire that
seemed to be stuck in the mud. "You know what I saw?"

"Fifty men with automatic rifles and a helicopter?" Quinn
scoffed.

Rowen placed another rock in front of the tire, then
straightened and looked at Quinn. "I saw Nevada," he
announced. "She drove past here like the devil was chasing
her."

"Marco?" Quinn asked.

Rowen grinned and nodded. "I'd stake my life on it," he
replied. "That girl's got some serious bloodhound in her. I
think we need to join forces with her. Three-way split is still a
hell of a lot of money. We're going to need to join forces if
we're going to stand a chance with all the hired guns chasing
Marco. We need the prick alive. Those bastards will gladly
take him dead. Easier that way." He nodded to the jeep's
driver seat. "Give it a try now."

Rowen moved behind the jeep while Quinn got behind the
wheel. As Quinn gave it gas, Rowen pushed. They easily freed
the jeep from the muddy ditch. Rowen approached the driver's
side and removed the keys from the ignition. Quinn leaped out
of the jeep.

"Hey!"

"Just making sure you don't leave without me," Rowen announced while casually dangling the keys, then walked back to his truck. "I need my gear."

Quinn frowned and cast his back against the jeep. Once Rowen had his duffel bag, he rejoined him and jumped in the passenger side. Quinn hopped into the driver's seat and was handed the keys. He started the jeep and drove down the road. They didn't drive very far before reaching the ambush site. Both men stared at the dead men on the road and the bullet holes in the remaining blazer.

"There's some serious shit going down," Rowen remarked and shook his head.

"Maybe getting Nevada on our side isn't such a bad idea," Quinn admitted.

"We need to get out of here before someone finds this mess and points fingers at us," Rowen insisted.

"You don't have to tell me twice."

Chapter 22

Nevada sat backward alongside the bound Marco throughout the helicopter ride and glared at Zack and Kirk, who sat facing forward. Kirk sat back in his seat with his arms folded across his broad chest and glared back at the young woman. Zack casually leaned against the corner with one leg resting on the seat across from him and shifted looks between Kirk and Nevada.

"I guess you two still hate each other's guts," Zack remarked with little emotion.

"She's the spawn of Satan," Kirk scoffed.

"Blow me," Nevada snarled with a sneer.

Kirk eyed Zack, giving him a stern, serious look. "Can I throw her out the door?"

"You're asking the wrong guy," Zack remarked. "I'm not in charge."

"This is going to be a fun ride," Marco muttered while shifting uncomfortably.

"No one asked your opinion," Nevada launched back at Marco.

"I don't even know why she's here," Kirk shot back, then glared at Zack. "Why is she here?"

"Because I caught the prick," Nevada shouted at Kirk. "He's my bounty!"

"If it hadn't been for Zack, you'd be a dead bounty hunter," Kirk snapped. "You're lucky he saved your ass because I certainly wouldn't have."

"The feeling's mutual, you gigantic talking dildo," she launched back.

Zack groaned and placed his hand over his eyes. "Will the two of you just kill each other and end my misery!"

Bogart glanced into the back, then cast a look at Jackie and nudged her. She eyed Bogart and noted his curious look regarding their female passenger.

"Something I should know?" Bogart asked his sister.

"I don't know what the deal is with the guys and Nevada," Jackie replied and shook her head. "Apparently, they bumped into her a while back."

The feuding between Kirk and Nevada continued, turning into little more than seeing who could use the most profanity. Jackie was growing weary of the fighting. It was bad enough when it was just her guys blowing off steam, but Nevada seemed to add a whole new spark to the powder keg. Jackie finally groaned, having had enough.

"If I have to land this helicopter, there's going to be hell to pay," Jackie shouted at the man and woman in the back. "Now sit down, shut up, and behave!"

Kirk and Nevada slouched in their seats and silently sulked, taking the threat seriously.

"I guess we know who's in charge," Marco muttered while raising a brow.

Kirk and Nevada sneered at Marco.

"Where are we going?" Nevada finally asked while half turning to look at Jackie in the pilot's seat.

"A predetermined rendezvous," Jackie informed her, not willing to give up too much information to the woman she didn't know or trust. "We need to regroup and figure out where we're taking Marco."

"We're taking him to Vincent Scartelli," Nevada announced with little hesitation while shooting up in her seat. "He put the bounty on his head."

"I didn't kill anyone," Marco insisted.

Nevada cast a look at Marco and sharply raised her brow. "I don't care, and it's not my problem," she announced. "That's between you and Vincent."

"Sorry, Nevada," Jackie casually informed her, lacking sympathy. "We're not turning him over to Scartelli. Giovanni contracted us to keep Marco alive, and that's what we're going to do."

"That's not what I agreed to. I'm turning him in for the bounty," Nevada snapped back.

"Four other people in this helicopter say you're not," Kirk informed her.

"Five," Marco chimed in.

"Giovanni will honor the bounty on him," Zack informed Nevada. "So just calm the fuck down."

Nevada sneered at Zack. "Don't tell me to calm the fuck down," she launched back.

It seemed as if Zack was also losing his patience. The last thing anyone needed was Zack getting involved in some feud. Jackie wasn't about to risk that. She pushed the stick hard forward, causing the helicopter to plummet into a field. Bogart, Kirk, Marco, and Nevada all screamed. Zack braced his hand against the interior and his foot on the opposite seat, barely reacting to the sudden descend. As the helicopter lifted back up on a steep incline, more screams followed.

"Jesus, Jackie!" Kirk yelled.

Jackie leveled the craft. "Unless you want to take the express elevator to hell, I don't want to hear another word out of any of you," she shouted back at them.

"Rock my world, baby," Zack exclaimed while grinning, obviously enjoying the thrill ride a little too much.

Jackie rolled her eyes and groaned. She should have known Zack would get some sort of sick pleasure out of it. The helicopter continued on course for another thirty minutes in silence before landing in a deserted field close to the edge of the woods not far from an old, structurally sound cabin. Jackie shut down the helicopter and removed her headset.

"Everyone out of my helicopter," Jackie scoffed in mild anger directed at her passengers.

Without further prompting, Zack opened the side door and jumped out. He immediately got down on all fours and scanned the underbelly of the helicopter. He found Nevada's tracking device and removed it. Nevada made a face, apparently thinking she had been too clever for them. Zack switched it off, sat on the ground, and looked up at Jackie as she got out of the helicopter.

"Want to do a little skeet shooting?" Zack teased while waving the tracker.

"Think it might come in handy later?" Jackie asked.

Zack considered the comment then nodded. "Yeah, that could be fun," he replied and slapped the tracker on the side of the helicopter.

Zack extended his hand up to Jackie. She slapped her hand into his and helped pull him to his feet. Kirk helped Marco out of the helicopter, being he still had his hands zip-tied behind his back, and kept him from falling.

"How long?" Nevada asked as she jumped from the back of the helicopter and joined them.

Jackie looked at her watch. "About an hour," she informed them.

"I have to take a leak," Marco announced.

"You can hold it," Nevada scoffed.

"He's your bounty," Kirk remarked and nodded to the nearby woods. "Take him to the bathroom." He then smirked deviously. "Remember, shake it three times before tucking it away."

Zack and Jackie hid their smiles and had to look away. Bogart was somewhat surprised by the comment even though he shouldn't have been because, well, it *was* Kirk.

Nevada sneered at Kirk. "You really want me to kick your ass, don't you?" she snarled at him.

"Give it your best shot," Kirk launched back while holding his arms out to his sides.

Nevada took a quick step toward Kirk, who offered a tiny, devious smile, prepared to escalate the situation with the sexy but dangerous woman.

Zack held his hand up between the two and eyed Nevada. "I need to be honest with you, Nevada," he remarked with little emotion. "You're not that good."

Nevada glared at Zack. "I'm damned good," she insisted. "I could kick your ass."

Zack snorted a laugh and shook his head. "Not on your best day and my worst," he replied.

"Not to interrupt the ass-whooping," Marco announced while eyeing Nevada and Zack, "but I still have to go to the bathroom."

"Fine," Nevada scoffed and removed a knife from her boot. She moved behind Marco and cut one of the zip ties. She replaced the blade to her boot, removed a fresh zip tie, and tied his wrists in front of him.

"You've got to be kidding," Marco grumbled. "You expect me to go like this?"

Nevada met his gaze with a hostile glare. "Ninety-nine percent of my bounties are men," she informed him. "They've all managed just fine, but if you need some assistance, I'll be happy to help you find the little fella."

Bogart had to turn away to keep from laughing.

Nevada pointed to the nearby woods. "Move it," she snarled.

"Somehow, I imagined this would be more of a turn-on," Marco muttered.

As Nevada escorted Marco to the woods, Kirk spun to face Zack and glared at him. "Tell me we're leaving her behind," he announced.

"Ross accepted her terms," Zack informed him and showed little interest either way. "As long as she maintains possession of him, he's her bounty."

"Meanwhile, we're the ones protecting him and chauffeuring them around for free," Kirk snarled. "I'm not risking my life just for her to reap the reward."

"Me either," Bogart announced and shook his head with some annoyance. "You saw what happened back there. Every hitman and bounty hunter is looking for Marco. It's not like picking daisies. We're going to be putting in overtime on this one."

"I'm not doing this job out of the kindness of my heart either," Jackie remarked and folded her arms across her chest. "Sal may be our friend, but Giovanni certainly isn't."

"I agree," Zack informed them. "I'm sure Ross will offer her a deal. If she doesn't take it, she's on her own."

"She needs us more than we need her," Kirk scoffed in anger.

"We need to wait and see what Ross has to say when he gets here," Jackie insisted with a sigh.

§

Almost an hour had gone by when they heard the sound of a jeep approaching within the woods despite that there was no road. Bogart and Nevada moved Marco into the helicopter while Jackie, Zack, and Kirk each grabbed a rifle and took cover in front and behind the craft. Jackie remained close to the front in case they needed to make a hasty getaway. The jeep took its time arriving, which meant whoever was driving wasn't in a hurry. All three recognized Kirk's jeep as it appeared at the edge of the woods. Once it stopped, Ross and Beck got out. Ross whistled, signaling everything was okay. Jackie, Kirk, and Zack lowered their weapons, slung them, and moved away from the helicopter. Bogart and Nevada removed Marco from the back in order to keep an eye on him.

Nevada approached Ross with an air of arrogance. "We need to be clear on this," she announced and indicated Marco. "I caught him. He's my bounty, and we're turning him over to whoever is paying the million dollars."

Ross stared into her eyes and nodded. "Cards on the table," he announced and cocked his head. "You may have caught him, but you'd be dead, and he'd be in a body bag if we hadn't saved your ass back there. That being said, here are my terms. We're taking Marco to a safe house until Giovanni can arrange for his safety." Ross then folded his arms across his chest and held up his head proudly. "Giovanni pays us the one point two five million, which we split nine ways. I know, for a fact, that's a bigger payday than you've ever received in your career. We work together to keep him alive. Those are my terms. If you don't like my terms, we'll drive you back to your beat-up, wreck of a rental car on the other side of the woods, and you can fend for yourself." He then raised his brows. "Just to be straight; if you run into trouble, we will not bail you out. We will leave you for hitman fodder. Once Marco is out of your control, we will proceed with our original plan without you." He then shrugged. "Not that you'll care because you'll probably be dead. Those are my terms. Make your decision wisely."

Nevada folded her arms across her chest and stared at Ross while showing little emotion. They stood in a stare-off for more than a minute. Marco looked a bit tense while waiting to hear her response, knowing it was his life that lay in the balance. Nevada frowned and allowed her arms to fall to her sides.

"Fine," she scoffed. "You win."

Marco breathed a sigh of relief.

"Where are we going?" Nevada asked, losing some of her earlier arrogance.

"Still working on that," Ross replied. "After what happened at the cabin by the lake, it's pretty obvious someone knows the whereabouts of Giovanni's safe houses. That puts us at a bit of a disadvantage." He then gave her a curious look. "How did you find the motel safe house?"

Nevada casually shrugged. "I put a tracker on Jackie's helicopter, waited for you guys to show up at the airport, and followed Jackie. Just a calculated risk."

"How did you know we were working for Giovanni?" Ross countered.

"I saw Giovanni visit Sal," Nevada informed him. "I placed a tracker on Sal's car and waited to see what he did next. When I figured out whose house he visited last night, I knew to go to the airport and watch Jackie's helicopter."

Ross shook his head and frowned. "Someone close to Giovanni must have betrayed him and gave up the safe house locations," he remarked. "Giovanni told Sal the three safe house locations when they were alone together, and we weren't even outside when Sal told us. That means no one overheard our conversation either."

"He's going to need to find out who betrayed him before we turn over Marco," Beck insisted. "Otherwise, he's as good as dead the moment we walk away."

"According to Sal, his two hired henchmen are the only ones he trusts with anything anymore," Bogart informed them. "It seems unlikely it was one of them."

"Finding the locations of my father's safe houses isn't exactly rocket science," Marco informed them, finally contributing to the conversation. "Anyone hacking into his computer can find a list of his properties. It's not really all that difficult."

"We'll need to notify him, via third-party, that his safe houses were breached," Beck remarked. "If that list can be found in his computer, it wouldn't necessarily have to be someone he trusts. Any third grader with an internet connection can hack into that."

Ross shook his head while frowning. "This has Vincent Scartelli written all over it."

"We need to come up with one hell of an amazing safe house," Beck informed him. "We need to make sure we're as far from collateral damage as we can get."

"We're on our own too," Jackie remarked. "We can't call in any favors on this one. With the number of eyes searching for Marco, they're going to be listening in on every phone associated with Giovanni and Sal."

"That's why we have Othello as a backup," Ross informed them. "Burner phones without tracking and coded messages through Othello. Everyone else needs to keep their phones on standby mode. We need to go dark on this one."

"So where do we find this safe house far from collateral damage?" Bogart asked, appearing curious.

All eyes were on Zack. He looked back at them with a strange look.

"Don't look at me," Zack announced and snorted a tiny laugh. "Most of my places are occupied. Major collateral damage, and plenty of volatile soldiers just looking for an excuse to go nuclear."

Ross eyed Nevada and indicated Marco. "Babysit that one," he ordered. "We need to collaborate in private."

Nevada frowned and motioned Marco back to the helicopter. Jackie grabbed a paper map from the aircraft and joined the team as they headed for the abandoned cabin. Jackie spread out the map on the wooden porch floor, and they all sat around it. Zack crouched alongside Jackie and rested his forearm on her shoulder for support while studying the map. Ross removed a pen and placed circles on the map, indicating areas where there were large parcels of land with few people and only small towns.

"Okay," Ross announced and released a deep sigh. "These are our choices. Start calling them out. We'll pick three locations and scout out each before determining where we want to take Marco."

Bogart took the pen from Ross and placed a large 'X' on one of the circles, then returned the pen. "Monique and Colleen live here," he announced. "We stay far away from that area. We can't risk a war anywhere near them. It's not up for debate."

"Agreed," Jackie replied.

Knowing their two young friends, they'd see Jackie's helicopter a mile away and ride out to investigate. They had to stay far away from those adventurous teenagers. The team studied the map for several minutes in silence, each attempting to find the perfect location that offered shelter, privacy, and far from people. Jackie and Zack suddenly placed their fingers on the map in the same spot. Everyone looked at them in question.

"What's that?" Ross asked.

Jackie and Zack exchanged looks then grinned at Ross.

Chapter 23

Jackie's helicopter landed at a remote airport more than one hundred miles south of Colorado Springs. The airport was small and out-of-the-way. It was the perfect place to refuel. The helicopter no sooner touched ground when Nevada leaped out of the craft with a bound man wearing a sack over his head. She and her prisoner appeared to be the only ones in the back of the helicopter. Nevada hurried the bound man across the tarmac for an awaiting gray, four-door rental car. She tossed the man into the back seat, where he lay unable to get up. Nevada leaped into the driver's seat, started the car, and sped off. As the helicopter shut down and the rotors slowed, Jackie jumped out of the aircraft, ran around the front, and watched the car speed away. She threw her hands in the air in anger and frustration. While muttering to herself, she leaped onto the pilot's seat and grabbed the hand radio.

"Eagle One, this is Reaper," she announced into the radio. "The pigeon has flown the coup. Reaper out."

Jackie tossed the radio down and proceeded to refuel her helicopter. As she refueled, she saw a dark blue sedan speed away from the private airfield in the same direction Nevada had gone. Jackie eyed the departing car and appeared curious.

§

Nevada drove at a leisurely pace through the small town, keeping an eye on the dark blue sedan following her. She cursed softly under her breath then peered onto the back seat where the bound man with the hood over his head struggled against the zip ties binding him.

"We're being followed," Nevada announced, then focused on her driving. "You may want to consider keeping your head down if you don't want to have it blown off."

Once Nevada reached the edge of town, she picked up speed. The car following her sped up as well, indicating it was definitely following her. A black SUV suddenly joined the pursuit and rammed the dark blue sedan that had been on Nevada's tail. Nevada glanced in her rearview mirror and cried out enthusiastically.

"Oh, yeah," she exclaimed while laughing, amused at what she was witnessing. "These guys are eating their own." She again glanced over her shoulder at the bound, hooded man across the back seat. "It's going to get a little bumpy. You may want to hold onto something."

Nevada flew off the main road, swerved sharply to the right, and turned onto a back road. The bound, hooded man cried out as he was thrown from the seat and onto the floor. Nevada took another sharp turn onto an old, abandoned dirt driveway, kicking up loose dirt and stone and leaving a dust trail behind her.

"Last stop, coming up," Nevada cried out. "Look alive back there!"

An old farmhouse and barn came into view and was approaching fast. The two-story farmhouse was in desperate need of demolishing. Nearly all the paint was missing from what was left of the wooden siding. The porch had mostly collapsed, and the yard contained tall weeds. The old, three-story barn, on the other hand, appeared sturdy and in decent shape despite needing some paint. Both cars remained on Nevada's tail. The black SUV rammed the dark blue sedan a second time, sending it flying into the cornfield on the right. Nevada barely slowed before the barn and busted through the large doors. A cloud of hay and debris seemed to explode out the large opening, indicating Nevada had possibly crash stopped the car. The heavily damaged black SUV approached the barn and slid to a stop not far from the entrance. Hawthorn leaped from the car with a semiautomatic, affixed with a silencer, in his gloved hands. He ran around the back of his SUV and hurried to the busted barn entrance.

A woman suddenly appeared from the cornfield with her own gun in hand. Judging by her stalking attire and the silencer on her weapon, she, too, was a paid assassin. Wilson, the woman gun for hire, was a slightly taller, athletically built woman in her early to mid-thirties. Her long, fiery auburn hair and her prominent cleavage gave her a sexy yet dangerous sort of appeal. Sex appeal aside, there was little to love about the hellcat trying to make her mark in a predominantly male field. The ruthless woman took cover behind Hawthorn's SUV and aimed her weapon at the man now positioned alongside the barn opening.

"Hawthorn, you prick!" Wilson cried out, catching his attention right before she fired two shots at him.

Hawthorn turned and fired back at the woman he'd obviously met before. She returned fire from her secure position behind his car. Uncertain what to expect from the bounty hunter within the barn, Hawthorn ran to the side of the building for cover from the lady assassin. Wilson fired several more shots at him, splintering the wood near his head. Another shot nearly struck Hawthorn in the head, but this one came from behind him. He spun and saw Nevada running for the porch of the dilapidated house. She slid on her hip near the side of the house and was soon out of sight. Nevada now fired at Hawthorn from where she lay on the ground beyond the collapsed porch. Nevada's hasty exit told Hawthorn everything he needed to know. Nevada abandoned Marco in the barn, and the barn had a back entrance!

Hawthorn bolted for the back of the barn to locate the rear entrance while avoiding gunfire from both women. Wilson suddenly panicked, coming to the same conclusion, and was now worried Hawthorn would reach Marco first. Wilson fired at Nevada as well while running for the destroyed front entrance and disappeared inside. Despite being abandoned, the barn contained several bales of old hay, which had been exploded when the gray car collided with them. The large barn was mostly open with a few old stalls on the right side and a hayloft above. Cobwebs clung to the tall rafters and a few old trinkets that were lying around. The car had stopped in the center of the barn, surrounded by piles of loose hay and a few solid bales still in front. Wilson looked around the dimly lit barn and immediately ran for the back of Nevada's car, taking cover from Hawthorn, who had to be somewhere in the back of the barn. Perhaps that had been Nevada's plan all along. Let Wilson and Hawthorn kill each other.

When Wilson didn't see Hawthorn, she made her way around the car while keeping low. She pulled open the back door of the vehicle and aimed her gun at the back seat. Marco was gone. Just his hood remained. Wilson spun around with her gun aimed and scanned the barn. She needed to find Marco wherever Nevada had stashed him while also avoiding Hawthorn. She pressed her back against the side of the car and made her way closer to the front end while keeping her gun aimed and ready for whatever Hawthorn had planned. As she reached the front of the vehicle, she aimed her weapon toward the dimly lit back section of the barn. Hawthorn lay face down not far from the back door, and his gun appeared to be missing. Wilson quickly crouched near the front fender of the car, keeping alert, and scanned the area. Marco was somewhere within the dimly lit barn, and he was now armed!

Old hay suddenly pelted her from the hay loft. Wilson straightened and aimed her weapon toward the dark rafters above her. An old bale of hay fell from the loft and came straight for her. She screamed and leaped out of the way of the falling, fifty-pound bale of hay. Wilson backed up along the side of the car and scanned the dark rafters with her finger on the trigger prepared to fire. It was too dark, keeping her from seeing anything. There was a loud, metallic bang from the roof of the car alongside her. Wilson jumped with surprise and spun with her gun aimed at the car roof. A booted foot kicked the weapon from her hand, startling her. Wilson barely had time to react when Bogart went for the return kick, striking her in the shoulder. Wilson was thrown backward and into the nearby support beam. She regained her balance and looked around the hay covered floor for her weapon. When Wilson turned, she saw Nevada standing in front of her while wearing a slightly twisted grin on her face.

"I know you," Nevada announced almost cheerfully as if happy to see the woman.

Nevada then spun into a roundhouse kick and struck Wilson in the face. Wilson was thrown to the ground, knocked out cold.

Nevada sneered at the unconscious woman with a look of disgust. "Never did like you," she muttered.

Bogart jumped off the roof of the car alongside Nevada and indicated the unconscious woman. "Another bounty hunter?" he asked.

"Worse," Nevada informed him, then sneered. "Killer for hire."

Bogart seemed surprised. "She's a hitman?" he asked, then reconsidered. "A hitwoman? Lady? What's the politically correct term?"

"Bitch," Nevada informed him.

"What do we do with them?" Bogart asked, then indicated the unconscious man across the barn.

"Tie them up," Nevada replied, then smirked while removing several zip ties from her pocket. "Seeing how they can't stand each other, I say we tie them up together." She then indicated Hawthorn. "Drag his sorry ass over here. Once we have them tied, we'll split up. You can take the black SUV out front. We'll rendezvous with the others when we're sure we're not being followed."

"I've had a lot of experience at shaking tails," Bogart informed her while grinning.

Bogart dragged Hawthorn's unconscious body closer to where Wilson remained out cold. Nevada now appeared exhausted and somewhat cranky. Bogart eyed her as she fumbled with her zip ties.

"Are you okay?" Bogart asked.

"Yeah," she muttered. "Flying commercial from the East Coast has finally caught up with me. I've been up almost twenty-four hours now. I'm going to crash and burn soon." She shook her head. "I need some coffee."

"You need to get some sleep," Bogart informed her.

"No kidding," she scoffed in irritation then indicated Hawthorn. "Get that one to his feet." Nevada then groaned and shook her head. "I'd kill for a hot shower right about now."

"We passed an out-of-the-way motel--"

Nevada glared at Bogart and snarled, "That *wasn't* an offer."

Bogart was slightly surprised then raised an arrogant brow. "I wasn't offering," he snapped back. "You really are cold-hearted, aren't you?"

She sneered at him then indicated Hawthorn. "Just get him to his feet."

§

A little while later, Hawthorn opened his eyes and saw Wilson just inches from his face staring at him with an annoyed sneer. He groaned when he saw her, shut his eyes, and rested his head against the support beam behind him.

"Get the hell away from me," he muttered.

"Believe me, I'd love nothing more," she snarled in response.

Hawthorn's eyes suddenly opened, and he realized his wrists were bound around the support beam behind him. To make matters worse, Wilson's wrists were zip-tied around his midsection and behind the same beam, keeping them snuggly against each other. Wilson cried out as Hawthorn struggled against his bindings.

"Stop it," she lashed out. "Our wrists are tied together as well as around the pole."

"We can't stay like this," he launched in anger. "Deal with it!"

As he once more fought to free himself, she again cried out from the pain he was causing her. Wilson thrust her knee into his thigh, causing him to yelp.

"How do you like it?" she snarled in anger.

Each time he struggled, causing her pain, she rammed her knee into his thigh. He finally stopped struggling and groaned with defeat.

"Your wrists are against the pole," she snarled in anger. "See if you can slice through the plastic against the corner of the beam."

"We're going to be here all night," he scoffed.

"So stop talking and start working," she snapped back while attempting to look anywhere but at the man's face only inches from hers.

Chapter 24

Jackie's helicopter touched down at a second, remote private airfield not far from the first one. Once again, the side door was thrown open before the rotors stopped. Kirk jumped out of the helicopter with a duffel bag over his shoulder and pulled a bound man wearing a hood from the back. He practically dragged the much shorter man away from the helicopter and into an awaiting SUV, much the same as Nevada had done. The brown, late model SUV had seen better days, and the doors creaked when opened, but that didn't stop Kirk. Beggars weren't choosers. Kirk tossed the duffel bag into the back with his prisoner, then jumped in the driver's seat and sped away from the airfield. Jackie again refueled the helicopter while casting looks around the surrounding area. A newer, black sedan, parked outside the private airfield, pulled away and followed Kirk. Jackie also spotted a gray compact car and a dark blue sedan joining the pursuit.

"Enjoy your wild goose chase, boys," she muttered, then smirked.

It didn't take much to fill the fuel tank since she had just refueled at the previous stop thirty minutes earlier. She then took a moment to move onto her hands and knees and search the underbelly of the craft. She spotted Nevada's tracking device, where Zack had replaced it when he turned it back on, and pulled it free. Nevada's tracking device was easily hackable, which the team had used to their advantage to lead the others on a wild goose chase. The tracker had served its purpose, allowing a few of their fans to pursue them, but it was now time to say goodbye to being followed. Jackie headed into the small, mostly empty terminal building. A man sat at the desk and smiled at the attractive woman. Jackie returned the smile and headed into the ladies' room. She dropped the tracking device into the toilet and flushed it. If the device was waterproof, the thought of others attempting to follow it was quite amusing.

§

Kirk drove through the small town while keeping watch through his side and rearview mirror on the black sedan and gray compact cars that were following. The man on the back seat cast his bindings aside and removed his hood to reveal Zack. He remained on his back, stretched out on the seat, and looked almost comfortable.

"Are we being followed?" Zack asked and shut his eyes as if about to take a nap.

"We've got two bogeys on our tail and possibly a third hanging back a little further," Kirk replied while seeming a little too relaxed as well. "I wonder how long it'll be before they discover one another?"

"If we play it right," Zack casually announced from his comfortable position on the back seat, "maybe they'll kill each other."

"Want to have a little fun and lead them around town a while?" Kirk remarked while grinning. "Give them time to see one another?"

"Is there someplace with drive-through service?" Zack then asked. "I'm starving."

"Yeah, me too," Kirk announced, although he always seemed to be starving. He then nodded up ahead. "There's a hamburger joint down the road."

"I'm kind of in the mood for tacos," Zack informed him.

Kirk cast a look over his shoulder and into the back seat. "This is a small town," he scoffed with a scowl on his face. "Consider yourself lucky they have anything with a drive-thru window."

"Fine," Zack groaned and placed his hands beneath his neck. "Get me a couple of burgers."

§

Zack and Kirk finished their take-out food while leisurely driving around town. Once they were finished, Kirk fiddled with the GPS on his burner cell phone while Zack remained out of sight on the back seat. Zack opened the duffel bag on the floor and removed an assault rifle.

"According to GPS," Kirk announced to his partner in the back, "there's state game land nearby. You know what that means?"

Zack chuckled and cocked his weapon. "Hunting season," he teased.

"Time for a little nature hike," Kirk announced and drove out of town.

The moment they were out of town and away from people, Kirk floored the gas pedal, sending the car flying along the back road toward the game land. The black sedan and a gray compact car following them now picked up speed. Quite possibly having seen each other earlier, the vehicles following them reacted to each other, attempting to run the competition off the road. While they were busy trying to eliminate the opposition, Kirk was able to put some distance between them and the cars following them. He made a sharp left hand turn onto an old roadway of sorts within the game land and raced down it until he reached the woods. The brown rental car skidded to a stop. The older car had no sooner stopped when Zack and Kirk jumped out. Zack tossed Kirk the assault rifle, grabbed one for himself, and slung the duffel bag over his shoulder. Both men ran into the woods and took a stake-out position.

They waited for the first car to approach. The black sedan stopped several yards from Kirk's borrowed car. A man, who was easily pegged as a hitman, leaped out of the car, kept low to the ground, and hurried for the older, brown vehicle with his weapon in hand. The hitman, Nolte, was a tall, somewhat muscular African American man in his early forties. He kept his head shaved bald but wore a goatee, giving him a bad-boy biker look. Nolte straightened and aimed his weapon at the driver's seat, but there was no one there. He looked in the back seat, appeared alarmed, and then looked toward the woods. Zack and Kirk remained still and silent with their weapons aimed at the man. He was still partially hidden behind the car, and they wanted a clean shot before advertising their position.

The gray, compact car suddenly appeared, flew up the old lane, and nearly rammed Nolte's car. Two casually dressed men in their mid-thirties jumped out and immediately fired at Nolte, who ran to the front of Kirk's brown rental car and took cover. He was quick to return fire on his hitmen brethren. Zack and Kirk remained hidden behind their respective trees and exchanged glances.

"Should have brought some popcorn for the show," Kirk muttered.

Zack then cast a look across the field and gave a tiny nod. "Oh, look," he announced casually. "The third act just arrived."

A dark blue sedan raced to join the party, purposely spun sideways, and rammed the gray compact car the two men had been taking cover behind. They fired at Nolte in front of them and ran for cover in the opening in front of their vehicle to avoid the new arrival. The man in the third car jumped out, took cover behind the front panel of his sideways car, and exchanged gunfire with all three men. The newcomer, Slade, was in his early forties. He wasn't exceptionally tall and was neither athletically nor muscularly built. Slade's medium brown hair was businessman short, and he kept his goatee neatly trimmed. The average looking man was easily unnoticed and just as easily dismissed, making him almost invisible. While the two men stranded in the middle fired in both directions, Nolte sneered at Slade.

"Slade, you fucking prick," Nolte called out. "Why am I not surprised to see your ass here?"

"Hey, Nolte," Slade announced almost casually and without care. "Didn't recognize you. Doing something different with your hair?"

"You're a funny man, asshole," Nolte replied while lacking the humor of his fellow hitman. "Been waiting a long time to put a bullet in your ass."

"Feeling's mutual," Slade called back.

"How about we kill each other later?" Nolte called out to Slade. "I can think of a million reasons why we should work together."

Slade considered the comment. "I accept your terms," he announced.

Both men turned their weapons on the two men in the middle and fired rapidly at them. When the men took cover, Slade slid over his car's hood and leaped onto the other side closer to the two men. Nolte stepped out from behind his car as well. They descended upon the two men and fired several shots into them, killing both. Nolte and Slade then turned their weapons on each other and remained silently staring while keeping their guns aimed. There was a tense moment. Both men then chuckled and lowered their weapons, seeming to relax.

Nolte indicated the woods. "They ran into the woods that way," he informed him. "We'll need to go after them on foot."

Slade nodded and replaced his empty magazine with a full one. They stepped over the two dead men between the cars, aimed their weapons into the woods, and made their way past Kirk's borrowed brown vehicle. Both men were surprised when they heard Slade's car burning out in the loose dirt. They spun with their weapons aimed and saw Slade's dark blue sedan making a tight circle, creating a large dust storm as it pulled away.

"Motherfucker!" Nolte cried out in anger.

As the dust settled from Slade's car, Zack could be seen standing on the old roadway. He dropped the pin to a grenade and tossed it beneath the gray car behind them. Both men cried out and ran for cover. As the gray car exploded, Zack threw a second grenade beneath Nolte's black sedan. He then ran for Kirk in Slade's borrowed, dark blue car. The grenade exploded, taking Nolte's black sedan with it. Slade and Nolte leaped to the ground and took cover from falling debris. Once the debris settled, both men looked up and stared in silent disbelief as Kirk and Zack sped away in Slade's car.

§

Nevada downed the last of her coffee while driving along the remote back road. Her eyes became heavy, and she nearly ran off the road despite the afternoon sun beating in on her through the windshield. She jerked awake and groaned loudly while rubbing her tired eyes. Nevada saw an out-of-the-way motel up ahead.

"Bates Motel it is," she muttered and turned into the parking lot of the small, three-roach motel.

The motel, consisting of a row of cabins, wasn't much different from the abandoned motel where they'd first found Marco. This one was in slightly better condition, but not by much. At least the windows weren't boarded up, and the porch wasn't falling apart. Nevada parked the car off to the side of the office so it wouldn't be easily seen by anyone passing through. She then headed for the office attached to the first cabin. She entered the office and found an older man sleeping behind the desk with his feet propped up. Nevada hit the bell on the desk with a little more vigor than necessary. The man jerked awake and nearly fell from his chair. His near fall amused her. The man quickly stood and managed his best, weary smile at the attractive woman.

"Afternoon," he announced somewhat cheerfully.

"I'd like a room for the night," Nevada informed him and placed fifty dollars on the counter. "Will that cover it?"

"Yes, ma'am," he announced. "It's actually only--"

"Don't care," she muttered. "Just give me whichever room has a comfortable bed and a hot shower."

He handed her the old-fashioned key on the keychain to cabin number one.

Nevada eyed the key and groaned. "I know how this movie ends," she muttered, then took the key and glared at the older man. "I don't want to be disturbed. If anyone comes looking for me, I wasn't here."

The older man nodded almost knowingly. Nevada left the office and headed for the first cabin. She unlocked the door, entered, and bolted the door behind her. Nevada glanced around the 'no frills' room. It was about as bland as a motel room could possibly get. It looked more like a 'charge by the hour' sort of place. The furniture and bedding seemed as old as the motel itself. The carpeting had large, colorful patterns on it, or it was possibly just stained from years of neglect. Nevada didn't even bat a lash at the condition of the room, apparently, having seen many like it in her day. Nevada removed her boots on the way to the bathroom. She started the shower then pulled her cell phone from her pants pocket.

She was about to toss her cell phone onto the bed when she noticed there was a missed call, which had apparently gone straight to voicemail. The number on the caller ID was from the hotel in Maine, where she had been more or less living the past few weeks. Nevada hesitated a moment, then switched the phone off 'airplane mode', and pressed in a code, allowing the message to play.

"Hey, Nevada," the familiar male voice announced. "It's Kane. Not sure if you're coming back before the 'mob convention' in a few weeks, but Scorpio wanted to move you and Hayden to the third floor, so all the convention guests are together on the second floor. Call back and let us know if this is a problem. If we don't hear from you, we'll assume it's okay and move your things for you. Talk later."

Nevada tensed while listening to the message. She drew a deep breath, held it a moment, and was about to press the call back button. She hesitated, then frowned, thinking better of it, and tossed the cell phone onto the bed. She removed her pants before heading into the bathroom. A few minutes later, Nevada nearly fell asleep standing beneath the hot streams of water within the shower. A faint clunking roused her. She jerked awake and listened a moment. Despite not hearing anything, she grabbed the towel from overtop of the shower curtain bar and wrapped it around her wet body. She didn't bother turning off the water. That would take away the element of surprise if there had actually been someone in her room. She quietly stepped out of the shower wearing her moderately wet towel, stood alongside the mostly closed door, and listened a moment. The sounds of someone moving around within her motel room was enough to spur a reaction.

She took a quick step to the sink, opened a folded towel on top, and removed her semiautomatic. She clutched the gun in her hand, threw open the bathroom door, and stepped into the bedroom doorway with her weapon aimed. Quinn and Rowen sat at the small table near the door and removed hamburgers from a fast-food bag. Neither man bothered looking at her as they tore into the hamburgers.

"Hey, Nevada," Rowen announced, seeming more interested in the hamburger than the wet woman wearing only a towel. He didn't even look at her.

Nevada eyed both men and sneered. "What the fuck are you doing in my room?" she demanded hotly while keeping the weapon aimed at them.

Quinn finally glanced at her with an almost innocent look on his face and indicated the take-out bag. "Late lunch," he announced, then hesitated to take in a sweeping eyeful of her in the towel. "Looking good, Nevada."

"Don't worry," Rowen replied and only briefly glanced at her. "We brought enough for you too."

"I should shoot you both," she snarled.

"But you won't," Rowen replied while eating and paying little to no attention to her.

Nevada sneered and lowered the weapon. She snatched her discarded clothes from the floor then glared at both men, who continued eating.

"You'd better save me some damned fries, or I'm killing you both," she muttered, then disappeared into the bathroom, slamming the door behind her.

Once she'd dried off and dressed, Nevada joined the men by the table. She dug into the bag and removed a carton of French fries. Nevada flopped onto the bed, picked at her fries, and glared at both men.

"What *are* you doing here?" she again demanded. "And did you bring me a drink?"

Rowen extended a soda and straw to her while Quinn held up a flask. Nevada eyed both, then snatched the soda.

Quinn frowned and returned the flask to his jacket pocket. "It was worth a shot."

Rowen stood, turned his chair, and sat in it backward, facing her. "Rumor has it you were in pursuit of our million-dollar baby this afternoon."

"Are you surprised?" Nevada demanded while raising her brows. "Every bounty hunter has Marco in their crosshairs. Why wouldn't I be one of them?"

Rowen grinned and chuckled deep in his throat, amused by her words. "Oh, sweetheart," he announced. "We're not stupid." He then hesitated and cast a look at Quinn. "Well, Quinn is, but I'm not."

Nevada's eyes narrowed while glaring at Rowen. "Don't call me sweetheart," she snarled.

Rowen held his hands up defensively and smiled. "Sorry," he replied, then lowered his hands. "We know you have some divine wisdom on this one. Giovanni is good friends with Sal Romano, and Sal Romano always liked you."

Quinn chuckled almost knowingly and spoke with a mouthful of food. "Got a real hard spot for you," he teased.

Nevada glared at Quinn. She wasn't amused. Despite being a moderately handsome man, Quinn's unrefined manners left much to be desired.

"Don't speak with your mouth full," Rowen snapped at Quinn. "What's wrong with you, boy? Ain't you got any manners?" He then looked back at Nevada and resumed what he was attempting to pass off as charm. "You share the same problem as the rest of us. Too many interested parties." He then pointed between him and Quinn. "Quinn and I are combining our forces, and we want to include you. A three-way split is still a lot of money."

"I don't need your help," Nevada informed him.

Rowen snorted a laugh and shook his head. "No way you're bringing Marco in on your own," he insisted. "You've seen what's out there. Holy hell, they've got themselves a helicopter." He leaned his elbows on the back of the chair and met her gaze. "Ain't none of us bringing that boy in, dead or alive, all by ourselves. You need us, and we could sure use you."

Nevada stared at Rowen a long moment and seemed to consider what he said. Quinn finished his hamburger and turned in his chair as well.

"I may have some inside information," Nevada finally announced.

Rowen and Quinn suddenly grinned and laughed.

"It's not going to be easy, though," Nevada insisted. "Giovanni sent men to protect him."

Quinn removed a wrapped hamburger from the bag and tossed it to Nevada. She caught it and eagerly tore into it.

"Tell us everything you know," Rowen remarked.

"I'll give you the short version," Nevada replied while eating the hamburger. "First, I need a few hours' sleep." She then eyed them suspiciously. "How did you find me?"

Rowen grinned, stood, and spun his chair around facing front. "I'm a lot smarter than I look," he informed her. "I have trackers on more than a dozen cell phones of my competition."

Nevada made a face and eyed her cell phone on the bed. "When I turned it on to check my voicemail--?" she muttered and raised a brow.

"We just happened to luck out that you hadn't gotten that far from our location," Rowen continued.

"Actually, I've put on quite a few miles," she remarked, although she didn't offer him any details. "Turned out it was just a very large U-turn."

Chapter 25

Hawthorn and Wilson were still zip-tied within the old barn in their compromising position against the support beam. Hawthorn repeatedly sawed his zip ties against the support beam behind him.

He groaned while panting and gave up. "We're going to be here all night," he snarled. "Your turn."

"Okay, this obviously isn't working," Wilson announced while attempting to control her growing hostility. "I have another idea."

"I'm willing to try just about anything at this point," Hawthorn grumbled.

"I have a knife in my boot," she informed him. "I'm going to lift my foot up. If you hold it, I might be able to reach inside my boot and get the knife."

"Well, that would certainly speed things up," Hawthorn insisted. "Why didn't you think of that earlier?"

Wilson met his gaze and appeared offended. "Your constant bitching may have interfered with my ability to think clearly," she snarled.

Hawthorn groaned and shut his eyes, allowing his head to fall against the beam behind him. "Okay, fine," he muttered. "Let's try working together a little more." He seemed to consider something, then suddenly smiled and laughed.

Wilson glared at him through squinting eyes. "What's so funny?" she demanded.

"This is the longest we've ever been this close without trying to kill each other," he remarked.

She rolled her eyes and groaned. "Yeah, well, I'm killing you after we're free."

"Maybe we're going about this all wrong," Hawthorn insisted and met her gaze. "We can work together just this once. Why fight each other? We have plenty of other people to fight on this. The only reason we're in this predicament is because we were too busy fighting each other. Had we been working together, they never would have gotten away."

Wilson stared into his eyes a long moment and seemed to consider what he was saying. "I never thought I'd hear myself say this, but you're right."

Hawthorn grinned and chuckled. "See," he announced. "We can get along." He then gave a nod. "Toss your foot up."

Wilson pressed her body against his for balance and swung her leg up and around him and the pole. His hand grazed the leather on her boot. She groaned in frustration.

"A little higher this time," he insisted.

Wilson swung her leg up and around him and the post, giving a little extra rise to her booted foot. Hawthorn caught her boot, maneuvered her foot in his hands, and firmly held onto the heel. As Wilson reached for the top of her boot, her zip ties strained against his. He cringed in discomfort.

"Just a little further," she groaned. "I can feel the handle. I just need to get my fingers around it."

"Just do it," he insisted.

Wilson tugged against his zip ties and gripped the handle of the knife with her fingers.

"Okay," she announced. "Don't let go. I need to slide my leg through your hand in order to remove the knife from this angle."

"I have it," he insisted. "Just don't drop the knife."

Wilson pulled the knife from her boot and breathed a sigh of relief. She turned the blade and carefully slit through the plastic zip tie. She then moved around the pole behind

Hawthorn and freed her left wrist as well. She hesitated a moment, rounded the pole, and met Hawthorn's gaze. Her look was sly and somewhat unpredictable.

His eyes suddenly narrowed despite the mild horror on his face. "Don't you dare," he snarled.

She smiled almost mockingly and played with the knife while taking a step closer to him. Hawthorn sneered in anger and fought his restraints.

"I kind of like you this way," she cooed while giving him a quick once-over.

Wilson seductively slid the knife blade down his jacket without taking her eyes off his. Hawthorn sneered while staring at her playful but mischievous look.

"Wilson--" he snarled.

She maintained her devious grin, then lowered her mouth to his and aggressively kissed him. Hawthorn tensed, uncertain of the psychopath's intentions. While kissing him, she slipped the knife behind the post and cut the zip ties binding his wrists. Wilson broke off the kiss and pulled back just far enough to mock him with her smile. Hawthorn glared back at her, not amused. He violently knocked the knife from her hand, grabbed her by the throat, and spun her around, slamming her against the support beam. Wilson gasped with surprise but didn't defend herself. Hawthorn sneered while staring into her eyes. He then kissed her while pinning her body with his against the post behind her. Wilson returned the aggressive kiss while swiftly slipping him out of his jacket. He was barely freed from his jacket when he just about ripped her shirt off her. She resumed kissing him and aggressively threw her legs around his waist. Hawthorn caught her beneath her buttocks, spun her around, and just about tackled her to the nearby pile of hay.

§

After their wild but brief romp in the hay, Wilson slipped back into her shirt while standing not far from

Hawthorn, who sat on one of the bales of hay and hurriedly laced his combat boots.

Wilson glanced at her watch and then frowned. "They got more than an hours' head start," she remarked while picking up her discarded knife and replaced it to her boot.

Hawthorn stood, found his semiautomatic on the ground partway across the barn, and replaced it to his shoulder holster. He then glanced outside the wide, main entrance where the barn doors had been demolished.

"They stole my car," he muttered, then looked back at her. "What kind of shape is your car in?"

"The wheel wells are clogged with corn stalks," she informed him, "but once we remove them, it'll run." Wilson then frowned. "Any idea how we locate them now?"

"It's obvious they were just a decoy and knew about the tracker someone had placed on the chopper," Hawthorn remarked as they left the barn together.

"I'm sure the trackers been disabled by now," Wilson muttered. "After they had their fun leading us on a wild goose chase."

"That means we're back to square one," Hawthorn scoffed. "We need to hack into the computer at that airfield and check the flight log for that helicopter. See if we can figure out where they were heading."

"Then we need to return to the airfield," Wilson remarked as they walked along the overgrown, dirt driveway in the direction of Wilson's abandoned car. "Let's just hope we can find some information on that helicopter."

"Shouldn't be too difficult figuring out where they're heading," Hawthorn replied with little concern. "We can find out who owns it and put some pressure on anyone who knows them."

"Providing we can secure that information," Wilson announced.

"They can't be that smart."

She shot a glare at him. "They have automatic weapons and a sharpshooter hanging out the side of a helicopter," Wilson reminded him while raising a cocky brow. "We're not exactly dealing with amateurs here."

"At best, they're a bunch of weekend warriors looking for a big payday," Hawthorn insisted and waved her off. "We can handle them."

§

Beck drove Kirk's jeep through the woods along a path that barely constituted a roadway. It was overgrown with tall weeds and had been washed out in many areas. The jeep finally stopped within a small clearing near a gently flowing stream. Ross and Beck got out of the jeep and looked around.

"Well," Beck announced with a sigh. "This is about as remote as it gets."

"Needed a compass just to find it," Ross teased with a humored grin then looked back at Beck. "We're going to be here a while. We may as well make ourselves and our guest as comfortable as possible." He then raised a curious brow. "Did you want to pitch the tent?"

"I can do that," Beck replied almost cheerfully and approached the back of the jeep.

Ross headed for the rear passenger door and opened it to reveal Marco with his wrists still zip-tied in front of him. "Welcome to your new home," Ross teased.

Marco got out of the jeep and looked around with some surprise. "You can't be serious," he announced.

Beck tossed a flat, round, five-foot disk into the clearing. It sprang open into a pup-tent. "Tent is pitched," he proudly announced to Ross.

Marco stared at the small tent that would barely fit one average-sized man. "A tent?" he practically gasped. "We're going to live in the middle of the woods in a tent?"

"We also have sleeping bags. Spared no expense," Ross announced cheerfully. "Although, we only have two of them, but Beck and I will take turns on guard duty, so it'll work out just fine."

Marco didn't take his eyes off Ross. "And I thought the safe house was roughing it," he muttered, then managed a tense smile. "You can't possibly expect to keep me out here a few days."

"Days?" Ross asked with some surprise, then smiled and shook his head. "No, absolutely not. It's going to be weeks, but don't worry. We have fresh water." He indicated the stream. "And plenty of MREs that'll keep us alive for months. Once we dig a hole, we'll even have a latrine."

"It's the beginning of fall," Marco insisted. "Do you have any idea how cold it's going to get in a few weeks?"

"I did mention the sleeping bags, didn't I?" Ross informed him.

Beck then poked his head into their conversation and raised his hand. "And we're good Boy Scouts. We know how to make a campfire."

"It'll be fun," Ross announced cheerfully while patting Marco on the back. "Like camping; military style." He then eyed Beck and turned serious. "You did tell Kirk to pack the bear repellent, right?"

"It was on the list right beneath marshmallows," Beck replied.

"I'm going to die out here," Marco muttered, then groaned and placed his hand over his eyes. He then looked back at the two men who were clearly mocking him and raised his zip-tied hands. "I can't exactly go anywhere. Could you at least cut me loose?"

Ross glanced at Beck.

Beck stared back at him with a look of surprise. "Don't look at me," he practically gasped. "If he takes off, I'm not chasing after him. Not without the bear repellent."

Ross looked back at Marco and shrugged. "Looks like you're shit out of luck."

"Were you hired to protect me or humiliate me?" Marco demanded.

Ross considered the question. "The first," he replied, then grinned. "The latter is just an added bonus."

Chapter 26

Gil's helicopter set down in a remote field, seemingly in the middle of nowhere. Once the aircraft shut down, Monroe climbed out of the passenger side and opened the side door. Darth leaped out of the helicopter and immediately ran across the field, checking out his new surroundings.

"Don't wander off," Gil announced as he climbed out of the pilot's seat.

Gil consulted the compass on his watch then pointed across the field. "It should be half a mile that way on the other side of the woods," he announced.

"I wish we could have circled it from the air," Monroe remarked as he removed a small backpack from the back of the helicopter then shut the door.

"If there's anyone around, they'd be alerted to the helicopter," Gil responded with little emotion and started walking in the direction he'd indicated.

"I know," Monroe replied while looking around as they walked. "Jackie's coded message put me on high alert, that's all."

"We knew there were going to be several interested parties when we accepted this assignment," Gil reminded him.

"Which is why I'd love a bird's eye view of the land," Monroe insisted, then groaned. "And this is going to be a lot of land."

"Which is why we get to scout it out," Gil reported and seemed almost cheerful at the prospect.

Darth raced across the field to catch up to them then continued past them toward the nearby woods. The men and Darth walked into the woods and hiked nearly half a mile before reaching an old roadway. Both stopped at the edge of the woods and glanced down the old, overgrown lane while Darth scouted out the area, marking a few more trees.

"Well," Gil announced with a deep sigh. "I guess this is it."

"This should be fun," Monroe remarked with limited enthusiasm.

Both men stared down the dirt road at the old, overgrown sign. It read 'Gosford Animal Sanctuary'. The old, heavy gate was chained shut with a large padlock. Ten-foot-tall, stone fencing encompassed the entrance area in both directions, although it changed from stone to chain-link deeper into the woods.

Gil glanced at Monroe. "Did you bring the key?" he asked.

Monroe removed a heavy-duty bolt cutter from his bag and smirked. "Right here."

§

*O*nce inside the sanctuary, Darth ran excitedly around the vast, cleared area before a large building with a faded sign that read, 'Visitor's Center'. There was no telling what smells, even from years past, Darth was detecting. Gil and Monroe looked around. From what they were told about their potential 'safe house', it was once an animal sanctuary housing hundreds of endangered animals as well as rescued, injured animals unfit to return to the wild. The sanctuary was nestled on more than eight-hundred acres of cleared and wooded land alongside state game land and surrounded by large farms, making it incredibly secluded. The sanctuary had dozens of large habitats with natural and man-made enclosures and many outer buildings. The tall, stone wall that surrounded a lot of the sanctuary had fallen down in many areas. Other areas within woodland contained chain-link fencing. Some remained intact, while others had been destroyed by falling trees over the years.

Monroe and Gil headed for the visitor's center, which was the closest building to the main entrance. They approached the building's large, heavy doors and attempted to open them. Neither was surprised that the doors were locked. Monroe removed his lock pick kit and had the lock sprung in under a minute. Despite having been running around, Darth was at the door the moment it was opened. He darted inside ahead of the two men and sniffed his way around, exploring the entire area. The main room to the visitor's center was a massive lobby of sorts with a large visitor's desk just inside the doorway to the right. The open, animal-themed area contained many comfortable chairs and sofas for guests to relax during their visit. There were men's and women's restrooms to the left, not far from a corridor leading to some offices in the back. A small gift shop and snack bar were located beyond the front desk on the right. Not surprisingly, everything was covered in dust and cobwebs.

"According to Othello," Gil announced while looking around. "There should be a generator shed out back and another outside the veterinary clinic."

"The veterinary clinic must be the building one hundred yards from here," Monroe remarked.

Gil approached the front desk and found an old brochure for the sanctuary. He opened it and spread it out on the desk. It contained a map of the park, the buildings, exhibits, and enclosures for the various animals. Each was well-marked, which would be a tremendous help for them to find their way around the massive property.

Gil pointed to a location on the map. "We're here," he announced. "The generator shed is here, and the vet clinic is here."

Monroe peered at the map as well. "This place has everything," he remarked. "A bird sanctuary, reptile house, dozens of animal habitats, and small shelters located in each habitat."

"There are supposed to be sleeping quarters in the clinic," Gil remarked. "That means there's a kitchen and at least one bathroom with a shower. We'll need to see if the water still works."

"Othello has it on good authority that the place was still functional when they shut it down," Monroe informed him.

"What happened?" Gil asked, then glanced casually at Monroe and raised a curious brow. "T-Rex get loose and eat a few tourists?"

"Actually, I believe they lost funding when a few of their main investors were bumped off," Monroe replied with all seriousness.

Gil suspiciously eyed him.

"Sal was on the board under the name of one of his lesser-known organizations, P.R. Corporation. That was back when the sanctuary was operational," Monroe remarked.

"Figures," Gil muttered, then raised a curious brow. "Can this place be traced back to Sal?"

"No," Monroe informed him. "The company can't be traced back to him, and it's no longer in existence."

"Good to know." Gil looked around the visitor's center and spotted the gift shop with the snack bar alongside it. "There's also a kitchen within the snack bar and public restrooms here as well."

Monroe grabbed one of the many brochures and stuck it in his pocket as a backup in case they made a wrong turn. "Why don't you and Darth have a look around the visitor's center, and I'll see about getting the generator running," he suggested. "Once the power is on, we'll meet back here at the front desk. After that, we can head over to the vet clinic together and check that out."

Monroe removed an Uzi from the backpack and handed it to Gil. Gil slipped the sling over his neck and shoulder, allowing the weapon to hang at his side. Monroe then removed one for himself and did the same. As Monroe left, Gil and Darth searched the main lobby area of the visitor's center. Gil didn't anticipate finding much of anything, but that was sort of the point. Seclusion and privacy were what they needed most in a safe house. Once Gil and Darth finished looking around the massive lobby, they headed down the corridor beyond the restrooms to the area containing office space. Gil opened the door to the main office in the back. Also animal-themed, the office, thick with dust, included a large desk, an old sofa that quite possibly pulled out into a sofa bed, and some old chairs. Despite being closed for quite some time, the desk contained some dusty items left behind. Nothing of importance, but it seemed as if those in charge expected they'd be returning one day.

After Gil and his canine partner finished their sweep of the back corridor, Gil made a pit stop in the public restrooms and discovered the water was working. The water came out brown-tinged at first but cleared after running a few minutes. Running water was a plus, considering how long they would potentially be stranded there. As Gil and Darth left the men's room, the lights flickered and came on. Several light bulbs immediately burned out the moment power was restored, but there would still be plenty of light even at night. Monroe finally returned to the visitor center's lobby and joined Gil and Darth, who had finished their sweep.

"The clinic is about one hundred yards from here," Monroe informed him. "I did a quick walkthrough. It'll meet our needs for 'operations'."

"Then let's take a quick tour of the sanctuary," Gil announced while removing his official map of the property. "We'll check out some of the exhibits. Scout out the habitats and form a perimeter."

Both men and Darth left the main building and traveled the walkway now overgrown with plant life that had taken over after the sanctuary had been abandoned. A maintenance shed was located not far from the clinic and housed old machinery, some rusting golf carts, and a few old ATVs. The ATVs seemed to be in decent shape, and Kirk could probably restore them. The zebra habitat was the closest exhibit to the visitor's center. Although the fencing remained intact, the lush grass had grown tall. In the opposite direction was the hippo habitat. Near the middle was a kiddie playland of sorts with a half-sized train sitting and rusting on tracks that circled the entire sanctuary. The lion habitat was near the back, snug against the state game land. Not far from that was the reptile house and the bird aviary. The reptile house was a massive building, while the bird aviary was essentially a tall, two-story, glass birdcage. The many ponds throughout the facility now looked more like swamps.

Once they finished their sweep, which took some time to accomplish, all three returned to the visitor's center and decided to sit on the steps outside, enjoying the late afternoon sunshine and solitude. Monroe removed the portable radio from his backpack and contacted their friend and middleman during this particular assignment.

"Othello, you copy?" Monroe announced into the radio. He waited a minute or two and tried again. "Othello, you copy?"

"Yeah, Othello here," the familiar voice with a mouthful of food was heard over the radio. It would appear they caught their friend during his dinner break. Although, Othello did enjoy his junk food and between-meal snacks. "What can I do you for?"

"Could you call Dad and tell him his favorite son would like him to visit?" Monroe announced. "B.Y.O.B., if he pleases."

"I'll let Dad know," Othello reported over the radio. "Over and out."

Monroe stowed the radio in the bag and then removed two bottles of water. He handed one to Gil, who took a swallow then shared the rest with Darth. Monroe looked around and smiled.

"I could chill here for a few weeks," Monroe remarked. "It's nice here."

"Kind of creepy," Gil added, then eyed the happy dog beside him and grinned. "Darth likes it."

"About a thousand smells for him to take in," Monroe teased, then chuckled. "How far away was that town we saw from the air?"

"From what I saw, about two miles from here," Gil informed him.

"Should probably check it out once the others get here," Monroe remarked. "Get some supplies. Maybe Othello could hook us up with an untraceable car."

"Wouldn't hurt to make sure the town is safe," Gil agreed. "We're going to need a lot of supplies. We'll wait and see what Ross has planned."

Chapter 27

Ross and Beck sat on the ground within the thick woods with their backs against the side of the jeep. The two men laughed and joked around before finally glancing at Marco, who was sitting on the ground alongside them with his left wrist zip-tied to the jeep's running board.

"How's it going?" Ross asked.

Marco frowned and glared at them. "While I appreciate that you unbound my hands," he announced, "this isn't really that much better."

"On the upside," Ross announced, "you're still alive. I guess that's a fair trade."

Marco groaned but didn't respond. They heard the sound of a car in the near distance. Ross and Beck leaped to their feet while drawing their weapons, although remaining mostly hidden behind the jeep. Marco panicked slightly but couldn't even stand.

"What is it?" Marco gasped.

"Quiet," Ross shushed him.

They saw an unfamiliar, gray, four-door car with a heavily damaged front bumper driving slowly along the rough terrain of what once constituted a road. Both men kept their weapons trained on the vehicle that stopped several yards away. The car remained running a moment, but there wasn't any movement from within the vehicle. The engine finally shut off, and the door opened.

"It's just me," Nevada called out before slowly poking her head out with her hands raised above the door. "Don't shoot, okay?"

As Ross and Beck relaxed and straightened, Nevada got out of the car. Ross nudged Beck and gave him a stern, commanding look. Beck seemed to read his mind and remained behind the jeep. Although Beck no longer aimed his weapon, he didn't holster it either and, instead, kept a close watch on the woman they had little reason to trust. Ross walked out from behind the jeep while replacing his weapon to his shoulder holster. He stood near the front of the jeep and watched Nevada close the door behind her. She appeared to be alone, but Ross remained rigid. Nevada looked around and shook her head.

"Well, this place was a challenge to find," she remarked. "No wonder you gave me such shitty directions."

"Did Bogart get away?" Ross asked while completely ignoring her comment.

"Yeah," she replied and folded her arms across her chest. "We had a pair of mafia hitmen flunkies after us, but we took care of them." Nevada grinned and chuckled. "I'd have given anything to see the looks on their faces when they came to."

"You didn't kill them?" Ross asked.

Nevada glared at him and raised an arrogant brow. "In my profession, we don't automatically kill everyone we meet. It's not really, you know, my *thing*."

"Can we assume you weren't followed?" Beck asked where he leaned on the jeep's roof while keeping his gun in his hand and concealed behind the vehicle.

She immediately turned defensive and glared at him. "I'm not on the JV squad," Nevada scoffed. "I'm a professional. I know what I'm doing." Her eyes then narrowed. "No one followed me. You can put the gun away."

Beck cast a look at Ross. Ross gave a slight nod. Beck returned his gun to his shoulder holster but remained alert and untrusting.

"And he's the married one?" Nevada scoffed then shook her head, allowing her arms to fall to her sides. "His poor wife."

"Yes," Ross announced with little emotion. "We all feel sorry for the poor girl." He then indicated her car as he approached. "Car belong to one of your tails?"

"No, this was the *loaner* from the airport," Nevada casually replied. "Bogart took the hitman's car."

Ross casually walked past her and approached the car. He peered into the vehicle then opened the driver's side door.

"What are you doing?" Nevada asked, somewhat bewildered.

Ross popped the trunk and smiled almost sweetly at her. "Nothing," he replied. "Just checking."

Nevada suspiciously watched as Ross walked around the back of the car with his hand under his jacket, touching the grip on his gun.

"You guys really don't trust anyone, do you?" she demanded.

"Nope," Beck announced from behind the jeep.

Ross took a wide birth around the open trunk and peered inside as he got closer. The trunk was empty. Ross closed the trunk, then looked back at Nevada and smiled. She sneered her irritation with him.

"Satisfied?" she scoffed.

"For now," Ross replied.

The radio on Ross's belt crackled. "Dad, you copy?" came the familiar male voice.

Ross removed the radio from his belt and spoke into it. "Yeah, Othello," he announced. "What's up, son?"

"Your favorite son wants you to drop by and visit," Othello announced. "B.Y.O.B."

"Copy that," Ross replied. "Over and out."

Ross glanced back at Beck. "Cut him loose," he announced. "Our home away from home calls."

Beck removed his Bowie knife from his boot and cut the zip tie binding Marco's wrist to the jeep's driving board.

Marco stood and eyed both men with renewed hope. "So we aren't staying here?" he asked.

Ross suddenly chuckled. "My days of sleeping on the ground are pretty much over," he remarked, then looked back at Nevada. "Leave the car. It can be traced back to you. It's best if no one finds it." Ross nodded to the jeep. "You're in the back with Marco."

"Fine by me," Nevada announced and removed another set of zip ties from her pocket.

Marco immediately moaned. "Oh, come on," he whined. "Is that really necessary?"

"Shut up," Nevada scoffed.

§

Beck drove Kirk's jeep cautiously along the old, overgrown roadway to the sanctuary. Ross and Beck stared out the windshield and scanned the entire area before the large entrance that was covered in vines and plant life.

"Cozy," Beck teased.

Marco strained to look out the windshield from the back, where he once again had his wrists bound in front of him. His disappointment was evident by the look on his face.

"This is your idea of a safe house?" Marco remarked.

Nevada nodded her approval. "I like it."

"It gets better," Ross teased as they drove through the entrance.

As the visitor's center came into view, Nevada grinned, and Marco frowned.

"It's so creepy," Nevada announced almost enthusiastically. "I can't wait to explore it."

"Should've let them shoot me," Marco muttered.

"Othello said it has working water, sewer, and its own generator for electricity," Ross informed them. "All the comforts of home. Even has functioning in-door plumbing, staff sleeping quarters, and a kitchen in both the visitor's center and the clinic."

Nevada appeared excited and moved between the seats, eyeing both men. "Can we lock Marco in the gorilla pens?" she teased.

"There aren't any pens," Beck informed her.

Nevada frowned and sank back in her seat. Marco appeared relieved.

"It's an old sanctuary," Ross informed her. "The habitats are wide open fields with mostly hidden fencing. I'm told there are shelters in each section, and there's a barn of some kind for emergency use."

They pulled up to the visitor's center and parked off to the side of it. Monroe, Gil, and Darth appeared from the building and approached the jeep. Darth happily greeted Ross and Beck. As Nevada removed Marco from the back, Darth approached and checked them out, seeming somewhat skeptical. Nevada crouched down and held her hand out.

"Hey, puppy," she announced in possibly the sweetest voice anyone would ever hear from the hardened woman. "You're a nice puppy."

Darth approached and checked her out. Once he appeared friendly, Nevada happily petted him.

"Such a good boy," Nevada announced in baby talk. "Who's the good boy? You're the good boy."

Darth excitedly licked her face.

Gil rolled his eyes. "The dog's a damned womanizer," he muttered.

"Dogs are better than men," Nevada announced while still using baby talk as she focused her attention on the dog. "Dogs are loyal and never fuck you over. Isn't that right? Such a good boy!"

All five men glared at Nevada with the same loathsome look.

"I thought you were a Marine," Gil muttered. "Did you feel that way about your platoon?"

Nevada looked up from where she continued to coddle the German shepherd and smiled. "That was different," she insisted. "They were my brothers. They covered my ass, and I covered theirs."

"I'll bet," Marco muttered while grinning cheaply.

As Nevada straightened, she backhanded Marco in the groin just hard enough that he felt the sting and reacted with discomfort. Her look hardened as she sneered at him.

"I never *fucked* my brothers," she snarled, returning to her less pleasant demeanor. "I earned their respect, and they earned mine."

Marco held his hand up in apology while recovering from the slap to his crotch. "My apologies."

Gil cast a look at Monroe and raised his brows. "I hope you were taking notes," he announced almost mockingly. "Nevada is off-limits."

"Duly noted," Monroe muttered.

As they headed for the front of the visitor's center, Ross looked around and appeared pleased.

"Looks downright homey," Ross announced, then glanced at Gil and Monroe. "What's the verdict?"

"I think we should use the visitor center as the 'decoy' camp for our cover, in case anyone happens along unexpectedly," Monroe informed him, then nodded across the property. "We can use the vet clinic as operations. It has everything we need, and it's a little more secluded."

"Sounds good," Ross announced, then eyed both men. "Just the two of you so far?"

"So far," Gil informed him. "I sent Jackie a coded transmission on her helicopter radio. She beeped back, so she should be heading this way soon."

"We'll just have to wait for the others," Ross remarked with a defeated sigh. "The others were instructed to come here once they were sure they weren't being followed."

"Wait," Nevada remarked, just about stopping them. "So I'm the only one you made meet you in the woods? Why wasn't I told just to meet you here?"

She received several looks and raised brows. Nevada sneered at them and their apparent distrust.

"We need to remain dark on this one," Ross announced. "Less communication is best."

"If anyone runs into trouble, they know to contact Othello using untraceable phones," Monroe replied.

"Let's get started cleaning the visitor's center," Ross announced and indicated the main building. "Once we're finished there, we'll make ourselves comfortable in the clinic. While we work, we can discuss our cover story in the event anyone stumbles upon us."

§

The clinic building contained small, dormitory-style, private sleeping quarters and a staff dining area with a small kitchen and vending machines. The staff area was certainly 'no-frills,' but the accommodations were better than most of the safe houses the team had used in the past. There was a communal locker room that had a large, co-ed shower area in the back. The vet's clinic itself was a broad room with an exam table surrounded by many large in-door cages for the bigger animals on the left and stacks of smaller cages on the right. The area was often used for sick or injured animals being cared for by the vet. Marco stared at the large gorilla cage, which now contained a neatly made cot and a small area partitioned off with a shower curtain. As Ross opened the cage door, Marco eyed him then managed a tiny laugh.

"You're kidding, right?" Marco announced.

"No, I'm not kidding," Ross insisted, then nodded to the large cage. "It's safe, secure, and you have your own private bathroom."

Marco's smile faded. "It's a cage."

"It's nicer than most prison cells," Ross insisted.

"Everyone wants me dead," Marco informed Ross. "I'm safe here. I'd think you'd just trust me. I mean, where would I possibly go?"

"I may be 99% sure you're not the killer they claim you are," Ross announced, "but there's still that one percent chance that you are. I'm not risking the lives of anyone here, and I'm certainly not giving you the chance to escape. Desperate men do desperate things."

Marco frowned and again looked inside the cage. "This is humiliating," he insisted and once more looked at Ross. "Where the hell is this 'private' bathroom?"

"Behind that curtain," Ross insisted. "One of those portable commodes like they use in hospitals. It was a lucky find."

"I disagree," Marco balked.

"We had considered rigging a toilet seat on a bucket for you," Ross announced while grinning. "Trust me; this was a lucky find." He again indicated the cell. "In you go."

"I'm not going in there," Marco insisted and folded his arms across his chest. "You're just going to have to trust me. My father--"

Nevada approached Marco and just about got in his face. "Get your fucking ass in that cage, or I'll toss you in head first," she snarled.

Marco met Nevada's gaze only a moment before he stepped through the opening into the cage. Ross shut the door and locked it behind him. He then turned to face Nevada, who maintained her sneer at their handsome prisoner.

"You're not really a people person, are you?" Ross teased while grinning.

Nevada shot her venomous look at Ross. "Some people are more tolerable than others," she scoffed. "But they all pretty much suck."

"I heard you went back to Sal's when you heard the gunshot," Ross remarked and raised a curious brow. "Sounds to me as if you're not nearly as cold-hearted as you'd like everyone to believe."

"You give me too much credit, Ross," Nevada casually informed him while smirking. "I knew Sal had information. Someone showing up at his house only proved that theory. He was worth more to me alive than dead." She then cast a look at Marco within the cage. "And it seems as if I was right on that theory."

"It's none of my business," Ross informed her. "If you want people to hate you, that's fine by me." He straightened proudly. "I heard Zack set you up at the hotel in Maine. Just one word of caution. When it comes to Scorpio and Kane, don't cross Zack. He will put you down with extreme prejudice."

"I have no intention of doing anything that puts either of them in harm's way," Nevada retorted. "I just want out of there."

"Why?" Ross asked, suddenly unable to help his curious nature.

"That's none of your business."

Ross smirked and nodded. "You and Scorpio clash?" he teased.

Nevada tensed slightly and folded her arms across her chest. "She's okay," she replied. "She's got some serious demons, but I suppose that's part of her charm."

"Is it Hayden?" Ross teased while grinning. "I know he can go from zero to psycho in six seconds flat."

Nevada groaned and allowed her arms to fall to her sides. "If you must know, it's Kane," she informed him.

Ross stared at her with some surprise. "Kane?" he asked. "Kane is practically a saint. He even won over Mac, and that's saying a lot."

"He's like the mother I never wanted," Nevada scoffed with irritation. "He makes me completely insane. That's not the way men are supposed to act."

Ross shook his head and sighed. "I feel sorry for you, Nevada," he announced, then walked away from her.

Chapter 28

Jackie's helicopter landed not far from Gil's helicopter in the field close to the tree line. It was a nice, secluded area with plenty of cover. Jackie almost didn't see Gil's helicopter, making the location ideal. As she shut down, Monroe emerged from the woods and approached. Although she was happy to see her teammate, Jackie had hoped for a few minutes to herself before the guys showed up. After several hours in the air, the first thing on her mind was a bathroom break. None of the guys ever complained about her frequent pit stops, not even Kirk, but it was one of the drawbacks of being the group's sole woman. She could literally kick their asses, yet when it came to matters of the bladder, she would lose that battle every time. She opened the pilot side door, eyed Monroe, and then looked around.

"Are you the welcome party?" she teased.

"The party has barely gotten started," Monroe reported while managing a tiny smile.

"Who's missing?" Jackie asked and appeared curious, her mind immediately straying.

"Bogart, Zack, and Kirk," he announced.

"Nevada?" she asked skeptically while climbing out of the helicopter.

"She arrived with Ross and Beck," Monroe remarked. "About six hours after you'd dropped her and Bogart off at the airport."

Jackie remained suspicious and now tensed slightly. "Where's Bogart?" Her mind was already reeling about the possible fate of her brother.

"She said they parted company about an hour after you'd dropped them off," Monroe insisted. "Said they'd meet at the rendezvous."

"This is the rendezvous," Jackie reminded him.

"Yeah, but Ross gave Nevada an alternate rendezvous," he informed her. "I guess he doesn't trust her yet."

"I don't blame him," Jackie muttered and looked at her watch. "I'm not even sure Zack trusts her entirely." She then sank into her own thoughts. "And you know Bogart. He's easily played by an attractive woman."

"But he's also an amazing con man," Monroe reminded her. "I doubt he put too much trust into her. He knows better." He then seemed to read her mind and turned reassuring. "I'm sure Bogart is fine."

"Yeah," Jackie muttered but couldn't stop thinking about the possibility of Nevada double-crossing Bogart. She wasn't as confident as Monroe.

"Ross asked me to meet you here," Monroe informed her. "You and I are going to hike to town, scope it out, and pick up some supplies."

"Town?" she asked and raised her brow. "That's over a mile from here. Why didn't you bring Kirk's jeep? We could have taken it partway."

"Too dangerous," he insisted.

"I wasn't suggesting we'd take it into town," she informed him.

"I know, but it's still too dangerous," he remarked. "Too many people have seen that jeep. Besides, Othello is having a friend of a friend of a friend meet us just outside town with a loaner car for our new cover."

"What's our cover?" Jackie asked.

"Photographers and documentarians," Monroe replied and appeared somewhat humored. "We're photographing Colorado's scenic wilderness and wildlife. He's sending some equipment with the car. I'll fill you in on the walk." He then nodded across the field. "We should get going. We want to get back before dark."

Jackie offered a tiny smile then indicated the tree line near the helicopter. "Let me use the ladies' room first."

§

Jackie and Monroe walked for quite some time through the woods before finally reaching a dirt road. They followed the dirt road for most of the journey and talked about everything but their current assignment. Jackie was worried about her brother, but she didn't need to bring her thoughts on the subject into the conversation. Monroe knew her well enough to know what she was thinking, and he, too, avoided the subject. Both were silently hoping Nevada hadn't double-crossed Bogart. Despite being an excellent conman, Bogart was easily corrupted by beautiful women, and Nevada was both sexy and lethal. Even Monroe had been checking out the woman. Of course, the last thing Monroe needed in his life was to get involved with *another* lethal woman. Whereas Bogart was a master at flings, Monroe tended to fall hard for just about every woman he'd ever slept with. That included Jackie, although, that was a long time ago. Their brief, one-time encounter left Monroe heartbroken for a long time.

Possibly one of Monroe's biggest mistakes was his brief, sexual encounter with Zack's mortal enemy, Mac. Jackie still wasn't convinced Monroe was over Mac. That being said, Monroe certainly didn't need to insert himself into whatever disastrous life Nevada was leading. The very fact that Zack felt the need to move the bounty hunter into his kid's cliffside hotel in Maine was reason enough for Monroe to avoid the dangerous woman. Zack had a thing for hard-luck cases, and Nevada was just one of many. Jackie had only recently learned that Zack was removing war veterans from bad situations and attempting to straighten them out by giving them a new purpose in life.

One might speculate he was building his own army, but maybe that was just her theory.

Monroe and Jackie weren't far from the main, back road into town when they saw a late model pickup truck and a jeep that had seen better days parked alongside the dirt road. Two shifty-looking men stood outside the vehicles smoking cigarettes. Both men were scrawny. One taller; one shorter. Their clothes and overall appearance screamed 'backwoods hillbilly'. Just by their looks, it was difficult to tell if they were friend or foe.

"What do you think?" Jackie muttered to Monroe.

"Oh, they're definitely the guys," Monroe informed her.

As they approached, the two men kept their eyes on Jackie and Monroe. They seemed almost as untrusting of them. There was a slightly tense moment with the looks they were receiving from the shifty men. Jackie and Monroe had to be cautious, considering everyone and their brother with a gun was looking to take a shot at Marco and anyone that got in their way.

"Are you Monroe?" the taller man asked in a gruff tone as his eyes narrowed.

"Yeah, I'm Monroe," he replied, playing the tough guy act, and then indicated the old, beaten up jeep. "You have something for us?"

The taller man's mood suddenly lightened as he nodded to the jeep then tossed Monroe the keys. "Sorry to hear about your truck and all your equipment being stolen," he remarked, then opened the back of the jeep and nodded at the box of cameras and equipment. Both men seemed to relax, almost as if they felt the same nervousness about Jackie and Monroe. "This is the best we could do on such short notice. All digital cameras, but they're just a little outdated. Got you some binoculars too."

The shorter man seemed to take a liking to Jackie, checking her out with more than a passing interest, and then smiled. "We hooked you up with some camping supplies, too," the shorter man reported more to Jackie.

Monroe checked out the cameras in the box and nodded his approval. "This will do," he replied, then focused his attention on the two men. "You really saved us. When those guys stole our truck and all our equipment, we thought we'd have to scrap the entire project."

The taller man shook his head in disgust. "I can't believe anyone in these parts would do such a thing," he remarked. "People don't steal around here. Sure, kids might steal candy from the corner store, but we've never had problems with anyone stealing from campers before."

"Well, there's a first for everything," Monroe informed him. "We had some pretty nice equipment. Probably someone from out of town. Any other campers around here that you know about?"

Both men shook their heads. "No, the woods pretty much belong to you," the shorter man insisted. "Not too many hunters yet. Not for a few more weeks, at least. Well, we do have the occasional poacher, but the local boys usually deal with them."

"Anything else we can do for you?" the taller man asked almost cheerfully.

Monroe considered the question then shook his head. "No, you've been more than helpful," he replied. "You really saved our documentary with this; I mean that."

"Anything for our friend, Gus," the shorter man insisted. "He must be pretty good friends with your friend. Gus doesn't trust many people. He's one of those odd-ball loners. Likes to tinker with electronics and computerized gadgets. Great guy, though."

"Yeah, sounds a lot like our friend," Monroe replied while grinning.

"Anyway," the taller man announced with a sigh. "You'll find whatever food supplies you need at the store in town. Beth will take care of you. When you're done with the jeep, just leave it here with the keys under the floor mat. We'll collect it when we see it."

"Thanks again," Monroe announced.

Jackie and Monroe pretended to sort through the supplies in the back of the jeep while secretly watching the two men get into the truck and leave. Monroe finally shut the back and turned to face Jackie.

"Looks like the woods are pretty much ours," Monroe insisted.

"Sounds like we may need to keep our eyes open for local good-old-boys scouting the woods for poachers, though," she remarked.

"That's why we have our cover," he reminded her. "Nothing is more natural than a photographer in the woods." He then nodded to the jeep. "Let's check out town, scope out the area, and grab a few groceries."

"Sounds like a small, hick town," Jackie remarked. "They're going to notice us."

"We've already established our cover with our new friends there," Monroe informed her. "And Othello's friend, Gus, is very popular among the locals. Their distrust of strangers will work to our advantage." He offered a mildly devious grin. "Anyone looking for Marco is going to really stick out. If any strangers are passing through, we'll probably hear about it on our next grocery run."

Jackie needed to have faith in Monroe. He wasn't a conman like her brother, but he was a master at the con game. He knew a lot about blending in, going off-grid, and staying under the radar.

§

Detrick sat behind the wheel of the black blazer and stared out the windshield at the activity up ahead within the woods of the state game land. There was a fire truck, police cars with their lights flashing, and several ambulances. Bart sat in the back seat toward the middle, leaning his large forearms on the backs of both seats, and stared out the windshield as well. In the midst of the chaos of police, firemen, and ambulance crew, Carter spoke to one of the local police officers. Carter flashed a badge, and the men continued to talk.

"He gets a lot of mileage out of that fake badge," Bart muttered from the back seat. He then indicated the incident. "Do you think it was them?"

Detrick snorted a laugh. "Two cars were reported stolen from the private airfield less than fifty miles from here after that same helicopter supposedly refueled," he remarked. "Less than an hour later, there's a report of explosions in the woods. There's no doubt this was them."

They watched as the officer led Carter to the sheet-covered bodies that had since been removed from the area containing the exploded vehicles. He pulled back the sheet revealing the slightly singed dead men. Carter shook his head, thanked the officer, and then headed back to the car beyond the police barricade. Carter nodded to the officers keeping people from entering the area and approached the blazer. He jumped into the passenger side with his colleagues.

"None of the dead men were Marco," Carter informed them, "but plates from the exploded cars matched the two stolen cars from the airfield."

"Who were the dead men?" Bart asked.

"That's up to forensics to figure out," Carter remarked. "Both had been shot then were partially burned postmortem in the fire." He eyed both men. "They believe some sort of charge destroyed the cars." He raised his brows. "They're guessing the explosion was caused by something similar to a grenade."

"A grenade?" Bart asked with some surprise. "Who goes around carrying grenades in their pockets?"

"People who shoot automatic weapons out of helicopters," Detrick muttered.

"Half an hour before the helicopter landed to refuel at the private airfield, someone secured a rental car online," Carter reminded them. "That has to be the car these guys were following. I have the make, model, and plates for that rental car. We're looking for an older, brown SUV. Before the police start connecting the dots, we need to find that car and realize what they're looking for. Judging by the tire tracks in the dirt, there had been a fourth vehicle as well that left in a hurry. It's possible someone else may be currently tailing them."

"Some heavy hitters are going to be looking for Marco," Detrick remarked. "There's going to be a lot of interested parties."

"We're going to need eyes in the backs of our heads," Bart scoffed.

Detrick put the car into reverse and backed up several yards to the main road. He stopped short of the road and eyed Carter. "Which direction?"

Carter consulted his cell phone and GPS. "I doubt they're heading back in the direction of the airfield," he remarked. "There's a larger town about twenty miles west of here. Let's head that way. They have maybe half an hour head start on us."

"How are we going to find them?" Bart asked as Detrick pulled onto the back road and started driving west. "With a half an hour head start, they could be almost anywhere by now."

"I'll call in the rental car make, model, and plates to Vincent," Carter informed his teammates while removing his cell phone. "He has people everywhere. We have to hope that someone will report seeing that car."

Chapter 29

Zack sat in the front passenger seat of Slade's black sedan and periodically eyed the brown SUV, now driven by Slade and Nolte, tailing them through town. Zack groaned and didn't even bother looking at Kirk behind the wheel.

"If I had been driving, they never would have found us," Zack insisted with some irritation. "I can't believe you haven't shaken them yet."

Kirk frowned his disapproval while watching the streets before him. "If I drive any faster, we'll have the police on our tail as well," he snapped back. "Considering the firepower you have in your 'fun bag', we'll be thrown in jail for the rest of our lives."

"No one told you to drive into the city in the first place," Zack muttered in response.

"It's not a city," Kirk scoffed while turning angry. "This hick-burg barely constitutes a town."

"We need to lose them long enough to ditch the car," Zack remarked.

"Well, I'm open to suggestions," Kirk snarled in response while slamming his palm on the steering wheel.

"I made a suggestion," Zack snapped back. "I told you to let me drive."

"I've driven with you before," Kirk huffed under his breath. "I don't care to repeat the experience."

"I'm an amazing driver," Zack corrected.

"Yeah, if we were taking the checkered flag at Talladega," Kirk remarked.

Zack grinned at the comment, seeming pleased with the response.

"Just keep an eye out for someplace to ditch the car where we can blend in," Kirk remarked.

Zack zeroed in on something then pointed as they passed. "Back there," he announced. "I saw a sign for a flea market. There should be a lot of cars and people at a place like that. We'll ditch the car and blend in with the crowd."

"Okay, we'll swing by the area first and stake it out, then lose the tail and double back," Kirk replied.

They approached the large flea market parking area and looked around without appearing as if they were casing the place.

Kirk suddenly laughed and grinned his approval. "Oh, that is so ironic."

"Could be fun," Zack teased.

They continued past the large flea market and made their way through the small city. After doing another lap around some roads they had already traveled along a few minutes ago, they had gotten a feel for the area. It was time to lose the men following them.

Zack eagerly pulled his seatbelt tight. "Let's take that checkered flag."

Kirk grinned and pressed the gas pedal to the floor. The black sedan they'd stolen from Slade picked up speed and then made a sudden sharp right onto a side street. The brown SUV sped up and attempted to follow them.

Kirk suddenly smiled. "I think the universe is smiling upon us," he announced while slowing down.

Zack was mildly confused about why Kirk had slowed and then saw the police car sitting at the intersection. Kirk waited for the light to turn yellow before passing through. Once they were through the yellow light, Kirk made another sharp right and picked up speed. The car tailing them raced through the red light. The police car's red and blue lights came on, and the siren wailed as the police car chased after the men following

Zack and Kirk. The brown SUV evaded the police car and attempted to lose it. Within the brown SUV, Slade clutched the strap above the passenger door and held onto the dashboard while glaring at Nolte, who tried to lose the pursuing police car.

"Are you out of your mind?" Slade demanded in anger. "You're going to bring down the entire police department on top of us!"

"How many can there really be?" Nolte launched back without looking at him. "We're driving a piece of shit car that doesn't belong to us, and there are bullet holes in the back end. Once they see those bullet holes, they're going to frisk us. I don't know about you, but I don't want to explain my freshly fired weapon to them."

"And this is why I don't partner up with other hired guns," Slade snapped. "You take a bad situation and make it a thousand times worse."

"Motherfucker, please," Nolte cried out in anger, allowing his rage to control him. "Unless you want me to kick your ass out of a moving car, shut the fuck up and let me drive!"

Nolte looked like a demon-possessed as he swerved to miss another car and veered down a one-way road the wrong way. Slade seemed to be the only one who noticed it was a one-way street. He was about to comment but thought better of it. It was already too late. A moving truck was parked in the alley blocking the road. Nolte slammed on the brakes, bringing the SUV to a screeching stop. Slade placed his hand over his eyes and groaned. The police car pulled up behind them, and an officer jumped out of the car with his weapon aimed while using the door as a shield. Nolte stared into the side mirror and frowned while watching the officer. Slade still had his hand casually over his eyes in disgrace.

"How do you want to play this?" Nolte muttered while shooting looks between Slade's profile and the side mirror.

Slade finally lowered his hand from his eyes and glared at Nolte. "I wanted you to pull over," he launched back in anger. "A little late to ask me how I want to play it now."

"I say we shoot our way out," Nolte announced while reaching for his weapon in his shoulder holster.

"I think you'll be dead before you even have a chance to aim your weapon," Slade remarked.

"Two of us and only one of him," he pointed out.

Slade rolled his eyes then glanced in his side mirror as well. His eyes suddenly narrowed at the officer who still hadn't moved from his position behind the open car door. "What's he waiting for?" he then asked.

"Backup, maybe," Nolte replied.

"Something doesn't seem right," Slade muttered and continued to watch the stalemate behind them.

A black SUV pulled up alongside the alley. Carter and Bart got out and approached the officer crouched alongside his police cruiser. Slade and Nolte continued to watch the arriving strangers through the mirror.

"Who are these motherfuckers?" Nolte demanded, his fight reflexes again rising.

"Never seen them before," Slade remarked.

Carter and Bart paused not far from the police officer, who briefly glanced at them.

"What do you want me to do?" the officer asked.

"We'll take it from here," Carter informed him. "You never saw us."

The officer holstered his weapon, got back in the car, and backed out of the alley. Carter and Bart approached the brown SUV while removing their weapons. Slade and Nolte suddenly tensed.

"Oh, that's not good," Slade remarked as his eyes widened. "We need a plan fast."

"Shoot the motherfuckers," Nolte replied while sneering as he pulled his weapon.

"Solid plan," Slade replied and removed his weapon from his shoulder holster as well.

Both men sprang from the SUV on either side with their weapons drawn. Bart and Carter darted behind the car with their own weapons raised. Despite that all four men had silencers on their semiautomatics, none seemed interested in firing. Nolte and Slade took the opportunity to dart in front of their car and kept their weapons aimed at the men concealed behind the SUV.

"We only want Marco," Carter called out to them.

Slade and Nolte exchanged puzzled looks.

"So do we and about a hundred other people," Slade called back. "What's your point?"

"Hand him over," Carter shouted back.

Slade and Nolte again exchanged looks then eyed the borrowed car. Both men came to the same conclusion and rolled their eyes.

"It's their stolen car," Slade moaned and indicated the SUV. "They tracked this piece of shit car looking for the guys who ambushed us."

Nolte snorted a laugh then shook his head. He returned his attention to the two men at the rear of the SUV. "Sorry to disappoint you," Nolte called out to them. "We don't have Marco, but we did have an altercation with the men who do."

Carter and Bart now exchanged baffled looks. "The car?" Carter demanded.

"Fuckers blew up my car," Nolte shouted at them. "This was their piece of shit car. We were tailing them before your asses got involved and stopped us. Now, they could be anywhere!"

Carter and Bart groaned with irritation.

"Why don't we make a deal?" Slade called out to them, attempting to keep the peace. "We could work together. Split the bounty four ways."

"Not interested," Carter called back. "Stay out of our way. We'll leave you with a warning this time. Next time, you won't be so lucky."

Nolte eyed Slade alongside him. "Who does this bitch think he is?" he demanded.

"He obviously doesn't know who we are," Slade muttered, then eyed Nolte and raised a sharp brow. "Take my advice just this once and let them walk away. Too many witnesses nearby."

Nolte frowned then looked back at the men hiding behind the rear of the car. "Fine," he called out. "Leave us! Be on your way!"

Carter and Bart moved away from the rear of the car and backed down the alley while keeping their weapons aimed. When they nearly reached their black vehicle at the end of the alley, Carter shot out the brown SUV's rear tire. There was a loud pop, and the air expelled from the tire.

"Mother--" Nolte glared at Slade. "I should have shot the fuckers when I had the chance. Why did I listen to your ass?"

Carter and Bart jumped into the black SUV and drove away. Nolte and Slade straightened with scowls on their faces.

"I'll get the jack from the trunk," Slade muttered in defeat.

Chapter 30

Zack and Kirk walked among the masses of men and women dressed in their finest Army surplus wear. The large outdoor flea market venue was lined with rows of vendors and tables containing all sorts of Army surplus. Zack and Kirk blended in with the crowd almost a little too well. Kirk dug into his bag of peanuts while Zack enjoyed a large, vanilla ice cream cone with colorful sprinkles.

"Honestly," Zack announced in all seriousness while licking the ice cream. "I could live here."

Kirk watched an attractive, large busted, blonde woman walk past. The young woman was dressed in an army green tank top without a bra and camouflage fatigues crudely cut-off into short-shorts. Her sexy attire was completed with a pair of black, lace-up combat boots. The only thing the young woman was missing was a rifle slung over her shoulder. Kirk nearly gave himself whiplash, unable to take his eyes off her. As she passed, the sexy woman seemed to be checking out Kirk as well, which wasn't surprising. Physically, Kirk was quite the specimen of manliness and gained more than his share of female attention. He grinned back at the woman.

"I wish we had a little more time to explore," Kirk announced and checked out the woman's backside.

The woman turned her head, looked back at him as well, and then smiled and winked. Kirk groaned and tossed his peanuts at Zack. Despite the quick action, Zack was able to catch the bag with little effort.

"The hell with it," Kirk announced without taking his eyes off the woman. "We have a few minutes." He just about tossed the weapon's bag at Zack and then hurried after the woman.

Zack shook his head in disgrace while slinging the bag over his shoulder. "He's so easily distracted," he muttered aloud. Zack suddenly stopped in his tracks and stared several yards ahead of him, lust in his eyes, at the massive Apache Attack Helicopter on display. "Oh, I think I'm in love."

Zack handed Kirk's bag of peanuts to a passing kid then continued toward the vision of beauty before him. The Boeing Apache Attack Helicopter was a menacing marvel with a twin-engine and enough firepower to be its own war machine. Weighing over twenty thousand pounds, it had seating for a crew of two. A pilot and co-pilot gunner. The Apache had sixteen Hellfire missiles, seventy-six Hydra 70 rockets, and over a thousand chain gun rounds. Zack tossed his ice cream cone into the nearby garbage receptacle then made his way closer to the massive, flying marvel. He lovingly caressed the Hellfire missiles launcher and groaned his approval.

"We prefer that you don't touch anything," a man announced from nearby.

Zack turned and saw an older man dressed in Army issued combat fatigues standing a few feet from him. The man in his late fifties had gray hair in an Army buzz cut and a meticulously clean-shaven face. He was built like a tank with a steely gaze in his eyes that screamed the 'real deal'.

The man's expression suddenly dropped. "Zack?" the older man gasped, unable to take his eyes off Zack. "But you're supposed to be--" The man suddenly grinned. "Well, how about that!"

"Gunny," Zack announced and laughed.

The men exchanged a manly hug. The man called "Gunny" pulled away, held his hands up in the air, and laughed. "I'm smart enough to know I shouldn't even ask," he remarked. "Even though I should be shocked that you're alive, I'm not."

Zack eyed the authenticity of the man's fatigues then noted his rank insignia. "Are you still in?" he asked, then indicated the colonel insignia. "Or did you steal someone else's valor?"

"Well, Zack," Gunny announced and indicated the helicopter. "They don't let civilians just take these bad boys out on day trips." He then laughed while maintaining his smile. "Truth is, every time I thought about leaving, they promoted me." He sighed. "The wife got used to the lifestyle, so I guess now I'm in for life."

Zack chuckled. "Do they still call you Gunny?"

"Only the old guys," he teased.

Zack's smile faded to a sneer. "Not funny."

"Jesus," Gunny announced and shook his head. "I haven't seen you since, well, since you died. You look good for a dead man. Still jumping from moving helicopters?"

"I guess the last time would have been two, maybe three days ago," Zack replied.

Gunny stared at him with a slightly surprised look, then laughed. "I believe you too." His eyes suddenly narrowed. "Wait a minute. You wouldn't happen to have anything to do with those nearby explosions earlier today." Gunny suddenly held his hand up and shook his head. "Don't answer that. I don't want to know."

"I wouldn't have answered anyway," Zack teased. "Plausible deniability."

"What brings you to this out-of-the-way town?" Gunny then asked.

"The usual," Zack replied. "Avoiding the men who are trying to kill me."

"That would have been my first or second guess," Gunny teased. He then nodded at the helicopter. "Want to check her out?"

"I thought you'd never ask," Zack remarked.

§

Several men stood around the green, 1953 Dodge, hard body MASH ambulance. They appeared to be admiring the vintage medical ambulance with the giant Red Cross contained in a white square on the side. A man in his late forties wearing green combat fatigues approached his MASH ambulance while balancing his lunch and several drinks in a holder. He noticed the collection of men standing around the ambulance and staring at it.

"Go inside and check her out," the owner announced and nodded proudly at the ambulance. "It's for sale."

"It's locked," one man informed him.

The owner appeared bewildered. "Locked?" he remarked. "It shouldn't be locked. Let me find the keys."

"I think there's someone inside," a second man announced with a strange grin on his face.

The owner now appeared bewildered and approached the ambulance. It started rocking harshly, and the faint sounds of a woman's screams of ecstasy could clearly be heard. The rocking turned into a heavy thumping, which met the woman's screams, now clearly heard by all. Judging by the grins on the men's faces, it was quite possibly the reason they had collected in the first place. There was a loud male groan, and the ambulance became still. The owner remained frozen in place without taking his eyes off the vehicle. The back door finally opened, and the attractive, young woman in the green tank top exited from the back. She smiled at the vehicle owner.

"Hey, Dad," she announced without care.

Kirk then appeared from the back of the ambulance, gave the woman a knowing smile, and headed on his way. The young woman's father watched Kirk walk away then looked back at his daughter with his mouth hanging open. Kirk headed for the first food stand he found and approached the counter.

"I'll have a hamburger, two hot dogs, and an order of fries," he announced to the man in the food truck.

Zack approached Kirk while he waited for his food. "I found us a ride," Zack announced, his weapons' bag conspicuously missing. "I ran into an old military friend."

"Anyone I know?" Kirk asked and accepted his food order.

Zack eyed the pile of food Kirk attempted to juggle, then met his teammate's gaze. "Before your time," he replied. "We need to meet him in twenty minutes."

"Good," Kirk announced with a devious smirk. "Enough time for me to eat."

"I guess someone got laid," Zack muttered with little emotion.

Kirk grinned, amused, and raised his brows suggestively in response. "I never kiss and tell."

"That would be a first," Zack muttered, then indicated for him to keep walking. "Eat while we walk. I don't want to miss our ride."

"Yeah, yeah," Kirk groaned and shoved half the hot dog into his mouth as they headed through the exhibits and flea market stands. Kirk finished his second hot dog and was about to start on his hamburger when his curiosity got the better of him. "So who's this old friend anyway?" he asked with a mouthful of food, then looked alongside him.

Zack had disappeared without warning. Kirk became alert but refrained from drawing attention to himself by looking around. Zack's stealthy departures usually only meant one thing. Without hesitation, Kirk casually approached a nearby garbage can and dropped his untouched hamburger and fries into the trash. While remaining in front of the trashcan, he wiped his hands on his napkin. He could feel the presence of a man moving behind him.

"Surprise, mother--" Nolte began.

Kirk rammed his elbow backward into Nolte's gut, then spun and swiftly disarmed him before anyone even saw the weapon. Nolte was taken by surprise by the fast, hard strike and disarm. Kirk grabbed the man by his jacket, pulled him closer, and rammed his knee into his groin, all without any bystanders witnessing the action. Nolte groaned loudly and just about doubled over, but Kirk held onto him, keeping him upright. Kirk smiled and laughed while patting Nolte's shoulder as he met a few stray gazes from those in the crowd.

"I told you not to drink so much," Kirk announced, then turned Nolte away from the crowd while holding him up. While turned away, Kirk gave him a quick, fast throat punch. Nolte began to sink. Kirk continued to laugh. "I think you'd better sit down before you fall down."

Kirk just about dragged Nolte to a nearby stand and lowered him to the ground, where he writhed in agony, attempting to catch his breath. Kirk straightened and scanned the crowded area full of attendees and vendors.

"He's just going to sleep it off," Kirk announced cheerfully to one man who seemed to be taking an interest in the situation.

Kirk then looked beyond the crowd, attempting to locate his missing counterpart. Zack casually made his way through the masses of people toward Kirk. Slade was seen sitting on the ground, his back against a tree. He was almost certainly unconscious, although there was the off-chance Zack had killed him. It could really go either way with Zack. Zack was almost to Kirk when he saw a man plowing his way through the crowd toward them. Carter had his eyes locked on Zack and touched his ear, which was obviously concealing a hidden transmitter. Zack and Kirk noticed the action and immediately looked around for the man's backup. They saw Carter's two large friends making their way through the crowd toward them. Although they hadn't personally met any of the three men, they knew they had been identified when they took down Slade and Nolte. Kirk and Zack attempted to disappear into the crowd, but the three men continued their pursuit. They needed to lose their tails before meeting with Gunny if they wanted to make a clean getaway.

Zack and Kirk knew the men following them were just as hobbled by the crowd. There were too many witnesses. That a good portion of those witnesses were former military or gun enthusiasts was enough to keep their little game of cloak-and-dagger away from prying eyes. Anyone in the crowd could insert themselves into the situation and make matters worse. Even the three mercenaries chasing Zack and Kirk didn't want to draw too much attention to themselves. Carter, Bart, and Detrick were pretty well spread out in order to watch as much of the area as possible. They exchanged looks to one another across the crowd. Zack and Kirk appeared to have vanished.

Carter touched his hidden ear transmitter. "They're around here somewhere," he announced. "They couldn't have gotten far."

From their strategic positions around the mildly crowded square, the three men scanned the area. Bart saw Zack standing before one of the blue, plastic rental toilets. Zack was looking around, making sure he wasn't being followed, and then darted into the port-o-potty.

"Found one," Bart announced to his teammates through his hidden transmitter. "He just ducked into one of the rental toilets."

"Secure him in there," Carter announced over his transmitter. "We'll meet you there."

Bart made his way through the crowd and reached the line of portable toilets. Instead of waiting for his teammates, he held a knife carefully hidden against his arm and gave the door a firm yank, opening it. The portable toilet was empty. Bart looked up and saw Zack's booted feet disappearing through the topside vent. Bart lunged inside the port-o-potty and attempted to grab Zack's foot when the door suddenly slammed behind him. Bart spun for the door and attempted to bust it open. Just outside the toilet, Kirk pulled the zip tie tight over the padlock latches and walked away. Within the toilet, Bart kicked the door, doing some damage and possibly drawing a crowd.

"You son-of-a-bitch!"

Something small clattered within the vent shaft and hit the water with a small splash. Bart eyed the open toilet seat and took a step closer. Just outside the row of portable toilets, Carter and Detrick hurried to the bathroom area and looked around for Bart. They noticed one of the toilets had been zip-tied shut. There was a soft rumble followed by a loud, male scream. Carter removed his knife and cut the zip tie holding the door closed as a crowd began to gather. Bart threw the door open but didn't move from the opening. The large man was drenched in blue liquid and covered in human feces. The look on his blue face was a mixture of horror and rage. Carter and Detrick got one whiff of the man and stepped back while attempting to keep from gagging.

"What the hell--?" Carter cried out.

Detrick had a difficult time holding back his snicker. "Cherry bomb down the vent shaft," he remarked while hiding his grin. "I did that to a friend when I was in high school."

Bart sneered at Detrick, revealing teeth with a slight blue tinge. Carter cringed, realizing Bart must have had his mouth open during the small explosion.

§

Zack and Kirk approached a roped off clearing where a large crowd had abruptly gathered. As they headed into the group of people, Kirk looked around.

"We're heading in the wrong direction for the parking lot," Kirk announced.

"Our ride is this way," Zack insisted and led the way.

Kirk hurried after Zack without further question. Zack moved beneath the roped off area and into the clearing with Kirk on his heels. Kirk suddenly stopped when he saw the Apache Attack Helicopter preparing for take-off, which was what had caused the crowd to collect.

Gunny approached Zack and raised his brows. "You're late," he announced.

"Ran into some old friends," Zack informed him.

"Some things never change, huh? In that case, you'd better get aboard," Gunny insisted. "I already stowed your gear."

Kirk stared at the helicopter then eyed Zack and Gunny. "That thing only seats two."

"Yeah," Zack announced, then grimaced. "One of us will have to sit on the other's lap."

Kirk snorted a laugh. "We know who's sitting on who, runt," he remarked.

Zack indicated the back seat of the helicopter. "Just get in," he snarled.

Once Gunny and Kirk were seated and belted in, Zack jumped into the back, took his place on Kirk's lap, and shut the door. Zack reached in front of him, slapped Gunny on the shoulder, and then twirled his finger in the air. As the helicopter lifted off, the crowd cheered. Bart, Carter, and Detrick arrived on the scene and looked around the cheering crowd. They didn't see any signs of Zack or Kirk. None of the men bothered looking at the helicopter as it lifted off. Carter nudged the men above the loud noise and indicated the area to the right. All three hurried away. Zack stared out the side window and grinned as the men scurried around, looking everywhere for them but up.

"What's the plan?" Kirk shouted to Zack situated on his lap.

"Gunny's going to drop us off at his house," Zack informed him. "He has an old car he's going to let us use."

Kirk gave a thumb's up sign, signaling that he understood. Zack saw the gunner's handstick in front of him and lovingly placed his hand on the machine gun control. Kirk smacked his hand.

Chapter 31

It was getting close to dark as Jackie paced the area outside the visitor's center. The area surrounding the visitor's center had a certain eeriness about it even during the day. Now that it was starting to get dark, the creep factor was rising fast. Jackie frowned while looking at her watch several times. Zack, Kirk, and Bogart were still among the missing, and she was starting to worry. She was almost certain Zack and Kirk were okay, but it was Bogart that had her concerned. What if Bogart trusted Nevada and she betrayed him? None of them knew the bounty hunter very well; admittedly, neither did Zack. The woman lacked empathy and would roll any of them over for a buck. Jackie hated that she was so distrusting of the woman, but with Bogart still being gone and so many hours between the time Nevada said she left him, it had her concerned that something had happened to him. She heard movement near the main entrance to the sanctuary and swiftly plucked her binoculars that had been hanging around her neck.

Through the binoculars, Jackie saw Zack and Kirk heading through the large entrance. Both seemed fine physically. Jackie was relieved that both were okay. Now, she just needed Bogart to join them. She was tempted to call Othello herself and ask if he'd heard from anyone regarding her brother. Othello would be their middleman in all of this, and everyone knew to rely on him. His equipment was near hack-proof. As the men approached the visitor's center, they smiled when they saw her.

"Awe," Kirk announced while grinning. "The little missus waited up for us."

"Everyone else report?" Zack asked.

"Just waiting on Bogart," she replied and attempted to hide her concern.

"Idiot probably got lost," Kirk scoffed under his breath. "I'm starving." He then indicated the visitor's center. "Is this operations?"

"No, that's the cover," Jackie replied, then nodded toward the back. "There's another building in the back. It's quite cozy. I believe they saved dinner for you two."

Without a word, Kirk continued past and headed around back. Zack remained out front with Jackie as Kirk disappeared. He then raised a brow while eyeing her.

"You okay?" he asked.

She frowned and shrugged. "Just a little worried about Bogart," Jackie replied and nervously rubbed her hands along her cold shoulders.

"I wouldn't worry too much," Zack remarked. "He'll be along."

Jackie stared into Zack's eyes. "He went with Nevada," she remarked. "She came back, and he didn't." She then turned insecure. "Can we really trust her? Could she have double-crossed him?"

"Nevada may be a lot of things," Zack informed her, "but she's not a cold-blooded killer. She's a bounty hunter, not a hitman."

Jackie frowned and looked down. "I'm sorry," she announced timidly. "I should trust your judgment more."

Zack pulled Jackie into his arms and held her a moment. Jackie relaxed and returned the embrace. Without releasing her, he muttered into her ear, "Want me to wait with you?"

Jackie pulled out of his arms, rubbed her cold shoulders, and forced a smile. "No, you must be exhausted," she announced. "I'll wait out here a little while longer then join you in the clinic."

Zack removed his jacket and placed it over her shoulders to help warm her. The night was cool, and she was without her jacket. Jackie was grateful for the added warmth. Zack placed his hand on her shoulder and squeezed it as he passed. Jackie felt a little bit better with Zack's reassurances, but that only lasted a short while before she was once again consumed with despair. She slipped into Zack's warm jacket and held it closed across her body, then resumed pacing.

"Come on, Bogart," she groaned and again looked at her watch as the area rapidly darkened.

Nearly half an hour later, Jackie sat on the steps to the visitor's center with her arms folded across her chest while attempting to keep warm. As it got darker, the night had turned much cooler. Darth trotted around the side of the building and excitedly ran up to Jackie, licking her face. Jackie managed a smile and affectionately cuddled the large dog. Someone must have left him out, and he tracked her scent to the visitor's center.

"Just a few more minutes," she told the dog, "then I'm coming in."

Darth suddenly spun toward the main entrance and snarled softly. He then perked up and ran across the clearing for the opening. Jackie quickly sprang to her feet and strained to see where the dog had gone. Bogart scratched Darth's head as they walked back toward the visitor's center. Jackie ran across the clearing for Bogart and threw her arms around him, eagerly hugging him. Bogart returned the embrace and laughed.

"I wasn't gone that long," he teased.

Jackie pulled away, releasing him, and managed a tiny laugh. "Maybe not, but Nevada's been back for hours."

"Well, I wasn't taking any chances on being followed," Bogart informed her, then grinned. "I know how to cover my tracks."

"Yes, you do," she announced and felt somewhat embarrassed for thinking anything could have happened to her brother.

Before she even knew Bogart was her brother, he was covering her tracks for her. It seemed like a long time ago, but it really wasn't all that long.

"Did you need something to eat?" she asked. "If Kirk didn't eat what was left of dinner, I could heat something up for you."

"No, I'm good," Bogart replied and managed a tiny groan. "I stopped at three diners; four, if you count the diner I accidentally stopped at a second time while doubling back on myself."

"Did you notice anyone following you?" Jackie asked as they headed around back and walked toward the clinic.

"No, I didn't see anyone," he informed her. "Even as it was getting dark. I didn't pass a single car in the last twenty miles before I got here. This place is about as secluded as it gets."

§

It was already dark when Holden's black SUV pulled up to his partially lit house in the rural development. Motion sensor lights came on as the vehicle approached the garage. The garage door electronically opened, and the SUV pulled into the empty bay. As the garage door closed, Holden got out of the car and took a little extra time to scan the well-lit garage. He had been more cautious these last few nights. Despite that the team seemed to spend almost as much time at his house as they did their own, Holden gladly accepted Othello's offer to beef up security for their home. Between Holden's work at the FBI and Jackie's affiliation with Whiskey Tango Foxtrot, it seemed the only logical thing to do. Holden carried a pizza box with him to the kitchen door. He unlocked the door, entered the dimly lit kitchen, and immediately turned toward the security system to shut it off. He suddenly hesitated when he saw it was already disabled.

Holden swiftly drew his weapon while simultaneously placing the pizza box on the nearby counter. He scanned the dimly lit kitchen with his gun and listened for any unfamiliar sounds. He heard strange, eerie music coming from somewhere within the house. With his weapon aimed, Holden quietly crossed the kitchen and approached the archway to the living room. He could see a glow from the television that was now on, emitting the ominous music. Holden aimed his weapon into the living room and nearly collided with a large, heavyset man.

"Dude!" the man cried out in surprise, saw the gun, and jumped back a step.

Holden stared at the man with surprise. "Othello?" he gasped while lowering his weapon.

Othello was almost six-foot-tall and moderately heavyset, weighing about three hundred pounds. His dark, curly hair was somewhat wild and untamed, and the growth of seemingly haphazard facial hair was his attempt at growing a beard, not merely a man who had forgotten to shave. The friendly, approachable man wearing a superhero novelty t-shirt didn't look like a computer genius or possibly a criminal mastermind, but, when it came to Jackie's close circle of friends, looks were deceiving.

Holden's surprise quickly turned to concern. "What are you doing here?" he just about demanded. "Did something happen to Jackie?"

"Last I heard, she was fine," Othello insisted. "Sorry I couldn't give you a head's up before just showing up and, like, raiding your frig and all, but I'm maintaining radio silence as much as possible."

Holden replaced his weapon to his shoulder holster and relaxed. "If everything is okay, what are you doing here?" he asked.

"I assure you the team is safe," he informed Holden, "but there has been a lot of interest in Jackie's helicopter."

"Really?" Holden asked with a curious look. "What sort of interest?"

"People are trying to put an address to her helicopter," Othello replied.

"You took care of that, though, right?" Holden remarked, only mildly concerned. "That was part of the arrangement when Jackie started regularly working with the guys. Nothing can be traced back to our home."

"Yeah, of course, totally," Othello replied, then tensed. "It's just, well, there's been quite a few interested parties, and it's kind of made me a little tense."

"Quite a few?" Holden asked while eyeing the man. "How many is that?"

"About fifty-two," he replied.

Holden stared at the large man with some surprise. "Fifty-two? What exactly does that mean?"

"It means fifty-two people have shown an interest in Jackie's helicopter," he replied and now seemed slightly animated. "Everybody and their brother is attempting to trace that helicopter back to its origin."

"So they're looking for Jackie?"

"No, they're looking for her helicopter," Othello corrected.

"You're saying they ran into trouble, and her helicopter was spotted," Holden remarked.

"And that information spread like wildfire," Othello informed him. "I'm 99.9% confident they'll never trace that helicopter back to Jackie, you, or this house, but I'd rather not gamble with that .01%. I thought I'd hang out here and help, you know, cover your back."

"It wouldn't be the first time people have tried to kill me," Holden insisted.

"Yeah, but not *these* people," Othello reminded him. "So I'll, you know, keep an eye on things while you sleep and watch the house while you're at work." He then raised his brows and a tiny smile. "Maybe set up a motion detector perimeter around the property."

Holden smiled and managed a tiny laugh. "It's not necessary, Othello, but since you're already here, you may as well stay," he announced. "I brought pizza. Did you want some?"

"I'd never turn down pizza," Othello announced cheerfully. His expression suddenly dropped as his brows rose sharply. "It's not some weird vegetarian pizza, is it?"

Holden raised a cocky brow and withheld his laugh. "I think you've known me long enough to know that's not the case," he remarked.

Both men headed into the kitchen. Othello grabbed two bottles of beer from the refrigerator while Holden placed the pizza box on the island counter.

"Any idea what's going on with the guys?" Holden finally asked.

Othello shrugged and handed Holden a bottle of beer. "Light on details," he remarked, "but I assume everyone is still alive and kicking." He removed a slice of pizza from the box and set it on a paper plate. Othello then eyed Holden. "Does it bother you?"

"What's that?" Holden asked and took a slice of pizza as well.

"Jackie spending so much time running around on dangerous assignments."

Holden shrugged and then managed a smile. "I can't exactly be bothered when it's something that I do myself," he replied.

"Yeah, but what she does is, like, a thousand times more dangerous," Othello remarked then hesitated when he caught Holden's glare. "I mean, she's fine, I'm sure."

"I know what she does is dangerous," Holden replied while carrying his plate and bottle of beer into the living room with Othello following. "But if I asked her to stop, I'd be asking her to give up her identity. It's who she is, and I'm not going to stop that or change her by giving her some unrealistic ultimatum. If she wants to quit, I'll support her decision. If she wants to go on missions with the team, I'll support that too." Holden sat on the sofa and set his beer on the coffee table. "I know the team has her back." He then hesitated and considered the comment. "And I know Zack won't allow anything to happen to her."

Othello plopped down on the opposite end of the sofa and took a swig of his beer. "That's possibly the strangest relationship I've ever seen."

"It used to bother me," Holden remarked, then shrugged. "But after I got to know him, I know it's more of a strange fatherly, best friend sort of thing." He sighed. "Kind of like a faithful dog, I have little doubt he's already made himself comfortable in her bed, but I've come to realize that Zack's not sexually attracted to Jackie."

Othello cast a strange look at Holden but seemed to reconsider inserting his opinion. "Yeah, I'm sure you're right," he remarked and minded his pizza.

Chapter 32

Jackie woke from her light sleep, although uncertain what roused her from her slumber. The dormitory-style bedroom was mostly dark, not that there was much to see when it was light. The rooms were small and bland. Despite being considered full-size beds, they were barely a grade above cots and just a little bit bigger than a twin bed. Every movement on the cot-like bed could be felt and heard. When the cheap bed creaked, she was well aware of the reason behind it.

"Out, Zack," she muttered. "There's not enough room for both of us."

She heard Darth softly whine. Jackie lifted her head, looked at the foot end of the bed, and saw the dog through the dim lighting, making himself comfortable despite her comment. Jackie managed a tiny laugh.

"Sorry, Darth," Jackie announced and smiled wearily. "I didn't know it was you."

"See," Zack announced from alongside her, startling her, "there's plenty of room."

Jackie rolled partially onto her back and looked at Zack, who was comfortably on his side facing her. "What the hell--?" she muttered.

"I've been here over an hour, and you didn't even notice," he insisted. "If there hadn't been enough room, you would have complained earlier."

Jackie rolled her eyes and groaned. "One of these days, Holden is going to shoot you in your sleep."

"Holden knows I'm not going to do anything," he informed her. "Believe it or not, he trusts me. A bit misplaced, but he does."

"Seriously," Jackie informed him, "you need a new security blanket."

"Why?" he asked and sounded almost surprised. "My old one works just fine. Besides, under the circumstances, we shouldn't be alone. Danger could be lurking around every corner."

"If I stop arguing with you, will you shut up and go to sleep?"

"That's the only reason I'm here in the first place," Zack insisted. "Are we done arguing?"

Jackie groaned and returned to her side. "Yeah, we're done arguing."

"Good," Zack replied and moved closer to Jackie from behind and placed his arm around her while nestling against her.

Jackie removed his arm from around her waist. A moment passed, and he returned his arm to its original position. Jackie groaned and gave up. If she continued to fight him, she'd never get any sleep. She knew she'd never win anyway. Zack was a whole other level of stubborn.

"Hypothetical question," he announced close to her ear from behind, breaking the silence.

Jackie groaned and rolled onto her back, just about bumping into him due to limited space on the small bed. She glared at him, not in the mood to play games.

"What's the hypothetical question?"

"Would you be able to fly an Apache Attack Helicopter?" he asked.

She eyed him with surprise and couldn't even imagine why he'd ask such a question. "I suppose I could," Jackie replied and sighed, giving in to his little game. "Why?"

"Again, just hypothetical," he announced and moved onto his elbow while looking at her, "but if I could get my hands on one, would you be willing to fly it?"

Jackie stared at him and was at a loss for words. "Zack, that's a military *war* helicopter. Attack is literally right in its name," she informed him, now wide awake from the bizarre question. "If you tried to steal one, they'd kill you if they ever caught you. The same goes for me if I were caught flying it. We'd both be shot on sight."

"Well, yeah, I know," Zack replied, then shrugged. "That goes without say. I mean, we'd have to disappear forever, but we'd have an Apache Attack Helicopter." His eyes then widened. "With sixteen Hellfire missiles, seventy-six rockets, and twelve hundred chain gun rounds." He cocked his head and studied her through the dim lighting. "Honestly, what more could either of us really want from life?"

Jackie stared at him for a long moment, then shook her head. "I honestly don't know if you're actually serious," she announced. "I find that deeply disturbing."

Zack frowned and appeared to sulk while falling back onto his side. "I don't really feel I'm asking for all that much," he insisted. "If you truly cared about my happiness, you'd give me this one thing."

Jackie rolled back onto her side away from him, groaned, and buried her face in her pillow. "Go to sleep!"

When Zack fell silent, Jackie assumed he'd given up whatever crazy thoughts that were going through his head. Well, for the time being, at least. Jackie then allowed her thoughts to stray a moment. Although she hated to admit it, the thought of actually flying an Apache gave her tiny goosebumps. She took a moment to silently curse Zack for putting such ideas into her head.

§

Late the following morning within the clinic, Nevada sat behind the vet's desk with her feet propped up and a magazine in her lap. She looked bored. Marco had his arms through the bars, leaned on them, and watched her.

"There's no reason to keep me in here," he insisted. "Where the hell am I going to go?"

"You should be happy you're no longer tied," Nevada muttered without looking at him.

Marco was silent a long moment, but it was apparent he was working on his next strategy to convince the young woman to let him out of the cage.

"Exactly why would an attractive woman decide to become a bounty hunter?" Marco then asked.

"I like kicking the shit out of annoying men," she muttered without looking at him.

"Most women don't think I'm annoying," he boasted, then grinned. "Most women rather enjoy my company. I know how to treat women." Marco then sized her up. "I think, given a chance, you and I would really hit it off."

"I'd be the one doing all the hitting," Nevada informed him while casting a quick look at him across the room.

"A sexually dominant woman," he announced, then raised his brows suggestively. "I like that."

"There'd be nothing sexual about it," she remarked in turn, then sneered. "Keep talking, and I *will* come over there and shut you up."

Jackie entered the clinic, looked around, and spotted Marco locked in the gorilla cage. "Nice set-up," she announced her approval.

Marco smiled at Jackie and straightened. "Well, hello, Jackie," he announced while giving her a quick once-over. "I know we haven't met under the best circumstances--"

"We've met before," Jackie informed him. "I was at your wedding."

Marco's expression dropped to something less jovial at the comment. "Did you have a good time?" he muttered, now seeming disinterested.

"Your bride-to-be nearly killed my friend's girlfriend, and my best friend almost died saving my life," Jackie announced, then considered the question. "So, no, I didn't have a good time."

"Look," Marco announced with renewed hope, ignoring everything she'd just said. "Maybe you're more reasonable than the others. Let me out of here. Where am I going to go? I'm being hunted by countless bounty hunters and hitmen who'll shoot me on sight. The safest place for me to be is next to you and your friends."

"Ross prefers you in the cage," Jackie informed him. "Which means you stay in the cage."

"What if I promised to remain glued to your side?" Marco then asked and added a charming, almost lustful smile and suggestively raised his brows. "Think about it. That could be fun."

"Happily married," Jackie announced while wiggling her ring finger at him. "And even if I weren't, you're about as far from my type as a man can get." She turned her attention away from Marco and approached Nevada at the desk. "I'm sure someone else will watch him for a while. Give you a break from all that testosterone."

"No, it's my shift," Nevada informed her. "His mouth doesn't bother me. Almost all my bounties are men. You can believe me when I say I've heard it all."

Jackie smirked and sat on the edge of the desk facing the attractive, volatile woman. "I'm guessing that doesn't end so well for many of them."

Nevada shrugged and offered a tiny, almost humored smirk. "I've bruised a lot more than egos in my time," she replied almost proudly.

"I'll bet," Jackie teased while offering a humored smile. "Are you going back to the hotel in Maine when this is all over? A nine-way split of a buck twenty-five is certainly a nice chunk of change, but it's not life-altering."

Nevada tossed her magazine aside and met Jackie's gaze. "I don't think so," she replied.

Jackie was surprised by the comment then attempted a smile. "I thought you liked it there."

"Not really," Nevada replied, then sneered. "Everyone's so nice. It makes my skin crawl?"

"Nothing wrong with people being nice," Jackie informed her.

"I'd rather not discuss it," Nevada muttered and looked away.

Jackie studied her a moment, then nodded. "I understand," she announced, then stood. She actually felt quite sad for the woman. Someone must have hurt her deeply to make her so hateful toward others. She wasn't sure if Nevada knew Scorpio and Kane were Zack's kids, but she doubted that would make a difference or change her mind. "I'll just leave you to your shift."

As Jackie headed out of the clinic, Ross entered. They exchanged looks as if having a silent conversation about Nevada. Ross entered and looked around.

"Everything okay in here?" he asked, then indicated Marco. "Is Marco behaving?"

Nevada shrugged. "About the same," she replied.

"Ross, you copy?" Zack was heard through Ross's ear transmitter.

He touched his ear. "Yeah, Zack," he announced. "What's up?"

"We have company," Zack reported over his boss's ear transmitter.

Ross became alert. "What sort of company?"

"Looks like a Girl Scout," Zack replied. "Arriving from the north."

"North?" Ross just about exclaimed. "That's across the reserve. Who'd be coming from that direction?"

"Park ranger," Zack replied.

Ross suddenly groaned then spun to face Nevada, who was alerted by the part of the transmission she'd heard. "Watch Marco."

"What is it?" Nevada asked.

"Park ranger," Ross replied with a frown. "Probably nothing, but we don't want her becoming suspicious." He touched his ear transmitter. "All hands on deck. I want Jackie, Beck, and Monroe to meet me out front. The rest of you, hold your position."

Chapter 33

Bogart hurried out of the clinic after Jackie only a step behind her and appeared mildly upset. Jackie attempted to ignore her brother as he hounded her.

"Why wouldn't I be on the front line for this?" Bogart demanded while keeping pace with her. "When it comes to dealing with women, I'm the best you've got."

"This," Jackie insisted while vigorously indicating their interaction. "You tend to talk too much. You'll be inviting her to stay for lunch. Just go back to the clinic."

Bogart frowned and returned the way they had come. Jackie joined Ross, Beck, and Monroe, who stood in front of the visitor's center. Monroe handed Jackie a professional camera, which she placed around her neck to keep up appearances. He had a similar camera over his shoulder as well. Beck set up a telescope while Ross hung a pair of binoculars around his neck. They officially looked the part of their cover story.

"What's her twenty, Zack?" Ross asked through his transmitter while attempting to look casually at the trees through the binoculars.

"Twenty yards from me," Zack replied over their ear transmitters. "About two hundred yards from the clinic. She looks suspicious."

Ross finally spotted the uniformed park ranger through his binoculars. She was in her early thirties and rode on a large, gray horse. The horse's head suddenly turned in the direction of Zack's tree and snorted loudly.

"Hell," Zack scoffed through their ear transmitters. "The horse spotted me! Ratted out by a horse!"

§

The female park ranger looked in the direction the horse stared and scanned the area. The woman was a vision of the girl-next-door with a flawless complexion, long light brown hair, and a slender body. The lady in her late twenties had a mildly timid appearance, seeming somewhat shy and docile. Her delicate features almost made it impossible to believe she could be a park ranger, roughing it in the woods on a daily basis.

She patted the horse's neck while keeping watch. "What is it, boy?" the ranger asked, taking the horse's reaction seriously. "What do you see?"

When she didn't see anything, the ranger finally seemed to relax, apparently not suspecting anything. Without warning, she removed a high-powered rifle from the saddle holster and swiftly aimed it at the tree where Zack remained perched. She stared at him through the scope.

"You, in the tree," she yelled out, no longer seeming timid. "Hands where I can see them!"

"Crap," Zack muttered to his teammates via the ear transmitter.

"Do what she says, Zack," Ross informed him through his earpiece. "Nice and easy. This reserve is supposed to be abandoned. She's suspicious and possibly nervous."

Zack showed the ranger his hands from where he sat high in the tree. "Don't shoot," he announced. "I'm a photographer, not a terrorist."

The ranger didn't lower the rifle and continued to watch him through the scope. "Come down, nice and easy," she called to him.

"Coming down," Zack announced, then made his way down the tree.

The ranger kept the rifle locked on him, then hesitated and just about marveled at the way he scaled the tree. "Jesus," she muttered while taking her eyes off the scope to better appreciate his descent.

Zack jumped the last five feet, landing in a semi-crouched position.

The ranger admired his landing then, once again, raised the rifle. "Hands where I can see them," she instructed.

Zack did as she said.

"Who are you? What are you doing here?" she asked while remaining highly suspicious of him. "Show me some ID."

"It's back at camp," Zack informed her, then nodded in the direction of the sanctuary. "My friends are back at our camp within the sanctuary. They can vouch for me. We're just photographers."

"This is private property," she informed him. "Do you have permission from the owners to be here?"

"The former chairman of the board gave us permission," Zack informed her. "His name is Othello with P.R. Corporation. I can give you his contact information."

"There's no cell phone service out here," she informed him while slowly lowering the rifle.

"I know," Zack replied. "We have a radio."

"So do I," she announced. "I'll check out your story later. Let's have a look at your camp." She nodded in the direction of the main building and offered a mildly arrogant smirk. "After you."

"Can I put my hands down?" Zack asked.

"Can you show me your camera?" she quipped in response while raising her brows.

Zack glanced at his chest, realizing he was a photographer without a camera. "No, but I have my binoculars," he replied and indicated the binoculars tucked partially inside his jacket.

The ranger frowned and nodded. "Yeah, you can put your hands down," she replied but didn't seem happy about it. "Just don't make any sudden movements."

"As you wish," Zack replied, then walked past her and back for the visitor's center.

She nudged the horse with her heels and let the reins rest over the saddle horn so she could keep the rifle in both hands. The horse seemed to take cues without use of the reins. As they entered the clearing before the visitor's center, Ross, Jackie, Beck, and Monroe were now seen. Ross looked past Zack, saw the woman ranger, and offered his most charming smile.

"Leave it to Zack to make new friends in the middle of nowhere," Ross teased.

Zack glared his disapproval at Ross since the ranger couldn't see his face.

"Who are you people?" the woman asked while keeping the rifle cradled in her arms, ready at a moment's notice.

"I'm Ross," he announced, then indicated the others. "That's Jackie, Beck, and Monroe." He then nodded to Zack. "And I see you've already met our acrobatic friend, Zack."

"Thanks for the introductions," she replied, then raised a skeptical brow. "But not really what I meant. What are you doing here?"

"Zack didn't tell you we're photographers?" Ross asked with some surprise.

"He mentioned it," the ranger replied. "And you have permission to be here?"

"We have a friend at P.R. Corporation," Ross informed her. "He said we could camp here for a few weeks collecting photos. It's actually very exciting for us. One in our 'abandoned' collection."

"Can any of you produce some ID?" she asked with limited patience.

All four reached into their pockets. Without use of the reins, the ranger prompted the horse closer to Jackie. The horse stopped on command. She glanced at Jackie's driver's license, eyed Jackie, and then smiled more naturally as she slung the rifle over her shoulder.

"Sorry for that," the ranger announced and managed a tiny laugh. "I'm not used to finding people out this far. It's pretty isolated up here." She drew a deep breath and tensed slightly. "Usually, when I do find people up here, they're poachers, and that can get a little dicey."

"Understandable," Ross replied and returned his wallet to his pocket.

"Do you mind if I have a look around?" the ranger asked.

"Of course not," Ross announced while maintaining his smile. "Jackie could show you around."

"That's okay," the ranger announced, then indicated Zack. "Zack volunteered."

Zack appeared somewhat baffled and eyed Ross. Ross ignored the look Zack gave him. She singled Zack out for a reason, and that couldn't be good. They weren't out of the woods just yet with the lady ranger.

"I should probably tag along," Jackie insisted, then gave a nod to Zack. "Zack's more of our location scout than an operations guy."

"That would explain why I found him in a tree," the ranger insisted, then dismounted her horse.

"Zack enjoys climbing," Jackie informed her while offering a tiny smile. "That's why he makes such a great scout." She then indicated the visitor's center. "Our base is located in the visitor's center. It has everything we need, including a generator and running water." Jackie then glared at Zack and indicated the visitor's center.

Zack reluctantly joined them and headed toward the main building. The horse followed the ranger toward the building despite the reins remaining around the saddle horn. Jackie and Zack eyed the horse, instantly reminding them of certain other horses they'd come across in the past.

The ranger noticed the looks they gave the horse and managed a tiny laugh. "Never mind Smokey," she insisted. "He thinks he's a dog."

Jackie then glanced at the ranger. "I'm sorry," she announced politely. "I didn't catch your name."

"Samantha," the ranger announced. "You can call me Sam."

All three entered the now cleaned visitor's center, where the team had set up several cots that were neatly made with blankets and pillows. There were a few portable ice chests and several duffle bags to keep up appearances. Zack approached one of the duffle bags and removed something.

"Well, Sam," Jackie announced cheerfully and indicated the lobby of the visitor's center. "This is our main operation right here."

Sam looked around at the arranged cots. "How many of you are there?"

"Well, there's the five of us you've just met," Jackie announced. "And four others."

Zack approached and handed the ranger his driver's license. Sam glanced at the license, eyed Zack, and then returned it. She then cast a look between Jackie and Zack.

"You two live together?" Sam asked.

Jackie immediately tensed and cast a look at Zack. The strange question caught her off guard.

"Yes," Zack replied without hesitation.

Jackie smiled and nodded in agreement, although she was somewhat stunned by the news. Sam seemed to focus her attention on Jackie and raised a curious brow.

"What's his last name?" Sam asked while shifting her eyes in Zack's direction.

Jackie felt her heart pounding at the question. She didn't know what name was on the identification Zack showed the ranger. Zack went by dozens of last names and had identifications to match each identity. What were the odds he actually had an ID with his real last name on it? Zack placed his fingers to his temple, scratching it in something resembling a salute.

"Remus," Jackie replied without hesitation.

Sam smiled and laughed. "Sorry about that," she replied and shook her head. "I'm far too suspicious for my own good. You just acted kind of strange when I asked if you lived together."

"Well," Jackie remarked and shifted slightly. "I didn't realize he had chosen my address as his home address. He divides his time between my house, a friend's house, and with his children."

Sam then glanced at Zack. "You have children?" she asked. "How old are they?"

Zack was uncomfortable talking about himself, but he took the personal question in stride. He had to suck it up and play along. Although, he might have been secretly cursing Jackie for involving him in the conversation.

"They're twenty-two," he replied, then shifted. "Twin boy and girl."

"Twins?" Sam remarked and offered a pleasant smile. "That must be great."

Zack shrugged. "My daughter hasn't exactly warmed up to me yet," he replied.

"You weren't around when they were growing up?" Sam asked.

Jackie was now feeling slightly uncomfortable. For the average person, it was just polite conversation. For someone like Zack, it was intrusive and more information than he'd usually give.

"Their mother died shortly after they were born," Zack announced and seemed tense admitting the truth, but it was a lot easier than making up something on the spot. "Her father didn't approve of me and kept them from me."

"I'm so sorry," Sam replied, then tensed. "I didn't mean to open old wounds." She fidgeted slightly. "I should probably be going. If you have any problems or spot any suspicious activity, you can contact me on the radio twenty-four hours a day." She then eyed both and smiled. "It was nice meeting you. Have a nice afternoon."

Chapter 34

Ross laid out a map of the reserve, showing where the different animals were kept back when it was operational. As the guys gathered around the vet clinic's examination table to look at the map, Nevada leaned against the cage bars. Marco leaned his shoulder against the bars on his side of the cage and watched the meeting of the minds across the room.

"What are they up to?" Marco asked while giving a nod in the direction of the guys.

"None of your fucking business," she retorted with little emotion.

Marco shook his head while staring at her profile. "I hope you never need another favor from my father," he remarked. "I know you used to do some work for him."

Nevada eyed Marco with little emotion. "You should be less worried about me needing favors from your father and worry more about your own issues with him," she snarled. "He may want the guys to keep you alive, but that doesn't mean he's forgiven you for being a shitty-ass son."

"Who says I was a shitty-ass son?" Marco demanded.

She cast a look at him and raised an arrogant brow. "You've been sulking around since your wedding day massacre, blaming everyone else for what happened," Nevada snarled with detest. "Never once placing blame on that psychotic bitch you were set to marry for her role." Nevada cocked her head.

"Boo hoo, Marco. You should be damned grateful that bitch was taken out before she had the chance to take you out. You have the world by the balls, yet you choose to be the poor, little victim all the time. I'd give anything to have *your* problems over mine."

"Your problems, huh?" Marco retorted and straightened. "Let's discuss Nevada's problems. First off, you're the one on the free side of these bars, and every bounty hunter and hitman isn't trying to kill you for something you didn't do. But let's not focus on the obvious."

Nevada glared at him and showed no emotion.

"As far as I can see, all of your problems are self-created," Marco announced while raising his brows. "You're so terrified of becoming emotionally attached to anyone that you run away the moment you have the slightest feelings for them. You're so afraid that no one will love you that you do everything in your power to keep people away, so you'll never know how they really feel."

"Shut up," Nevada snarled.

"Make me," Marco snapped back and moved just far enough away from the bars while holding his arms out to his side. "That's why you want out of that new safe house Zack found for you, isn't it? What's his name? Kane? I overheard what you were telling Ross. It's not his clinginess that's the problem, is it? It's your fear of allowing yourself to like him that's the real problem. You're so terrified of emotional commitment that you'll do anything to avoid it."

Nevada sneered and lunged for him.

Marco smirked at her anger and cocked his head. "Hit a nerve, didn't I?" A strange grin crossed his face. "He's young and good looking, isn't he? A real catch, I'll bet. Your worst fear is that you're not good enough for someone like him. You know it, but you're afraid to actually hear it."

"I swear," she snarled. "I will take you in dead if you don't shut up."

"Knock it off over there," Kirk yelled at them.

Nevada stormed away from Marco.

Ross rolled out a larger map of the county that clearly showed every road anywhere near the sanctuary. He pointed at the map. "This is the bird aviary at the north side of the reserve," he announced, then pointed to another area just a short distance away. "So this has to be the ranger station just half a mile from the back edge of the sanctuary."

"That puts Sam in close proximity. Only about a mile from the visitor's center," Beck muttered while shaking his head. "We have a beautiful set up here. I'd hate for her to ruin it for us."

"My thoughts too," Ross announced while deep in thought. "I'd like to see what sort of set up she has there. How many rangers work there? How much contact do they have with the rest of the world?"

"How do you intend to do that?" Zack asked while leaning against the nearby support beam. "Her horse is like a bloodhound. It's as if they communicate telepathically or something."

"Kind of like Monique and Colleen with their horses," Bogart teased.

"We'll just have to outsmart her horse," Ross informed them.

"How do you outsmart a horse?" Monroe asked suspiciously.

"Jackie and Gil will pay Sam a little visit tomorrow morning," Ross replied. "Darth should be enough of a distraction for the horse. That should give Zack and Kirk enough room to scope out the rest of the area around the ranger's station." He eyed the guys. "Any questions?"

"I have one," Jackie announced, then looked at the guys while raising a curious brow. "According to what's on your IDs, how many of you are living with me?"

Bogart raised his hand in the air, but that was to be expected since he did live with her some of the time. The rest of the guys avoided looking at her.

Jackie's expression dropped. "All of you?" she gasped, stunned that they'd all do that to her.

"Just on our fake IDs," Beck insisted while flashing an innocent smile. "I mean, we can't exactly use our real addresses on our fake IDs."

"What happened to the backup address in Colorado Springs?" she demanded. "Why aren't you using that address anymore?"

"They turned that building into a convenient store," Monroe informed her. "We just didn't see the point to renting out another place just for a fake address. You live in Colorado Springs. It's convenient."

"Yeah, until someone checks our IDs and question our living arrangement," Jackie huffed. "Miss Park Ranger thinks we're living in some sort of free love commune. Very nice of you guys to at least give me a head's up."

The men chuckled.

"Sorry about that," Ross replied despite hiding his grin that suggested he wasn't really all that sorry. He was quite possibly amused.

"In the spirit of full disclosure," Gil announced. "I have, on occasion, used Holden's office fax number as my home phone number."

Kirk suddenly snorted a laugh and leaned back in the nearby desk chair. "Who doesn't?"

There was a round of chuckles.

Jackie shook her head. "You guys are the worst."

§

The following morning, Jackie and Gil made the hike across the sanctuary and to the ranger station, which was almost a mile from the visitor's center. Darth led the parade, sniffing and marking every tree along the way. Zack and Kirk made the hike as well, but they lagged behind by several yards, keeping to Jackie and Gil's right and left. If Sam's horse noticed them, Sam would assume it was just the man and woman that caught the horse's attention.

"This is nice," Gil announced while looking around and smiling. "Just you and me for a change. Ross rarely pairs us up together."

"Probably because he needs both of us to fly. Let's face it," Jackie remarked. "You and I are glorified chauffeurs."

Gil chuckled, amused at the comment. "Air taxi," he teased.

"Sky Uber."

Both laughed.

"He's only sending me because of my gender," Jackie informed Gil. "I get it. Sending two guys might make Sam uncomfortable. She may feel less threatened with another woman."

"Yeah, but when you're not teamed up with Zack, Ross usually teams you up with Monroe," Gil remarked. "I wonder why he didn't send him."

"Probably because you're low-key, whereas Monroe is a bit high-strung," Jackie replied and shrugged. "If not for Sam's benefit, then for mine."

Gil suddenly chuckled and eyed her. "Why's that?"

"I love Monroe dearly, but the guy needs a girlfriend," Jackie informed him. "He gets in his moods, and then he turns nostalgic. When he turns nostalgic, he brings up uncomfortable subjects, and I don't want to keep revisiting that part of my life. I don't need that constant reminder."

"I hear you," Gil replied and watched the German shepherd roaming the woods ahead of them. He then looked back at her. "Have you ever been paired up with Beck or Kirk?"

Jackie suddenly chuckled loudly and shook her head. "Hell no!"

Gil appeared curious. "Is that by design?"

"I don't have anything against Beck," Jackie insisted, "but he and I *don't* see eye-to-eye. We fight more than Monroe and Beck when we're alone together."

"I never knew that," Gil remarked. "What's the story with you and Kirk not working together?"

She cast a look at Gil. "Are you serious?" she practically demanded. "The man has no filter between his brain and his mouth. If he got laid that week, he's telling me about it in graphic detail."

"Oh, he does that with you too?" Gil asked, then chuckled. "I guess he's comfortable around you."

"A little too comfortable," she replied. "I'd like to assume it's because he thinks of me as one of the boys, but then he'll ask me if Zack and I are *doing it*." Jackie then eyed Gil. "But, of course, in Kirk's unfiltered language."

Gil snorted a laugh and shook his head. There was a long moment of silence between them. Gil then looked at her. "You aren't, right?"

Jackie looked at Gil with some surprise. "No, of course not," she practically shouted, then turned defensive. "What's wrong with you?"

"Sorry," he quickly announced and recoiled. "It's just one of those 'guy thoughts' that we have. I mean, it's definitely possible. Zack's been known to jump into bed with some pretty wild women, and everyone knows there's nothing wrong with your sex drive."

Jackie suddenly stopped and stared at Gil with surprise. She was stunned to hear him say something like that. Any of the other guys, but not Gil. Gil realized she was no longer beside him, stopped, and turned to face her.

"Since when do you talk like that?" she practically demanded.

"Come on, Jackie," Gil replied and held back his tiny grin. "You and Holden woke up the entire house the other morning, and Bogart's complained on more than one occasion about the noise coming from your bedroom."

"The bastard," Jackie scoffed.

"It's nothing to be ashamed of," Gil remarked. "I think it's good for a healthy relationship."

Jackie shook her head and continued along the path past Gil, who then hurried to catch up with her. "From now on, I'm insisting on being paired with Zack," she muttered.

They walked the rest of the way to the ranger's station in silence. As the station and barn came into view, Gil stopped Jackie at the woods' edge and forced her to face him. His look was apologetic and sincere.

"I'm sorry, Jackie," Gil announced somewhat timidly. "I didn't mean to upset and or embarrass you."

Jackie managed a tiny smile. "You're forgiven," she replied. "Fortunately for you, I like you."

Darth entered the clearing and approached Sam as she tossed some hay to her gray horse in the paddock. Sam saw the dog and appeared surprised.

"Hey, there," Sam announced and crouched down to the friendly dog. "Are you lost?"

She scratched Darth's scruff and then checked his collar. As Gil and Jackie entered the clearing, Sam straightened, recognized Jackie, and smiled.

"Oh, hey," Sam announced, then indicated Darth. "Does this guy belong to you?"

"Yeah," Gil replied cheerfully. "Darth is friendly."

"I see," Sam replied and again petted the dog, then eyed Gil. "I don't believe we've met."

"Sam, this is Gil," Jackie announced, then indicated the dog. "And you've met Darth."

"It's a pleasure to meet you, Gil," Sam replied, then looked around, seeming a little overly curious as if looking for others. "Just the two of you?"

"The rest of the guys are around somewhere," Jackie informed her as they approached. "We were exploring the area and saw the ranger's station." She looked around then smiled at Sam. "Nice little set up you have here."

"Not the Ritz," Sam remarked, then indicated the satellite dish on top of the barn, "but I have satellite television and internet."

"The place is bigger than I thought it would be," Jackie remarked.

The ranger's station looked more like a three-bedroom ranch house than an out-of-the-way fort. The siding was recently power washed, giving it a clean appearance. There was a small front porch containing two rocking chairs and some hanging plants. There wasn't much in the way of landscaping, but the few bushes were neatly trimmed, and other plants were meticulously tended. The place certainly benefited from a woman's touch.

"Where are the rest of the guys?" Gil asked while looking around. "Sleeping in?"

Sam snorted a laugh. "Hardly," she replied. "No, it's just me. Well, me and Smokey." She indicated the horse. "Other than the occasional lost hiker or stray poacher, the job's not very demanding." She then indicated the station. "I just put on the kettle. Did you want some coffee or tea?"

"We'd love some," Jackie announced.

§

While Jackie and Sam had tea and talked at the table, Gil wandered along the main living area and studied the old framed photos on the walls. Some were from over one hundred years ago. Sam happily played with Darth, who sat at her feet almost the entire time. He was enjoying the ear scratches a little too much. The cabin's main living area was an open concept with the kitchen, dining area, and living room all in one large room. The walls were natural wood as well as the ceiling with exposed beams. There were several ceiling fans on the cathedral ceiling, and the many windows allowed plenty of daylight to flood the room. The ranger's station was warm and inviting with a large screen television, a full library of DVDs, and a large bookcase filled with hundreds of books. There were two bedrooms and at least one bathroom that Jackie could see from where she sat at the kitchen table.

"I hope I don't sound disrespectful," Gil announced while glancing at the photos, "but don't you get bored up here by yourself?"

Sam smiled and chuckled in her throat. "It's not disrespectful," she announced. "Unfortunately, I'm a bit of a recluse. I like being alone with nature."

Gil paused by the large bookcase and eyed hundreds of books, both hardcover and paperback. "I'm guessing you spend a lot of time reading."

"What gave me away?" she teased, then smiled eagerly. "Everything from romance to horror. I love fiction of every genre." Sam retreated into her own thoughts a moment and shrugged. "I enjoy writing too."

"What do you write?" Jackie asked while sipping her tea.

Sam seemed somewhat bashful now as if reluctant to talk about it. "Oh, a little of this and that."

Jackie suddenly grinned and leaned a little closer. "Is that code for erotica?" she teased just loud enough for Sam to hear so she wouldn't embarrass her in front of Gil.

Sam giggled and waved her off. "I wouldn't mind a little of that, to be honest," she replied. "But my ex-boyfriend killed whatever lust I'd had pent up inside me." She met Jackie's gaze and raised her brows. "In other words, I write mostly crime fiction and horror."

Jackie couldn't help but laugh.

Sam then shifted her eyes in Gil's direction while staring at Jackie. "Are you two, you know, together?"

Jackie tensed slightly then laughed. "No, Gil and I are just friends."

Sam then indicated Jackie's ring finger. "But you are married, aren't you?"

"Yes, I'm married," she replied. "But my husband isn't into photography." Jackie then shrugged. "Or the outdoors. Or camping."

"He doesn't mind you going away with a bunch of guys for weeks at a time?" Sam asked.

"He's used to it," Jackie replied. "His work keeps him very busy."

"My ex-boyfriend was a bit of a workaholic too," Sam muttered, then frowned. "Even though he wasn't around much, that didn't stop him from keeping tabs on my every move. That's why I love it up here. No one keeping tabs on me every second of the day. I don't answer to anyone, but my superiors, and even they leave me alone unless there's a problem." She smiled and sighed. "I love the freedom."

"I hear you," Jackie replied. "Out in the woods, alone, with just a camera." She smiled. "That's bliss."

"I feel the same way about writing," Sam informed her almost excitedly. "Smokey and I go out for hours and just take it all in. Sets the mind free."

Jackie couldn't exactly admit it to Sam, but that's how she felt when she was flying, especially when she was flying solo. It was peaceful in the sky by herself. During solo flights, she mostly reminisced about her father and all the time they'd spent together flying.

"If you're interested," Sam announced, snapping Jackie out of her thoughts. "There's an amazing spot a little further up the mountain. It's kind of steep. There's an old tower at the top. Climb up that tower, and you can see for miles. I travel up there once a month just for a little extra inspiration. You'd probably get some great pictures."

"Thanks," Jackie announced. "We'll check it out another time. Maybe sunrise or sunset one of these days."

"I'll try to swing by and check on you and your party every couple of days," Sam informed her. "In the meantime, if you have any problems, just give me a shout over the radio. I always have it on."

Chapter 35

Zack relaxed within the crook of the tree that afternoon and shut his eyes a moment. The sun was shining, it was pleasantly warm, and the reserve was peaceful and serene. The faint sound of saddle leather creaking could be heard, breaking the silence. Zack's eyes popped open, and he looked around without barely moving. He saw Sam on her gray horse almost thirty yards away and heading toward the visitor's center. Zack groaned and lightly touched his ear transmitter.

"Look alive, the Lone Ranger is twenty clicks and closing," he announced.

Zack remained completely still and watched as the horse and rider seemed to pass without noticing him. He again shut his eyes.

"Hey, Zack," Sam's voice was heard.

Zack's eyes suddenly popped open. He looked around and saw both Sam and her horse now turned and riding back toward him. The horse gave him away again! Damned horse and its enormous ears that heard everything!

"Catnapping in the tree?" Sam teased as she stopped her horse not far from his tree while staring up at him.

"Seemed the logical thing to do," Zack reported, seeming slightly uncomfortable. It wasn't often he was caught doing his thing.

"Understandable. It's an unseasonably warm afternoon," she informed him. "Most of the photogenic wildlife will be taking the afternoon off."

"The photographer too," he replied and even managed a tiny smile. At least this time, he had a camera to back up his story.

"I found some homemade fudge in the freezer," she announced and patted her saddlebag. "I thought maybe you and your friends would like it. I'm seriously addicted to the stuff and don't trust myself around it."

"Kirk will relieve you of it, I'm sure," Zack informed her with little emotion.

Sam appeared curious and cocked her head. "I don't think I've met him yet," she replied.

"Show up with food; he'll appear out of thin air," Zack remarked.

"Are you going back to the visitor's center for lunch?" she asked with what seemed like more than a passing interest.

Zack considered the comment. "I suppose I should," he remarked, opting to do whatever it took to lower the ranger's suspicions.

"Want a lift?"

Zack eyed the horse with a curious look then met Sam's gaze. "Can I drive?"

"Well, I'm not sure what you mean by that," Sam teased then smiled, "but, yeah, sure."

Zack swiftly descended the tree and jumped the last few feet, once again sticking the impressive landing. Sam watched him and appeared equally as astonished as she had the first time she'd watched him make the jump.

"You're really very good at that," she marveled.

"I've had a lot of practice," he replied, then approached the left side of the horse.

Sam removed her foot from the stirrup and extended her hand to him. She was a little surprised when he grabbed her wrist in a combat catch. He easily scaled the horse, barely using the stirrup, and swung behind her. Sam was slightly set back by his spry mounting style.

"I've been riding a long time, and I couldn't do that on my best day," she informed him.

"I do quite a bit of climbing," he announced while situating himself behind her.

As Zack reached around her for the reins, she jumped with some surprise. Despite agreeing to let him 'drive', she obviously hadn't been expecting him to reach around her as he did. He certainly wasn't shy about it. For as surprised as she was with his hand reaching around her for the reins, she was twice as surprised when he anchored his right arm around her waist. He gently nudged the horse with his heels, having learned his lesson after riding a friend's horse. Sam seemed undecided about where to put her now free hands, consciously aware of the man's arm around her waist. She finally rested one hand on the saddle horn and the other on the cantle beneath that. They rode a short distance on the trail in the woods before reaching the clearing about one hundred yards from the visitor center. Zack sent the horse into a canter, just about startling Sam.

As they approached the visitor center, Jackie, Bogart, and Monroe watched the riders on the horse approaching at a fast pace. Zack slowed the horse and stopped near his friends. All three seemed to be paying more attention to the woman ranger than Zack. Sam wore a strange smile on her face and attempted to cover her flushed cheeks.

"That was fun," Zack announced, then swiftly slid off the horse without using the stirrups, although he had little trouble holding onto Sam's knee as he dismounted.

Sam seemed excessively giddy now and couldn't even look at the others. "I, uh, picked up a hitchhiker," she announced, then finally found the courage to look at Jackie, Monroe, and Bogart.

"Sam brought fudge," Zack informed them.

As Sam dismounted, Kirk suddenly appeared near them and approached. "Did someone mention fudge?"

Sam appeared surprised and glanced at Zack. "Is that Kirk?"

Zack grinned and nodded. "His stomach has good hearing," he replied.

Sam stared at Kirk as he approached them. Her expression dropped at the sight of the large man. "Jesus, he's big," she gasped a little too loudly.

Jackie tensed slightly and eyed the guys as Sam opened her saddlebag. They all shared the same concerned looks. They had to play nice or risk seeming suspicious. As Sam turned with the brick of fudge wrapped in foil within a plastic bag in her hand, Jackie immediately smiled.

"Did you want to stay for lunch?" Jackie asked and just about cringed at the offer. It was the polite and least suspicious thing to do.

"I have my lunch with me," Sam announced, "but I'd love to have someone to eat with for a change."

"There are some clean tables in the visitor's center," Jackie reported, then nodded to the main building. "Grab your lunch and join us. We have water, soda, and iced tea."

"Thanks," Sam replied, then extended the brick of fudge to them.

Kirk reached for it.

Monroe glared at Kirk and took the package from Sam. "We're not falling for that trick again," he snarled at his brawny teammate.

§

In order to keep up appearances, the guys joined Sam for lunch in the visitor's center. Gil and Nevada were the only two who remained mysteriously absent. Someone had to stay with Marco, and someone had to watch the perimeter. Nevada was more than happy to remain on prisoner detail since she was anti-social anyway. Gil just happened to have a better stake-out position when Sam called, so he stayed out to keep watch for intruders. Sam seemed typical for someone who had gone without social interaction for a while. Initially, she was slightly introverted, but she was soon happily striking up conversations with the guys. Despite Zack's unique ability to avoid people and socialization in general, Sam seemed to keep her attention focused on him. The rest of the team found humor in Zack's forced socialization and his obvious discomfort for the role he had to play.

Once lunch was over, and the fudge was devoured, it was time for Sam to take her leave. She was grateful to use their bathroom before leaving since she didn't often have an actual toilet while out patrolling away from the ranger's station. While she was in the ladies' room, all eyes were on Zack, and his teammates seemed to be sharing strange smiles.

"What?" Zack demanded with some irritation by their stares. "I played nice."

"She likes you," Monroe teased.

"What are you talking about?" Zack snapped back while shooting a glare at Monroe.

"She was flirting," Monroe pressed, finding humor in Zack's inability to read women.

"I'd think I'd know if a woman were flirting with me," Zack remarked and attempted to ignore the looks he was receiving.

"Zack," Jackie announced with a sigh, unwilling to let her comrades continue their torment of her partner. "She was definitely flirting with you."

"Anyone else find that weird?" Kirk asked while downing the last piece of fudge.

"Personally, I have no idea what any woman would find appealing about Zack," Beck insisted, then shrugged. "Especially an intelligent woman like that."

"Fuck you, Beck," Zack scoffed, then stood and snatched his camera from the counter. "Excuse me; I have photographer things to do."

As Zack headed for the visitor's center door, Ross called after him. "Stick around to thank Sam for stopping by and bringing fudge," Ross announced.

Zack didn't respond to Ross as he headed out the door. Sam returned from the ladies' restroom, which was on the other side of the large lobby. She immediately noticed Zack's disappearance and looked somewhat disappointed. It only seemed to prove the point the guys were attempting to make. Sam wasn't suspicious of Zack; she *liked* him.

"Thanks for letting me join you for lunch," Sam announced to the guys.

She was greeted with a round of thanks for the fudge. Jackie then walked her to the door. Sam now seemed uncomfortable.

"Zack had to leave, huh?" Sam asked, seeming somewhat disappointed.

"He's not the most social person," Jackie informed her, then managed a tiny smile. "I'm kind of amazed he stuck around as long as he did."

Sam stopped Jackie just before the door, now that they were out of earshot of the others. "I was kind of curious. How is it Zack lives with you, you know, being you're married to someone else?" She immediately backtracked the question. "I mean, it's really none of my business; I'm just trying to understand the situation between you two."

Jackie managed a humored laugh. "I suppose it can seem strange to some," she replied, then more or less answered truthfully. "Zack served in the military with my father, so he's always been a large part of my life. It's made us close. I guess you could say he lives a bit of the nomad life, but he's slowly transitioning to a more stable home life, especially now that he's trying to bond with his kids."

"It's kind of ironic," Sam remarked.

"What's that?" Jackie asked.

Sam frowned and shrugged. "Every guy I've ever taken an interest in is never emotionally available," she reported, then sighed. "It's a curse of mine."

"Well, I wish I could tell you you're wrong about Zack," Jackie remarked, then sighed. "But he's about as emotionally unavailable as they come. Bonding with his son has been a very good experience for him." Jackie then frowned. "I just wish his daughter would warm up to him, but she shares a lot of his less charming traits."

"That's too bad," Sam remarked then hesitated. "I mean that she hasn't warmed up to him."

"She tends to keep her emotions buried pretty deep inside, too," Jackie remarked. "Although everyone believed her reserved boyfriend was what she needed most, I often wonder if she'd do better with someone more outgoing."

"Sounds like Zack needs that too," Sam remarked.

"Zack's done the 'outgoing' girlfriend type," Jackie remarked. "Unfortunately, they've been outgoing in a bad way."

"So he has a type?" Sam teased, then seemed a little embarrassed.

"Yeah, pretty much," Jackie replied with a tiny sigh. "I suppose mild to moderately psychotic would be his preferred type."

Sam managed an embarrassed laugh. "Good to know," she replied, then seemed defeated but forced a tiny smile. "Thanks for the talk, Jackie. I appreciate it. If you're in the area, feel free to drop by the ranger's station any time. I don't mind the company."

It was painfully obvious Sam was extremely lonely, despite her insistence that she enjoyed the solitude. Eventually, everyone looked for some form of human bonding. Jackie never had that problem. She'd rarely been alone a day in her life. Growing up, her father's military buddies were always in and out of her life. Now that she was an adult; that was still the case.

"Well, I do want to check out that tower one of these mornings," Jackie replied. "Maybe I'll drop by after I've taken some photos."

"I'd love to see them," Sam announced, then finally left the building.

As Sam walked outside, she paused when she saw Zack nuzzling with the horse, who appeared to be enjoying a good ear scratching. Sam hid her smile and approached.

"You boys getting along?" she teased, then approached the side of the horse and tightened the girth she had previously loosened.

Zack moved away from the horse's head as if he'd been caught doing something wrong. "Just 'guy talk'," he casually replied.

"Not sure if that's good or bad," Sam remarked, then glanced at Zack, almost unable to make eye contact with him while hiding her smile. "I thought you'd be back up in your tree already."

"If you're heading back that way, I thought you could give me a lift," Zack remarked.

Sam glanced at Zack with some surprise, then immediately hid her smile. "Uh, yeah, sure," she replied. "But if it's okay with you, I'd like to drive this time."

"Yeah, I get that a lot," Zack remarked with little emotion. "I've been told I'm an aggressive driver."

Sam chuckled at the comment then mounted the horse. She removed her foot from the stirrup and extended her hand to him. Zack grabbed her wrist, although she was prepared for it this time, and swung on the horse's back behind her. Despite that he wasn't 'driving', he still anchored his right arm securely around her waist. Even though she had been anticipating the action, she was still taken somewhat off-guard by it. They rode at a leisurely walk across the clearing and eventually into the woods. It only took a few minutes, even at a walk, to reach the area where she'd found him.

"I believe this is your stop," Sam teased, then seemed to curse herself for the bad joke.

Zack appeared hesitant to dismount. He then placed his foot in the stirrup, despite not needing it to dismount last time, and reached around her with his left hand, catching onto the saddle horn. As Zack moved from the horse's back, he placed his knee on the saddle behind her and stood in the stirrup to her side, positioning himself securely. Sam eyed his action with bewilderment. Without warning, Zack placed his hand to her face, kissing her passionately and with some aggression. Sam immediately tensed at the aggressiveness of the kiss. Zack broke off the kiss and met her moderately stunned gaze. She seemed almost shocked.

Zack immediately looked away as if realizing his mistake. "Sorry," he announced, then frowned. "I took some bad advice."

Before Sam could even respond or react, Zack jumped backward off the horse. He no sooner landed on the ground when he returned to his tree. Sam finally snapped out of her shocked state and watched him scale the tree with little to no effort.

"I'll, uh, see you around," Sam replied, then kicked the horse and took off across the woods, in a hurry to get away as fast as possible.

Zack sat on the thick branch, leaned back against the tree, and groaned with some irritation. He then tapped his ear transmitter. "Jackie, you copy?"

"Yeah, Zack," Jackie replied over his earpiece.

"You were wrong about Sam," he snapped with irritation. "She wasn't flirting, and she's certainly not interested in me. Next time, keep your advice to yourself."

"My advice?" Jackie announced over his transmitter. "What advice? What did you do?"

"Zack out," he scoffed and angrily tapped his ear transmitter.

Chapter 36

Zack lay on his back on the tallest rock formation within the lion's enclosure and watched the sunset. The top of the tall, faux rock gave a fantastic view of most of the sanctuary. The habitat itself had a tall, chain-link fence covered in fake vegetation to conceal it, giving the impression of an open enclosure while keeping the predatory animals secure from their would-be prey. Jackie stood at the bottom of the rock formation and looked up at the man who was quite possibly sleeping. Zack looked a little too 'at home' in the predator's habitat. It was almost fitting, except the fences that kept in the wild cats would never contain Zack. Jackie groaned, knowing Zack was purposely ignoring her calls over his transmitter, and she was forced to climb the man-made rocks to the top. Despite that she now stood over him; he didn't bother opening his eyes.

"What do you want?" he snarled.

"Why the hell are you mad at me?" she demanded and sat down beside him.

Zack opened his eyes and sat up, glaring at her. "You told me the ranger was flirting with me," he scoffed. "I foolishly made the first move, and now she probably thinks I'm some sort of pervert." He angrily held up his finger as if making a point. "And, although that may be true, I'm only a pervert among close friends."

Jackie stared at him with a strange look, latching on to the part of the conversation that struck a chord with her. "First move?" she asked with some concern. "What do you mean?" A concerned look crossed her face. "Please tell me you didn't just grab the poor girl and kiss her."

"Well, that would be the first move, now wouldn't it?" he demanded, then shook his head. "This is why I prefer letting the woman make the first move. At least then I know what's expected from me."

Jackie groaned softly, placed her hand over her eyes, and shook her head. There were times Zack could be impossibly clueless, and it usually involved women. "I said she was flirting, Zack," she insisted, then shot a look at him. "That doesn't mean she was looking for you to jump on her."

"How the hell am I supposed to know what you mean if you don't say what you mean?"

"Only in your world would 'flirting' possibly mean 'take me now'," Jackie snapped back.

"This coming from the woman who handcuffed a federal agent to a bed the third time they'd met," Zack scoffed.

"Okay, that was different," she huffed and recalled the erotic moment with great fondness. Jackie returned to reality. "And it was the fourth time."

"How was that different?" he demanded.

"I handcuffed Holden to the bed in order to escape being taken into federal custody," she insisted.

Zack rolled his eyes and avoided looking at her. "So we're going to pretend you didn't hump him, huh?"

Jackie felt her cheeks redden at being called out. She now wished she'd never told Zack about that incident. "It's still different," she insisted. "Sam isn't one of your 'hit and runs', Zack. She's not Katya or any of your other fuck buddies."

Zack shot a glare at Jackie. "I don't find that amusing," he snapped.

"It wasn't meant to be," Jackie replied, then held her breath a moment and sighed. "I sincerely doubt that Sam is looking for a hook-up, and, if she were, she most certainly isn't looking for a 'hit-and-run'. She wants the whole sexual-emotional experience."

Zack frowned and looked away. "I don't do that," he remarked. "Not since Maggie."

"I think you should apologize to Sam," Jackie informed him.

"Will that be enough?" he asked while eyeing her. "I feel really bad about kissing her like that. She seemed pretty upset by it."

"You can only apologize," Jackie insisted and drew a calming breath. "It was a misunderstanding."

"Should I go up there right now?"

Jackie stared at him with horror in her eyes. She sometimes wondered what went through his head. "Yeah, I'm sure that won't freak her out in the least," she muttered, then groaned. "No, just wait for her to come back this way in a day or two. You don't want her to feel cornered, especially if she's fearful of you now."

Zack groaned and lay back down on the rock. "Women are complicated," he muttered. "It's no wonder I can't connect with my daughter. You're all crazy."

§

The following morning, Jackie emerged from her dormitory-style bedroom, still dressed in her sleep shorts and a tank top, looking disheveled after a mildly rough night. She had her towel and shower kit in hand and headed for the locker room and shower area. Most of their safe houses had individual bathrooms with showers or tubs. She wasn't used to the dormitory-style shower facilities, particularly the co-ed kind. The facility only had one shower room. Jackie felt reasonably confident the showers wouldn't be in use by the other guys this early in the morning. Zack was already up and about for nearly an hour, so she wasn't worried about him occupying the showers. Kirk wouldn't be up until noon if left to his own devices, and the rest of the guys were probably just dragging themselves out of bed right about now.

Jackie knocked on the closed locker room door. When there was no response, she tried the door. Since it wasn't locked, the shower was available. She entered and locked the door behind her. The locker room was less than impressive, with several rows of old lockers containing benches. The concrete floor was coated but bland, and the walls were basic cinderblock. It reminded her of gym class in high school. Jackie walked past the rows of lockers and headed for the shower area. The communal shower area didn't contain a door, although there was a short privacy wall before the large shower area just beyond it. By the time Jackie heard the showers running, it was already too late. She nearly ran into Monroe, who was wearing only a towel around his waist, as he emerged from the showers.

Monroe was possibly more surprised than Jackie was. She jumped when she saw her teammate wearing nothing but a towel wrapped around his wet body. Given their many missions together, it wouldn't be the first time she'd seen the guys in towels or just their boxer briefs, but that didn't make it any less awkward, especially when it was Monroe.

"Damn it, Monroe," she cried out in anger and mild embarrassment. "Under the circumstances, would it kill you to lock the door?"

Monroe could do little more than stare at her, certainly not expecting to see her in the locker room.

"Is that Jackie?" Beck was heard calling from the showers. His tone then turned mocking. "I didn't think we were doing the whole co-ed shower thing!"

"Hey, Jackie," Gil cheerfully called from the shower area above the running water. "Nice of you to join us! Come on in!"

Jackie could hear the guys laughing within the showers. Monroe appeared mildly embarrassed and seemed to fumble over himself.

"Yeah, sorry about not locking the door," Monroe remarked. "We weren't thinking--" He then pointed to the shower room. "I'll, uh, just--"

Monroe didn't even finish the sentence before bolting back into the shower room. Darth suddenly appeared from the shower area, soaking wet, and happily greeted her. Jackie groaned and shook her head.

"There are days when being 'one of the boys' sucks," she remarked, then deposited her towel and shower kit on the nearby bench and quickly left.

Since taking her morning shower was out of the question, at least for the time being, Jackie decided to venture into the kitchen and see if Zack had breakfast available. She walked along the corridor in her bare feet, not bothering to change from her sleep shorts and tank top. She didn't mind parading around in her sleep attire in front of the guys. Being the sole woman on the team, she had to give up some modesty, but she drew the line at co-ed showers. It was bad enough she'd seen Kirk naked on numerous occasions, and she had given her virginity to Monroe before she went to college. She didn't need to add seeing the rest of the guys naked to that list. She was almost to the kitchen when she heard a thump followed by a loud crash. Jackie ran for the kitchen and slid into the doorway.

Kirk and Nevada were entwined on the floor together among scattered dinnerware. At first glance, they appeared to be playfully tussling, but when Nevada delivered a sharp elbow blow to Kirk's side, Jackie knew it wasn't just friendly horseplay. Kirk was attempting to put some sort of wrestling move on the nimble woman. Despite his size advantage on every level, Nevada was holding her own against the big man. It was about to turn ugly fast.

"Hey!" Jackie shouted in anger, attempting to break them up without inserting herself into the mix.

Honestly, Jackie didn't want to get between the two. Kirk wasn't the most reasonable man on the team, and Nevada was a ticking time bomb. Attempting to separate them would require turning her back to the one least likely to go through her. Unfortunately, Jackie didn't trust either in their current state. Nevada managed to whack Kirk in his groin with her palm before he could put her into a chokehold. The shot was enough to jolt him but not disable him. In short, it just pissed him off. Nevada attempted to scramble to her feet, but Kirk sat up, caught her ankle, and easily pulled her down to the floor. Once he had her down, he pulled her across the floor, feet first, toward him. She looked like a cat being pulled by its tail, clawing at the smooth, hard floor. The moment he had her close enough, she thrust her foot backward and clocked him in the mouth.

Despite the clean shot, he managed to grab her hips and keep her from escaping. It almost looked like some bizarre mating ritual, forcing Jackie to cringe. Jackie needed to end their fight before they once again became entangled. She bolted to the kitchen sink near them, turned on the faucet, and grabbed the spray nozzle. Jackie sprayed both with cold water. It was enough to startle them, getting their attention. Nevada cried out in anger while Kirk yelled profanities. Jackie sprayed Kirk in the face a second time just to silence him. She turned the water off and glared at the moderately wet man and woman sitting on the floor.

"What's the big idea?" Nevada cried out while flinging back her wet hair, then glared at Jackie.

"You tell me?" Jackie snapped in response. "What the hell is wrong with the two of you?"

"He ate the last toaster pastry," Nevada snarled, genuinely angry about it.

"It didn't have your fucking name on it," Kirk snapped back while casting an evil glare at her.

"I'm the one who put it in the toaster, garbage gut!"

Jackie couldn't believe what she was hearing, although she actually shouldn't have been too surprised. "You're fighting over a toaster pastry?" she demanded, then rolled her eyes and shook her head. "I'm surrounded by children."

"You shouldn't even be here," Kirk lashed out at Nevada from where the two remained on the floor. "And you wouldn't be if Zack didn't have a weak spot for you." His eyes then narrowed. "Or is it a *hard* spot?"

The fire in Nevada's eyes revealed her next move. As Nevada lunged for Kirk, Jackie again turned on the water and sprayed both in the face.

"Hey!" Kirk cried out while glaring at Jackie and pointing demandingly. "She's the one doing the attacking here!"

"You both need a time out," Jackie snarled back.

Nevada attempted to control her anger while sneering at Kirk. "I never *slept* with Zack."

"Enough," Jackie shouted while glaring at both. "Both of you!"

Nevada sprang to her feet while Kirk seemed to be in less of a hurry to stand. When he did stand, he towered over Nevada, folded his arms across his broad chest, and glared at her. Whatever their problems were, they were far from resolved.

"Why are the two of you at each other's throats?" Jackie demanded while shaking her head. "Don't we have bigger problems?"

Nevada turned and left the kitchen without responding.

Kirk sneered as she left the room then looked back at Jackie. "Stop playing mother hen with me, Jackie," he scoffed. "You can't control me the way you do the others."

"What's that supposed to mean?" Jackie snapped with surprise and a touch of anger.

Zack stood in the kitchen doorway with his arms folded across his chest and glared at Kirk. "Got something to say, Kirk?"

Kirk saw Zack then sneered and shook his head. "No," he replied, then headed for Zack and the kitchen door.

Zack and Jackie watched Kirk leave. Once he was gone, Jackie shook her head and groaned.

"I'd blame cabin fever," Jackie remarked, "but we haven't been here that long."

"Nevada doesn't bring out the best in people," Zack informed her while straightening. He then approached and eyed the water on the floor. "She's fighting her own demons. The demons are winning."

"The way those two are acting, I'd swear there was something between them," Jackie remarked while tossing a dishtowel onto the puddle of water on the floor.

"Nevada's a bit of a black widow," Zack announced and helped wipe the water from the floor. "If she's ever mated, none has lived to tell about it."

"Well, I'm glad it's not unresolved sexual tension between those two," Jackie muttered as she wrung the rag into the sink. "So what is their problem?"

"Don't know, and I wouldn't ask," Zack replied. "None of my business."

"Becomes our business if they're going to rip each other's throats out."

"Then call it a clash of personalities," Zack remarked as he leaned against the counter. "You have Nevada, who's almost certainly sexually frigid, and Kirk, who's a bit of a man whore. Combine those two chemicals, and what do you get?"

"Two people who can't stand the sight of each other," Jackie remarked. "I get that Kirk's a bit of a prick around Nevada, but what's his newly found irritation with me? I've never done anything to the guy."

"Kirk's not exactly complicated," Zack remarked. "Plenty of food, lots of exercise, let him kill something, and unlimited access to vitamin F." Zack considered the comment. "Huh? I think I just described myself."

"Joke all you want," Jackie insisted. "You're a lot deeper than you think. Somewhere, buried deep inside you, there's a locked box filled with emotions."

"You'd like to believe that," Zack informed her, then smirked. "I'll just let you keep thinking that if it makes you happy."

"Kirk is singling me out lately," Jackie announced, then shook her head. "When it comes to Kirk, I'm pretty much 'hands-off', and I certainly don't *mother* you guys."

Zack hid his grin. "No, of course, you don't."

Jackie shot a glare at him and suddenly felt offended. "Was that sarcasm?"

§

Sam rode along the wooded trail on game land nearly two miles from the sanctuary visitor's center. Her horse suddenly snorted, alerting her to something within the woods. Sam stopped the horse and looked around. She scanned the ground first, then checked out the trees in the distance, possibly anticipating Zack.

"What do you see?" she asked the horse while patting its neck.

The horse remained alert while staring slightly off to the right. Sam lifted her binoculars and slowly scanned the area. Alarm swept through her when she caught a glimpse of a man dressed in black combat fatigues and carrying a rifle cradled in his arms. Sam released the binoculars and swiftly removed the rifle from her saddle holster. She aimed the rifle at the man in the distance.

"Drop the weapon," she cried out. "Hands where I can see them!"

The man stopped at her commanding words, slowly and carefully set the rifle on the ground, and then straightened, holding his hands in the air where she could see them. Sam nudged her horse with her heels, leaving the reins draped over the saddle horn, and rode closer to the man. The horse suddenly snorted loudly and bolted in a tight circle to something behind them.

Sam cried out a loud, firm, "Whoa!"

A rifle blast echoed loudly from behind her.

Chapter 37

Later that morning, Jackie sat on the clinic desk while Marco listlessly picked at his breakfast within his cell. Nevada would be showing up shortly for her shift after she had a chance to shower. Jackie wondered if Nevada's shower would contain fewer Navy SEALs. The guys needed to keep their distance from Nevada and her wrath. She just hoped Monroe and Bogart were smart enough to keep their hormones in check around the volatile woman.

"You seem like the most sensible, intelligent one in the group," Marco announced while setting his tray aside and ripping Jackie out of her own thoughts. He stood and approached the bars. "Where am I going to go? Honestly? We're in the middle of nowhere. Wouldn't life be so much easier on everyone if you guys just trust me? I'm not suicidal. I'm not going anywhere."

"Sorry, Marco," Jackie replied and released a sigh. "That's Ross's call, not mine."

"Then maybe you could talk some sense into him," Marco announced and clung to the bars. "Let me out of here. This is ridiculous."

"No, what happened at that cabin safe house," Jackie announced and raised her brows, "*that* was ridiculous. Ross told you who we were, and why we were there, yet you still took off, endangering all our lives in the process."

"When I saw the helicopter, I didn't know who to trust," Marco informed her. "I know the score now. Talk to Ross. Get me out of here." He then gave her his best puppy dog eyes. "I'll behave; I promise."

"Yeah, sorry. Your charm isn't going to work on me either," Jackie informed him.

Marco groaned and walked away from the bars. Bogart entered the clinic and approached Jackie while grinning somewhat deviously.

"I heard you tried to shower with the boys this morning," Bogart teased.

Jackie rolled her eyes and shook her head. "They just couldn't wait to spread that around, could they?"

"I hear they're fighting over who gets to tell Holden," Bogart continued with his torment. He was starting to settle into his role as her annoying brother.

"I need better friends," Jackie muttered. "Maybe I can adopt *another* SEAL team."

Zack and Nevada entered the clinic while lightly arguing. When they saw Jackie and Bogart, both became oddly silent and didn't even look at each other.

Bogart raised his brows and gave Jackie a quick look. "That's not at all suspicious," he muttered as Nevada and Zack approached.

"Okay, I'm here," Nevada announced and flopped into the desk chair. "Everyone out."

"Someone got up on the wrong side of Kirk this morning," Bogart remarked.

Nevada's eyes narrowed as she glared at him. "That's not even the slightest bit funny."

"Don't poke the bear, Bogart," Jackie muttered to her brother.

"No more in-house fighting," Zack announced with little interest in the subject.

Jackie, Bogart, and Zack heard chatter over their concealed earpieces.

"Something's wrong," Kirk's voice was heard over their ear transmitters, alerting them to the situation outside. "Sam's coming in hot. Real hot."

All three bolted from the clinic and ran outside, straight for the visitor's center. Ross, Gil, and Monroe met them out front and scanned the area with their binoculars.

"I don't see her," Jackie announced while searching the area.

Gil touched his ear transmitter. "Which direction?" he demanded.

"Heading straight for you due northwest," Kirk replied over their earbuds.

All six turned and saw the gray horse galloping for them with Sam slumped over his neck. The horse was approaching fast. As the guys bolted for the running horse, the horse slammed on the breaks. Sam was thrown to the side of the horse, held partially on the horse's back with both feet still in the stirrups and the reins looped around her hands. She must have been conscious for part of the journey, knew she was fading out, and attempted to ensure she wouldn't fall off before making it to the visitor's center. Bogart easily controlled the excitable horse, being he had the most experience with horses. He held the heavy breathing, excitable horse still while Monroe and Gil supported Sam's unconscious body.

Jackie darted to the horse's right side and removed Sam's foot from the opposing stirrup while Zack and Ross removed the reins wrapped around her tight fists. Once she was free, they lowered her to the ground.

Monroe eyed his shoulder and the fresh blood soaking his shirt. "Shit, she's bleeding," he gasped while quickly backing up. "I'll get the field kit. Meet me in the clinic!"

The guys immediately searched Sam for the wound. Her entire shoulder was covered in blood. The horse snorted several times while angrily stomping its hind leg. Zack plucked Sam from the ground and into his arms, then hurried her back to the clinic more than one hundred yards from the visitor's center. Gil removed his shirt while running alongside Zack and attempted to hold pressure on the wound.

"That's a gunshot," Ross announced and immediately lifted his binoculars while scanning the area. "Kirk, keep your eyes peeled. We may have a bogey."

The horse again stomped its back hoof. Bogart looked at the horse's back leg and saw the bright, red blood running down its hind end.

"Ah, hell, no," Bogart cried out. "The bastard shot the horse!"

Ross touched his ear transmitter. "Beck," he barked in anger. "Get a rifle and get to Kirk's location. See what you can see." He then spun to face Jackie. "Get to the helicopter and wait for my orders. We may need to evacuate Marco and the ranger. If I give you the order, you'll need to get here fast."

Jackie nodded and ran east of the visitor's center to where the helicopter was hidden. Ross then turned to Bogart, who attempted to look at the uncooperative horse's injury. Ross could see the concern for the animal in Bogart's eyes.

"Take the horse to the clinic through the wildlife entrance," Ross informed him. "See if you can assess the damage."

Bogart nodded and led the horse to the infirmary. Despite the blood, the excitable horse just about pranced alongside him, showing no signs of limping.

§

Sam lay unconscious on the metal examination table within the veterinarian clinic. Nevada paced the area before Marco's cell and watched the commotion surrounding the injured ranger. Ross fumbled with the bottle of numbing solution while Zack ripped open one of the sterile syringes. Gil tore Sam's shirt away from the wound, quickly assessed it, and applied pressure again.

"Can someone hand me some gauze pads?" Gil just about demanded. "I need to take a better look at the wound."

Ross handed Zack the bottle of solution and hurried to Gil's side. Nevada watched Zack as he was about to insert the syringe into the bottle.

"What the hell are you doing?" Nevada suddenly cried out and bolted for him. She snatched the syringe from his hand. "You just contaminated the stopper on the bottle. Jesus. Do you want to give her an infection?" Nevada removed an alcohol prep from the bag and sterilized the stopper on the bottle of solution. She drew up some numbing agent into the syringe, flicked out any air bubbles, and then approached the unconscious woman. Without regard to the men working around her, Nevada sterilized an area near the injury and injected the solution near the wound. She then glared at Zack, lacking patience. "Make yourself useful and find the bottle of morphine in that bag."

Zack found the morphine and approached Nevada. While holding pressure to the wound, Ross watched Nevada remove a clean syringe from the supplies laid out on the table. She then snatched the bottle from Zack and sterilized the stopper before drawing up solution.

"Find the rubber tourniquet," Nevada ordered while carefully drawing up a small amount of the morphine. "Tie off her arm above the elbow."

While Zack found the yellow band in the bag and tied off Sam's arm, Nevada swabbed the crook of her arm. Once the blood flow to her arm was stopped, Nevada searched for a vein. Ross and Zack watched as Nevada poked around the woman's arm. She again swabbed the area after finding a vein and then inserted the drugs directly into her bloodstream.

"Where did you learn to do that?" Ross asked.

"Marines," Nevada announced without looking at Ross. "I've seen my share of gunshot wounds and shrapnel."

Gil removed the bullet and dropped it into a pan on the table. "Hit the bone," Gil announced. "The angle was damned near perfect. She's very lucky." He then looked at Nevada. "You're more useful than these guys. Want to help me clean this up and stitch the wound?"

Nevada nodded. Bogart stood on the other side of a set of bars to one of the pens with the tied horse and watched the activity surrounding the ranger.

"If you don't need all those hands over there, I could use a few over here," Bogart remarked.

Ross slapped Zack on the shoulder, nodded to Bogart, and both men joined him by the horse with some supplies.

"What's it looking like?" Ross asked.

"The bullet grazed the horse's hindquarters," Bogart informed them. "It's not nearly as bad as it looked. Some cleaner and blood stop, if you've got."

"Ross, you copy?" Beck's voice came over his ear transmitter.

Zack entered the cage through the smaller interior door and joined Bogart on the opposite side of the bars with the injured horse.

Ross handed Zack the supplies through the bars while responding to his man. "Yeah, Beck," Ross replied. "I copy. What do you have?"

"Kirk heard several rifle shots more than twenty minutes ago," Beck announced over his ear transmitter. "It was at least two miles away. We're taking the four-wheelers in that direction."

"The verdict?" Ross asked while watching Zack and Bogart attempt to clean the horse's injury.

"We're going with poachers," Beck replied over his ear transmitter."

"The bullet Gil dug out of the ranger is pretty uninspiring," Ross reported while remaining in thought. "Not really something you'd find on a hitman or mercenary, that's for certain." He then sighed and continued to talk to the guys over his ear transmitter. "You and Kirk see what you can see. If you run into anyone looking like poachers, give them a good old-fashioned Navy SEAL scare."

"With pleasure," Kirk replied, then chuckled.

"Jesus Christ," Sam gasped while coming too and attempted to look around, but she was obviously disorientated. "What the hell happened?"

"Maybe you could tell us?" Gil asked and offered a tiny, sympathetic smile.

She attempted to look at her shoulder. "What the hell are you doing?" Sam cried out. "Is that blood?"

"Well, you *were* shot," Gil casually informed her.

Sam's expression suddenly dropped. Her eyes rolled back, and she again passed out.

"And she's out again," Nevada announced with a sigh. "Let's finish stitching her up before she wakes up again." Nevada removed her sterile gloves and reclaimed the bottle of morphine while grinning. "I think she could use some more happy drugs. If you can't fly high after being shot, what's the point?"

Chapter 38

Jackie sat in one of the visitor center's more comfortable lobby chairs while Sam slept peacefully on one of the cots. When the woman woke, Jackie set aside the old magazine she had found and smiled.

"How are you feeling?" Jackie asked, having been in Sam's position more than once.

"Like shit," Sam replied while cringing. "Why do I feel so spaced out and sore?"

"Well, you were shot," Jackie informed her while raising her brows. "And Nevada may have been a little generous with the morphine."

"Shot?" Sam asked. Her eyes suddenly widened. "Oh, shit!" She attempted to sit up then immediately cringed and regretted the action. "What happened? How did I get here?" She then whispered while staring at Jackie. "I had the weirdest dreams."

"I'm not surprised," Jackie informed her. "Whether intentional or not, your horse brought you here."

"Is Smokey okay?" she asked with concern.

"He's recovering nicely in the zebra paddock," Jackie replied. "A bullet grazed his rump."

"It all happened so fast," Sam groaned and shook her head. "I saw one guy, but there must have been another guy behind me. If Smokey hadn't reacted the way he did, the bastard would have shot me in the back." She seemed lost in her thoughts. "I barely remember my rifle firing; it was pretty much a blur. I knew Smokey had been hit by the way he took off." Sam stared off, reliving the moment. "I thought for sure I'd never make it here. I could feel myself fading out." She then met Jackie's gaze. "It was the strangest thing I've ever experienced."

"I've been there," Jackie muttered but didn't elaborate. "Your horse got you here safely, and you're both going to be fine."

"I should get to my radio," Sam moaned and again attempted to sit up. She groaned in agony and lay back down on the cot.

"Kirk and Beck are at the ranger's station on the ATVs they fixed from the maintenance shop," Jackie informed her. "They're taking care of everything."

Sam seemed to have trouble processing the information. "What did my superiors say?" she asked with a concerned look on her face. "The last time someone used my radio without permission, they sent half the department to the cabin to check on me."

"I believe they spoke to the local authorities," Jackie reported. "They didn't mention any problems."

"I'll need to give them a description of the poacher I actually saw," Sam remarked. "I never saw the one behind me. He was just a blur. When Smokey spun, I only caught a glimpse of him before he shot me."

"You don't have to worry about that," Jackie replied. "Kirk and Beck caught the guys. The local police are meeting them at the station to collect both men."

"I really need to get back to the station," Sam remarked and again attempted to sit up. The pain was too much. She fell back down and groaned in agony.

Jackie laughed and shook her head. "Gil just dug a bullet out of your shoulder. You and your horse are in no condition to go anywhere," she remarked and attempted to keep the ranger calm. "If you're going anywhere, it's going to be the hospital." Jackie drew a deep breath and straightened proudly. "You have two choices. You can stay here for a few days with your horse to recover, or you can go to the hospital and recover there."

Sam seemed to consider her options then managed a tiny smile. "Your friend, Gil, dug the bullet out, huh?"

"He had medical field training when he was in the military," Jackie informed her. "He's actually quite good at digging out bullets. Better than Zack, that's for sure." Jackie subconsciously rubbed her left shoulder, still feeling the phantom pain from the time Zack had patched her up.

Sam managed a tiny, almost embarrassed smile. "I'm very grateful to you and your friends," she announced. "I don't even want to think about what would have happened if you hadn't been here when I needed help."

"We're happy to help," Jackie replied. "Kirk and Beck are going to pack a bag for you from the ranger's station. Is there anything else you need? I can radio them."

"A change of clothes, a toothbrush, and a hairbrush are all I really need," she insisted. "Thanks."

"Did you want something to drink?" Jackie asked. "You should probably stay hydrated."

"Thanks."

"I'll make you a cup of tea," Jackie insisted, then stood. She was about to walk away then looked back at Sam. "Oh, and heads up. While you were flying high on morphine, compliments of Nevada, you told all the guys they were so handsome, you loved them all, and you may or may not have grabbed my brother's ass. Jury's still out on that one."

Sam shut her eyes and groaned. "Great."

"Don't worry," Jackie remarked and grinned. "They had a good laugh over it."

Jackie headed across the visitor's center, where Ross stood before what used to be the snack bar. As Jackie plugged in the electric kettle to make tea, Ross attempted to remain casual in case Sam was watching them.

"Think she's buying it?" Ross asked.

"Yeah," Jackie replied, then frowned, "but your lie is a little short-sighted. What happens when she returns to the ranger's station and finds out we never contacted anyone and that the poachers were never even reported or found?"

Ross smiled and patted Jackie on the shoulder. "You seriously underestimate my ability to stretch the truth," he teased. "Beck contacted the local authorities about the poachers and gave their general location. You and Monroe met the local sheriff when you checked out the town. Even if the rangers contact him, his arrogance will keep the lie alive."

"So you're counting on the left hand not knowing what the right hand is doing?" Jackie remarked.

Ross grinned. "Exactly."

"And we're absolutely positive those men were poachers?" Jackie asked.

"Kirk and Beck found their camp not far from where she'd been shot," Ross replied. "Everything there suggested they were hunters. Their camp had been there long before we arrived. They weren't looking for us."

"And what about Sam staying here for a few days?" Jackie questioned, uncertain how she felt about that. "I know we can't send her back to the station, but the thought of keeping her here is very stressful."

"One of us will need to keep an eye on her the entire time," Ross replied. "For Sam's comfort, that should probably be you or Nevada for now. She may feel less intimidated in the company of other women than with strange men."

"Have you met Nevada?" Jackie remarked and raised a curious brow. "Compared to her, Kirk even seems friendly."

He considered the comment. "You may have a point," Ross muttered. "Sam should remain on bedrest here in the visitor's center the rest of the day. Tomorrow, when she's up and moving around, we can all take turns keeping an eye on her. As long as we keep her away from the clinic, we shouldn't have any problem."

§

Later that evening, Holden entered his home through the kitchen entrance carrying a bag of take-out. He saw the mail neatly piled on the island counter and eyed it suspiciously.

"Othello," he called out while approaching the island counter, "I'm home. I brought fried chicken for dinner."

Holden glanced into the living room and saw Othello planted on the sofa with several empty cans of soda and empty bags of chips surrounding him. He wore a headset with a microphone while working on his computer.

"Yeah, that's great," he announced without looking at Holden.

"I'm glad you're making yourself at home," Holden remarked while eyeing the mounting collection of junk food wrappers.

"No, that's nobody," Othello announced into his headset microphone.

Holden set the bag down on the counter and eyed Othello. "What?"

Othello harshly waved off Holden while continuing to work on his laptop. "No, nothing yet, but I'll continue tracking that storm system."

Holden appeared puzzled and entered the living room, now realizing Othello was talking to someone else. He peered over Othello's shoulder and eyed the laptop screen.

Othello looked back at him and lowered the lid partway. "A little privacy, dude," he announced.

"Seriously?" Holden demanded.

Othello again waved him off with a little added vigor. "Thanks for calling, Dad," he announced. "Talk soon. Give my brothers all my best." Othello pressed a button on his computer screen then looked at Holden as he rounded the sofa. "Not cool."

"Were you talking to Ross?" Holden asked, now interested in what had transpired.

"Well, I certainly wasn't talking to my real dad," Othello insisted. "He's rotting in some Russian prison."

"What did he--?" Holden began then waved his hand. "Never mind." He then indicated Othello's laptop. "Are they okay?"

"Yeah, they're fine," Othello replied and shut his laptop lid. "You mentioned fried chicken?"

Holden frowned then nodded. "Yeah, help yourself," he announced while running his fingers through his hair. "Did you talk to Jackie?"

As Othello stood, several potato chips fell to the floor. He shuffled across the room in his plush Anime slippers to the island counter.

"No," Othello replied while opening the food bag. "Limited communication. Just a few brief words with *Dad*."

"Is there anything you *can* tell me?" Holden asked with mounting frustration.

"No," Othello replied while removing several pieces of chicken and placing them on a plate.

Holden stared at Othello, watching him lick the fried chicken grease from his fingers. "Will you just tell me something?" he finally demanded. "Anything!"

Othello groaned, collected his plate, and headed back to the sofa. "Fine," he announced with a defeated sigh. "They ran into a park ranger who'd been shot. The guys are taking care of her now."

"Her?"

Othello glared at Holden then plopped down on the sofa. "No, that's all you get," he announced sternly. "I shouldn't have told you that much."

Holden moved onto the nearby chair, sat on the edge, and stared at Othello. "Who shot the ranger?" he asked with concern. "Was it some hitman? Mercenary? Who?"

"You're impossible," Othello moaned and glared at Holden. "It was an accident. Just some poacher. Nothing to get all worked up over."

Holden sank back in the chair, covered his eyes with his hand, and groaned. "I know I said I was okay with this," he announced, then lowered his hand and eyed Othello, "but I'm really not. Do you have any idea the kind of people who are out there right now looking for them?"

Othello didn't bother looking at Holden while cleverly raising his brows. "I have a pretty good idea," he remarked. "Anyone who's anyone on the who's who of hired assassins' registry."

Holden shut his eyes and rubbed his temples. "There has to be something I can do."

"Yeah, find the killer and clear Marco's name," Othello casually announced. "No bounty; no reason to kill him."

"Easier said than done," Holden muttered. "The guy is smart. Most serial killers are. That's why it takes so long to catch them. You have to wait until they make a mistake."

"Might be easier taking down Vincent Scartelli," Othello remarked while biting into the fried chicken leg.

Holden stared at Othello a moment, then slowly sat up. "That's an interesting theory," he remarked. "What sort of trouble would Vincent have to be in for that bounty to be null and void?"

"I sincerely doubt being arrested would be enough," Othello remarked. He then hesitated and eyed Holden. "You weren't thinking about turning dark on me, were you?"

Holden appeared stranded in his own thoughts a moment, then snapped back into reality. "No, of course not."

Othello seemed slightly tense and kept his eyes on Holden. "Good, because that would be bad." He then shifted on the sofa and wiped his mouth on a napkin. "Jackie is fine. That girl has survived worse on solo gigs. They've got this."

Chapter 39

The following morning just before sunrise, Sam sat up on her cot with some discomfort and rubbed her sore shoulder. Since Sam had to stay with them, most of the team needed to spend the night in the visitor's center on their prop cots to keep up appearances. They needed to avoid the clinic and the more comfortable staff bedrooms. Despite the early hour, Zack was already up and gone, and Nevada was again keeping an eye on Marco. The rest of the team would be getting up soon since none of them were much for sleeping in, except Kirk, who would sleep all day given the opportunity. Gil was now awake and saw Sam gingerly rubbing her shoulder. He moved off his cot, approached her, and crouched before her cot while offering a comforting smile.

"How are you feeling?" he asked.

"Like I was hit by a freight train," Sam remarked and cringed.

"Would you like some pain killers?" Gil asked.

Sam snorted a laugh. "I'll take whatever you got," she teased.

"I'd like to change the dressing on your wound," Gil remarked then appeared curious. "Unless you'd rather wait for Nevada."

"I don't suppose there's much point to being modest now," Sam teased, forcing a timid smile.

Gil chuckled at her observation and straightened. "I'll get the medical kit and meet you in the bathroom in five minutes," he replied.

As Sam wearily headed for the bathroom, Jackie's eyes opened. She waited for the woman to enter the ladies' room across the visitor's center then sat up on her cot when Gil returned with the medical bag.

"Did you want me to change the dressing?" Jackie asked.

"No, I've got this," Gil informed her. "She doesn't seem bothered by me looking at it, and I'd rather see the wound for myself. If it gets infected, we'll need to take her to the hospital, and none of us wants that."

Gil approached the ladies' bathroom and tapped on the closed door. "Everyone decent in there?" he teased.

Sam laughed from the other side. "Yeah, we're all good in here."

Gil entered as Sam had just finished washing her hands after using the facility. She turned, leaned against the sink, and seemed slightly apprehensive as she unbuttoned her shirt. Sam wore a tank top beneath the shirt, which allowed Gil unobstructed access to the bandage while maintaining some of her modesty. Gil gently removed the dressing and eyed the stitches.

"Looks good," he informed her somewhat cheerfully. "It's healing nicely."

He handed her a bottle of pills then fished around in the medical bag for a clean dressing. Sam read the label on the pill bottle.

"Oxycodone," Sam remarked, then cast a look at Gil. "You pack a pretty serious medical kit."

"When you spend weeks out in the field, it's good to be prepared," Gil informed her.

Sam took one of the pills without water and then returned the bottle to him. "I won't even ask how or why you had Morphine."

Gil cast a quick look at her, then covered with a slightly humored smile. "That's probably best," he teased.

The ranger was obviously a little suspicious of their well-stocked medical bag, particularly after Jackie had let it slip that Nevada gave her a morphine injection, not your average medical bag drug. Their medical bag was a little too well-stocked for the average person, although not unusual for someone used to treating gunshot wounds. Gil finished dressing her wound and shut the bag before she could sneak a peek inside and see what else they had stocked in there.

"Which way is the zebra paddock?" Sam asked while slipping back into her shirt. "I'd like to check on Smokey."

Gil offered a pleasant smile. "I'll walk over with you," he replied.

"I'm sure I could find it on my own," Sam informed him. "I don't want to put you out. I've been a big enough burden on all of you already."

"It's no trouble," Gil insisted. "The gate to the paddock is heavy and a bit rusted. I don't want you straining and tearing out any stitches."

Sam smiled and nodded, seeming to buy his excuse for tagging along.

§

Gil and Sam approached the zebra paddock from the rear, shelter side entrance. He hadn't lied. The gate was thick steel and contained a fair amount of rust. Gil opened the gate with some effort and extended his hand for her to enter. Sam entered the paddock with Gil a step behind her and crossed the large field. The zebra paddock was a large, open area filled with tall grass and a few trees near the back. A wooden shelter was made from trees to give it a more natural appeal, although the shelter was partially collapsed now. The disguised fencing gave the habitat an open appearance while keeping the horse confined. The gray horse immediately lifted its nose from the lush grass and snickered when he saw her. Sam held her hand out.

"Hey, boy," she announced. "How are you feeling?"

The horse whinnied excitedly and trotted over to greet her. She affectionately held the horse's head and petted him as he nuzzled her.

"I'll just wait outside the gate," Gil announced and left her alone with the horse.

The gray horse lifted its head and snorted at something behind her. Sam patted the horse's nose and didn't bother looking over her shoulder.

"Good morning, Zack," she announced.

"Damned horse," Zack muttered from nearby.

Sam turned and saw Zack in a tree near the fence. Zack climbed from the tree to the top of the fence and walked across it, skillfully balancing himself as if he were walking in the park. He then jumped off without effort. Sam stared at him and shook her head.

"What I wouldn't give to be able to do that?" she remarked, then grinned. "So were you spying or stalking?"

"Neither," he replied. "I was watching the horse. You just happened along."

"Then I don't know if I'm relieved or disappointed," she teased.

Zack gave her a slightly bewildered look, seeming somewhat suspicious. "Jackie would suggest you were flirting just now," he remarked and paused near the horse, scratching its withers.

The horse lifted his head in the air and made low grunting sounds, enjoying the scratching.

Sam laughed at his interaction with her horse. "You found his itchy spot," she remarked, then attempted to hide her embarrassment. "And Jackie would be right."

Zack cast a slightly bewildered look at her. "Now I'm back to being confused again."

"Don't many women flirt with you, or am I doing it wrong?" she teased while hiding her embarrassed smile. "I mean, I know it's been a while for me--"

"According to some, I'm clueless when it comes to women and the subtle art of flirting," Zack replied, then placed his arm over the horse's withers and eyed her. "If you were flirting, why did you recoil the other day when I kissed you?"

Sam stared at him with some surprise and seemed to blush. "Well, that was direct and to the point."

"Sorry; I don't have much of a filter," he remarked. "I tend to say what I think."

"I'm guessing that doesn't always work out for you, huh?" she teased.

"Are you avoiding my question on purpose?"

Sam tensed slightly, then managed a tiny smile. "I guess I just wasn't expecting you to, well, kiss me like that. It kind of took me by surprise."

"I don't typically initiate, and I should probably stick with what I know," he remarked. "If my aggressive behavior upset you, I'm sorry."

She hid her smile and avoided looking at him. "It didn't upset me. It just caught me off guard," Sam replied, then finally met his gaze and smiled with embarrassment. "It's funny how when you read romance novels, you fantasize about that sort of thing, but when a man actually does it, you find yourself paralyzed with fear."

"A few shots of tequila fixes that," Zack reported.

Sam gave him a strange look. "I don't think we're talking about the same thing."

"I've read a few chapters from Jackie's romance novels," Zack announced. "That thing was loaded with deviant behavior. I got the general gist."

"Yeah, I don't think she was reading the same kind of romance novels I read," Sam insisted while managing a tiny laugh. She took a step closer to Zack and seemed apprehensive. "Although I admit I was taken by surprise when you kissed me, I won't deny it was possibly the single most erotic moment in my life."

Zack stared at her a moment and removed his arm from the horse's withers. "Now that sounds a lot like a proposition," he remarked.

"I'm pretty sure it was meant to," she remarked while maintaining her tiny smile.

Without further prompting, Zack took a step toward her, pulled her against him, and kissed her passionately and with a fair amount of aggression. Sam immediately tensed with surprise. Zack broke off the kiss and pulled away.

"You did it again," he insisted and once more appeared confused. "You recoiled."

Sam quickly took a step toward him and placed her good arm around his neck before he could retreat. "I've been alone a long time, Zack," she insisted. "I assure you, my hesitation is not rejection. Just go with it. I'll catch up."

Zack again pulled her against him and kissed her passionately. She eagerly returned the kiss this time. As Zack's passion started to rise, Sam stopped him and met his gaze with a tiny, seductive grin.

"Is there someplace a little more private around here?" she cooed while gently caressing his chest.

"More than a hundred private places," he informed her. "Care to narrow down that request?"

Sam thought about it a moment, then grinned. "Well, it's been a long time since I've had intimate contact with any man," she informed him. "So I'd say somewhere without fear of interruption, being caught, and the need to rush."

Zack seemed somewhat hesitant by her words.

Sam noted his expression and tensed slightly. "Is something wrong?"

"No," he replied, despite his expression. "Most women I meet seem to prefer the rushed version."

Sam chuckled while staring into his eyes. "Am I throwing you off your game?" she teased.

"A little," he replied, then hesitated. "I'll adapt, though." A sly grin then crossed his face. "I think I know the perfect place. Wait here. I just need to get a sleeping bag."

§

Zack carried a rolled sleeping bag slung over his shoulder while walking with Sam through the overgrown sanctuary property. They approached the large, glass aviary. Despite vines growing over the sides of the glass building, which looked more like a two-story greenhouse, the glass seemed to be mostly intact, possibly being shatterproof.

Sam appeared curious. "What is this?" she asked. "A greenhouse?"

"It's an aviary," he informed her, then opened the door containing frosted glass and extended his hand for her to enter first.

Sam entered the aviary and stopped just inside. The aviary was thick with trees and various plant life, now growing mostly wild. The natural watering system still functioned even without human interaction and provided a warm, tropical setting despite being abandoned. The walkway was still intact, although somewhat overrun with plant life along the edges. Sam marveled at the romantic setting and grinned her approval.

"I am very impressed," Sam announced, then looked back at Zack.

Zack indicated the romantic jungle setting. "Secluded," he announced, then shut the frosted glass door and bolted it. "And completely private."

Sam smiled her approval. "Very nice," she announced, then raised her brows. "And very romantic."

"That's something I've never been accused of before," Zack remarked, then guided her deeper into the aviary.

He stopped her near the center of the building, where many types of trees had grown over one another, giving the area an even more secluded, romantic appeal. Zack unrolled the sleeping bag then removed his cell phone. Sam carefully sat on the sleeping bag to avoid using her injured arm then watched Zack. The sounds of birds and nature were heard from his cell phone. He turned up the volume, set the phone down, and joined her on the sleeping bag. Sam watched him and smiled.

"Are you sure no one's ever accused you of being romantic before?" she teased.

Zack removed his combat boots while considering the question then looked around. "I know how to coordinate things, sort of like setting the stage," he informed her. "I suppose with a little stretch of the imagination that could be the same thing as 'being romantic'." He set his boots aside and turned on the sleeping bag to face her where she sat. "The real challenge will be adjusting from the quick version to the extended version."

"You haven't done that in a while?" she teased.

"I know a lot of aggressive women," he replied. "It's much easier letting them set the pace, and I'm pretty good at taking orders."

Sam suddenly grinned and raised her brow. "Well, then," she announced with some humor. "I think we just found our common ground. I'm good at giving orders."

She placed her good arm around his neck, moved against him, and kissed him warmly but passionately. Zack returned the kiss with a little added aggression.

Chapter 40

It was just after breakfast that morning. While Zack was busy entertaining Sam, Ross and Gil were patrolling the grounds, leaving Nevada on guard duty. Jackie stood at the main desk within the visitor's center with Monroe, Beck, and Bogart. They were studying a map of the sanctuary with matching frowns at their new dilemma.

"Can't do it," Beck finally announced and straightened with disgust. "There's no way we can pull it off."

"Stop being so negative all the time," Monroe scoffed and shook his head. "We have a ton of resources. We've pulled off more with less."

"I hate to agree with Beck," Jackie informed them, "but he's right."

Beck glared at Jackie and cocked his head with something resembling a smirk. "Thanks," he scoffed. "I take back all those disparaging remarks I've made about you."

Jackie sneered at Beck.

"Stop your fighting; all of you," Bogart announced with a groan while raking his fingers through his hair. He then indicated the map with some irritation. "Can we just get back to our current situation? We need to think of something and fast; before Zack returns and wants in."

"Don't worry about Zack," Beck announced, then offered a cheap grin. "If he's doing what I think he's doing with that

Girl Scout, we have plenty of time while she earns her 'roughing it' merit badge."

"That's disgusting, Beck," Jackie remarked.

"Yeah, well," Beck announced while eyeing her, "so is Zack."

Jackie rolled her eyes, which only managed to fuel Beck's bad behavior. He chuckled at Jackie's disapproval. Kirk entered the visitor's center, headed for one of the nearby storage containers, and removed a bag of chips. Without hesitation, he tore into them. All four glanced at Kirk. While the others returned to the map and their mission, Monroe kept his attention on Kirk.

"We just had a big breakfast," Monroe insisted. "How can you be hungry?"

"I'm a big boy," Kirk casually announced while crunching on some chips as he approached them at the counter. He appeared curious and eyed the map. "What are the four of you plotting this time?"

Monroe looked back at the map, leaned on the counter, and sighed while shaking his head. "We want to have a little target shooting competition, but even with our weapons' suppressors, there's a risk of Sam hearing us."

"Not to mention anyone else close by," Beck added. "There's no telling who's out there. We don't need to fuel someone's suspicions and blow our cover."

"You'd think between the four of you, you'd be a little more creative," Kirk remarked while crunching on his chips. "You don't need firearms to target practice." He tossed his bag of chips onto the counter and removed his Bowie knife from his boot. He flipped it in his hand then slammed it on the counter on top of the map. "Knife throwing."

Jackie, Monroe, Bogart, and Beck exchanged looks. Jackie couldn't help but wonder why she hadn't thought of that first. Why did it take Kirk, of all people, to come up with such a great idea?

"I'm suddenly feeling pretty stupid," Beck remarked, then looked back at the map. He pointed to the kiddie land. "We can hang a target here in the kid's playland."

Jackie grinned her approval. "I'll grab some knives," she remarked.

"I'll find material to make a target," Bogart announced excitedly.

"I'll get some snacks," Kirk informed them and immediately received several looks.

§

As Jackie entered the clinic later that afternoon, Nevada saw her and slipped her cell phone into her pocket. Jackie noticed the action as she approached the desk and wondered what the woman was doing. They had gone dark, which meant no contact with anyone from the outside world except coded messages to their go-between, Othello. Jackie paused before the desk and managed a tiny smile, pretending she hadn't noticed the action.

"Everything okay in here?"

"Yeah," Nevada replied while leaning back in the chair, then indicated the nearby cage. "Thankfully, he's been sleeping all afternoon. I've been enjoying the peace and quiet for a change."

"Did you need a break?" Jackie asked.

"I could use a little fresh air and an hour's nap," Nevada remarked, then stood.

Jackie felt compelled to comment on what she'd just witnessed. Despite not wanting to accuse the woman of anything, she felt she had to mention it and casually nodded to Nevada's pocket.

"You weren't communicating with someone, were you?" Jackie asked.

Nevada was confused by the question then managed a tiny smile and a laugh. "No," she replied. "There's no reception in the clinic even if we were allowed to use our cell phones. I was reading some books I had downloaded on my phone. Don't worry; I have my phone on airplane mode."

Jackie managed a tiny laugh. "I keep forgetting you already know the drill," she remarked with some embarrassment. "Force of habit."

Nevada waved her off. "I don't blame you," she remarked. "It's your ass too. One of us screws up, and we're all screwed." She then hesitated. "In case you're interested--" Nevada indicated the lower desk drawer. "There's an old smut magazine in the bottom desk drawer. It has a great raunchy article, if you're into that."

Jackie laughed and shook her head. "Thanks, but I'm good."

Nevada shrugged and grinned. "Your business; not mine," she remarked, then left the clinic.

Jackie cast herself into the desk chair, leaned back, and stared at the ceiling a moment. Her eyes then shifted to the bottom desk drawer. She glanced across the room toward the door, saw that no one else was around, and then opened the drawer. She removed the dirty magazine and searched for the aforementioned raunchy article. As she read the article, she gasped with surprise. She laughed and continued reading, becoming completely immersed in it. A few minutes later, Jackie had finished reading the long article, shut the magazine, and held her breath a moment.

"Wow," she gasped, then fanned herself with the magazine. She suddenly missed Holden all over again.

The magazine was snatched from her hand, startling her. Zack sat on the desk and eyed the cover with a mostly nude woman sprawled on it. He then glanced at Jackie and raised his brows.

"All this time," he announced. "Something else we have in common that we could have been enjoying together."

"I was just reading it for the articles," Jackie informed him matter-of-factly.

Zack grinned and laughed. "That's what they all say," he teased, then casually flipped through the magazine. He paused on one page in particular and tilted his head while raising his brow. "Hmm, nice." He then looked at Jackie. "Where did Nevada go?"

"I gave her a break," Jackie replied. "She went to get a little sleep."

Zack gave her a strange look. "I saw her heading across the sanctuary."

"Maybe she went for a walk," Jackie remarked.

He sank into thought then nodded. "Yeah, maybe," Zack replied and tossed the magazine on the desk as he stood. "I'm going to tail her. See what she's up to." He then eyed Jackie and offered a slightly mocking grin. "Are you okay? You look a little flushed."

Jackie glared at him and sneered.

"I find a cold shower usually helps," Zack teased with a chuckle as he left the clinic.

§

Around ten o'clock that evening, Jackie, Kirk, Beck, and Bogart had gathered in the visitor's center. Kirk strode across the large lobby with a scowl on his face, cast himself onto one of the cots, and groaned in disgust.

"This is bullshit," Kirk snarled, sharing his foul mood with everyone. "Perfectly good, private bedrooms, and we have to sleep refugee style in the visitor's center because we have *company*."

"Quit your whining," Jackie snapped as she approached one of the cots and sat on it. "The rest of us are the ones who have to suffer listening to you snore."

Kirk sat up on his cot and glared at Jackie. "The others may think you're cute, Jackie," he announced, "but your feminine wiles don't work on me."

"Wiles," Beck remarked, then chuckled from where he sat on his cot across the room. "Who talks like that?"

"Educated people," Kirk scoffed.

"From the 1800s, perhaps," Beck remarked while laughing at Kirk's expense.

"I like you better when you're exclusively living at the lodge," Kirk informed Beck.

"My wife does too," Beck remarked while stretching out on the cot. "But you're stuck with me until it's time to go home."

Bogart was about to take the cot alongside Jackie when she eyed him. "You don't want to do that," she insisted.

"Why not?" Bogart asked.

"Because Zack is just going to dump you onto the floor," she informed him.

Bogart rolled his eyes and took the next cot over. "One day, I'm going to be able to kick his ass," he announced.

"Yeah, well," Zack announced from behind him, startling him. "It's not today."

Zack sat on the empty cot alongside Jackie and looked at her as if he had something on his mind. She stared back at him and cocked her head.

"What's up?" Jackie asked.

"I won't be bunking with you tonight," he informed her.

Despite the sexual connotation of the comment, she gave him a slightly surprised look. "Really? Why?" she asked, although almost sure she already knew the answer.

"I'm bunking with Sam," he replied and shifted slightly. "You don't mind, do you?"

Jackie stared at him with complete disbelief. She sometimes wondered what went through his head. Did he actually think he needed her permission?

"Of course, I don't mind," she replied with a tiny chuckle then grinned. "I'm happy for you."

Zack groaned, revealing some irritation by her response. "Don't make a whole *thing* out of it," he announced.

"I'm not making a *thing* out of it," she insisted while attempting to hide her humor.

He glared at her and raised his brow. "Really?"

Jackie hesitated, then shrugged. "I mean, I think it's wonderful that you're actually having a sleepover date with a nice girl."

Zack groaned and stood. "That's the *thing* I was talking about," he remarked. "It's not a sleepover. It's sex with some sleeping afterward. Well, I doubt I'll sleep, but I kind of want the sex, so it's a fair trade-off."

Jackie considered the situation and suddenly felt curious. "Where are you spending the night?" she then asked. "Not in the clinic bedrooms."

"No, of course not," Zack replied, then nodded past the restrooms. "There's a pull-out sofa bed in the office in the back."

"So Zack gets an actual bed?" Kirk demanded from two cots over, obviously listening in on their conversation.

"Don't start," Beck moaned from his cot.

Zack groaned and approached one of the plastic tubs alongside the portable cooler. He removed a bag of potato chips and tossed them to Kirk. Kirk caught the bag and eagerly tore it open without another word.

"It's as if you people haven't learned anything," Zack muttered, then glared at Jackie while pointing at Kirk. "When he barks, feed him. That'll keep him quiet until he falls asleep."

Sam entered the visitor's center and appeared somewhat shy upon seeing the others settling in for the night. "Where's everyone else?" she asked while approaching.

Zack met her halfway and indicated the empty bunks. "Night photography," he replied. "We find it's safer in groups."

She smiled and nodded, then sheepishly met his gaze. "So, uh, where are we bunking?"

Zack nodded past the restrooms then showed her the way. Bogart moved back onto the cot alongside Jackie's cot and watched Zack disappear into the nearby hallway with Sam.

"Someone really needs to do a documentary on Zack's mating rituals," Bogart remarked, then sighed. "Because I really don't understand how he gets laid."

"Aggressive women love him because he's so fucking quiet," Kirk announced from his cot while crunching on chips.

Beck groaned in frustration and placed his pillow over his head.

"They like me because I'm tall and muscular," Kirk continued without even looking at Bogart. "And you because you're funny."

Beck removed the pillow from his head and glared at Kirk. "And what about me?"

Kirk cast a look at Beck. "They feel sorry for you," he replied.

Beck frowned and threw his spare pillow at Kirk's head. Kirk deflected the pillow without losing a chip.

Jackie sat hunched over on the edge of her cot, groaned, and held her head. "Would someone just shoot me now?"

Bogart glanced past Jackie, shifted uncomfortably, and then placed his hand over his eyes. "Now I want to be shot too," he muttered.

Jackie lifted her head and looked across the room. Kirk strolled across the lobby toward one of the beverage coolers wearing only his maroon-colored, form-fitting boxer briefs that proudly displayed his package. There was no denying he had an amazingly muscular body that most women would fawn over, but Jackie had grown tired of seeing him strutting around in his colored boxer briefs.

"Jesus, Kirk. Can't you wear shorts in mixed company?" Beck moaned and dramatically threw his hands in the air. "No one wants to see that."

Kirk removed a bottle of water from the cooler and cast a stern look at Beck. "Plenty of women want to see this," he announced, then indicated Jackie. "Even Jackie."

"No, not Jackie," she insisted and refused to look at him.

Kirk smiled at Jackie then looked back at Beck. "She's afraid I'll ruin her for Holden."

§

Jackie had just about drifted off to sleep on her cot within the dimly lit visitor's center when a loud clunk from the back office area woke her. Bogart nearly jumped from his cot with his gun in his hand.

"What was that?" Bogart gasped and looked around the dimly lit room.

"Nothing," Kirk muttered while half asleep on his cot closest to the back hallway. "Go back to sleep."

"I should check it out," Bogart insisted.

"It came from the back office," Kirk moaned without opening his eyes. "It's just Zack being, well, Zack."

Bogart glanced at Jackie, who was now sitting up as well. She glanced at her watch and was also wondering if they should check it out. There was another clunk from the back office area. Bogart shook his head defiantly.

"I'm going to check it out," Bogart announced, then headed for the hallway alongside the bathrooms.

Jackie groaned, moved from her cot, and followed Bogart with less enthusiasm. She didn't want him wandering into trouble by himself, although she was pretty sure Kirk was right. Bogart stopped outside the closed office door. As Jackie approached, they heard the loud thump again, like someone moving furniture. Bogart knocked on the door.

"Zack?" he announced. "Everything okay in there?"

"Go away!" Sam screamed then cried out in ecstasy.

Bogart stepped back from the door with an embarrassed look on his face, then glanced at Jackie. She winced slightly, hid her own embarrassment, and quickly hurried back for the main room with Bogart only a step behind her. Zack may have been clueless when it came to reading women, but even Jackie was aware of his reputation as an aggressive lover. Of course, Holden would say the same about her. As they returned to the main room, Kirk eyed them from where he remained comfortably resting on his cot and grinned.

"Amateurs," Kirk teased, then shut his eyes.

§

A small light dimly lighted the back office within the visitor's center on the table alongside the wall. The old, leather sofa bed had been opened into a full-sized bed but still remained neatly made. What few items had been on the nearby desk had been hastily cast onto the floor during Zack and Sam's impromptu desktop romp. Zack tossed his naked body into the chair behind the desk as he took a moment to catch his breath. The old chair creaked beneath his weight. Sam leaned against the desk for support while panting, a permanent smile on her face. She finally reached for Zack's discarded shirt and slipped into it. Sam cringed with some discomfort from the thumping pain in her injured shoulder then buttoned the three middle buttons. She sat on the desk facing Zack and eyed the naked man leaning back in the chair with his bare feet crossed and propped on the desk.

"You have a bit of a wild streak in you," Sam teased while attempting to contain her grin.

Zack opened his eyes, peered at her, and then chuckled. "I've been accused of worse."

Sam attempted to lean seductively on the desk but found it difficult with her injured arm. "I've been alone too long," she remarked and offered a tiny smile. "I forgot how much fun mixed company could be."

"I'm mildly useful," Zack remarked.

Sam moved off the desk and climbed onto the pull-out sofa bed. She managed a somewhat seductive pose on the much softer surface and offered her best come-hither look. Zack studied her a moment, then seemed to take his cue and joined her on the sofa bed. Sam immediately snuggled up against him. Zack tensed slightly but then relaxed with her in his arms. Sam lightly ran her finger over one of his many scars visible within the dim lighting.

"You saw a lot of action in the military, huh?" she asked without meeting his gaze.

"My share, I suppose," Zack replied.

"And then some," she added while moving her hand to another scar on his chest. "Jackie said you served with her father."

"Yeah, he and I served together," he replied.

"I assumed that's where you got most of your scars," she remarked, then offered a playful smile. "Either that or you're incredibly accident-prone. A man who can climb a tree the way you do has probably had his share of falls."

"Yeah, but I mostly land on my feet. I have a low center of gravity," he insisted. "Gives me excellent balance."

Sam lifted her head, met Zack's gaze, and grinned. "You're not real good at pillow talk, are you?"

"No, not really," he replied. "I don't have a lot of relationship experience."

"Yeah," she replied, then sighed softly while nuzzling his chest. "Me either."

"Kind of hard to meet people when you live alone in the woods," Zack informed her.

"That was sort of why I wanted to live alone in the woods in the first place," she insisted, then sank into her own thoughts and frowned. "Better to be alone *without* someone than alone *with* someone."

"I get that."

Chapter 41

Late the following morning, Sam stood in the large zebra paddock with her horse and scratched him behind his ears while he nuzzled her.

"Don't worry, boy," Sam announced and seemed a little preoccupied. "We'll be going home soon. A change of dressing today for both our injuries, and then we're out of here."

The horse resumed grazing on the lush grass within the zebra paddock. He didn't seem to share her enthusiasm to return home. His accommodations at the sanctuary were a little larger with thicker grass than what he had back at the ranger's station.

"Fine, you can have the afternoon to graze down the rest of the paddock," she informed the horse. "But then we're definitely going home."

Sam patted the horse's rump while again lost in her own thoughts. She then headed for the gate. As she slipped through the gate, she saw Nevada hurrying from the clinic and across the sanctuary. The bounty hunter seemed unusually distracted, possibly even frustrated, while frantically pressing buttons on her cell phone. Sam appeared curious regarding the mysterious woman who'd patched her up, but yet she'd only met a handful of times. Sam considered it only a moment and then hurried after her.

§

More than an hour later. The visitor's center was relatively quiet that afternoon. Most of the team was patrolling the perimeter, keeping an eye out for anything unusual. Ross, Jackie, and Beck stood at the front desk and discussed their plans for the day.

"If Sam isn't showing any signs of infection from her shoulder wound, we need to send her back home," Ross remarked. "It's getting harder to keep an eye on her without her suspecting we're keeping tabs on her movements."

"Are we sure sending her home is a good idea?" Jackie asked with some concern. "Despite what we told her, we still don't know who actually attacked her."

"Ross is right," Beck announced. "She needs to go back to the ranger's station before her superiors start looking for her." He then straightened and eyed both. "Someone should go back with her. Make sure the ranger's station is safe. Maybe even spend the night."

Ross glanced at Jackie and raised a commanding brow. "She might feel more comfortable having another woman stay with her," he remarked. "You're nominated."

"Actually, I'm guessing this is more of a job for Zack," Jackie informed him.

Beck hid his smirk, but Ross didn't seem to get the inside joke.

"Why Zack?" Ross finally asked.

"They're, uh, *hitting* it off pretty good," Beck remarked while trying not to laugh.

Ross rolled his eyes and shook his head. "I would have put money on Bogart, myself," he muttered. "Fine. Zack will accompany her back to the ranger's station and stay with her tonight."

The visitor's center door was just about thrown open, and Sam stumbled in while holding her bruised and bleeding cheek. She appeared relieved when she saw them and limped toward the desk. All three turned and stared with stunned surprise when they saw her.

"What happened?" Ross asked.

Jackie hurried to Sam's side and removed her hand from her bleeding cheek. "Did your horse kick you?" she asked.

"No," Sam announced with some irritation and shuttered slightly. "Nevada attacked me."

All three stared at her with surprise.

"Nevada?" Beck gasped.

"What do you mean she attacked you?" Ross demanded as his mind reeled with his own theories.

"I saw her heading across the back of the property," Sam informed them. "I think she came from that building in the back. She was heading toward the habitat beyond the zebra paddock." Sam shuttered slightly and looked at all three with stunned disbelief. "I called out to her, but she didn't seem to hear me. I guess she was distracted by something on her cell phone." Sam held her breath and tensed. "Like the friendly person I am, I followed her and again called out to her. That's when she turned and kicked me in the face. I mean, she *literally* kicked me in the face."

"You said she was on her phone?" Ross suddenly asked and appeared somewhat concerned.

"Yeah, I thought maybe she was texting someone," Sam insisted, "but I don't know what sort of reception she'd expect to get out here." She then sank into thought. "She must have been meeting that man."

"What man?" Beck asked while cocking his head.

"I don't know," Sam replied and shook her head. "I guess he's someone from your party I hadn't met yet. Tall man; dark hair; extremely handsome. He looked Italian. I barely got a glimpse of him where he was sitting on the ground before she attacked me."

Ross glared at Beck and pointed demandingly. "Stay with her," he announced, then motioned to Jackie. "You, come with me."

Jackie and Ross ran from the visitor's center.

Sam gingerly touched her bruised cheek, grimaced slightly, and seemed to tense while eyeing Beck. "Are Nevada and Ross a couple?" she whispered with some concern. "Is that why he was so upset about the other guy?"

Beck eyed the innocent look on Sam's face. "Uh, yeah, something like that," he easily lied. "Let's get some ice on your cheek."

§

Jackie followed Ross into the seemingly empty clinic, which lacked anyone on guard duty. Ross just about ran past the unmanned desk and hurried to Marco's closed cell door. Ross looked inside the gorilla cage. Marco was gone. He slammed his palm against the bars causing a dull, metallic clang. He then cursed under his breath while spinning to face Jackie with a hostile look on his face.

"She double-crossed us," Ross snarled as his rage spiked. "Head to the habitat where Sam said she had been heading. See if she's there or any sign of which way she headed. I'll send Zack to meet you there."

Jackie nodded as a thousand thoughts raced through her mind regarding the bounty hunter. She couldn't believe the woman betrayed them, yet it didn't seem so far-fetched. Jackie turned and ran from the clinic.

Ross touched his ear transmitter with added vigor. "All hands on deck," he announced in anger. "Nevada went AWOL and took our friend with her. Zack, meet Jackie at the rhino habitat. I want Gil and Monroe to the helo pad. Standby and await my orders. We'll do a flyover as a last resort. Kirk and Bogart will head north in the direction of the ranger's station. I'll check the jeep and then head south."

§

Ross hurried across the sanctuary, past the visitor's center, and for the area where he had parked Kirk's jeep and the older jeep that Othello graciously had friends send to Monroe. He seemed relieved to find neither jeep had been stolen, but it didn't alter the fact that Nevada and Marco were gone. They could be just about anywhere with the hour's head start they'd already gotten. It was doubtful Marco willingly left with Nevada, and if he did, he was playing her. He knew Nevada intended to turn him over to Vincent for the bounty on his head. Vincent would slowly torture Marco before eventually killing him, and Marco knew that. Beck and Sam approached Ross by the jeep.

"Is she gone?" Beck asked, pretending he hadn't heard anything over his ear transmitter in order to keep up appearances for Sam's sake. She couldn't know they were communicating through secured ear transmitters.

"I don't understand what's going on," Sam announced while eyeing both men. "Am I a little pissed that she attacked me? Of course, but there's no reason to go after her for that. I'm not interested in pressing charges. The woman obviously has mental issues. Getting the law involved isn't going to resolve any of them."

"I'm afraid it's a little more complicated than that," Ross informed her with a defeated sigh. "The man you described seeing with her has stolen all our digital files from our work here. Once they get to the open highway, all our work will be gone forever."

"Well, if you want to find them," Sam insisted, "you should probably start by heading south. That's the direction she was heading when I saw her meeting with that man. If you continue south through the woods, you'll eventually run into town. Through the woods is the more direct route."

"What's between the sanctuary and town?" Beck asked the ranger.

"Once you reach the end of the woods," she informed him, "there's a large farm. The town is on the other side of that farm."

Ross tossed Beck the jeep keys. "Take the jeep," he announced. "Drive out to that farm. See if you can cut them off there. Explain the situation to the farmer. I don't want to frighten anyone." Ross then frowned. "If Nevada hasn't already given them a scare--"

Beck jumped into the loaner jeep, started it, and then raced away from the sanctuary. Ross then turned to Sam and managed a tiny smile.

"We should get you back to the visitor's center and put more ice on your cheek," Ross announced.

"You don't need to worry about me," Sam insisted, then smiled warmly. "I'll be fine. You should help your friends find Nevada. I'd hate to see you lose everything you've worked to achieve. I can take care of myself. I'll just wait in the visitor's center."

Ross smiled and nodded. "Again, I'm sorry for what happened," he insisted and attempted a tiny, reassuring smile. "Nevada had us fooled too."

"I've come to understand the cruel realities of the human condition," Sam replied and shrugged. "It's why I chose such a remote position in the first place. Smokey's never betrayed me."

§

Kirk and Bogart hiked across the sanctuary in the direction of the reptile house. It would make a great hiding place, although it seemed more likely that Nevada would be attempting to find a town or someplace that had a car she could boost. Once they'd check the reptile house, they'd continue onward for the woods in the direction of the ranger's station. It would be a bit of a hike, but Sam had a jeep at the ranger's station. It was possible Nevada would be heading there. The two men approached the children's play area, which was on the way to the reptile house. The children's adventure land had a nice sized play area with typical attractions found in most playgrounds. There was a swing set, jungle gym, and sawhorses. The tall weeds had taken over most of the play items, giving the play area a somewhat creepy appeal

Kirk appeared disgusted and shook his head. "We should never have brought her with us," he snarled in anger. "The fact that she's in Zack's relocation program should have been enough of a red flag."

"He seems to trust her," Bogart insisted. "When has Zack ever been wrong about people?"

Kirk paused alongside the smaller version of a working train now overgrown with vegetation. Back when the sanctuary was in operation, the half-sized train would take visitors around the sanctuary and past the back end of the habitats for greater viewing.

"When has Zack ever been wrong about people?" Kirk demanded in disbelief. "Just about every woman he's ever slept with has tried to kill him. That should tell you everything you need to know. When he *doesn't* trust someone, his instincts are spot-on. Since he rarely trusts people, that's something you can count on. When it comes to his hard-luck cases, Zack is a little too confident that there's good in every soldier."

"I don't know," Bogart remarked and seemed preoccupied. "Nevada doesn't come across as a bad person. I think she's just a little broken."

"She's a lot broken," Kirk insisted. "And she has one point two-five million reasons to betray us."

The two men continued onward toward the nearby reptile building. The reptile house was a large building with tinted, double glass doors and was in decent shape despite years of neglect. There was a large wooden sign out front depicting the reptile house as being home to many species of snakes, alligators, and various other creatures.

"Zack has made mistakes regarding former soldiers on many occasions," Kirk continued. "His biggest one to date is that mess of a man, Hayden Vandyke." Kirk shook his head. "I can't believe he left that man at the hotel in Maine with his kids."

"Is he that bad?" Bogart asked.

Kirk snorted a laugh and shook his head, then sneered. "He should have put that piece of shit down when he had the chance," he remarked. "You don't rehabilitate men like that. You shoot them in the head like a rabid dog. Hayden has a corrupt and indecent soul. If he ever stops feeling sorry for himself, he'll revert back to his old ways." Kirk shook his head. "The idea of that man anywhere near Zack's kids is concerning. I doubt Zack even told them what sort of monster he left with them.   The man's a cold-blooded killer, and that's putting it politely.   I had an opportunity to take him out, but Zack stopped me."

"What about Nevada?" Bogart asked and fidgeted slightly. "How bad is she?"

"I don't think she's the cold-blooded killer type," Kirk replied, then seemed to consider the question.   "But I think she could easily turn down that dark path, given the proper motivation."

Chapter 42

Jackie wandered around outside the rhino habitat where Sam said Nevada had attacked her. The rhino habitat was a large area with a natural-looking containment meant to keep the animals secure without looking like a cage. The large, open field was now tall with weeds. Jackie studied the area and noticed the ground and grass had been disturbed. It seemed almost certain that a scuffle had taken place in that area. There was no sign of Nevada or Marco. Although there was no evidence to support it had actually been Marco Sam had seen, it seemed a fair assumption based on the facts. Jackie wanted to believe Nevada wouldn't betray them, but it wasn't looking good. Still, she wanted to hold out further judgment until she spoke with Zack. The area had been so trampled; it was difficult to tell which way they had gone. Jackie turned and collided with Zack.

She gasped with some surprise, allowing him to support her elbows with his hands to keep her from stumbling. Jackie wasn't sure where her head had been. Zack was great with his stealth mode, but his ability to sneak up on her had decreased considerably considering all the time they'd spent working together. She had a good handle on his routines, habits, and stealthy comings and goings. Jackie was a little mad at herself for not being nearly as alert as she should have been. If Nevada had betrayed them, Jackie would need to watch her back. It was possible Nevada didn't intend to escape with Marco but possibly bring others to them to help her remove him. She couldn't deny the thought of Nevada joining forces with other bounty hunters had crossed her mind. Nevada probably knew a lot of the bounty hunters looking for Marco.

Zack released Jackie's elbows and gave her a slightly bewildered look. "What's with you?" he asked. "I thought you heard me a mile away."

"I guess I was lost in my own thoughts," she informed him and attempted to hide her insecurities.

"About what?" Zack asked, then looked around the area surrounding the rhino habitat, noticing signs of a struggle as well. He frowned his disgust and shook his head. "Well, this isn't good."

"You shouldn't have to ask where my head is," Jackie replied and looked around as well. "Can you tell which way they went?"

Zack again looked at Jackie and raised a curious brow, seeming somewhat surprised by her question. He pointed north from the habitat. "How can you not see which way they went?" he asked and again tilted his head. "It's obvious which way they went. What's wrong with you?"

Jackie frowned with defeat and headed north of the habitat. Zack walked with her and observed the ground and the nearby plant life that showed subtle signs of someone recently passing through.

"At least two people went this way," he informed her while scanning the area. "Definitely a man around Marco's size." Zack indicated the partial footprint then frowned as well. "I'm guessing those are Marco's footprints. Anyone out this far would be wearing decent hiking shoes or combat boots. Not expensive loafers."

"I won't even ask," Jackie muttered.

Jackie understood the basic concept of tracking people, but she wasn't nearly as good as Zack. He could probably give Darth a pretty good run for his money.

"What has you so preoccupied?" Zack again asked without looking at her.

For a man who seemed clueless on emotions, he certainly knew Jackie's moods inside and out.

"I suppose I don't want to believe Nevada would betray us," Jackie remarked and now lagged a step behind Zack, allowing him an unobstructed view of the ground.

"She's not a saint," he reminded her. "Nevada is a huntress. She enjoys what she does. And when there's a lot of money at stake, it only fuels her instincts."

"So you actually think she took off with Marco?" Jackie asked.

"It wouldn't surprise me if she did," Zack replied without looking back at her. "She has no loyalties. No real family. Her only family was her Marine buddies, and most of them continue to serve. She was left behind all alone to fend for herself."

"Why didn't she stay in the Marines?" Jackie felt compelled to ask.

"She said she needed a change of scenery," Zack informed her. "My personal opinion? Something happened. Possibly involving one of her teammates, but she won't talk about it. She's not really good with emotions."

"Seems to me the two of you would speak the same language," Jackie remarked.

Zack cast a sly look back at her and appeared almost offended. "Are you implying I have no emotions?" He rolled his eyes then resumed following the tracks before him. "You, of all people, should know that's not the case."

"You have emotions," Jackie replied, then considered the comment. "They're just *complicated.*"

Zack chuckled without looking back at her. "See? You get me," he remarked and again turned serious. "I think Nevada fears becoming too attached to people. That's why she's having such a difficult time at Scorpio's hotel. The comradery is strong with them, and she doesn't know where she fits in."

Jackie frowned and continued to scan the area while momentarily lost in her own thoughts. She couldn't imagine her life without her father's team, without the dozens of military men parading in and out of her life while growing up and even now. It shaped her life and defined who she was as a person. She couldn't imagine what it would be like if she suddenly lost that. Was that the world Nevada found herself in outside of the military? Jackie could understand how the woman might feel 'lost'. Something then dawned on her, and she eyed Zack in front of her.

"You were going to see what Nevada was doing yesterday afternoon after she left the clinic," Jackie remarked. "Were you able to find her?"

"Yeah, I found her," Zack casually replied while following the trail.

"Was she doing anything, well, suspicious?" Jackie pressed.

"Suspicious?" he asked. He considered the question then shook his head. "No, she wasn't doing anything suspicious. Just, you know, lady things."

"Lady things?" Jackie asked with some surprise, wanting to laugh at the way Zack's mind worked. "What exactly does that mean?"

"You know," he pressed without looking back as they continued along the path. "*Lady* things."

"No, I don't know," she demanded, now feeling her frustration increasing with his non-answer. "You're going to have to elaborate. Stop talking in code."

Zack considered the comment only a moment, although he still didn't look back at her. "You know," he announced. "That thing you do when Holden's not around to do it for you."

Jackie suddenly stopped on the path and stared at Zack's back as he pressed onward. She was mildly surprised by his comment. She wanted to know if he meant what she thought he meant, but she certainly didn't want to hear any further explanation. Zack must have realized she'd stopped, causing him to turn and look back at her.

"What?" he asked almost demandingly. "Guys joke all the time about jerking off. Do you think your solo act is off-limits just because you're a woman?"

Jackie could feel her cheeks turning red, but she wasn't about to let Zack know he had successfully embarrassed her. "I don't know what makes you think that I--"

"Are you really going to pretend you don't self-pleasure?" he boldly announced, then rolled his eyes before turning and continuing along the path. "Please, Jackie! The buzz from your vibrator can be heard through the bedroom walls at the lodge.

We were actually discussing chipping in and buying you a quieter model."

Jackie groaned, rubbed her eyes while enduring the embarrassment, and then hurried after Zack. "You're not funny," she snapped.

"Wasn't trying to be," he replied.

"How the hell did we get on this subject?" Jackie muttered while shaking her head.

"You asked what Nevada was doing in the woods when I found her."

"Of course, you'd remember that," she remarked under her breath. "Please tell me you didn't spy on the woman while she did that."

"Why would I?" he asked without looking back at her. "I have no interest in having a sexual relationship with Nevada. Therefore, her solo act doesn't interest me."

For some men, that may have sounded difficult to believe, but Jackie knew Zack was a different breed altogether. Bogart wasn't wrong. Someone *should* do a study on Zack's mating rituals. Although he'd readily jump into bed with just about any sexually aggressive woman, he wasn't the kind of guy you'd catch watching porn. Jackie couldn't even remember the last time she'd caught Zack lusting after a woman. He could go months without sex, and it wouldn't even faze him. Yet he was ready and willing at a moment's notice, almost as if there was some secret 'on' switch.

"Well, I'm glad to hear you have some morals when it comes to things like that," Jackie reported, actually feeling better on account of her own situation. "I'd hate to think you're listening through the walls back at the lodge. At least I don't have to worry about that."

Zack cast a glance back at her, giving her an odd look. He then smirked and snorted a laugh while continuing along the path. "You obviously weren't paying attention to the first part of that statement," he remarked, then shrugged, "but whatever makes you comfortable."

Jackie hesitated, stopped in her tracks, and again stared at Zack's back. "Wait," she announced, then felt a strange rush of panic and hurried after him. "What?"

§

Gil and Monroe followed Darth through the woods to the makeshift helicopter landing pads in the small clearing. The car Zack and Kirk had borrowed from Gunny was parked alongside the black SUV Bogart had 'borrowed' from one of the hitmen. Nothing appeared to have been disturbed. Darth excitedly ran to Gil's helicopter and jumped at the door, then sat while patiently waiting. Like all good dogs, he thought they were going for a ride.

Monroe touched his ear transmitter. "Ross, we're at the landing pad," he announced. "No sign that any of the cars have been tampered with. It doesn't look as if Nevada has been here."

Gil approached Darth and stared down at him. "No, we're not going for a ride."

Darth turned and ran for Jackie's helicopter and sat by the side door. He let out a loud, demanding bark while keeping his eyes locked on the side door.

"The answer is still no," Gil informed the dog with a little more insistence.

Darth whined while staring at the door as his tail happily wagged.

"That dog is so spoiled," Monroe muttered.

"He's spending too much time with Aunt Jackie and Uncle Zack," Gil remarked. "I don't know who to blame, but one of them has been wrestling with him. Found that out when my wife and I were having a romantic evening. We were sitting on the floor, and he tackled me to the ground."

"Yeah, I'm sure that's Zack," Monroe muttered. He again touched his ear transmitter. "Do you copy, Ross?" He then eyed Gil. "Reception is bad this far out from the visitor's center."

"There's a lot of interference between here and there," Gil informed him. "I got better reception when I was closer to the woods."

Darth stood on his hind legs and began pawing at Jackie's helicopter.

Gil groaned and shook his head. "No, we're not going for a ride," he insisted to the dog. "And stop scratching Aunt Jackie's helicopter. You know how she feels about her toys. You're going to get me in trouble."

Darth whined loudly. Gil sighed with defeat and approached the side door.

"Fine," he muttered and pulled open the door. "You can sit inside--"

Darth suddenly snarled and leaped into the helicopter. Rowen was seen just beyond the doorway. He bolted against the opposite side door and stared at the dog with concern. Gil swiftly drew his weapon and aimed it at Rowen.

"Call off the dog," Rowen cried out. "I was just looking for a place to sleep!"

Darth continued to bark and snarl. Monroe pulled his weapon and hurried for Gil's helicopter. Darth spun, leaped from Jackie's helicopter, and bolted across the field to Gil's helicopter. Monroe pulled open the door with his weapon aimed. Darth placed his front feet on the helicopter floor and snarled at Quinn, who sat on the end seat in the back and held his hands in the air.

"I'm with him," Quinn announced. "We didn't know anyone was coming back. Honest. It looked like a cozy, safe place to sleep."

"Who are you?" Monroe demanded.

"I'm Quinn, and that's Rowen," he announced while indicating the man in the helicopter further away, although not taking his eyes off the seemingly vicious excited dog. "We were camping back there." He nodded toward the woods. "A bear came along and destroyed our tent. We were just looking for a place to crash for a while before heading back for our car."

"Gil," Monroe announced without taking his eyes off Quinn. "Options?"

"Fresh out," Gil called back while keeping his gun trained on Rowen.

They were in a bit of a predicament now. Should they hold the two strangers, possibly innocent men, prisoner? Or let them go and risk blowing their cozy safe house? Gil lowered his weapon. Despite being uncomfortable with it, Monroe followed suit.

"Where's your car?" Gil asked Rowen.

"Out by the road," Rowen insisted and attempted to relax. "A good mile from here. We were tired and didn't want to make the long trip back to the car."

"And where is this destroyed campsite?" Gil continued his line of question.

Rowen pointed toward the woods. "About two miles that way," he announced and nodded at Quinn. "Just like my friend said."

"Did you see the bear?" Gil asked.

"See it?" Rowen asked with some surprise. "No, we didn't see it. Why?"

"How do you know it was a bear?" Gil asked.

"The entire camp was destroyed," Quinn chimed in, perfecting his innocent country boy look. "I don't think a man would do something like that."

Gil and Monroe exchanged looks. If hitmen were attempting to clear out the woods of hunters and campers, they would do something like that.

"What are you thinking?" Monroe asked Gil.

"Do you have keys for either car?" Gil then asked his teammate.

Monroe approached the black SUV Bogart had taken off Hawthorne. Since it couldn't be traced back to any of them, it seemed the logical choice. He checked under the floor mat and removed the keys.

"Yeah," Monroe announced in response. "I have keys to this one."

"Darth and I will drive these gentlemen to their car and see them off safely," Gil announced. "Darth wants to go for a ride anyway."

"You sure?" Monroe asked.

Gil nodded. "Darth can ride in the back with our guests," he replied.

Rowen and Quinn tensed slightly at the suggestion but immediately covered. "That's awful kind of you," Rowen announced with his perfected country boy smile. "We appreciate that."

Gil then looked back at Monroe. "You wait here, in case our *friend* shows up."

Chapter 43

Kirk and Bogart continued across the sanctuary and reached the last habitat before the woods, which was the lion habitat. A pair of sliced zip ties were on the pathway not far from the faux rock formation that contained the habitat entrance. They heard the rattling of chain-link fencing. Both men drew their weapons and hurried around the fake rock wall. Nevada was within the enclosure, kicking the chain-link fence that constituted an entrance gate. Her boot knives were outside the fence, and the gate was held shut with one of her own zip ties. She appeared relieved when she saw the men and attempted to collect her emotions.

"I'm glad to see you guys," Nevada announced, then touched her bleeding temple. "Get me the hell out of here!"

Kirk placed his finger to his ear transmitter. "Hey, we found Nevada within the lion habitat," he announced. "She's alone. It looks as if she'd been in a scuffle."

Nevada glared at Kirk and raised her brows. "Someone jumped me," she snarled in response. "Will you get me out of here?"

Bogart frowned and shook his head. "I'm very disappointed in you," he remarked to the caged woman.

"We all have our off days," she retorted, then turned demanding. "Are you going to let me out or not?"

"Copy that," Kirk announced and removed his finger from his ear transmitter. He then looked at Nevada and raised an arrogant brow. "Ross says to sit tight."

"Sit tight?" Nevada demanded with surprise, then turned angry. "Whoever clobbered me could be heading for Marco as we speak."

"We already know who clobbered you," Kirk informed her while sneering his disgust. "You tried to take off with Marco. I wouldn't doubt you're working with those two men Gil and Monroe caught by the helicopters."

"What two men by the helicopters?" Nevada demanded in what almost appeared to be surprise. "Why would you think I took off with Marco?"

"Because Marco is gone," Kirk informed her, then indicated the sliced zip ties in his hand. "These are yours, aren't they? We found them around the corner, where Marco attacked you before locking you in the lion habitat."

Nevada stared at Kirk with a strange look on her face. "He got away?" She shook her head and then turned angry. "I didn't take off with Marco," she insisted. "Someone jumped me, and it certainly wasn't Marco. A professional. They must have gotten to him." She became enraged. "We need to find him!"

"Oh, stop with the lies!" Kirk shouted in anger. "We already know it was you. Sam told us that you attacked her beyond the zebra paddock."

Nevada stared at Kirk with horror. Her expression then turned hateful and angry. "She's a lying bitch!"

"She said she saw you texting someone on your phone," Bogart remarked while frowning, disappointed in the woman. He shook his head. "Why, Nevada? You put us all in danger. There's no telling who's going to show up because of your greed."

"I *didn't* betray anyone," she cried out in frustration. "You're taking the word of some park ranger you don't even know over me!"

"In all fairness, we don't know you either," Bogart informed her.

Kirk slapped Bogart's arm while nodding in agreement. "That's right," he announced boldly and glared at Nevada. "We don't know you. Sam said she saw you on your cell phone. She followed you to where you had Marco and that you attacked her." His eyes narrowed. "Well, guess what? Marco is gone. We find you locked in a cage and your zip ties on the ground. You sound pretty guilty to me."

Nevada stared at him in stunned silence with her mouth hanging open. Rage overtook her. "You're an idiot! I'd never betray Zack," she cried out, then pointed demandingly. "No matter what shitty things I'd do, he always has my back. I wouldn't do anything that might get him killed."

Kirk sneered at her and touched his ear transmitter. "Do we have names on those two guys by the helicopters?" He hesitated while listening to the response then looked at Nevada. "Rowen and Quinn."

Nevada's expression suddenly dropped.

Kirk smirked at her reaction and nodded. "Yeah, that's what I thought."

"I didn't give them our location," she announced and again turned angry. "They tracked me down at a crappy roadside motel, but I didn't give them any information."

§

Rowen and Quinn climbed into the back of Bogart's stolen SUV, sliding across the seat. Gil opened the back door on the opposite side for Darth to join them. Gil then hesitated, hearing chatter over his earpiece, and touched his hidden transmitter.

"Huh--?" Gil hesitated only a moment, then drew his weapon and pointed it at the two men. He commanded to the dog in German, "Darth, halten!"

Darth snarled viciously and lunged for the men while bearing his teeth. Both men slid across the back seat and stared at the snarling, enraged dog that seemed to be waiting for the command to strike. Monroe ran to the opposite side of the car, opened the back door, and aimed his weapon at the men. He had received the same message from Ross over his earpiece as well.

"It seems we almost made a mistake," Gil announced to the motionless men frightened by the snarling dog. "It was nice of Nevada to confirm your identities to us."

"Out of the car," Monroe ordered, indicating his side. "Nice and slow."

§

Kirk glanced at Bogart and indicated Nevada still locked within the enclosed habitat. "The guys are on their way," he announced. "We'll just keep her locked away until they get here."

Bogart frowned, then eyed Nevada and shook his head with disappointment. "I went to bat for you," he huffed at the woman. "I thought they were judging you too harshly." He then eyed Kirk with shame. "I'm always fooled by a pretty face."

"It's not your fault," Kirk informed him, almost showing compassion for once. "Attractive women will always be our downfall." He then indicated Nevada. "Watch her. I'm going to the woods. See if I can catch up to Marco before he gets too far ahead of us."

Bogart frowned and nodded. Once Kirk disappeared into the woods, he looked back at the gate. Nevada was gone. It wasn't as if she could go anywhere. The habitat had chain-link fencing meant to keep lions contained. If lions couldn't escape, Nevada certainly couldn't. The sound of the chain-link fence rattling could be heard. Bogart groaned and hurried around the side of the habitat just to make sure she didn't do anything stupid. He stopped and watched Nevada climbing the eight-foot-tall fencing. Bogart folded his arms across his chest and shook his head while indicating the three rows of barbed wire lined across the top.

"You won't make it past the barbed wire," he informed her.

Nevada easily scaled the fence and ignored his words. When she reached the top, she grabbed onto the support pole angled inward, which contained the rows of barbed wire. Bogart stared in silent disbelief as Nevada maneuvered to the end then heaved herself up with astonishing agility, only touching the barbed wire with the soles of her boots. She stood on top of the angled support pole and caught her balance. Bogart stared at her eight feet up in the air and watched as she cautiously walked along the support pole closer to the edge of the fence.

"Don't do it," Bogart warned her and hurried closer to the fence.

It now seemed possible that she'd find a way to make it back to the chain-link fence and climb down. Nevada leaned down before Bogart reached her, grabbed the top of the fence beyond the barbed wire, and back flipped, allowing her body to strike the chain-link fence. She released the top of the fence and dropped the remaining couple of feet. Bogart was just about on top of her while reaching for his weapon. Nevada hit the ground and immediately spun into a roundhouse kick for Bogart, knocking the gun from his hand. Bogart was a little surprised by her quick reflexes but took a defensive step back, prepared to take on the nimble woman. She threw a punch for his face, which he immediately blocked and attempted to catch her wrist. Nevada saw the move coming and grabbed his wrist instead, then punched him in the chest with her left fist. The hit wasn't excessively hard, but it was enough to catch his attention.

Bogart broke free from her grip and attempted to kick her in the side. She delivered a sharp elbow to his leg, which stung like a bastard, then delivered a soft kick to the groin. Bogart went down from the blow, feeling the intense pain. She could have easily gone for the field goal kick in order to disable him effectively, but that didn't seem to be her objective. Bogart took several deep breaths while pulling himself to his hands and knees. He watched Nevada snatch his discarded weapon along with her boot knives, then take off deeper into the sanctuary. Bogart groaned in discomfort and frustration then touched his ear transmitter.

"Nevada got away," he announced, alerting the others. "She's heading deeper into the sanctuary. South, toward the train. She could be leading us to Marco."

§

The guys were now on the hunt for Nevada after she disappeared from the lion habitat. Jackie and Zack had been heading in the direction she was last seen, but they didn't find any trace of the crafty woman. While Gil and Monroe drove back to the sanctuary with their two prisoners, Ross and Beck left Sam at the visitor's center so they could help hunt down Nevada and maybe locate Marco before they breached the security of the sanctuary. Kirk was now backtracking to catch up with Bogart in his search for the missing woman. The sound of Sam's horse loudly snorting and squealing sent Jackie and Zack to the nearby zebra habitat. They entered the habitat with their weapons drawn and discovered Nevada clutching the saddled horse's reins while holding Bogart's gun aimed at Sam. Sam, refusing to be intimidated, had her rifle aimed at Nevada. The two women appeared to be in a stand-off. Both saw Jackie and Zack arrive, but neither took their eyes or weapons off each other.

"I caught her," Sam announced to Jackie and Zack while keeping her weapon aimed. "She was trying to steal my horse and make a run for it."

"You lying bitch," Nevada growled in anger while keeping her attention focused on Sam. "She's playing you! I never attacked her. She attacked me!"

Sam stared at Nevada and shook her head without lowering her weapon. "She's a fucking psycho ninja or something," Sam remarked.

Zack was reluctant to aim his weapon at either woman while attempting to sort out what was happening. It seemed very unlikely that Sam could get the slip-on someone like Nevada.

"Nevada," Zack calmly announced. "Put the gun down. We'll sort this out. There's no need for anyone else to get hurt."

"I didn't betray you!" Nevada cried out in anger and possible frustration while keeping her weapon aimed at Sam. She then sneered at the woman ranger. "You're being played by her. She's been slinking around here ever since she'd supposedly been shot by poachers."

"I *was* shot," Sam snarled back defensively. "Do you think I shot myself?"

Jackie saw Nevada's cell phone on the ground not far from them. She picked it up and fiddled with it, hoping to find some of her own answers.

Sam cast a quick look at Zack. "She attacked me because I caught her conspiring with that man and whoever she was exchanging texts with on her phone."

"I wasn't conspiring with anyone, and I certainly wasn't texting anyone," Nevada scoffed, although it was unclear if it was directed at Sam or Zack.

Zack stood alongside Sam and watched Nevada with a hard to read expression. "Just put the gun down, Nevada," he insisted. "We can resolve this without aiming weapons."

"Tell her to put hers down first," Nevada snarled while sneering at Sam. "I put mine down, and she's liable to shoot me."

"You attacked me," Sam shouted back in anger. "I'm not putting my weapon down. I don't trust you as far as I can throw you."

Jackie hacked into Nevada's cell phone and pressed several buttons. She suddenly tensed then looked up. "Zack," she announced in a firm tone, alerting Zack even though he didn't look at her. "Sweep her."

Without warning, Zack grabbed the barrel of Sam's rifle with his left hand, jerked it up in the air, and swept Sam's legs out from under her from behind. Sam crashed to the ground, clutching her injured shoulder from the impact, and groaned. Nevada released the breath she'd been holding and lowered her weapon. Sam scrambled to her knees while clutching her injured shoulder and glared at Zack.

"What the hell--?" Sam cried out then pointed demandingly at Nevada. "You trust her over me?"

"Nope," Zack casually replied while slinging the rifle over his shoulder. "I trust Jackie." He then pointed a stern, warning finger at Sam. "Stay down."

Sam remained on her knees while staring up at Zack and shook her head. "I can't believe you'd take her side over mine."

Zack ignored the comment and eyed Jackie as she approached them with Nevada's cell phone. "What did you find?"

Jackie glanced at Nevada and raised her brow. "You didn't make any phone calls or send any texts, did you?"

Nevada shook her head. "I told you I didn't," she scoffed, still fuming from the incident.

Jackie then looked back at Zack. "Her phone is still in airplane mode, and there aren't any new text messages," she informed him, then looked back at Nevada and raised her brows. "Tell Zack what you were doing on your phone when Sam saw you leaving the clinic."

Nevada frowned and shifted uncomfortably. "I was looking at photos."

Jackie held up the phone to Zack and showed him the photo of Nevada with Zack's kids and their friends at the hotel in Maine. Jackie then showed the picture to Nevada.

"This picture?" she asked.

Nevada frowned and looked away without answering.

Jackie then looked back at Zack. "She wasn't conspiring with other bounty hunters," she announced. "She misses her family."

"They're not my family," Nevada muttered without looking at either. "I don't even like them." She then frowned and seemed almost insecure. "And I'm pretty sure they don't like me either."

"I somehow doubt that," Jackie informed her, then tossed her cell phone to her.

Nevada caught the phone and placed it in her pocket without another word.

Jackie looked back at Zack then indicated Sam. "Sam took Marco," she insisted. "We need to find out what she did with him."

Zack glared at Sam, who remained on her knees. "Where's Marco?"

Sam sneered at Zack. "Fuck off," she snarled and looked away.

Without looking at Nevada, Zack held up his hand. Nevada tossed him a pair of zip ties. Zack caught them and, without emotion, swiftly zip-tied Sam's wrists in front of her, not the least bit concerned about the pain it caused her injured shoulder. He pulled her to her feet and nodded toward the clinic. Sam sneered and reluctantly headed in the direction he'd indicated with Zack only a step behind her. Nevada watched them leave, fidgeted, and finally looked at Jackie with some embarrassment.

"Are you going to tell Zack what else you found on my phone?" Nevada asked in a somewhat docile tone.

Jackie managed a tiny smile and shook her head. "I didn't see anything else," she replied, then turned and followed Zack.

Nevada stared after Jackie and smiled with relief. She then hurried after them.

Chapter 44

Zack escorted Sam into the clinic with her wrists zip-tied in front of her and stopped her in front of Ross, who sat on the vet's desk. Beck leaned against the gorilla cage bars and watched them in silence. Sam didn't bother looking around and immediately made eye contact with Ross. Her lack of emotion told them everything they needed to know about her intentions coming into the sanctuary, although it wasn't clear when she knew what.

"Where's Marco?" Ross asked with little emotion as he folded his arms across his chest and stared back at her.

Sam then smirked in a mildly unsettling manner and raised an arrogant brow. "Fuck you."

Ross glanced past Sam at Zack. "Charming girl," he announced.

"Consistent with the type of trash I attract," Zack replied, not even seeming affected by it.

Nevada and Jackie entered the clinic but remained near the entrance and observed from a distance.

"Lock her up," Ross announced and indicated the cage they had used for Marco.

Zack escorted Sam to the nearby cage, where he emptied her pockets and checked her shoes for any lock pick devices. She glared her displeasure with his indifferent treatment of her. Kirk and Bogart soon joined them in the clinic. Monroe and Gil were only a minute behind them and entered with Quinn and Rowen. Both men had their wrists zip-tied behind their backs. When they saw Nevada, they became enraged.

"You double-crossed us," Rowen shouted while attempting to reach Nevada.

"I was trying to save your worthless lives," Nevada scoffed back while glaring at both men. "Even if the three of us did combine forces, we'd never make it out alive. We're no match for what's out there!"

Gil and Monroe placed them in a separate cage not far from Sam's cage. Monroe cut the zip ties binding them since they weren't getting out of the pen anytime soon.

"I'll remain here and watch our prisoners," Ross informed them. "Jackie and Zack will hike to the ranger's station. I want the two of you to search every inch of that place." He then indicated Sam within the first cage. "I want you to find out everything there is about *Ranger* Sam." He then eyed the others. "The rest of you need to split up into your usual teams and find Marco."

As the guys buddied up and began leaving the clinic, Nevada frowned and insecurely rubbed her arms. "What about me?" she then asked, seeming almost apprehensive.

"Beck is going with Gil and Monroe," Ross informed her. "You can go with Kirk and Bogart."

Kirk groaned while sneering. "Great," he muttered.

Bogart managed a tiny smile at Nevada while waving off Kirk. "Kirk's an asshole, but you get used to him," he announced.

§

Bogart appeared defeated as he walked with Kirk and Nevada through the sanctuary overgrown with vegetation. "Finding Marco is going to be next to impossible," he informed them. "If she hid him somewhere within the park, he could be almost anywhere."

"Not anywhere," Nevada informed Bogart, then nodded to an old, rotting sign that pointed out the different areas of the park. "This way; toward the gorilla habitat."

"Why that way?" Kirk asked while reluctantly following her anyway. "It's not very far from the clinic. That sounds a little too easy."

"She jumped me near the lion's habitat," Nevada informed them. "She got me out of the way first, and then went back for Marco. It's a straight shot across the park from the lion's habitat past the gorilla's enclosure to the clinic. I caught up with her in the zebra habitat where she was saddling her horse, preparing for a hasty getaway." Nevada eyed both men. "That means Marco has to be somewhere nearby. We were in the zebra habitat, and Zack and Jackie had checked the giraffe paddock. That just leaves the gorilla habitat."

"Your logic escapes me," Kirk muttered, "but I don't have a better suggestion."

Nevada groaned and rolled her eyes. "I'm a bounty hunter," she informed them. "Finding people who don't want to be found is sort of my job." She threw her hands in the air in frustration. "Just trust me, okay?"

They headed into the gorilla habitat and looked around. The habitat had a large open area overgrown with tall weeds, natural fencing, and tall, faux stone for climbing. Bogart entered the fake stone cave that was meant to be a shelter for the gorillas. Once inside, he discovered Marco sitting on the cement floor with his hands and ankles zip-tied and a piece of duct tape over his mouth."

"He's in here," Bogart called to them.

Kirk and Nevada entered the stone shelter. Nevada removed one of the knives from her boots and easily sliced through the zip ties while Bogart removed the duct tape covering his mouth. Marco groaned a sigh of relief and gingerly rubbed his sore wrists.

"I'm so glad to see you guys," he announced, then eyed Nevada. "Even you."

Nevada rolled her eyes then returned her knife to her boot. Kirk lent Marco a hand, which he accepted, and pulled him to his feet.

"That ranger woman came into my cell, waved a gun in my face, and tied me up," Marco informed them then cringed. "The way she looked at me, I thought for sure she was going to kill me."

"She had us all fooled," Bogart remarked.

"We should get him back to the clinic before something else happens," Kirk announced.

§

After announcing they'd found Marco, everyone except Jackie and Zack returned to the clinic. Marco joined the others near the desk while glancing across the clinic room. He saw Sam occupying his old cell and sneered at her.

"Psycho bitch," Marco scoffed at her.

Sam sneered back at him.

Marco then eyed the two men in the end cage. "Who are they?"

"They're bounty hunters," Nevada informed him while moving closer to the cell containing the two men. She glared at both men with loathe. "Don't worry; they're not the 'kill you' type of bounty hunters."

"We might just make an exception for you," Rowen remarked to Nevada while offering a slightly cocky grin.

Nevada sneered at Rowen. "Give it your best shot," she scoffed.

Ross sighed while eyeing Marco, leaned against the vet's desk, and folded his arms across his chest. "It might be easier if we just left you on your own recognizance," he remarked to Marco. "Do you understand the importance of staying with us?"

"Trust me," Marco announced as his eyes widened. "I'm not going anywhere without you guys."

"Kirk and Bogart will take first watch," Ross announced. "Take him to locker room and let him shower, then get him something to eat." Ross approached Nevada, who still remained near the cell containing the two bounty hunters. "I think, under the circumstances, it'd be best if you distanced yourself from these two."

Nevada cast a skeptical look at Ross. It was possible she realized Ross didn't exactly trust her with the bounty hunters with whom she'd had a known history. She didn't respond but, instead, turned and walked away. Ross eyed both men, then returned to the vet's desk, casting himself in the chair, and propped his feet on top.

"Girl's going soft," Rowen muttered to Quinn while watching Nevada leave the clinic.

"No, she just got a better offer," Quinn remarked with a defeated sigh. "She knows better than to bite the hand that feeds her."

"Nah," Rowen remarked while shaking his head. "Ever since she took up residence at Zack's home for wayward mercenaries, she's been different. I think he broke her."

"She was pretty much broken before," Quinn reminded him. He then hesitated and considered something else. "Maybe he's fixing her."

Rowen glared at Quinn. "You don't fix someone like Nevada," he remarked. "Girl's got no emotions."

§

Zack entered the ranger's station with Jackie only a step behind him. Both headed in separate directions to begin their search. Jackie entered the bedroom while Zack started his search in the living room at a bookcase filled with fiction novels. He pulled each book from the shelf and flipped through it in search of anything hidden within them.

"Who reads this many romance novels?" Zack called to Jackie.

"Plenty of women read romance novels, Zack," she called back from the bedroom.

"You don't," Zack replied.

"I do, but mine are all digital," she announced.

"What you read doesn't constitute 'romance'," he informed her. "I've seen what you read. A lot of throbbing, thrusting, and panting."

Jackie poked her head out of the bedroom and glared at Zack's profile with annoyance. "Stay out of my cell phone," she scoffed.

"Why do you need to read that trash anyway?" Zack asked without looking back at her. "Doesn't Holden give you enough throbbing and thrusting?"

A flying pillow struck Zack in the back of the head. He jumped and looked back at the bedroom doorway, but Jackie was gone. Zack grinned slyly and returned to the books on the shelf.

"Zack," Jackie called out from the bedroom. "I found something!"

Zack replaced the book to the shelf then hurried for the bedroom. Jackie kneeled over a hidden compartment within the floor. She removed a large metal box. Zack lowered himself to his knees on the floor beside her. Jackie attempted to open the box, but it was locked.

"I need something to pick the lock," she announced, then turned toward him while still on her knees, knowing he had just about everything a good Boy Scout would need. Jackie patted down his thigh pocket closest to her. "Do you have a lock pick kit on you?"

"Would it kill you to carry shit in your own pockets?" Zack teased.

Jackie eyed him and raised an arrogant brow. "I shop in women's stores," she informed him matter-of-factly. "Women's clothes don't have pockets."

"Is that why I'm always carrying your lip balm?" Zack asked.

Zack then removed his Bowie knife from his boot, slipped the blade between the lock and the box, and gave it a hard flick. The lock flew from the box. Jackie eyed him skeptically. She could have done that.

"Not exactly state-of-the-art technology," he informed her, flipped the knife in his hand, and returned it to his hidden boot sheath.

Jackie opened the box revealing several identifications, passports, credit cards, and a few bundles of cash. While Zack routed through the IDs, Jackie removed an envelope with several newspaper articles inside.

Zack suddenly groaned and shook his head. "Son-of-a-bitch," he muttered.

"What is it?" Jackie asked and glanced at the ID in his hand.

"All these IDs are fake except this one," he informed her and showed her the real one. "Sam was girlfriend to Vinnie the knife's grandson, Vincent."

Jackie's expression dropped. "Oh, that's not good," she remarked. "Meanwhile, we're sitting on the man who's accused of killing his brother."

"Oh, but it gets worse," Zack informed her. "About five years ago, back when Sam's real name was Kelsey, she witnessed Vincent killing a police detective. Kelsey went into witness protection; only it didn't end very well. It was believed she'd died along with several U.S. Marshalls when the safe house was blown up."

Jackie shuttered, reliving one of the less fond memories from her own past. She frowned and sifted through old newspaper articles, scanning them.

"Yep, it's all here," she remarked. "Sam did one hell of a job going off-grid."

"She couldn't get too much further off-grid than this," Zack agreed. "Question is, how far did she go to disappear? What happened to the real ranger?"

"How do you suppose she learned of the bounty on Marco?" Jackie then asked. "She doesn't exactly have access to that sort of news up here."

"She has internet," Zack informed her. "With all the free time she has on her hands, it wouldn't take much for her to put it together."

"Okay, so she dated Vinnie the knife's grandson and was about to testify against him," Jackie remarked. "That means he wanted her dead five years ago. What would she hope to accomplish by snatching Marco?"

"Absolution?" Zack suggested while raising a brow. "Maybe she just wanted her life back."

"I doubt Vincent would give her that," Jackie remarked. "She'd have to know the chances of Vincent simply killing her would be great."

Zack placed Sam's ID into his pants pocket then sat on the floor near the secret compartment. His mood seemed to change drastically. "You know, I'm no stranger to women using me," he informed her, then ran his fingers through his hair in disgust, "but I usually know that going in." He then met her gaze. "I actually believed she was who she said she was. That she thought I was just some average guy and she was some average girl." Zack tossed the remaining IDs and passports into the metal box. "Something almost normal, like when I first met Maggie." He then stood and seemed almost angry, which wasn't often. "*This* is why I prefer women like Katya. I know where I stand with women like that. There are no games, no pretending to be something we're not. We're who we are and do what we do."

Jackie stood and met his gaze. "You know damned well you can have a normal relationship with a normal woman if you just put a little effort into it," she informed him. "Just because Sam turned out to be a fraud--"

"I'm not broken, Jackie," he announced boldly while staring into her eyes. "I know the kind of person I am. You don't have to feel sorry for me."

"I'm not feeling sorry for you," she insisted while moving closer to him, then placed her arms around his neck and moved in to hug him.

"This certainly feels like pity," he gruffly remarked.

"Shut up and accept the hug," Jackie announced without releasing him.

Zack placed his arms around her waist and held her only a moment before pulling her tightly against him as if he'd never let go. "Okay," he announced while burying his face into her neck. "You can feel sorry for me just this once."

Jackie suddenly tensed at what she felt then groaned in disgust. "And you ruined the moment," she firmly announced while attempting to push him away.

He refused to release her. "I swear," Zack protested. "That *is* my gun."

Jackie managed to pull away, then looked down and saw the handle of the semiautomatic sticking out of the waistband of his pants. She smiled with some embarrassment.

"My mistake," she remarked.

Zack shook his head with disapproval. "You always go there," he huffed.

"Sorry," she replied while smiling timidly, then crouched beside the metal box and returned it to the compartment in the floor.

While she wasn't looking, Zack quickly turned away and attempted to adjust himself without her noticing.

Chapter 45

Sam stared at the ID Zack held up to the bars containing her photo and the name Kelsey. She frowned, walked away from the bars, and flopped onto the cot.

"So now you know who I am," Sam scoffed then glared at the guys on the other side of the bars. "Why don't you tell me who the hell you are?"

"We're doing some contract work for Giovanni," Ross informed her. "We're here to keep his son alive."

Sam lifted her head and glared at them. "If I intended to kill Marco, I would have done it," she insisted. "I'm not a killer."

"No," Nevada scoffed while glaring at her. "You were only dating one."

Sam sprang up from the cot and glared at Nevada. "Not intentionally," she scoffed, then attempted to control her temper. "I'll admit; I'd heard the rumors about Vincent's family, but Vincent told me he was nothing like them. I dated him for a little more than a year, and I never noticed anything even remotely suspicious. He seemed legitimate." She then frowned. "Until that one night." Sam drifted off into her own world. "I couldn't sleep and went downstairs. That's when I walked in on Vincent executing that police detective. I suppose I was in shock, but I just stood there wondering if he was going to kill me for having seen it." She managed a tiny, almost painful smile and snorted a laugh. "He handed the gun to his man, took me back upstairs, and made love to me as if nothing had ever happened. I was just waiting for him to kill me, but he didn't."

Everyone stared at Sam and quietly listened to her story. Sam remained lost in her own thoughts.

"I remember every detail of that night like it was yesterday. He told me he loved me, rolled over, and went to sleep as if everything was perfectly fine." Sam looked up and realized everyone was staring at her. "I was too scared to go to the police. I was sure he'd have his men follow me. I waited until two days later when I had a spa treatment scheduled." She drew a deep breath and held her head up proudly. "Once I was at the spa, I called the FBI. I wasn't sure if any of the local police were on Vincent's payroll, and I didn't know who to trust. That was the day my life ceased being my own." She then eyed the others. "You heard about what happened at the safe house, I'm sure. I took off after that, and I've been in hiding ever since."

"What happened to the real ranger?" Monroe was the first to ask. His look was commanding, revealing his concern for the actual ranger's fate.

"There wasn't any ranger," Sam informed him while raising her brow. "The ranger station was abandoned for a few years already. I found uniforms, working equipment, and even a badge. I guess they couldn't find anyone to take the job and just locked the door. There was an older man who lived within walking distance from the station at the time. When he passed away, no one claimed anything from his estate, including Smokey. I found a lot of his daughter's belongings at his house. I proclaimed myself the park ranger, and no one ever questioned me. Well, not that I actually came into contact with a lot of people. Mostly, I made small talk with hunters and campers and chased off my share of poachers."

"Have you been hiding out up there all these years?" Gil asked with surprise.

Sam nodded. "No one cared," she insisted. "No one questioned me." She then shrugged. "I know you never found the guys who shot me because if you had, you would have discovered there hadn't been a ranger in that station for more than five years.

"Who were the guys who shot you in the woods?" Ross then asked.

"I assumed they were hitmen looking for me," she announced. "I knew right away by the way they were dressed that they weren't poachers."

"So when did you realize we had Marco?" Bogart then asked her.

"I knew something wasn't right about you guys," Sam informed them, "but it wasn't until the morning I was shot that I put it all together." She cast a look at Gil. "Your medical kit was a little too professional for a bunch of photographers. That's the kind of kit carried by people who see a lot of action."

"And what was your plan for Marco?" Jackie felt compelled to ask.

"I've spent the last five years of my life alone in these woods," she informed them. "I kind of miss people. I had no interest in the money I'd heard being offered for Marco. I just wanted my freedom."

"And you thought if you handed Marco over to Vincent, you'd be off the hook?" Zack asked while raising a brow.

"It had crossed my mind," Sam informed him.

"You would never have walked out of there alive," Zack informed her.

Sam stared back at him. "Maybe I don't care anymore," she snapped in response. "Being alone is pretty much the same as being dead."

"You're breaking my heart," Ross muttered without emotion, then straightened and eyed his team. "I've heard enough. Thanks to Vincent's girlfriend, we need to discuss our options for possible extraction. I'm not sure if it's safe to stay here. Who's on first watch?"

"I'll take first watch," Gil announced with a sigh and flopped into the desk chair. "I could use the rest."

The others started filtering from the clinic while muttering to one another over the possibility of locating a new safe house. Zack turned to leave as well.

Sam clutched the bars and stared at him. "Zack, wait," she announced.

Zack looked back at her and showed little emotion.

She managed a timid, sympathetic smile. "I wasn't using you," Sam insisted. "What I felt for you was real."

"It doesn't matter," Zack casually informed her and shook his head. "I never had any feelings for you."

Sam stared at him a moment and appeared mildly disappointed by the response but managed a tiny smile. "Ouch, that hurt."

Zack didn't react. He simply turned and left.

§

Colorado Springs. In a quiet, rural area not far from the city, the newly-built Huntington Country Club was nestled alongside a well-groomed, eighteen-hole golf course. The two-story building looked more like a massive mansion with gray, stone siding, immaculately kept lawn, and detailed landscaping. The parking lot was filled with expensive cars belonging to wealthy members. Men and women in their finest fall golfing outfits zipped around the course in their luxury golf carts. It was a beautiful, sunny, autumn day, which meant every serious golfer was out and about. The country club catered to its upscale clientele, offering fine dining, various indoor and outdoor recreation, and its popular luxury spa.

The country club spa contained every amenity, from manicures and pedicures to massages and saunas. No luxury was spared to pamper and spoil its members. Rather than having the typical waiting area, the spa contained staging areas for its guest's comfort. Upon arrival, each guest was whisked away to their own private room, which included expensive furniture, a bar, and changing area. A man of undeniable wealth in his early forties sat on the comfortable, white lounge chair in his plush, white bathrobe with matching slippers. His expensive suit hung neatly on a special suit rack near the door. Armani Visconti had dark hair with some graying on the sides, adding to his distinguished appearance. He was a handsome, sturdy man with a strange mix of regal and ruggedness. He looked to be a serious businessman with no interest in anyone or anything outside of his little world. Armani remained casually reclined, sipping champagne from a crystal flute and texting on his cell phone while he waited.

There was a soft tapping on the door, which he didn't acknowledge. The door opened to reveal the young, attractive receptionist, who was possibly in her mid-twenties. She was professionally dressed, looking the part of welcoming wealthy clients to the spa. Most men would find the woman unbelievably attractive, but Armani didn't even give her a first glance, let alone a second. She was beneath him. The attractive receptionist wore an unnaturally pleasant smile on her face, undoubtedly programmed to be polite toward their wealthy clientele. It was obvious the young woman was doing her best to maintain her friendly demeanor despite Armani's lack of pleasantries.

"Mr. Visconti," she announced and waited for him to look up.

Armani finished his text then stood almost without acknowledging the young, attractive woman. The wealthy man met and socialized with his share of attractive women, and this particular woman had nothing to offer him that he couldn't find in someone from the proper upbringing.

"Right this way," the woman continued with her forced pleasantries.

Armani placed his cell phone in his bathrobe pocket and passed through the doorway. The young woman managed to get ahead of him and took him through what seemed to be an endless cluster of rooms and corridors. The system was designed with their guest's privacy in mind. Despite being completely booked for the afternoon, the spa guests wouldn't run into each other. The young woman opened one of the doors and politely extended her hand.

"Make yourself comfortable," she announced. "I'll let Angela know you're here."

Armani didn't acknowledge the woman's politeness as he continued into the room. The receptionist's smile faded into a slight frown when she knew he wasn't looking. She shut the door, giving him his privacy. The young woman obviously had her share of Armani's. The private massage room was crisp, white, and sterile. The massage table, covered in white linen, was in the center of the room. The room had a private bar for their guests while they waited, a small, soothing waterfall, many scented candles, and fresh flowers. Armani removed his robe from his naked body and tossed it onto a nearby chair. He then wrapped the plush, white towel around his waist, pulled his cell phone from the robe pocket, and climbed onto the table, positioning himself face down. He placed his face through the padded hole in the table and continued texting on his cell phone. A few minutes passed when the door opened.

"Good afternoon, Angela," Armani announced without interrupting his texting. "The usual with your customary tip for the extended happy ending."

A black-gloved hand grabbed a handful of his dark hair and swiftly pulled his head back, nearly stunning him. He barely had time to react as the sharp dagger was firmly and swiftly slashed across his throat. Armani just about managed a gasp. The cell phone fell from his hand as blood poured from the gash across his throat. The gloved hand released his hair. Armani's head flopped back into the padded hole while his blood continued to flow from the deep slit in his neck. The killer wiped the blood from the blade onto the white towel covering Armani's buttocks, leaving long, bloody streaks. As the blood continued to flow from Armani's body onto the sterile, white floor, the spa room door was heard opening, and the killer slipped out.

§

The seedy, single-story motel was located just on the edge of town, not far from where Carter and his team had lost Zack and Kirk. The three men were staying in two bland, uninspiring rooms with the connecting door open between them.

Bart and Detrick were on their respective beds and watched Carter pace the small room while on his cell phone with Vincent.

"It's as if they disappeared without a trace," Carter informed their boss over the phone. "No one has reported seeing the helicopter or any of the known vehicles anywhere. We've even resorted to sharing information with bounty hunters and rent-a-killers. They're all coming up empty."

"They've gone into hiding," Detrick muttered while flipping through an old magazine.

"Must be one hell of a hiding place," Bart remarked while staring at the ceiling. "You'd think someone would have seen them somewhere."

"Gotta be someplace real secluded," Detrick continued. "Away from people. Maybe camping on state game land."

"They aren't camping on state game land," Bart scoffed while glaring at his partner.

"Why not?" Detrick bellowed and glared back at the large man.

"Because it's getting colder at night," Bart insisted. "They won't want to be out in the cold weather for weeks."

"There are cabins all over the place," Detrick insisted.

"Not on state game land."

"Near state game land," Detrick launched back.

"Will you two shut up," Carter snarled, then returned to his cell phone. "Okay, we'll do that." Carter disconnected his call then tossed the cell phone onto the small table in disgust. "His people don't know anything either." He collapsed into the chair, rubbed his eyes, and then looked at the two men occupying the two beds. "They have a helicopter, AKs, and enough manpower to lead us and a handful of bounty hunters on a wild goose chase. We have to assume these guys are professionals. They didn't contact Vincent about the bounty, so that means they have to be working for Giovanni."

"We checked all his safe houses," Bart reminded him.

"Including the one next to the casino where he'd been staying," Detrick muttered without taking his eyes off his magazine.

Carter groaned and rolled his eyes. "Yes, you were right, Detrick," he scoffed, then glared at his man. "Can we move on already?"

"What's our next move?" Bart asked. "We can't just cool our heels in this dump forever. Who knows how long it'll be before they poke their heads out of whatever hole they're hiding in."

"We don't even know how many of them there are," Detrick added, then tossed his magazine aside and sat up. "The two we ran into were extremely resourceful. They're not giving up Marco without one hell of a firefight."

"Then we'll give them one," Carter insisted.

"We're a little outnumbered for that, and they have home-field advantage," Detrick reminded him. "I highly doubt they're going to be scared of us three."

"It doesn't have to be just the three of us," Carter insisted. "We can join forces with the competition. Use them to fight the front lines." Carter's cell phone buzzed and vibrated across the small table. He grabbed his phone, pressed a button, and placed it to his ear. "Yeah?" There was a moment of silence. Carter suddenly perked up. "Yeah, got it." He disconnected the call and sprang up from his chair. "Look alive. Vincent just got word from one of his contacts. A man was admitted to the hospital less than an hour from here with a gunshot wound. Probably two or three days old. The man's name is linked to some car that had been found abandoned alongside the state game land near there." Carter grabbed a map and spread it out on the table. He pointed to a location on the map. "Right around here."

Detrick and Bart sprang from their beds, joined Carter at the table, and eyed the map. Detrick pointed to an area adjacent to the game land.

"What's this right here?" Detrick asked.

Carter eyed the spot and shook his head. "Farm maybe," he replied. "The game land is surrounded by large farms."

Detrick whipped out his cell phone and searched the internet. He suddenly grinned and held up his phone. "It's an old animal sanctuary."

All three men exchanged looks then grinned in response.

"That's one hell of a hiding spot," Carter remarked. "Probably have themselves tucked in real nice."

"Yeah, that means we're going to need that army," Bart informed him.

Carter chuckled and nodded. "I'll rally the troops," he announced. "Give them an offer they can't refuse."

"You do realize they'll shoot us in the backs the moment we're close to Marco," Detrick insisted.

Bart snorted a laugh. "And we won't?"

"We let the bounty hunters and hitmen lead the charge," Carter announced, then grinned. "Then we'll take out whoever's left."

Chapter 46

Ross stood with Beck before the counter within the visitor's center later that afternoon. A map of Colorado was spread out before them while both seemed to ponder over it. Nevada approached them and eyed the map.

"Zack said you wanted to see me," she remarked and again eyed the map. "What's going on?"

Both men straightened and looked at the young, serious woman.

"Your two friends--" Ross began.

Nevada folded her arms across her chest and raised an arrogant brow. "They're not friends," she scoffed. "More like disgusting acquaintances."

"Irrelevant," Ross remarked. "What are the chances they were followed here?"

Nevada frowned and allowed her arms to fall to her sides. "They're not nearly as stupid as they look," she insisted. "They specialize in tracking men. If you're good at tracking, you're good at covering your tracks as well. They wouldn't want anyone else moving in on their bounty." She then shook her head. "No, they wouldn't have allowed themselves to be followed."

"That's reassuring," Ross remarked, although he didn't seem convinced.

Beck remained tense and shook his head. "As far as safe houses go, this place is just about perfect," he remarked, "but we've had two breaches in one afternoon. We should consider bugging out before someone else decides to drop in unannounced."

Ross touched his hidden ear transmitter. "Zack, you copy?" he bellowed.

"I copy," Zack remarked over Ross's earpiece.

"Grab Jackie and escort her to the landing pad," Ross announced. "Prepare for dust off on my command."

"Are we bugging out?" Zack asked over Ross's ear transmitter.

"I'm afraid so," Ross replied. "By the time you reach the helicopter, we should have a new location."

"Yes, sir."

Ross turned to face Nevada with a stern look. "You know where to find Marco?"

"I left him in the shower room," Nevada replied, revealing her displeasure with the plan to bug out.

"Get him," Ross instructed.

Nevada was about to walk away when Ross and Beck both flinched and touched their ear transmitters, hearing an urgent message from one of the men.

"Kirk?" Ross announced with tension in his voice. "What's going on?"

"We have company," Kirk replied over his ear transmitter. "I've got half a dozen men on foot coming from the east and another half a dozen or so coming from the north."

"I have at least a dozen coming in from the south and west," Gil announced over their radios. "They haven't reached the landing field yet, but they're closing in."

Ross cursed under his breath. "Zack, you copy?" he announced.

"I heard," Zack announced over his ear transmitter with some urgency. "What's the plan?"

"You and Jackie get to that helicopter ASAP," Ross announced with his finger on his ear transmitter. "If you can take off without being shot, do it. Meet us back here for extraction."

"Yes, sir."

§

Nevada stormed into the clinic, startling Monroe, who had been reclined in the chair behind the desk. She darted across the clinic for the end cage and lunged through the bars for Rowen. He jumped back with surprise then laughed.

"You bastards!"

"Oh, someone is riding her broomstick today," Rowen announced while chuckling. "What's wrong, darling? Marco slip away on you?"

As Nevada made another attempt to grab Rowen, Monroe approached with some surprise.

"What's going on?" Monroe asked while glaring at the enraged woman.

Sam remained casually reclined on her cot in her cell with her head resting against the cinder block wall and watched the unfolding scene with little interest.

"They gave away our location," Nevada shouted in anger without taking her eyes off either man behind the bars.

"What do you mean?" Monroe asked with concern.

Sam now appeared interested in the conversation and sat up on the cot.

Nevada spun to face Monroe and appeared surprised. "Haven't you been listening in on your comlink?"

Monroe tapped his hidden ear transmitter and immediately heard a lot of chatter. Ross hurried into the clinic with his finger on his ear transmitter.

"All hands on deck," Ross announced while on high alert. "We have men coming at us from every corner. They're surrounding the sanctuary. Kirk and Gil have visual on them. They're moving in on foot."

Monroe turned to face Ross and appeared concerned. "Are we evacuating Marco in the helicopters?"

"We'll never make it to the helicopters," Ross informed him. "At least not with Marco. Zack's going to cover Jackie's ass and see if he can get her to her helicopter, but it's not looking good."

"How many men?" Rowen asked while moving directly in front of the bars. The look on his face was that of genuine concern.

Nevada punched Rowen in the face through the bars. He clutched his mouth then glared at Nevada while holding his bleeding lip.

"We didn't give away our location. We weren't followed," Rowen insisted, now turning angry. "Do you think we weren't careful?"

"The last thing we want or need is dozens of hired killers crawling up our asses," Quinn announced in their defense. "We were careful."

"Then how did they find us?" Nevada launched in anger. "More than two dozen men are coming this way from every corner. It's a coordinated attack."

"Let us out," Rowen insisted while looking at Ross, almost pleading with him. "There aren't enough of you to handle that many men, especially if you can't reach that chopper. You need us."

"No one trusts you enough to let you out," Nevada shouted back in anger.

Quinn glared at Nevada. "We're sitting ducks in here," he informed her. "Whether you like it or not, we're in this together. They'll kill us the same as they'll kill you."

"He's right," Rowen announced and again looked back at Ross, possibly hoping he'd be more rational than Nevada. "There is nothing, and I mean nothing, that we can offer to those men that would spare our lives. We're dead men either way. We may as well go down fighting alongside you."

Ross seemed to be mentally calculating his options while under extreme pressure of how fast things were going down. He looked at Nevada, who vigorously ran her fingers through her hair.

"How well do you know these men?" Ross finally asked Nevada.

She groaned and threw her hands in the air with disgust. "They're idiots, not killers," Nevada announced. "But they are right. Those men coming will kill them the same as us. The only way they get out of here alive is to fight with us."

Ross cursed under his breath and unlocked the cage. He indicated Monroe to the men. "You two stick with Monroe," he announced. "He'll get you some weapons and set you up within the sanctuary." Ross then pointed a warning finger at both men. "Anything funny, and my men will shoot you without thinking twice."

Rowen held his hands in the air and shook his head. "No funny business," he announced. "On my mother's head, I swear."

Monroe and Ross exchanged concerned looks. Monroe then motioned both men to the entrance. Ross was about to leave when Sam sprang to the cell door.

"Let me out," she insisted with something resembling fear in her eyes.

"You're not going anywhere," Ross informed her.

"I can help," Sam announced while pleading with her eyes. "I have just as much to lose as you do. Maybe more. If any of those men work for Vincent, they'll recognize me. I'm dead where I stand."

"You're a liability," Ross informed her while raising an arrogant brow. He then turned and started walking across the clinic.

"I know you only see me as some mob boss's whore," Sam cried out, "but I wouldn't have survived all these years if I wasn't resourceful."

Ross paused and looked back at Sam, who clung to the bars while staring at him. The desperate look on her face was hard to read.

"Your relationship with Vincent was never the issue, Sam," Ross informed her. "No one here cares that you were dating a mob boss or that you ratted him out. It's your desire to get back in his good graces that makes us not trust you." He again turned to leave.

"Everyone is so quick to think I'd want to get back in Vincent's good graces," she shouted after him. "Do you honestly think I'm that stupid? I just wanted to get close enough to Vincent to kill him!"

Ross paused and looked back at Sam. The look in her eyes could easily be the truth, but there was something cold and calculating as well. It was what made women more frightening than men. The uncertainty. A rage most men couldn't even hope to understand.

"We're all safer with you right where you are," Ross informed her. "If it goes sideways, we'll unlock the door and let you go."

As Ross left the clinic, Sam sneered and slammed her palm against the bars.

§

Zack sat in the crook of a tall tree and scanned the nearby area with his binoculars. Through his binoculars, he could see several men standing guard over the helicopters. He frowned and shook his head.

"We could take out the men standing guard over the helicopters," Zack announced, "but we wouldn't make it very far before alerting the others."

Jackie stood on the branch within the same tree directly beneath where Zack sat and lowered her own binoculars. She had to admit; it didn't look good. "I'm seeing at least six men positioned within the woods on the other side. "Extracting Marco by helicopter without being shot down would be next to impossible."

"With the woods and man-made rock formations, taking them out from above would be counterproductive," Zack remarked. "We'd be sitting ducks in the helicopter."

"They're coming this way." She lowered her binoculars and tapped Zack's combat boot not far from her face. "We need to get back to the visitor's center before they close in."

Jackie quickly descended the tree and jumped the last few feet. Zack quietly followed. Once he landed on the ground, they hurried through the woods.

Zack touched his hidden ear transmitter. "Ross," he announced. "A helicopter evac is a no-go. We have at least a dozen men heading for the sanctuary from the west. Jackie and I should reach the sanctuary before they do, but they won't be far behind."

"All hands on deck," Ross announced over their ear transmitters, alerting the others. "We need to maintain a perimeter around the sanctuary and hold them off. Keep them from the clinic as long as possible. The clinic will be our last stand."

Once they reached the sanctuary, Jackie and Zack shut the metal gates behind them. Zack placed a large padlock on the thick chain, then removed a sanctuary map from his pocket and showed it to Jackie.

"Okay. According to Ross, Beck's going to provide some cover here at the visitor's center," he informed her. "Ross will stay with Marco here at the clinic. We have Monroe and those two bounty hunters here by the train." He continued pointing to different locations on the map. "Nevada and Bogart are here at the reptile house, and Kirk and Gil are here at the bird aviary."

Jackie briefly studied the map then pointed. "So you and I should be somewhere around here," she announced and indicated a place on the map.

"The hippo habitat," Zack remarked, then eyed Jackie and raised a curious brow. "There's a huge pond in there that's been covered over by plant life. Mostly a swamp now. One wrong step--"

"Yeah, I know," Jackie informed him and grinned. "It's a great place to lose someone."

Zack chuckled and shook his head. "I love your devious mind."

"Let's stake out our spot for the show," she announced.

Chapter 47

Jackie followed Zack along the overgrown walkway close to the tall stone wall surrounding the west end of the hippo habitat. Left of the walkway was the massive pond now overgrown with plant life. It looked more like a swamp. Jackie eyed the murky water and made a face while keeping close to Zack ahead of her. On the other side of the small, man-made pond was a fake stone cave, which would provide shelter for the animals during severe weather. Although there was an open field and some trees, most of the habitat was based around the pond.

"There's a stench you don't come across every day," she remarked and wrinkled her nose from the foul smell. "What is it?"

"Decay," Zack replied without forethought. "Rotting vegetation and possibly the remanence of an animal or two that fell into the pond and couldn't get back out."

"That's a pleasant thought," she muttered.

Zack paused before a tree blocking the path. He looked up the large tree and nodded his approval. "This is perfect," he informed her. "His and her branches." He indicated the branches on either side of the tree. "And the wall is about three feet above the branches. We'll have the safety of the wall as a shield, and yet be able to fire over the wall at anyone approaching." He extended his hand to the tree and grinned. "Ladies first."

Jackie cast a look at Zack and raised her brows. "Yeah, I'm not falling for that one again," she remarked and extended her hand to the tree. "Age before beauty."

Zack didn't appear amused. "I can run circles around you," he informed her. "Don't mock my age."

Without another word, Zack scaled the tree to the first branch halfway up the ten-foot wall. Jackie watched and waited. As Zack was about to climb to the second branch, they saw something move beneath the surface of the murky pond. Jackie took a step closer to the edge for a better look. Zack's hand was suddenly in front of her as he reached down.

"Jackie," he cried out.

Jackie wasn't sure what he saw, but she grabbed his wrist without question, allowing him to hoist her from the ground. An alligator lunged from the murky water and nearly caught her booted foot. Jackie grabbed onto the lower branch while digging her boots into the tree trunk. She screamed at the sight of the alligator's teeth so close to her. Zack pulled her onto the branch with him. She just about leaped onto Zack, where he crouched, and clung to him. Her heart was racing while she stared in horror at the close call.

"What the hell--?" Jackie cried out in terror.

Despite everything she'd ever been through, that had to be her most frightening moment with the team. Zack held onto her with one arm while clinging to the tree behind him with the other.

"Now there's something you don't see every day," he remarked, seeming less rattled than she was. Of course, it hadn't been his foot either.

"Let me go down in a fiery ball of flames," Jackie announced while staring at the alligator moving beneath the surface. "Being eaten alive is *not* how I want to die."

"You don't need to worry about that," Zack casually remarked. "You and I are going to die "Butch Cassidy and Sundance Kid" style."

Jackie finally caught her breath and cast a look at Zack. "We're going to jump off a cliff together?" she just about demanded.

"Well, yeah, but in a helicopter after being struck with a heat seeking missile," he replied.

Jackie stared at him without releasing him. "Pretty detailed image," she muttered. "Do you fantasize about us dying together a lot?"

"No," he replied. "Only two or three times a day."

She stared into his eyes a moment and had to wonder if he was kidding. Jackie pulled away from him and braced one hand against the branch beneath her and the other on the stone wall behind her. She glanced into the murky water below. Zack remained crouched on the branch and casually leaned his shoulder against the tree trunk. He observed the water as well then pointed with little reaction.

"There's another," he casually informed her. "At least now we know where the smell was coming from."

"Even if they were left behind when the sanctuary closed, how could they possibly survive winter?" she asked. "I thought alligators couldn't handle the cold, especially with how cold Colorado gets."

"The habitats have plenty of cozy areas," Zack informed her. "I guess they find warm spots and hunker down for the winter." He then indicated the tree. "We'd better get into position."

Jackie remained perched on the branch and stared at the ripples in the murky water below. Zack was about to continue his climb when he hesitated and studied Jackie.

"Are you scared of a couple of alligators?" Zack asked, seeming surprised.

She shot a horrified look at him. "Shouldn't I be?"

"Would it make you feel better if I shot them?" he asked.

Jackie cast a look at him then shivered slightly. "No," she muttered. "We can't risk alerting the intruders to our presence."

Zack removed his Bowie knife from his boot and playfully flipped it in his hand. "I always wanted to wrestle a gator," he remarked. "I'll just go for a quick swim and take care of them for you."

Jackie stared at him with a strange look. She suddenly smiled and laughed. "You would do that, too, wouldn't you?"

"Of course," he replied. "And not just because it'd make you feel better. It'd make for a great story. I need some new material."

"I think, under the circumstances," she announced, "we should just let them be."

Zack replaced his knife to his boot. "Okay, but I offered," he announced. "Let's get into position."

§

Monroe took a lookout position within the old, rusted half-size train sitting on tracks that once carried the train around the entire sanctuary. He sat on the warped, wooden bench with his assault rifle across his lap and peered out the glassless windows with his binoculars. While watching the surrounding area leading up to the sanctuary, he periodically cast looks at Quinn and Rowen in nearby cars that were situated on the curve in the track. Monroe wasn't particularly happy trusting a pair of bounty hunters who arrived with the sole purpose of snatching Marco out from underneath them. Ross trusting them may very well have been a mistake. Giving them weapons was possibly even the bigger mistake. Did they really have his back when he needed it? Or would they shoot him in it?

Rowen made a strange bird call sound, alerting Monroe and Quinn. Quinn and Monroe scanned the area with their binoculars in an attempt to see what Rowen had seen. There was movement within the woods. Although Monroe could only make out one man, the movement within the underbrush was consistent with soldiers moving in formation. Monroe moved to the train floor, kneeled alongside the glassless window, and positioned his rifle toward the woods. He tapped his ear transmitter.

"We have at least half a dozen men approaching from the northeast," Monroe announced. "They're too far out to make visual confirmation." He glanced back at the train and saw Rowen signaling something to him. Monroe frowned and touched his ear transmitter. "Elmer Fudd is trying to tell me something." Monroe looked at Rowen, made a face, and shook his head, indicating he didn't understand. He again tapped his ear transmitter. "I don't know what branch of the military this guy served, but I'm pretty sure it was in another country."

Quinn rolled his eyes and shook his head at Monroe's confusion. He, too, started gesturing and making hand signals, as if that would help clarify what he was attempting to convey.

Monroe groaned. "Great, now Daffy Duck is in on the act as well," he remarked.

"Does it look as if he's asking you to steal third base?" Nevada chimed in over Monroe's ear transmitter.

"A little," Monroe remarked.

"He wants you to wait until they're in the clearing," Nevada informed him. "Let them get past your position and then take them from behind."

"That's not the plan," Monroe announced through his transmitter. "We're not supposed to let them inside the perimeter."

"He sees something you don't," Nevada insisted. "Listen to him, Monroe. Once they start shooting back, there's only a thin wall of wood protecting you."

"Ross?" Monroe asked while scanning the area through his riflescope.

"Any change in movement?" Ross asked.

Monroe continued to scan the area. "I'm seeing more movement now. We're looking at close to a dozen men coming from this direction."

"Listen to Elmer Fudd," Ross insisted over his earpiece. "Let them get past you and then do a sneak attack from behind."

Monroe frowned, then looked back at Rowen and gave him a thumbs up. Rowen nodded and disappeared inside his car. Once the men came into view, Monroe kept out of sight as well. Nearly a dozen heavily armed men made their way past the half-sized train and headed into the sanctuary. Once the last of the men had passed, they were now in a larger clearing. Before the men got too far into the sanctuary and would reach the next area of shelter, Monroe signaled to Rowen and Quinn. All three opened fire upon the men. Three men went down while the rest darted for cover and fired back. Before they reached shelter, three more men went down. The six remaining men reached cover within the children's play area not far from the train and fired back. All three men within the train took cover as bullets pierced the small train's thin wood and metal sides. Monroe cursed under his breath.

Rowen was heard laughing and hooting from within his train car. "Woo hoo," he cried out. "Just like Billy the Kid at the O.K. Corral!"

"Billy the Kid was never at the O.K. Corral," Quinn shouted back.

"Buzzkill!"

§

Within the country club spa, Holden approached the police officer standing just outside the roped-off corridor. He flashed his badge while slipping under the yellow police line without waiting for permission. He walked along the hall to the back room and paused within the doorway. As the forensic photographer took pictures of the crime scene, Holden looked at the dead man lying face down on the massage table. The bright red blood soaked onto the white cloth covering the table, and a pool of blood collected on the white, marble floor. The medical examiner attempted to briefly examine the body without disturbing it. He straightened while shaking his head then seemed to notice Holden.

"Special Agent Falcone, I presume," the examiner announced, then managed a smirk. "I was expecting you but not nearly so fast."

"Another 'family' killing gets my immediate attention," Holden remarked, then indicated the body with the sheet just covering his buttocks. "Who do we have?"

"Armani Visconti," the examiner reported, then raised his brows knowingly.

Holden groaned and rubbed his eyes. "That's not going to go over well with his family," he remarked. "Are we sure it's the same killer?"

"Well, I haven't been here long enough to do a thorough investigation, but from what I can see, the knife used to slit his throat was similar to the other murders," the medical examiner reported. "There aren't any security cameras in the private spa rooms, but those within the spa itself suddenly stopped working about twenty minutes before our friend got his ticket punched. He was shown to this room by the receptionist. Ten minutes later, his therapist shows up and finds him dead."

Holden shook his head in disbelief. "This guy is like a homicidal ninja," he remarked. "Daring killings in a small time frame with a high risk of being seen."

"And somehow no one ever does," the medical examiner replied. "Detective McGrath is with the two young women from the spa who last saw him alive. He has them in the room down the hall."

Holden stuffed his notebook into his pocket and removed his cell phone. "I'll read their statements from the detective," he announced. "I need to call this in."

Holden hurried from the room and pressed a button as he headed down the corridor for the police officer and the yellow police line. He ducked under the tape and walked across the empty waiting room.

"Othello," Holden announced with some urgency. "Contact the team. There's been another killing. It wasn't Marco."

"I'll get right on that," Othello responded from the other end.

"Tell them to sit tight," Holden remarked. "I'll see about getting word out to call off the dogs."

Chapter 48

Othello paced Holden's living room that now contained stacks of old food containers, empty pizza boxes, and various other trash. The once immaculate room looked like a home away from home for the computer genius. Othello held his cell phone to his ear while pacing.

"Come on, guys," he groaned with concern. "Why aren't you picking up?"

Othello finally disconnected the call, cast his cell phone aside, and removed a second cell phone. He pressed a button and waited for a response. The kitchen door opened, and Holden bolted into the house.

"What's the word?" Holden asked.

"Holden," Othello announced with concern and disconnected the call he'd been attempting to make. "I tried both of my special numbers. No one's answering."

"What does that mean?" Holden demanded with concern in his voice.

"It means they're not answering," Othello responded with frustration then appeared animated. "I'm 9-1-1, man. When I call, they pick up! I can see not getting through on one phone but not both." He shook his head in concern. "I've got a bad feeling."

"You call Sal," Holden just about exploded while pointing at Othello. "He needs to contact Giovanni. We need to get the word out far and wide that Marco was in custody during the last murder."

"Yeah, okay," Othello replied, then tensed. "What are you going to do?"

"I'm going to call Vinnie and hope he can get through to his grandson," Holden replied. "Vincent is the one who put the bounty on Marco's head. He's our best chance to call them off."

While Othello recovered his untraceable burner phone and made his call to Sal, Holden found the number for Vinnie the knife. Othello was already talking to Sal as Holden's call to Vinnie went straight to voicemail. Othello appeared animated and immediately stopped pacing.

"Sal?" Othello announced into the phone. "Sal? Are you there?"

Holden disconnected his call and glanced at Othello with some concern. Whatever was being said, it was a one-sided conversation from Sal's end.

"I hear you, but--" Othello remarked into the phone but was interrupted. "No, Sal. That's not a good--" Othello then groaned and disconnected the call.

"What's up with Sal?" Holden demanded.

"Nothing good," Othello announced while seeming tense. "Sal just got word that half a dozen rogue bounty hunters had teamed up with a whole bunch of mercs and hitmen. They were reportedly heading toward the state game land a couple hours' drive from here."

Holden appeared alarmed while staring at Othello's concerned look. "That's not good," he announced.

"It's worse than that," Othello responded as his eyes widened dramatically. "Sal had tried calling Vinnie, apparently having the same idea as you. He and Giovanni are just pulling up to Vinnie's mansion now. He hung up on me."

"Of all the stupid--"

"Right before he hung up, he said Vincent's car was already there," Othello continued while cringing.

Holden ran his fingers through his hair and sank into thought before shifting his attention back to Othello. "Keep trying the guys. Hopefully, we're not already too late to warn them about the onslaught heading their way."

Othello stared at Holden with concern. "You're going to do something stupid, aren't you?"

Holden frowned. "Yeah, I'm doing something stupid. I'm going to confront Vincent and tell him to call off the dogs," he remarked.

"He may not listen," Othello quickly announced with a nervous look on his face. "He may just decide to shoot you instead."

"I'll make him listen," Holden insisted. "And if he doesn't call off the bounty--? Well, they can't collect a bounty off a dead man."

As Holden stormed from the house, Othello tensed and held his breath. "This is not going to end well," Othello groaned softly.

§

Holden's official black blazer pulled up to Vinnie Scartelli's mansion, driving past two unfamiliar vehicles and one he recognized as Giovanni's black sedan. Holden parked his blazer near the front entrance, parking in such a way that he wouldn't be exposed to the house windows or doors on his driver's side. Just as a precaution. He got out of his vehicle and stood behind it a moment while surveying the mansion and listening for anything that sounded remotely like a gunfight. The mansion was eerily silent.

"That can't be good," Holden muttered, then shut his car door.

He again looked at the mansion, seeming to have his reservations, cautiously eyeing each window for movement. When he still didn't see anything, he walked around his vehicle and approached the main entrance. Holden paused before the door and was about to press the doorbell when he saw the front door was ajar. Holden removed his weapon from his shoulder holster while moving to the side of the door. He slowly pushed the door open a little wider in order to peer inside.

"Vinnie?" Holden announced and took a sweeping eyeful of the familiar foyer and grand hallway. "Vinnie, it's Holden with the FBI."

There was still no response. Holden drew a deep breath and held it a moment. With a man like Vinnie, there was no right or wrong way of handling this situation. They were all equally fatal. Holden cautiously walked through the grand hallway toward the lounge at the far end, being the room he had first met Vinnie the knife. As he got closer to the back lounge, he could hear angry voices. Holden paused outside the lounge and pressed his back against the wall, listening to the heated exchange. When he heard Sal's voice, he shut his eyes and withheld his groan. He clutched his gun close to his chest and listened a moment longer before peering around the corner, hoping to go unnoticed by those within the room. He needed to scope the layout for hostiles. From his brief glance into the room, he saw Vincent and four of his mercenaries with their backs to the doorway. The four rough types had their weapons aimed at Giovanni's two goons and Vinnie's two aging bodyguards, who returned the favor by having their guns aimed at them.

From what Holden could see, Vinnie was in the less comfy chair near the fireplace while Sal and Giovanni were standing just in front of the old, thick portable bar. If any of the three wise guys were armed, Holden didn't see their weapons. Holden again pressed his back against the wall and swiftly contemplated several scenarios of how it would play out. Holden shut his eyes a moment, drew a deep breath, and went with the option that would possibly cause the least amount of bloodshed, although none of them was exactly ideal in this situation. A gathering of volatile killer types with guns pointed at each other wasn't going to end well for anyone. Holden moved into the doorway just far enough to aim his weapon at the men with their backs to him.

"FBI. Put your guns down," Holden announced, just bold enough to get their attention. He didn't want to provoke any of the men to--

Two of Vincent's mercenaries spun and immediately fired their weapons at Holden. Holden ducked back around the corner just in time to avoid the barrage of bullets coming at him. Their gunfire prompted the beginning of World War III, with Giovanni and Vinnie's men firing back at Vincent's mercenaries. Holden could hear Vinnie's mercenaries thumping across the floor for the hallway. They were running for cover from the shootout and to take out Holden. Being Holden was no match for the number of men coming at him, he bolted down the hallway and into the nearest room. Holden sought shelter within the game room doorway and looked back into the hallway to take down the men who were almost certainly coming for him. When he looked in the hallway, the four men were outside the doorway, firing into the lounge, leaving themselves exposed to Holden.

Holden was mildly surprised that they'd leave themselves open and exposed like that, but he saw his chance and took it. As Holden was about to step into the hallway, despite the gunfire from the next room over, he heard a floorboard creak within the game room behind him. Holden spun just in time to see Vincent directly behind him, having slipped through some sort of concealed doorway connecting the two rooms. Holden raised his gun, but he wasn't fast enough. Vincent pulled his trigger first, and the gun fired with a loud bang.

§

Within the sanctuary, gunshots were heard from every corner. The men plotting their attack knew they were discovered and no longer bothered with the silent approach. Back in the visitor's center, Beck fired shots out the broken window at the men now running just outside the main entrance. Several men fired back while others continued on to the next area, fanning out. With men running everywhere, it was nearly impossible to stop all of them. Despite Beck's best effort to keep the men from approaching, they were getting through. There was a loud crash from the back of the visitor's center.

The men were coming at him from behind and had successfully surrounded him. Beck had to abandon his post or risk being shot from behind. He darted into the back hallway and could hear someone closing in on him. He slipped into the closest office and darted behind the door. Beck slung his rifle over his shoulder and removed his Bowie knife from his boot.

If any gunshots were heard, it would bring the rest of the men upon him. He had to keep his attack silent yet deadly. The office door was slowly pushed open, and the barrel of a rifle came into Beck's view. As soon as the man moved into the doorway, Beck had to intercept him. A trained professional would look to the side of the door first, giving him only precious seconds to make his move. Beck grabbed the barrel of the rifle, pushed it up into the air, and lunged forward with his knife. He struck the man in the neck, holding him in place while he gasped and spat up blood. Beck caught the man before he fell and pulled him into the room. He lowered the man to the floor, pulled his knife free, and wiped the blood from the blade onto the man's shoulder.

Beck listened but didn't hear anyone else approaching. He kept his rifle slung and removed his semiautomatic from his shoulder holster. He cautiously looked into the dimly lit hallway, being the lights were off, only limited natural light filled the corridor. When he didn't see anyone, he slipped into the hallway. There was no telling how many intruders had successfully infiltrated the visitor's center. Beck cautiously returned to the lobby, looked around, and then headed for the snack bar. He slipped behind the counter and positioned himself where he could look over the counter and still remain hidden. He replaced his semiautomatic and removed the rifle slung over his shoulder.

Three armed men entered through the main entrance. So much for keeping quiet and not alerting anyone to his position. Beck straightened and fired several rounds, taking all three men down before any could return fire. Beck ducked behind the counter and waited. When no one else appeared, he hurried for the back exit of the visitor's center, which would be the quickest route to the clinic.

Beck tapped his ear transmitter while on the move. "Ross, you may have some bogeys coming your way. I'm heading to you."

"Copy that," Ross replied.

§

Within the vet's office inside the clinic, Ross handed Marco an automatic rifle and gave him a stern look. "You do know how to use one of these, right?"

Marco managed a strange, twisted smile. "I think I can figure it out," he replied while accepting the weapon.

"I need to greet Beck at the side entrance," Ross informed him. "Stay in here with the door locked until I get back. If anyone other than someone from the team arrives, shoot first and ask questions later."

Marco nodded. Once Ross left the room, Marco locked the door behind him.

"Come on, Marco," Sam announced from her position within the large cage. She now appeared concerned or possibly frightened. "Let me out of here. I can help, I swear. If those men find me, I'm as good as dead. At least let me defend myself."

Marco glanced at her, frowned, and shook his head. "I have no reason to trust you."

"You have no reason to trust anyone else either," she insisted. "Sometimes, you just need to have a little blind faith." Her eyes pleaded with his. "Do what's right. I won't ask again."

"Sorry," Marco informed her and returned his attention to the door, attempting to listen for any sounds just outside the clinic. He suddenly hesitated and turned his head to look back at the cage.

Sam now stood behind him with a tiny, almost sympathetic smirk on her face. She punched him in the stomach and snatched the rifle, turning it on him as he reacted to the hit.

Marco gingerly rubbed his abdomen and stared at Sam, holding the weapon on him.

She smiled sweetly. "In my defense, I did ask nicely," Sam announced.

§

Beck followed Ross along the corridor heading for the clinic. Ross paused before the door and tapped on it. The door slowly moved inward from the pressure of his knock, indicating it wasn't even shut, let alone locked. Ross appeared somewhat concerned and pushed the door open while securing his handgun. He moved into the doorway and aimed his gun across the room. Beck kept his rifle aimed as well. Marco stood behind the bars of the gorilla cage and looked at Ross while frowning.

"She got away," Marco informed Ross.

"Well, at least she didn't take Marco this time," Beck remarked to Ross and found the keys for the cage lock.

"She must have slipped out the back while we were at the side door," Ross scoffed.

Beck unlocked the cage door and released Marco from the cell.

"I say good riddance," Marco muttered in annoyance, now freed from the cage. "She probably would have gotten us killed anyway."

§

The sanctuary sounded like a war zone as intruders ascended upon the team from all ends. Not far from the bird aviary entrance, Gil had a secured position behind a large, heavy sign. Darth, who was sporting his bullet-proof vest and a small doggie saddlebag, kept low and watched the area behind Gil, despite that the building offered some protection. Gil had his rifle scope trained on the tree line but kept his shots to a minimum. He needed to conserve ammo. It was unclear how many men were still out there. Kirk was heard firing from nearby and took shots anytime someone poked their head out. There was no telling how much ammo he'd gone through already. When Kirk stopped firing, it was a pretty good indication he'd gone through all his spare magazines. One or two men suddenly felt confident he was out of ammo and made their move into the clearing. Gil waited for them to move out and shot both. Two men; two clean shots.

Darth suddenly snarled from behind Gil. Gil spun with his rifle aimed. Kirk came into view, darted behind the large sign, and took cover. Being there were no shots fired from the woods, they must not have seen him.

"I'm out of ammo," Kirk informed Gil, then went for the small saddlebag Darth wore over his bulletproof vest.

"I'm not surprised," Gil remarked and again focused on the woods. "Were you even aiming?"

Kirk removed two large magazines from Darth's bags and placed one in his pocket. He slapped the other into his rifle and glared at Gil.

"Hey, I took more of them down than you did," Kirk informed him. "Neatness doesn't count."

"It's quiet out there," Gil remarked while ignoring Kirk's comment and kept his focus on the woods. "I thought there were more."

"I think one or two took the long way around," Kirk informed him. "Probably heading deeper into the sanctuary." He aimed his rifle and scanned the area. "Ross is going to need reinforcements."

Darth suddenly became alert and snarled. Both men turned to the same opening Kirk had slipped through. A bullet struck the side of the sign.

"Or they could be behind us," Kirk remarked and fired back.

"Into the aviary," Gil announced and indicated the nearby door.

"Are you kidding?" Kirk cried out without looking at Gil in horror. "Damned building has glass walls!"

"It also has a forest inside," Gil informed him, then motioned Darth to the open aviary doorway.

Darth ran inside the aviary. Gil darted after him, stopped by the doorway, and covered Kirk as he ran for the door. Both disappeared inside. Kirk and Gil ran deeper into the massive bird sanctuary and darted behind larger trees. They aimed their weapons at the door and fired at the two men who bolted inside after them. The two men were Nolte and Slade. Both men immediately took cover while blocking the exit.

"Why are we wasting our time with these two?" Slade demanded. "While we're here, the others are moving in on Marco."

"The others don't know where Marco is any more than we do," Nolte snapped back, then nodded deeper into the aviary. "We get one of these stupid assholes to talk, and they tell us where they're hiding the mother."

"And that doesn't get us any closer to Marco," Slade insisted while becoming annoyed. "It's obvious he isn't being held in a glass birdcage. We should be going for one of the stronger buildings. Anywhere but here."

Nolte glared at Slade, and his eyes narrowed. "You want to terminate our agreement?" Nolte demanded, then sneered at him. "You're free to go your own way, but I'm the only reason you got this far."

"No, that asshole laying in a hospital bed insisting a park ranger shot him is the only reason we got this far," Slade launched back in anger. "And following those mercenaries got us into the sanctuary. None of that had anything to do with you."

Nolte nodded to the open door. "There's the door, motherfucker," he snapped. "Use it."

"I will," Slade announced and patted Nolte on the shoulder. "Have a nice life, asshole."

Slade partially stood and made his way for the door. Nolte sneered and turned with his gun aimed, prepared to shoot Slade before he could reach the exit. He was surprised to discover Slade wasn't there. Slade moved out from behind a tree and shot Nolte in the chest. Nolte gasped and fell to the ground while clutching his chest.

"You mother--" the dying hitman gasped with his last breath.

"Serves you right for thinking about shooting me in the back," Slade scoffed without sympathy, then bolted for the glass doors.

As Slade slipped through the open door and ran from the aviary, Kirk and Gil exchanged bewildered looks.

"Did they just turn on each other?" Kirk asked in surprised disbelief.

"Hitmen and mercenaries aren't exactly a trustworthy bunch," Gil replied while shrugging. "They'll work together until the last moment and then turn on each other."

"Good. It'll make our job that much easier," Kirk muttered.

Chapter 49

Nevada and Bogart stood alongside the reptile house and fired at several mercenaries attempting to get past them and closer to the clinic. One of the men slipped past them and ran into the building.

"Does the building have a back exit?" Bogart asked with concern.

"I assume it would have multiple exits," Nevada reported, then nodded to the nearby door. "I'll go after him. You hold our position here."

Before Bogart could respond, Nevada ran for the reptile house door. Bogart fired several shots across the clearing, providing cover for the woman. Nevada entered the building, immediately threw her back against the wall, and looked around, attempting to get her bearings in the dimly lit building. There was no telling which way the man ran, and she didn't need him sneaking up on her. When there was no sign of the man who had entered, Nevada walked along the dimly lit area lined with glass walls, enclosing what used to be different reptile habitats. Nevada took the first right into another section when she heard the main door creaking as it opened and then closed. There was additional light that flooded the main area, further indicating someone had entered behind her. Nevada remained still and listened, unwilling to call out to Bogart in case it wasn't him. The habitat must have been soundproof, considering the war outside could no longer be heard. The silence was almost deafening.

When she didn't hear anything, Nevada continued along the dimly lit exhibit. She finally reached the back exit and pushed on it. The door opened to the outside, flooding light into the area she now occupied. She peered outside but didn't see signs that anyone had left the building in that direction. When Nevada released the door, allowing it to close slowly and the light fading with it, she turned and saw a man standing only a few feet from her with his gun aimed. Nevada raised her weapon before the area would become too dark as the door closed. A gun fired, startling her. As the man gasped and fell to the floor, Bogart lowered his rifle and suspiciously eyed Nevada.

"Did the others escape through the back?" Bogart asked.

"Others?"

"While I was taking care of our friends out there, two others slipped inside," Bogart replied.

Nevada looked around the dimly lit area, as her eyes once again adjusted to the darkness, and shook her head. "No, that means they must be in here somewhere," she insisted. "There are plenty of corridors leading to other exhibits. I've got this. Why don't you head back to operations and give Ross some additional backup."

"No, we stick together," Bogart insisted.

Rather than argue, Nevada moved past Bogart while keeping her weapon aimed and ready. Bogart kept close to her and watched the area behind them. As they proceeded cautiously across the corridor, something moved behind the glass wall from within one of the enclosures. Nevada spun and stared at the glass covering the habitat near her. In the darkness of the habitat beyond the glass, it was nearly impossible to see anything.

"I swear I saw something move," she whispered to Bogart.

Both kept away from the glass with their weapons raised. Bogart removed his cell phone from his pocket, turned on the flashlight, and held it up to the glass. They saw a large snake on the other side of the glass staring back at them. Nevada let out a startled gasp.

Bogart looked at her with surprise, stunned at what sounded like fear from the hardened woman. "What the hell was that?" he demanded.

Nevada composed herself and sneered at him. "I don't like snakes," she snarled in response. "You got a problem with that?"

"It's one little snake," he insisted, "and it's behind the glass."

"Obviously, it's not locked in there," Nevada scoffed. "It wouldn't have survived without food if it were."

"It's fine," Bogart insisted. "It's not coming to get us. Let's just continue our sweep and then get the hell out of here."

"I'm all for that," Nevada muttered, then shivered. "This place gives me the creeps."

Nevada walked past Bogart and led the way along the corridor. She suddenly stopped, holding her hand in the air, indicating for him to hold his position. Bogart took his cue and stopped as well. There was a strange sound, almost like the sound of the wind blowing.

"You hear that?" Nevada whispered.

Bogart listened a moment, then shook his head even though he couldn't see anything. "Probably a broken window," he replied.

"Then why don't I feel a draft?" Nevada asked, remaining suspicious of the sound.

"We need to keep moving," Bogart insisted with a sense of urgency. "There's no telling how many are making their way to the clinic."

Nevada took a few steps forward and again stopped. "Where's that flashlight?" she announced.

Bogart removed his cell phone and again turned on the light. Both looked around, then simultaneously hesitated and slowly looked down. The floor was covered with dozens of snakes, and Nevada and Bogart were already a couple of feet into their area. Nevada let out a shrill scream, which was immediately silenced by Bogart's hand covering her mouth.

"Shh," he whispered. "Don't scream. You'll give our position away."

Bogart slowly removed his hand from Nevada's mouth. Rather than being hostile about him having touched her, instead, she was mildly panicked.

"Back up," Nevada whispered with fear in her tone. Her fear increased. "Back up! Back up now!"

Bogart stepped around the snakes and moved past them. Nevada nervously followed while keeping her eyes on the creatures slithering close to her boots.

"Get me out of here," Nevada whispered in panic. "Get me out of here now!"

"Almost there," Bogart quietly informed her.

The moment they were away from the snakes, Nevada shivered and turned squeamish. "I never want to do that again," she muttered.

Bogart turned and hurried Nevada away from the snake-filled corridor. As Bogart rounded a corner first, Hawthorn was suddenly in front of him with his weapon aimed. Bogart froze, holding Nevada back and out of sight just beyond the corner.

"Well, well," Hawthorn announced and grinned. "Looks as if we meet again. What a small world."

Bogart held his rifle in a motion of surrender. He started to set down the rifle, then thrust it upward and knocked the gun from Hawthorn's hand. Without hesitation, he rammed the rifle stock into the man's chest, winding him. Nevada leaped out from her concealed position with her weapon aimed at Hawthorn. Wilson suddenly appeared in front of Bogart, spun into a roundhouse kick, and struck him in the chest. The rifle flew from his hands as he crashed into Nevada, knocking them both against the nearby wall. Nevada took the brunt of the impact, leaving her slightly dazed. Bogart recovered almost immediately and took a quick step closer to Wilson.

When Wilson went for the return kick, Bogart blocked it with his forearm, but he was unprepared for the punch that immediately followed. Bogart took the hit to his cheek and stumbled backward and into the wall near Nevada, who had now recovered and appeared moderately enraged. Before Bogart could even get his bearings from the punch and impact with the wall, Wilson was practically on top of Bogart and hit him in the gut. Nevada was about to intervene when she saw Hawthorn going for his discarded rifle. Nevada bolted across the hall and tackled Hawthorn into the glass wall, just about winding him with her shoulder to his chest. Hawthorn managed to stumble away from Nevada but quickly turned to face her, prepared to battle hand-to-hand with her.

Wilson swiftly kicked Bogart in the ribs, momentarily incapacitating him. She then took a step back and went for a roundhouse kick meant to disable him permanently. Nevada saw what was going down. She kicked Hawthorn in the chest and sent him flying into Wilson's path. Wilson kicked Hawthorn in the chest instead, sending him flying backward into another wall of glass. Wilson's surprise reversal was enough to catch her off guard. Nevada kicked Wilson in the chest with her booted foot, hurling the woman across the reptile atrium and into the exhibits' glass wall. Nevada eyed Bogart, then pointed demandingly at Hawthorn sitting on the floor.

"He's yours," Nevada informed Bogart, then charged across the atrium for Wilson, who was now gathering her bearings.

Nevada didn't even bother stopping to kick or punch the woman. She maintained her speed and tackled the woman to the floor. In a well-coordinated roll, Nevada landed on top of Wilson and punched her in the face. For a brief moment, both Hawthorn and Bogart stared at the demon-possessed woman. When the two men exchanged looks, it was as they suddenly remembered they were supposed to kill each other. Hawthorn pulled a knife from his boot, leaped to his feet, and attempted to slash Bogart. Bogart jumped back, avoiding the blade, and threw a left-legged kick, striking Hawthorn in the side. He pivoted around, knocking the knife from his hand with his right forearm, and then punched him across the face with his left fist. It happened so fast; Bogart even surprised himself. Bogart's moment of hesitation after his coordinated attack victory left him open to Hawthorn's uppercut punch.

Bogart was thrown back and struck the glass enclosure with enough force to moderately daze him. Hawthorn seized the opportunity and lunged for him. The man was plowed down by the two women flying down the corridor with their hands on each other's throats. Wilson was screaming like a banshee while Nevada roared like a tiger. Bogart flattened himself against the glass to keep from being taken down with them as they flew past like a tornado. Both women disappeared into the nearby, darker corridor. Hawthorn stumbled to his feet, dazed by the force of the two women plowing through him. Bogart lunged forward, threw himself into a roundhouse kick, and struck Hawthorn in the chest with a hard, fast kick. Hawthorn flew backward and hit the thick glass enclosure with enough force that it cracked. Despite having nailed the kick, Bogart lost his footing on the landing. It took him a second to regain his bearings.

Hawthorn was obviously in agony from the kick to his chest and then the sudden stop against the glass wall, but he still managed to pull himself together enough to lunge for his discarded knife. Bogart saw him leap for the knife and jumped on top of him to keep him from securing the weapon. Bogart placed his arm around Hawthorn's neck from behind and applied pressure. The man gasped while fighting Bogart's arm around his neck and attempted to grasp the knife with his free hand. Bogart pulled himself up to his knees without releasing Hawthorn and applied added pressure to stop him. When he heard the man's neck snap, Bogart gasped with surprise. Hawthorn went limp beneath his arm. Bogart cried out and released him, springing backward and away from the man. Bogart stared at the dead man with the realization that he'd unintentionally snapped the man's neck. Bogart ran trembling fingers through his hair, stunned at what he had done.

"Oh, shit!"

There was a loud thump from the nearby corridor, and the women could be heard screaming profanities. Bogart grabbed his discarded gun, sprang to his feet, and ran for the nearby passageway to check on Nevada. The two women broke free from each other's grip and immediately threw punches. Both were already a few feet into the snake-infested corridor, although neither seemed to notice. Nevada blocked Wilson's right fist then kicked her in the side. She immediately went for a second, higher kick. Wilson went low, avoided the kick, and swept Nevada's legs out from under her. Nevada crashed to the floor but went with the fall. She rolled across the floor, landing on her hands and knees, and then saw the snakes on the floor just about surrounding her. Some of the snakes seemed quite agitated. Nevada cried out with something resembling horror. Most were non-poisonous, but that didn't seem to matter much to Nevada, who was obviously terrified of the more than two dozen snakes.

The sound from a couple of rattlesnakes could be heard just a few feet away from her. Nevada's eyes went to the sound. There was a small cluster of rattlesnakes just beyond the angry but non-lethal snakes. Nevada, still on her knees, spun to face Wilson. Wilson wore a sinister grin and thrust her foot for Nevada's chest, intending to kick her backward and into the poisonous rattlesnakes. Nevada ducked the flying foot and sprang to her feet. Wilson sneered and immediately threw a fist for Nevada's face. Nevada blocked the punch, caught her wrist, and thrust her shoulder into Wilson's abdomen. With all her energy and anger, Nevada elevated the woman off her feet and threw her over her shoulder. Wilson was thrown through the air and landed on the floor just about on top of the rattlesnakes. The snakes angrily and repeatedly bit Wilson while she screamed.

Nevada bolted away from the snakes and practically leaped into Bogart's arms while staring in horror at the woman being repeatedly bitten by the venomous creatures.

"We need to get out of here," Nevada gasped while clutching and clawing at Bogart, unable to take her eyes off the terrifying scene before her.

Bogart hurried Nevada away from the snakes and into the safer corridor.

§

Jackie and Zack remained on their respective branches of the large tree behind the wall. They easily remained hidden while firing shots at the men attempting to advance closer to the visitor's center. More than a dozen men had already made it past the main gate after busting through it. Jackie and Zack fired at the six men within their range, unable to do anything about the others that had gotten past by heading further north where the wall was demolished. Keeping the invaders in smaller groups meant fewer men attacking the clinic at once. They knew Beck had been defending the visitor's center as a last stand before the clinic. Jackie and Zack took their time lining up their shots, making each one count. With all the trees, it made less sense to spray the entire area with bullets in the hopes of hitting something.

Zack looked through his scope and hesitated. "Son-of-a-bitch," he muttered just loud enough for Jackie to hear.

She gave him a curious look. "What is it?"

"I recognize one of the men," Zack informed her while watching Carter through his scope. He was able to advance while remaining out of Zack's line-of-sight. "We ran into him and his friends the other day."

"I'm sure we've run into a lot of these guys the other day," Jackie remarked.

"No," Zack replied. "These guys are different. Like pieces on a chessboard, you send the pawns in first. This guy--he's a bishop. He's letting the pawns clear a path for him."

"You think he's one of Vincent's men?" Jackie asked.

"I don't know, but he's definitely higher up the food chain," Zack remarked while keeping an eye on Carter through his scope. "I can't get a shot. It's like he knows I have him in my sights. He's just playing with me."

The remaining men made another attempt to advance. Zack and Jackie fired a few shots, winging two of the men. Several return shots were fired back at the tree, and a stray bullet struck the tree near Jackie's head. The bark splintered, hitting Jackie in the face, which caused her to recoil. She lost her balance, fell backward from the branch, and plummeted into the murky water below. Although no stranger to taking unexpected swims, Jackie felt terror the moment she went under the dark surface into the cold water. She knew what was down there, and, for a brief second, she attempted to see the danger coming her way. Unfortunately, the water was so murky; she couldn't see much.

Jackie no sooner hit the water when Zack yanked the Bowie knife from his boot and leaped into the water not far from her. Jackie surfaced with a gasp while her heart raced, and she immediately looked for the nearest embankment. She then saw the water crest not far from her, not needing to see the alligator to know it was coming for her. Without delay, she swam on pure adrenalin for the nearby embankment deeper within the habitat. The alligator was just about upon her when it suddenly disappeared beneath the water. Jackie heaved herself onto shore, flipped onto her backside, and saw the water churning violently beneath the surface. She looked up at the tree and realized Zack was gone. Jackie sprang to her feet and looked back at the dark water with horror, realizing Zack must have jumped in after her.

Despite the dull brown color of the churning, murky water, she saw it suddenly turn red. Jackie gasped with horror and took a step closer to the edge. The second alligator, who had been further away on land, suddenly slid into the water. It would reach her in a matter of seconds, but she couldn't just leave if there was a chance Zack was alive. Zack surfaced with a large gasp, spit out the foul water, and swam for Jackie. She reached down, caught his hand, and just about hoisted him from the water with urgency. Zack scrambled to his feet with the Bowie knife still in his hand.

"Those boys don't go down without a fight," Zack gasped while again spitting out the foul water, then looked toward the murky pond. "I lost my weapon."

"You're not going in there after it," Jackie snarled.

"That's my Honey Badger PDW," Zack informed her matter-of-factly. "I like that one."

"Too bad," Jackie huffed while clutching his wet jacket sleeve. "We have to move before that alligator's very pissed off girlfriend reaches us."

They saw someone enter the habitat with eyes on their location. Zack hurried Jackie for the nearby man-made rock formation, which provided shelter for the hippos when the sanctuary was operational. They weren't a second too soon. A bullet ricocheted off the faux stone near them as they bolted inside the shelter. Jackie and Zack took cover and removed their semiautomatics from their shoulder holsters. Both pulled the slide bolts back to drain any water that may have entered the weapons during their unexpected swim. Jackie tapped her ear transmitter and then frowned. She ripped it from her ear and tossed it aside.

"I lost communication after our little swim," Jackie reported. "We can't get any intel from the others."

Zack tapped his ear transmitter as well and shook his head. "Mine's dead too," he informed her. "Cheap crap Monroe picked up."

"Options?" Jackie asked while looking around their manufactured shelter.

Zack looked behind them and indicated the rest of the fiberglass cave. "Check for another exit," he announced. "I'll cover our asses from here."

Jackie nodded, then hurried through the fake cave. Zack looked back out the opening while remaining against the wall near the entrance. He saw one of the three familiar men from the military show. Detrick ran across the hippo habitat and ducked behind a large tree. Zack aimed his semiautomatic at the tree and kept his sights locked on it, waiting for the big man to poke his head out for a clean shot. While focused on the shot he was waiting to take, he was also listening for Jackie. He then heard the sounds of movement close to him. Zack aimed his weapon at the side of the entrance near him. Carter suddenly appeared before him and knocked the gun from his hand. The man seemed a little too arrogant with his stealthy move while simultaneously aiming his weapon at Zack. Zack swiftly struck Carter's wrist, dislodging the gun from his hand, surprising the man.

Jackie hurried along the shelter, which was more of a large corridor in a semi-circle and able to accommodate several hippos. She heard what sounded like running water and glanced at the cement floor designed to look like ground. There was a sizeable grate against the back wall. Jackie peered through the rusted grate and heard the water a little more clearly. It must have been some sort of sewer drainage system, allowing employees to hose down the shelter when necessary. She continued along the wide, fake tunnel and saw another entrance up ahead. Jackie slowed her approach and aimed her semiautomatic at the opening. She hesitated a moment, then moved alongside the entrance with the gun raised and moved closer to check the corner. Bart suddenly appeared, plowed into her, and slammed her into the opposing wall. Her gun flew from her hand and slid across the floor, stopping alongside the rusted grate. Jackie felt the pain surging through her back while gasping to catch her breath.

Bart took a step back and raised his assault rifle at the moderately stunned woman. Jackie suddenly lunged forward, grabbed the barrel in her left hand, and pointed it up in the air. As the rifle fired, she released the barrel and punched Bart in the face. He took the hit but was barely fazed. Jackie withheld her surprised gasp and immediately spun into a kick, striking his hand with the weapon. The rifle flew from his hand and slid across the fake ground. Bart sneered at Jackie and threw a punch for her face. She ducked his large fist, successfully allowing it to strike the fiberglass wall. His fist went partway through the wall from the hard hit. In the brief moment he was trapped, Jackie nailed him twice in the side with her knee, accidentally helping him dislodge his fist from the fiberglass. He was quick to swing at her. She again ducked and delivered another kick to his side.

§

Zack threw three quick, sharp blows to Carter's face, successfully knocking him back a step. Zack heard the echoing clatter of a weapon hitting the concrete floor deeper within the fake cave. Carter immediately retaliated and punched Zack in the face. Zack was slightly surprised that he was distracted enough to let Carter land a shot. When Carter smirked and threw another fast fist, Zack deflected the blow, held onto his arm, and kicked Carter in the leg. Carter just about went down to the ground. Zack maintained control over Carter's arm and gave it a healthy twist, driving Carter the rest of the way to his knee. There was a loud thud echoing from deeper within the shelter. Zack's attention seemed to stray only a split second, but that was all Carter needed to break free from the hold. Carter thrust his fist upward and nailed Zack in the hip rather than the intended groin shot. Zack was forced to release the man.

Carter swiftly sprang to his feet with a little more arrogance and threw a punch for Zack's face. Zack ducked the flying fist and sprang back up with a high kick that Carter hadn't been expecting. His booted foot connected with Carter's shoulder and knocked him back a step. Zack immediately spun into a roundhouse kick and struck Carter in the chest, throwing him against the wall with some force. Carter appeared slightly dazed and mildly concerned. Zack went for another high kick. Carter managed to duck the kick with only an inch to spare, then leaped to the ground and grabbed his discarded weapon. Zack lunged for his own weapon. As Zack sat up, Carter was already shooting while fleeing. Zack fired a shot at him, but Carter had already ducked behind a nearby tree just outside the shelter. Zack threw himself against the side of the fake cave just in time to avoid the bullet striking the wall.

§

Jackie knew she had to take the big man down while she had the advantage. She went for another kick since her fist seemed to do little more than tickle the big man. Bart managed to block her kick to his chest. She went for the return kick, connected with his abdomen, and doubled him over while again planting him against the wall. She always thought Kirk would be a bear to take down, and she realized this was a similar matchup. She seemed to be winning at the moment, but she was wearing herself down as well. She needed to disable him fast before she had nothing left. Why couldn't he be cooperative and just let her kill him? Jackie moved in for a knee kick to his side, botched the kick, and gave him the opportunity to grab her leg under her knee. He clutched her leg close to his body and attempted to throw her off balance. She was too close to him to use her leg beneath her. Jackie went for a throat punch, knowing it would be one of the few blows that would possibly disable him.

Bart caught her by the wrist, stopping her punch midair. When the big, intimidating man grinned, Jackie was somewhat panicked. A left-handed blow wasn't going to do anything to the man. Bart whipped her around, now holding her against his chest from behind, and put her in a stranglehold. Jackie clutched his thick arm while gasping for air. She wasn't moving that arm, and she could feel herself unable to catch her breath. He could just as easily break her neck, but it was possible he wanted a slower, more satisfying kill. Jackie summoned all her strength, clutched his arm, and threw herself to her knee.

Somehow, she managed to heave the large man over her shoulder and bowled him across the shelter. Bart struck the wall, landing on the rusted grate. He was only mildly disoriented and immediately saw the nearby, discarded weapon and scrambled to his knees on top of the grate.

Jackie panicked at his accessibility to the weapon and her lack of shelter. She saw his discarded rifle a few feet from her. It was her only option. Jackie threw herself into a roll across the concrete floor, snatched the rifle, and popped up into a sitting position while aiming the weapon. To her surprise, Bart was no longer there. Jackie slowly moved to her feet while keeping her weapon aimed and took a step closer to the opening in the habitat shelter. She quickly scanned the area, just in case Bart had managed to get up and take off, but she didn't see him. Jackie then saw the opening in the floor that had once contained the rusted grate. She took a step closer to the opening, switched on the scope's night vision, and aimed the rifle into the drainage sewer.

The pit was almost eight feet down, with murky brown water in the bottom. Bart pulled himself to his hands and knees within the foul-smelling, sludgy water inside the underground sewage system. Bart looked up and saw her. He moved to his feet, covered from head-to-toe in brown goo, and sneered at her.

"You bitch," he cried out in anger. "I'm going to kill you!"

Jackie smirked and lowered the rifle. "You can try," she replied, "but you might want to shower first."

She turned and headed for the opening that would take her out of the large, faux cave shelter on her quest to find Zack. She kept the rifle aimed and ready for whatever she might find. Jackie paused just before the opening, prepared herself, and spun around the corner with the rifle aimed. A man's hand grabbed the rifle barrel and slammed it against the side of the faux cave wall. Detrick aimed his semiautomatic at her face. Jackie stared down the barrel of the handgun and didn't move. He was too close and wouldn't miss if he pulled the trigger. Jackie released the rifle and kept her hands where he could see them. Detrick stared at her with some surprise and perhaps a bit of confusion. He tossed the rifle aside while keeping the gun trained on her.

"Who are you?" Detrick asked while maintaining his strange look.

Jackie's mind was racing at the question and the way he stared at her. Was it possible he'd seen her before? She didn't recognize him, but she'd crossed paths with many men, particularly former military, mercenary types, which wasn't necessarily a good thing.

"Jackie," she replied, not wanting to give up too much information.

Detrick seemed to be struggling to place the name. A strange realization suddenly crossed his face. "Remus?" he just about gasped while staring at her. "Commander Jackson Remus's daughter?"

She wasn't sure she liked her odds enough to answer the question. The wrong answer could mean a fate worse than death. Her father was a respected man, but his position in the military and with the team also brought its share of enemies who'd love to get their hands on his daughter. Silence seemed the best answer, under the circumstances. Detrick seemed conflicted and relaxed his finger on the trigger. He shook his head while seemingly cursing under his breath.

"You shouldn't be here," Detrick informed her. "If Carter finds out who you are--" His eyes suddenly widened. "The men protecting Marco--?" Detrick then tensed as if figuring it all out. "It's your father's team." He kept the gun aimed at her but with less conviction. "Jackson Remus and his team saved my life."

"You don't have to do this," Jackie informed him, hoping to return a soul to a man without one. "You don't have to do Vincent's dirty work. You can walk away."

Detrick frowned and shook his head. "It's too late for that," he replied, then relaxed and lowered his weapon. He gave a firm nod. "Consider this a free-pass."

Jackie knew he could easily kill her and took him up on the 'free-pass'. She walked past him and the murky pond, confident he wouldn't shoot her in the back. In the spirit of fair play, Jackie wouldn't take any cheap shots either, but she knew this man's fate was sealed the moment he resumed his quest for Marco.

"Hey," Detrick announced while turning his back to the pond as she passed him.

Jackie tensed and looked back at the big man, concerned he'd changed his mind about shooting her. Detrick placed his booted foot on the discarded rifle and slid it across the ground toward her.

"You're going to need that," he insisted and offered a tiny smirk. "You won't get far without it."

Jackie cautiously reached down to pick up the weapon while keeping an eye on the man before her. Just because it seemed as if he was letting her go, that didn't mean she trusted him. The brownish green-tinged water suddenly erupted behind Detrick. Jackie saw the alligator leap from the water's edge, grab Detrick's booted foot, and pull his leg out from under him. He was partially dragged into the murky water. Detrick cried out in horror while frantically grasping at nearby vegetation to keep the creature from pulling him into the water. Jackie instinctively leaped forward and grabbed his wrist. Detrick grabbed onto her while attempting to kick the alligator in the face with his free right foot. The alligator was reluctant to release his left, booted foot, and attempted to drag him into the water.

"Don't let go," Detrick cried out.

Jackie was practically on her backside while digging her heels into the soft ground just outside the pond. She was losing her footing and was slipping in the wet vegetation. A drenched and dirty Bart stumbled upon the scene, saw what was happening, and grabbed Jackie's discarded rifle. Detrick saw his comrade and indicated the alligator that he continued to kick with his free foot.

"Shoot the damned thing, Bart," Detrick cried out to his man.

Bart sneered, offering a devious smile, and aimed the rifle at Jackie instead.

Horror crossed Detrick's face. "Bart, what are you doing?" Jackie was the only thing keeping the alligator from pulling him into the water with it. "Shoot the alligator!"

Jackie looked at the man not far from them and saw he had the rifle aimed at her. She barely had time to gasp, let alone rationalize whether or not she should let go of the man. If she let go, she had no hope of escaping the shot out in the open and in her vulnerable position. A shot suddenly rang out. Bart clutched his thigh and stumbled backward partially into the water. Detrick again kicked the alligator with his free foot. The alligator released Detrick and lunged for Bart instead, grabbing onto his injured thigh. Bart cried out in pain and surprise as the alligator attempted to pull him into the water. Jackie flew onto her backside while still clutching Detrick's wrist and kept him on the embankment. Jackie looked behind her and saw Zack standing nearby with his rifle aimed at the alligator.

"Shoot it," Bart cried out in agony and panic while clutching and grasping at vegetation to keep from being pulled into the water.

Jackie pulled Detrick the rest of the way from the water and safely onto shore. The large man panted and flipped onto his back to watch the unfolding scene. Rather than shoot, Zack lowered the rifle and stared at Bart with no emotion. Bart yelled profanities at Zack as the alligator yanked him into the water.

Detrick stared at the churning water and sneered. "Dick," he scoffed in anger. He gasped several times, flexed his foot inside his moderately sliced boot, and then looked back at Jackie. "Thanks. I owe you."

"Actually, that kind of makes us even," Jackie announced with a tiny smile.

"The other one got away," Zack informed Jackie, then indicated Detrick with an untrusting nod. "Making new friends?"

"Well, you know me," Jackie replied while panting to catch her breath.

"Are you okay here?" Zack asked her while indicating Detrick.

"Yeah," she replied. "Find the other one. I'll be right behind you."

Zack nodded and headed for the habitat entrance not far from the pond. Jackie helped Detrick to his feet, letting him lean on her as they put some distance between them and the murky water. Detrick was limping badly, but his injuries weren't life-threatening. Jackie needed to get both of them away from the pond in case they had been mistaken about there only being two alligators.

§

Zack hurried across the sanctuary in the direction of the visitor's center and paused by some nearby trees. He scoped-out the cleared area in front of the main building but didn't see anyone. Once the area seemed secure, he hurried across the clearing for the visitor's center and paused before the door. As Zack opened the door, Carter suddenly lunged from the entrance with a knife in his hand and tackled him to the ground just outside the building. Carter landed on top of Zack and attempted to plunge the knife into his throat. Zack punched Carter twice in the face, knocking him off him and onto his back. Zack moved to one knee, spun from his crouched position on the ground, and nailed Carter in the chest with the heel of his boot. Carter gasped and wheezed several times while clutching his chest, severely winded from the impact. As Zack sprang to his feet, Carter flailed his arm in an attempt to reach the discarded knife. Zack kicked the knife away from his hand and stared down at the man.

"For the man giving the orders, I thought you'd be tougher," Zack remarked.

Zack heard the sound of a gun cocking and spun around just in time to see another intruder with a semiautomatic aimed at him. The man smirked as his finger tightened on the trigger. A rifle blast suddenly echoed loudly. The man's head snapped back, taking the shot directly between his eyes, and he fell to the ground. Carter scrambled to his feet, not waiting to see who came to Zack's aid, and darted inside the visitor's center. A bullet struck the doorframe where Carter's head had just been, nearly clipping him as well. Zack spun and saw Sam sitting on her horse less than fifty yards away. She lowered the automatic rifle she'd taken off Marco, smiled at Zack, and then sent her horse into a gallop away from the visitor's center. Zack snorted a tiny laugh, then turned and approached the visitor's center. He cautiously entered and looked around, but Carter was gone.

§

Vinnie, the knife, Scartelli sat reclined in the chair alongside the fireplace within the lounge with a cigar in one hand and a glass of scotch in the other. He puffed on the cigar, blowing smoke up toward the ceiling. The sound of gunfire seemed to echo throughout Vinnie's once-quiet lounge, bullets ricocheting off the marble fireplace, and men shouting profanities at one another. Vinnie seemed almost too casual, a tiny smirk on his face as if he'd been listening to a symphony of sorts. Vinnie's older henchmen, taking cover behind an antique sofa, fired at Vincent's men, who were just outside the lounge entrance. Sal and Giovanni took cover behind the large, portable bar, resting their backs against it while Giovanni's goons joined Vinnie's goons, shooting multiple rounds at Vincent's men.

Giovanni casually removed one of the bottles of brandy from the bar near where they sat and looked at the label. He then eyed Sal.

"You know, we're probably going to die here," Giovanni announced, revealing little concern.

Sal glared at his old friend and didn't appreciate his carefree attitude. "Maybe that's your intention, but I have other plans," he announced.

Giovanni shrugged and found two glasses. He opened the bottle and poured each of them a glass of brandy. As he handed one of the glasses to Sal, Sal again glared at him.

"Seriously?" Sal demanded.

Giovanni again shrugged, showing little emotion. "There's not much else we can do," he remarked. "Unless, of course, you want me to find you a baseball bat and let you have a go at them."

"Not funny," Sal scoffed.

"I thought it was." Giovanni sipped the brandy and shut his eyes, savoring it. "Oh, that's the good stuff." He then eyed Sal and gave a general nod. "Is Vinnie still alive?"

Sal glanced around the sturdy bar and eyed Vinnie, still sitting in his chair without a care in the world. Sal looked back at Giovanni and shook his head.

"Miraculously, yes," Sal replied.

"And Holden?" Giovanni asked while gently swirling the contents of his brandy snifter.

"He's probably dead," Sal scoffed, then lifted his glasses to rub his eyes. "Jackie's going to kill me."

§

Holden lay unconscious on the hardwood floor within Vinnie's game room with his left wrist cuffed to an old radiator. He'd been shot in his right shoulder, and the gash on his temple suggested he'd been pistol-whipped. His head injury seemed to have stopped bleeding, but there was still plenty of blood down the side of his face and covering his white shirt beneath his jacket. Holden slowly woke to the sounds of gunshots one room over and realized where he was and what had happened. He pulled himself into a sitting position, immediately feeling the pain in his injured right shoulder and the throbbing of his head. He looked around the room a moment, then realized he'd been handcuffed to the radiator. Holden groaned at the realization that he'd been shot, coal copped, and detained with his own handcuffs. Not his finest moment. He attempted to reach into his pants pocket with his free right hand. The gunshot wound was enough to make him cringe in agonizing pain.

Not too surprising; the keys were gone. Naturally, Vincent had taken the handcuff keys when he cuffed him. Holden groaned and took a moment to rest his head against the old-fashioned radiator. The sound of gunshots continued in the next room. With his eyes still closed, Holden suddenly smiled and snorted a laugh. He opened his eyes and slid his foot closer to him. He reached inside his shoe and removed a spare handcuff key. Keeping a spare key was something he learned after the first time he'd been handcuffed by someone he had been pursuing. One of his fonder memories of Jackie when they'd first met.

§

Vincent's four men took turns poking their heads through the lounge doorway, firing at the two sets of enforcers within the room. Both sides of the doorframe were splintered with bullet holes. None of Vincent's mercenaries seemed willing to shoot at the old man still casually reclined in his chair near the fireplace. Did Vinnie believe he was untouchable? Or did he just not care if anyone shot him in the head? Vincent paced the hallway not far from the foyer and the grand stairs, far enough from the raging war just down the hall.

"I thought you guys were tough mercenaries," Vincent boldly announced to his four men attempting to take the lounge by force. "You can't take down a couple of old bodyguards and two meatheads?"

The man closest to Vincent turned and glared at his boss. "Those old bodyguards and meatheads have guns the same as us," the man snarled with irritation. "Bullets don't discriminate." He then resumed firing into the room, alternating with his cohorts.

Vincent rolled his eyes and groaned. "Spare me the dramatics," he remarked.

"You just worry about the fed," the man snarled back at his boss.

"He's been taking care of," Vincent snapped back. "Just end this!"

The mercenary by the lounge doorway sneered and again turned to face Vincent. The hallway and foyer were empty. Vincent was gone.

The man frowned and shook his head. "Dick."

Just off the foyer, within the nearby game room, Vincent struggled against the arm wrapped tight around his neck, holding him in a chokehold. Holden sneered while applying pressure to Vincent's neck and kept his lips close to the struggling man's ear.

"You're going to listen to me, you son-of-a-bitch," Holden snarled into his ear, "or so help me, I'll snap your fucking neck."

"You're a fed," Vincent gasped while attempting to sound confident despite his obvious panic. He managed a tiny chuckle and even smirked. "You can't do anything to me. You have rules--"

Holden applied pressure to Vincent's neck, forcing him to gasp for air. "At this very moment, there are no rules," he snarled in Vincent's ear. "And, right now, being a fed only means I know how and where to hide your body." He loosened his grip just enough to let the man breathe.

Vincent gasped in an attempt to catch his breath. "What do you want?"

"I want you to listen to what I have to say, and then I want you to do what's right," Holden growled close to his ear with a rarely seen anger.

"I'm listening," Vincent announced while breathing heavily and grasping at the arm around his neck.

"The man responsible for your brother's murder struck again," Holden informed him in a less threatening tone, although he didn't lessen the pressure on Vincent's neck. "Marco has been in federal custody for the last few days. It wasn't him. He's innocent."

"Why do you care?" Vincent just about demanded despite his bad position.

"Because every hitman and mercenary on the West Coast is descending upon Marco at this very moment," Holden informed him. "My team, the ones protecting him, is in danger, and you can stop it."

"I can't stop them," Vincent declared, now seeming fearful for his life. "I don't have every hitman listed in my phone contacts. These things take time."

"We don't have time." Holden tightened his grip around Vincent's neck and forced him to gasp. "I suggest you get creative. Either you call them off, and I let you walk, or I'll snap your fucking neck. Clock's ticking."

Chapter 51

Bogart and Nevada hurried across the sanctuary with their weapons cradled in their arms, prepared for action. Monroe, Rowen, and Quinn stepped outside the old train as the two approached and looked around.

"Have you seen any others?" Monroe asked.

Bogart and Nevada shook their heads.

"I'm sure some got through, though," Bogart replied and continued to look around. "It's a big place."

"We'd better get back to operations and make sure they're still good," Monroe announced. "Ross has been unusually quiet, and that can't be good."

Rowen and Quinn's cell phones simultaneously dinged. Both men seemed oddly surprised and removed their phones. Nevada peered over Rowen's shoulder at the text on his cell phone. Her stunned look turned hostile.

"Son-of-a-bitch!" she shouted in anger.

"What is it?" Monroe asked and peered at Quinn's cell phone as well. He appeared equally shocked and turned anxious. "We need to report this."

"You take Nevada and Quinn to the clinic and check on Ross," Bogart announced, then indicated Rowen. "Rowen and I need to get to the visitor's center."

"The visitor's center?" Nevada asked with surprise. "Why would you want to go there?"

"Trust me," Bogart announced. "I know what I'm doing."
He motioned for Rowen to follow him.

§

Ross slammed and bolted the clinic door behind Beck.
Both men backed across the clinic while keeping their rifles
aimed at the door and joined Marco near the gorilla cage, which
seemed to be the securest place.

"Marco, take refuge in the gorilla cage," Ross firmly
instructed and handed Marco a semiautomatic pistol.

Marco clutched the gun and stared past the men at the
door. "How many are out there?"

"I don't know," Beck informed him. "They just plowed
down the main entrance. I didn't wait around to take a
headcount."

Marco hurried into the gorilla cage and remained just out of
sight alongside the cement block wall. They heard gunfire
coming from outside the door, but they were confident the
gunfire wasn't aimed at the door itself. Ross and Beck
exchanged confused looks.

"One of us?" Beck asked.

"I don't know," Ross replied. "I lost contact with the rest
of the team. Too much interference."

The corridor beyond the clinic door became still and quiet.
Ross and Beck toppled the metal examination table, took refuge
behind it, and aimed their weapons at the door.

"It's too quiet out there," Beck muttered.

For a moment, the silence was almost deafening. A loud
explosion suddenly shook the building, and the metal door was
blown inward, straight for the metal exam table. Ross and Beck
were thrown from the blast that rattled the entire clinic. The
cinderblock construction was the only thing that kept the whole
building from collapsing. Smoke and dust filled the large clinic
room. Carter stormed inside only a second later with his
weapon aimed. Ross lay motionless on the opposite side of the
room from the gorilla cage. Beck saw the intruder and
attempted to grab his discarded rifle while gagging on the thick

smoke. Carter shot at him, nearly hitting him. Beck rolled out of the way, without his weapon, and behind a small piece of wall. Carter fired several shots at Beck, but the bullets ricocheted off the cinder block. Carter took two cautious steps closer to where Beck had taken cover just beyond the gorilla cage.

"Come on out," Carter snarled while keeping his rifle pointed at the small wall. "I won't shoot you if you turn over Marco."

Carter heard a thump from the opposite end of the room and spun with his weapon aimed. Ross was gone! As the smoke and dust settled, Carter scanned the room with his weapon. Marco remained hidden alongside the gorilla cage wall, barely poked his head out while aiming his gun, and fired at the armed intruder. Before Carter had a chance to aim his weapon, the bullet struck his lower arm near the rifle. Although it was just a deep scratch, Carter dropped his weapon and clutched his bleeding arm. Successfully unarmed, he leaped out of the way before Marco fired the next shot. The bullet whizzed past his head, almost taking him out. Carter rolled across the floor out of Marco's line-of-sight and sprang to his feet while reaching for his holstered semiautomatic. Ross was suddenly standing before Carter and punched him in the mouth, sending him back several steps. Despite the hard hit, Carter collected himself and lunged for Ross.

Carter tackled the much older man to the floor and punched him in the face. Ross took one hard hit to the jaw but immediately shot back with a throat punch. Carter gasped and wheezed from the hit. Ross tossed the man off him and moved back to his feet with less vigor than Zack always managed. Despite gasping to catch his breath and the agony he must have been feeling, Carter managed to jump back to his feet and again charged Ross since it worked the first time. Ross seemed to anticipate the action this time. He dodged to the side and caught Carter around the neck in a chokehold. Carter attempted to break the hold, but Ross refused to release him. With some effort, Ross snapped Carter's neck. The cracking sound echoed throughout the entire room. Ross let out a groan of exhaustion and released Carter. The man fell lifelessly to the floor. Beck snatched his discarded rifle and joined Marco as he hurried for Ross, who gasped several times before straightening.

"Zack makes it look so easy," Ross announced, clearly winded from the added exertion.

They could hear more gunshots outside and the sound of movement coming from the corridor.

"There are more of them," Marco gasped with alarm. "What do we do?"

"They're already inside," Ross announced and indicated the gorilla cage. "Take cover. The exterior entrances are reinforced from the outside. There's no place left for us to go."

Ross grabbed Carter's discarded rifle, and all three men darted inside the gorilla cage behind the cinderblock wall, which would provide some safety.

§

Zack cautiously hurried through the corridor outside the sleeping quarters within the clinic building. Several men lay dead on the floor, almost certainly killed by one of their own. It was apparent Carter no longer had any use for the additional men. More of Carter's expendable men were seen up ahead near the clinic itself. A few of them spotted Zack and spun to fire at him. He fired back and leaped into a nearby, open bedroom doorway. More gunfire came from the back entrance to the sleeping quarters behind Zack. Zack poked his head out with his rifle aimed and saw Jackie firing at the men near the clinic. Zack grinned, spun, and fired at the men as well, providing cover for Jackie. She joined him in the bedroom doorway and safety.

"Where's your new boyfriend?" Zack teased.

Jackie ejected the magazine from her rifle and fished around Zack's thigh pants pocket for a fresh one. She removed the full magazine and slapped it into the rifle.

"Halfway to his parked car by now," Jackie informed him while cocking her weapon. She then nodded down the hall. "What do we have?"

"Half a dozen men outside the clinic," Zack reported. "I heard gunfire from inside the clinic, so they've already breached the barrier. We'll need to distract them."

"Okay," Jackie replied, then stepped into the doorway behind Zack and fired at the men down the hall.

Zack crouched down and fired from his lowered position. He turned his head and saw Jackie's leg was bleeding just above the knee.

"Were you shot?" he asked.

"Not now, Zack," she announced while concentrating on returning fire with the men in the hallway from her partially hidden position.

Zack removed gauze wrap from his large, leg pocket, turned in the doorframe, and swiftly wrapped her leg while she fired at the men. Jackie didn't even pay attention to Zack tending to her injury except when he tightened the wrap with a little added vigor.

She gasped slightly, looked down, and then snarled at him, "That hurt."

"That'll teach you to get injured without permission," he retorted, then secured his weapon and again returned fire down the hall.

"I'm running low on ammo," Jackie announced. "What do you have left on you?"

"That was my last magazine," he informed her. "I just have two mags left for my 9mm."

Jackie groaned with disgust and tossed the empty rifle aside. She removed her semiautomatic and remained in position without firing.

"Gotta conserve ammo," Jackie announced. "If we can get to my room, I have a few more 9mm mags."

"How about you start hitting some bad guys?" Zack snapped back. "Who the hell taught you to shoot?"

"I'm pretty sure it was you," she scoffed.

§

Bogart hurried Rowen into the visitor's center and bolted toward the welcome desk off to the right side. Rowen ran after him, keeping pace.

"Will this work?" Rowen asked while keeping an eye out for any unexpected visitors.

"It has to," Bogart replied, then slid alongside the PA system for the park and threw several switches.

There was a loud humming sound that nearly shattered their eardrums. Both men cried out with surprise as Bogart quickly adjusted the volume. They could hear gunfire close by and getting closer. Kirk and Gil were heard shouting inaudible words through Bogart's ear transmitter, which wasn't helping. Bogart did his best to ignore the idle chatter, but he was able to take away that everyone was getting low on ammo, and there were still endless bad guys in sight. The rifle fire now turned to handgun fire. Bogart moved away from the PA system and indicated the microphone to Rowen.

"Do it," Bogart announced.

§

Slade appeared from the clinic's kitchen area and shot two of the men attempting to make their way into the nearby vet's office. He approached the open kitchen doorway and saw some men by the sleeping quarters' corridor firing in the opposite direction. They were busy fending off someone else, giving Slade free access to the vet's office. Slade grabbed one of the dead men's rifles and stepped into the clinic doorway. From where he stood, the vet's office appeared to be empty. Deeper within the clinic, Ross remained hidden along the gorilla cage's edge with his semiautomatic in hand and looked at Beck, who was crouched against the wall close to his legs.

"How many rounds do you have left?" Ross whispered.

"Two," Beck replied and briefly glanced up at Ross.

Ross eyed Marco and indicated his weapon, then Beck. Marco reluctantly gave Beck his pistol.

"We need to make them count," Ross insisted.

Slade darted across the clinic and dived behind the doctor's desk. He now had a clear shot at them from his hidden vantage point. All three men leaped behind the cot, overturning it, but it wouldn't be enough.

"Hand over Marco," Slade called out while crouched behind the desk. "I'm not interested in the rest of you. No one else needs to die!"

Marco tensed at their dire situation then eyed Ross and Beck, who kept their weapons aimed across the clinic. "Let me go out there," Marco announced to them. "We're sitting ducks in here. I can buy you enough time to get one shot at him before he shoots me."

Ross and Beck eyed Marco then exchanged looks. Ross looked back at Marco. "Bad idea," Ross informed him. "We won't get much of a shot."

"He's in position to take us all out," Marco insisted, then offered a sympathetic look. "He's getting me one way or another. This is your only hope to get him. I'd rather die here than be taken to Vincent alive."

Before either man could protest, Marco stood with his hands in the air. He managed his usual charming smile and cocked his head.

"Is that you, Slade?" Marco asked almost cheerfully while moving in such a way that it would force Slade to reposition himself, possibly giving the guys a viable target.

"It's nothing personal, Marco," Slade replied while smirking, keeping his weapon trained on the man. "A bounty is a bounty."

"Can I convince you to take me in alive?" Marco asked while maintaining his smile, although it was obviously painful for him. "For old times' sake?"

"I'd love to oblige you, Marco," Slade announced. "But I'll never make it out of here with you alive."

Slade moved just enough to get Marco's head in his sights. Ross carefully aimed his weapon, needing just a sliver more to take the shot. The PA system suddenly crackled loudly, catching everyone's attention.

"This is Vincent Scartelli," the familiar voice announced over the loudspeakers, obviously coming from a cell phone voicemail. "Authorization code Alpha Bravo Foxtrot. The bounty on Marco is canceled. There will be no bounty paid on the head of Marco. That is all."

Slade had his finger tight on the trigger while holding Marco in his sights. He hesitated then removed his cell phone from his pocket. Slade pressed a button and saw the text message on his phone. There was a link to the voice message. Slade relaxed his finger on the trigger.

"Everyone relax," Slade announced, then slowly straightened from behind the desk. He replaced his weapon to his shoulder holster and held up his cell phone. "The bounty has been lifted. There's no need for further bloodshed."

Beck eyed Ross and raised an arrogant brow. "Can I shoot him?"

Ross shook his head. "No, I don't think you should," he replied. "He'll take it personally and shoot back."

Slade adjusted his jacket and offered a tiny smile at Marco. "Sorry for almost killing you," he announced. "Maybe next time." He then turned and headed for the doorway.

§

As the firing within the corridor ceased, Jackie and Zack listened to the near silence a moment, then exchanged curious looks. The remaining armed men simply turned and walked away without further conflict. It was as puzzling as it was creepy.

"What just happened?" Jackie asked, remaining rigid in the bedroom doorframe. It was difficult to trust what she was witnessing.

Zack shrugged and sighed while seeming to relax. "No bounty. They no longer have any reason to kill Marco," he announced, then considered his own words. "Or us or even each other, for that matter."

"Just like that?" Jackie asked.

"Just like that," Zack replied.

Jackie groaned while lowering her semiautomatic and shook her head. "That's messed up," she huffed.

"Well, we could declare war on them and continue the battle, if you'd like," Zack announced while raising a curious brow. "Although it might be fun, it'd probably be counterproductive and maybe get us killed."

Jackie firmly patted Zack's shoulder and smirked. "Yeah, but then that would ruin our plans for going down together in a fiery blaze of glory."

As she walked past him, Zack grinned and replaced his pistol to his holster. "I love it when you talk dirty."

§

Nevada stood with Quinn and Monroe outside the main entrance to the clinic building. She folded her arms across her chest and watched several men with their rifles slung heading from the building as if nothing had ever happened. Nevada and Quinn shared the same expressions as the other men.

"So that's all, huh?" Monroe remarked and motioned at the defeated men leaving in an orderly fashion. "They just take their toys and go home?"

"Pretty much," Quinn replied.

"There goes that bounty," Nevada scoffed in disgust. "I wasted all that money on airfare out here for nothing."

Quinn shrugged, then eyed her and grinned. "You and I could slip off to some fancy hotel for a wild weekend of fun," he announced.

Monroe stared with surprise at Quinn, possibly wondering why he himself hadn't thought to make that suggestion first.

Nevada sneered at Quinn and gave him a disgusted once-over. "There's a good chance you're still going to be shot," she snarled in response.

Monroe secretly hid his smile, having been saved the wrath Quinn was now facing.

Quinn frowned and shook his head. "You're probably the least fun lady bounty hunter out there," he remarked. "Which kind of sucks considering you're the best-looking one."

Chapter 52

Jackie's helicopter prepared for touchdown at a private airfield not far from the animal sanctuary. She set the craft down near Gil's helicopter, which had arrived several minutes earlier. Gil brought reinforcements to the remote, private airfield just in case they needed ground support before Marco's arrival. Giovanni stood just outside his sedan with his two large enforcers on either side of him. All three looked a little worse for wear after their own coup d'état. The men watched the second helicopter touch ground and then shut down. Kirk's jeep pulled up and grinded to a halt as the rest of the team piled out of Jackie's helicopter. Quinn and Rowen got out of Kirk's jeep with matching frowns on their faces. It had been a long week for everyone, and, in the end, there was no prize to be had. Kirk and the two bounty hunters joined the others by Jackie's helicopter.

Marco hurried to his father, and the two men hugged in a joyful reunion. After a brief greeting with Giovanni, Ross and the notorious mobster spoke a moment in private. Ross eyed Giovanni's facial scratches and bruises that resembled a man who'd been in a fight. Giovanni's two goons looked equally banged up.

Ross offered a tiny smirk. "Is it possible we weren't the only ones in the war zone?" he asked.

Giovanni touched his bruised face and chuckled lowly. "You should see the other guy," he teased.

Ross snorted a laugh. "I can only imagine," he muttered. "And I doubt I'd want to know."

"No, probably not," Giovanni remarked, then grinned and shrugged. "We had a little disagreement with Vincent and his Boy Scouts."

"Oh, so can I assume you're the reason Vincent called off the hit?"

"Me?" he remarked, then laughed and waved off Ross. "Nah, Sal and I hid behind the bar and got plastered. Your fed friend really came through for us. I'm not sure what he said to Vincent, but I'm pretty sure he wasn't playing good cop when he said it."

Ross stared at Giovanni and appeared somewhat surprised. "Really?" he asked and cocked his head. "Holden? He's too much of a Boy Scout for that."

"You go ahead and think that," Giovanni teased while grinning. "That fella has a trigger word, and I'm pretty sure it's 'Jackie'."

"Yeah, he's pretty fond of her," Ross teased. "Enough that he puts up with us in his life."

Giovanni shrugged. "You can't pick your family."

Back by Jackie's helicopter, Nevada shared the same, uninspiring expression as her two bounty hunter colleagues while scanning the private airport.

"Not even a cab to take me to the Colorado Springs airport," Nevada muttered and shook her head. "This has been a real kick in the ass."

Jackie moved away from her helicopter while refueling and approached Nevada. "I'm heading to the Colorado Springs Airport to meet my husband," she announced. "I'll give you a lift."

Nevada managed a moderately humbled smile. "Thanks, I appreciate that."

"Are you heading back to Maine?" Jackie then asked.

Nevada shrugged while insecurely folding her arms across her chest. "I have little choice, do I?" she muttered, then sighed.

"We always have choices," Jackie informed her, then studied her a moment as if attempting to read her emotions. "You know, you can admit you like Scorpio and Kane."

"I can't stand them," Nevada scoffed in response and immediately straightened. She then fidgeted. "I mean, Scorpio is okay. She's got a bit of a dark side to her, but Kane is too clingy and affectionate." She sneered. "It's unnerving."

Jackie stared at the hardened woman for a long moment. "Kane's a good man," she remarked gently, then hesitated before speaking what was on her mind. "You don't have to deny your feelings for him."

Nevada suddenly stiffened, looking angry and ready to strike. "I *don't* have feelings for him," she scoffed a little too quickly.

Jackie smiled and nodded. "Why don't I believe that?"

Nevada frowned and looked away. Rowen and Quinn approached Nevada, who quickly pulled herself together, once again turning stern and unfeeling.

"Kirk agreed to give us a ride to the nearest car rental dealer," Rowen informed her. "You want to hang around Colorado Springs with us for a while?"

Nevada drew a deep breath then shook her head. "No, I have someplace else I need to be," she replied.

All four watched Giovanni drive away with his son and his guards. Once again, Nevada, Quinn, and Rowen wore matching frowns.

"Life sucks," Quinn muttered while shaking his head.

Ross approached them and eyed Jackie while grinning. "How much longer?"

"Almost finished," she informed him.

Ross turned to Nevada, Quinn, and Rowen while maintaining his smile. "I appreciate your assistance back there," he announced. "You didn't have to help us, but you did. The team and I are grateful, and so was Giovanni."

Ross handed each a check. Nevada, Quinn, and Rowen looked at the checks in their hands. The name was left blank, but the checks were written out for one hundred thousand dollars each.

"Our deal with Giovanni was to keep his son alive," Ross informed them. "The team and I agreed to include the three of you in an eleven way split, more or less, of the one and a quarter-million dollars."

Nevada stared at the check then looked back at Ross with surprise. "Is this for real?"

"Yes," Ross replied somewhat cheerfully. "So I recommend you fill in your names as soon as possible."

Nevada snatched Rowen's pen from him before he could even use it and wrote her name in the blank spot on the check. She then returned the pen to Rowen.

"Look at that," Jackie announced while grinning. "You have enough money that you don't need to go back to Maine after all."

Nevada seemed to tense and shifted. "Well, there's this party going down in a few weeks," she announced, then straightened proudly and smiled for the first time. "Might be a good place to make some new connections."

Jackie smiled almost knowingly. "I hope that works out for you."

Ross handed Jackie a check that already contained her name on it, which she immediately folded and stuffed in her back pocket. He then looked around with one last check in his hand.

"Where's Zack?" Ross asked. "I thought he was coming with you."

Jackie took Zack's check from Ross and placed it with hers in her pocket. "He's on a scavenger hunt," she announced. "He'll be along in a few days with the rental car we'd left behind."

Ross suddenly groaned and shook his head. "Scavenger hunt, huh?" he remarked with disapproval. "Adding a few more weapons to his arsenal, I presume."

Jackie shrugged, almost disinterested. "I'm sure there'll be some of that," she replied, then frowned. "I just hope he's not going diving for his Honey Badger."

"You'll bring him back to the lodge then?" Ross asked.

"When he's ready," Jackie replied.

"Did you talk to Holden?" Ross asked, now curious. "Since the bounty was removed from Marco's head, does that mean they found the killer?"

"When I talked to Holden, he said the killer struck again while Marco was in our custody," she replied. "I guess that was good enough for Vincent to pull the bounty."

"So the man who killed Vinnie's grandson is still out there?" Nevada asked with some surprise.

Jackie nodded. Rowen and Quinn listened in on the conversation and suddenly perked up while straightening.

"Well, maybe we can all do this again sometime real soon," Rowen teased while grinning. He then nudged Quinn and motioned him toward Kirk's jeep.

Nevada indicated the small, private terminal building. "I'm going to hit the ladies' room and grab us some drinks for the road," she announced to Jackie. "Don't leave without me."

Jackie nodded, then glanced at Ross as Nevada headed for the terminal building.

Ross tensed while eyeing Jackie. "Rowen's not wrong, you know," he announced. "Someone out there is executing mobsters, and it's not going to end well."

Jackie nodded and released the sigh she'd been holding. "Yes, it's far from over," she replied, then offered a tiny smile. "But when that particular war breaks out, I assure you, we won't be in the middle of it next time."

"I can almost guarantee we won't," Ross teased, then affectionately hugged Jackie. He pulled away and smiled. "See you in a few weeks. Give Holden my best."

Jackie smiled and nodded.

§

The sun had set, and all seemed peaceful at the ranger's station in the woods not far from the animal sanctuary. Within the station building, Sam tossed another log onto the fire to ward off the evening chill. She gingerly rubbed her sore shoulder before moving to the nearby sofa where her blanket and romance novel awaited. Smokey could be heard snorting from outside in his paddock. Sam snatched the assault rifle she had recently acquired and headed for the door, a look of concern on her face. She unbolted the door and threw it open while aiming the weapon. Zack casually leaned in the doorway and eyed the weapon aimed at him. Sam stared at Zack a moment, smiled, and lowered the rifle.

"I was hoping you'd drop by and say goodbye before you left," she announced, then raised her brows suspiciously and with a hint of concern. "You are here to say goodbye and not to turn me in, right?"

Without a word, Zack took a step toward her, grabbed her by the back of the neck, and aggressively kissed her. Once he broke off the kiss, Sam hid her flustered smile.

"Even better," she replied and stood aside, allowing him to enter.

Zack entered the ranger's station, shut the door behind him, and tossed his damp Honey Badger rifle onto the nearby chair. Sam remained still and cautious while watching Zack as he approached her. Without warning, he swept her off her feet and carried her into the bedroom.

The End

Other books by Holly Copella!

"The Battle for Andrea Maria"

A cruise ship attack turns six survivors into overnight celebrities after they take credit for the heroic act of a stowaway who died saving them.

The cruise is just what Jess needed--a bit of harmless fun far from her daily grind. But what begins as a relaxing vacation turns into a desperate fight for her life when terrorists take over the ship and start piling up bodies. Teaming up with a mysterious stowaway, Jess attempts to send out a distress call but knows they cannot wait for help to come. If she or the few remaining passengers have any hope for survival, Jess must act now. The papers dub it "The Battle for *Andrea Maria*," but to Jess it is the moment she fought side-by-side with her enigmatic Romeo, saving the ship--and losing him. She thinks the story ends there, but really, the nightmare is just beginning...

"Insanely Deadly"

When the dead return to life, it's up to an admiral's daughter and a mildly insane, former war hero to save their small town.

Jetta Cross, a Navy Admiral's daughter, is tasked with keeping her father's comrade, a former war hero turned town crazy, grounded in the real world. Capt. John Hunter is still fighting the war in his head, where imaginary dead people are part of his world. When a viral outbreak brings about a zombie uprising, Hunter is left to his own devices. He must resume his role as a one-man commando unit in order to destroy the ravenous undead. With Hunter still fighting his own inner demons as well as the undead, the townspeople fear their zombie neighbors may not be the only threat. Stranded at the island's luxurious resort with a handful of workers, Jetta is forced to live up to her father's reputation and take charge of the deteriorating situation at the hotel. She must wage her own war against the infected before the government declares her hometown a total loss.

"Deadly Institution"

A town recluse suspected of killing his wife teams up with a young woman in order to stop a killer.

After being accused of murdering his wife, Konrad Churchill turns his back on the town that once adored him. Ten years later, he still holds his grudge and the title of the most feared man in town. With the reopening of the burned mental institution, where his wife had died, former employees are now murdered one-by-one, throwing suspicion back on Churchill. A young local reporter, Jacey, is forced to reveal her long-time friendship with the infamous recluse in order to clear his name not only in the recent murders but to exonerate him in the death of his wife as well. Will Jacey's relationship with Churchill invite the killer closer to her? Or is the killer already in her life?

"Death Displacement"

A grief-stricken man travels back in time to seek revenge on the woman who murdered his girlfriend but inadvertently falls in love with her.

Kane is about to marry the woman he loves. A few weeks before the wedding, a vindictive woman from his girlfriend's past kills her. He learns of a traumatic accident that happened five years earlier, which triggers Riley's hatred for his girlfriend. Distraught over his girlfriend's death, Kane uses an antique time machine to travel into the past in order to find and destroy the woman responsible. When he runs into Riley's younger self, he realizes she's not the monster she later becomes, and he can't bring himself to destroy her. With a little help from his oddball friend from the past, they formulate a plan to prevent the accident that sends Riley down her destructive path. Kane's plan backfires when he falls for the younger Riley. His new tortured existence is further complicated when future Riley, his girlfriend's killer, shows up with her own devious agenda that doesn't include him. Will he be able to stop the time ripple, which ultimately ends with his girlfriend's death? Or will future Riley take him out of the timeline forever--

"Dead Village"

After strange happenings isolate a small resort town from the rest of the world, nearly one hundred residents seek refuge at the closed hotel. Only eight survive the night. And that's just the beginning...

One day after the entire population of Fox Ridge Village disappears, a car wreck forces several unsuspecting crash victims to seek help at the closed summer hotel. Within the hotel, they discover the grisly aftermath of a brutal slaughter. Crash victims Vander and Devon, a reluctant clairvoyant, team up to solve the riddle of the "haunted hotel" and the mass hysteria plaguing the remaining survivors. By the time they discover the hotel's secret, they're already drawn into the hysteria. As the body count continues to climb, it's a race to isolate the source and bring everyone back to reality before they kill one another. Will Devon be able to communicate with the traumatized spirits before their fate becomes her own?

"Town Darling"

After surviving a brutal attack that claims the lives of those she loves, a young woman seeks revenge on a corrupt town.

Going back home is never easy, but for Casey, it means returning to her corrupt hometown where she barely survived a brutal attack. Accompanied by two family friends, she seeks justice for the night that destroyed her life. Her physical scars are nothing compared to her emotional ones, forcing the local sheriff to believe that the town darling is back for revenge. As the conspiracy for her revenge appears to be leading up to the coveted town fair, the sheriff is determined to stop her from fulfilling her vengeful scheme...but guilt over his role on that fateful night continues to haunt him. Will his desperate need for Casey's forgiveness be his undoing? Or will Casey's desire for revenge destroy them both?

"Basement Dwellers"

A viral outbreak at a hospital leaves a mortician, sheriff, and coroner fighting for their lives against a horde of undead and the CDC.

After a massive car wreck leaves several survivors in critical condition at the local hospital, a surgeon uses experimental drugs on his critical patients and accidentally causes a zombie outbreak. When local mortician, Lexx, receives an infected corpse as her client, she becomes stranded in the hospital basement during CDC quarantine along with the local sheriff and the coroner. The infamous surgeon struggles to find a cure for his infectious blunder by using the other survivors as test subjects. Meanwhile, Lexx and the sheriff attempt to locate his missing sister, who's stranded somewhere in the battle zone that once was the emergency room. It's a race against time and the ravenous undead. Can they survive the undead before CDC sanitizes the hospital of all infection?

"Misfits, Inc."

A seemingly ordinary, young woman meets four misfits who claim she has given them supernatural powers.

While on a business trip to a remote island paradise, a bored secretary, Hailey, has her world turned upside down when her path collides with a psychic freak, Skyler. He attempts to convince her that they had met in his dreams, and she had chosen him as one of her four mystic warriors. After Skyler foresees a woman's death, they discover an unidentified creature has killed one of the guests. They are joined by a lounge pianist and a rich playboy, who also claim they had met her in their dreams. If Skyler's prophecies are genuine, the evil entity controlling the ravenous creatures needs to destroy Hailey to ensure its survival. Reluctantly accepting her fate, Hailey has to locate the last and most powerful of her chosen warriors, The Guardian. Their fate is in doubt when The Guardian turns out to be a self-absorbed, former cat burglar with a bad attitude. Can Hailey turn her company of misfits into an elite team of mystic warriors? Or will The Guardian's secret agenda destroy them all?

"Deadly Institution 2"

When blackmail turns into murder, a young woman finds herself caught in the killer's crosshairs.

The small town of Stony Ridge is no stranger to scandal and persecution of the innocent. When a brutal killing shakes the town's prestigious country club, Jacey McMurray seeks help from a self-proclaimed vigilante, Konrad Churchill. As her professional and personal worlds collide, Jacey fears the stress of the country club killings have finally taken their toll on Churchill. Can a stressed out vigilante stop the killer before he strikes again?

"Witness Protection"
Also available in audiobook!

After witnessing an execution, a resourceful young woman attempts to disappear while being pursued by a hitman and a handsome federal agent.

A helicopter pilot, Jackie Remus, reluctantly agrees to go on a date with one of her clients, but her date is unexpectedly cut short when she witnesses a man being murdered. After narrowly escaping with her life, she is placed into protective custody. When the safe house is breached, Jackie makes a daring escape from both the hired killers and the handsome FBI agent, who wants to return her to protective custody. With a little help from her sly and crafty friend, Monroe, Jackie is convinced she can disappear until the trial. While on her journey to meet with her friend, she solicits help from a few shady but lovable characters along the way. Although she manages to stay one-step ahead of the hired killers, the federal agent remains in hot pursuit. Will Jackie reach Monroe before she's captured by the FBI and returned to protective custody? Or will the hired killers silence her first?

"Unconditional"

A young woman puts her life on hold to care for an unstable, highly skilled combat soldier, who believes someone is trying to kill him.

A botched military coup leaves a team of elite fighters injured with one clinging to life in a coma. When Harlan wakes from his coma, he's left with no memory of his past life. His commander's daughter, Indy, takes it upon herself to care for the fallen war hero. She's challenged with more than just his physical care as she combats with not only his memory loss but also his newly found desire for her. His infatuation with her becomes the least of her worries when he sinks back into his role of a combat soldier. Believing his life is in danger, his fighting skills surface, turning him into an unpredictable and dangerous man. Will his memory return to him before Indy is forced to commit him? Or will he finally find his nemesis, "the coyote", and possibly claim the life of an innocent person?

"The Pen Pal"

In order to save her friend, she must enter the mind of a serial killer.

When her best friend is abducted, no one believes Jolynn saw it in a psychic vision. With nowhere to turn, Jolynn reluctantly joins Agent Harris Slade and his team on their hunt for a sadistic serial killer known only as "The Pen Pal". Finally confronted with the killer, Jolynn realizes she must enter the mind of the psychopath in order to stop the brutal killings. But when her vision reveals a particularly disturbing death, can Jolynn sacrifice her lover for her friend?

"Witness Protection 2"
The Return of Whiskey Tango Foxtrot

Believing she holds the clue to millions in missing laundered money, a young woman is placed into the protective care of a former Navy SEAL team.

Feeling sorry for her recently separated co-worker, Leeann invites Wiley to join her and her friends on their night out. Little does she know that finding her co-worker murdered is just the beginning of her nightmare. Leeann unknowingly holds the key to fifty million dollars in potentially laundered mob money. With hired killers pursuing her, the FBI places her into a different kind of protective custody. Former Navy SEAL team Whiskey Tango Foxtrot reunites to keep Leeann alive at their secret hideaway. What should be an easy assignment takes an unscheduled turn when secrets, lies, and betrayal threaten to derail their mission. Is the team prepared for a war on their own doorstep? Will Leeann's misguided trust endanger the lives of those sent to protect her?

"Witness Protection 3"
Alpha Mike Foxtrot

A helicopter pilot risks her life to help a team of retired Navy SEALs rescue two girls from a killer.

When former Navy SEAL team Whiskey Tango Foxtrot asks for a simple favor, Jackie reluctantly offers her air-taxi services. What could go wrong? What begins as a search and rescue for two girls turns into a fight for survival against a heavily armed drug cartel. Wanted by the law with the cartel in hot pursuit and their home base breached, the team is forced to call in a favor from a questionable ally. Unfortunately, their new safe house isn't what it seems. Without knowing who the real enemy is, can Jackie and the team save their young witnesses from the hands of a killer?

"Already Dead"
Supernatural Collection

From the already dead to the undead. Three supernatural tales of "things that go bump in the night".

"Bloodletting" - A vampire themed resort allows guests to *participate* in their Bloodletting Ritual to celebrate the island's legendary vampires.

"Reaper of Souls" - A young woman must outwit an evil sorcerer in order to save her brother or become one of his minions forever.

"Already Dead" - When Flight 220 crashes, ten passengers make it to an isolated island, but only one man lives to tell the lie.

"Witness Protection 4"
O-Dark-Hundred

A simple assignment turns deadly when a retired Navy SEAL team uncovers a plot to kill a notorious mob boss.

When Whiskey Tango Foxtrot embarks on a simple stalking case, they're not prepared for a trip to a private island paradise owned by an infamous mobster. With one of their own suffering from traumatic head injuries, the team is left scrambling to decide what is real or imagined. The situation escalates even further when they uncover an assassination plot where everyone is a suspect. Now targets themselves, can the team survive their trip to paradise?

"Witness Protection 5"
Outside the Wire

After suffering several casualties on their last assignment, a retired Navy SEAL team discovers their misery is just beginning.

When Whiskey Tango Foxtrot returns home after suffering a devastating loss, they're hit with even more bad news regarding the rest of their team. Their grief is cut short when they discover their names are all on the same hit list. Hunted by relentless assassins, the scattered team must decide whether to remain safely hidden or find the man who put the price on their heads. Against the wishes of her teammates, Jackie strikes out on her own in order to save a friend who wants her dead. In a kill or be killed situation, will Jackie's emotions finally betray her?

"The Murder of Emily Fisher"

After finding their favorite teacher murdered, the lives of two teenage girls are forever changed.

Everyone loved Emily Fisher. While walking home one afternoon, two teenage girls, Sidney and Trisha, stumble upon a gruesome murder scene. The brutal murder of Emily Fisher, a young, attractive schoolteacher, shocks the small town of **Marilina**. After graduation, Sidney moves far away from the memories of the small town while Trisha retreats deeper into denial. Eight years after the murder, Sidney receives a desperate call from her childhood friend, forcing her to return home. Trisha believes Emily's killer was falsely accused and she manages to turn the entire town against her while attempting to prove it. When Trisha receives a death threat, Sidney realizes there may be some credibility to her friend's wild accusations. Is Trisha's mental breakdown a result of childhood trauma? Or is the real killer actually attempting to silence her? In order to save her friend, Sidney must answer the eight-year-old question. Who murdered Emily Fisher?

"Once Upon a Disaster"

A young homicide detective finds herself at the mercy of a hitman in the aftermath of an earthquake

While investigating the murder of a hitman, Detective Jade Wesson pursues a lead connecting the dead man to a break-in at a computer programming company. She's drawn into the world of nightclub owner and front man for the mob, Cody Riley. Her investigation keeps pointing to Cody's right-hand man and possible hitman, Vahn Lott. Despite her efforts to keep her investigation on track, Vahn has plans of his own for the attractive detective. When an unprecedented earthquake rocks their east coast town, Jade must put her life in Vahn's hands if she wants to survive. Can she trust a man who might be the killer she's hunting?

"Awaken the Dead"

A grieving innkeeper struggles to keep her haunted hotel out of foreclosure.

After losing her parents in a suspicious boating accident, Harley Brandon is determined to keep the family hotel out of foreclosure. Unfortunately, the hotel ghosts have other plans. Built with tainted money, the century old Horizon Hotel thrives on a tradition of murder, scandal, and suicide. As the paranormal activity increases to alarming levels, Harley discovers the truth about the hotel and its residents. Can Harley save her friends from the hotel's frightening hidden secrets?

"Castle Bloodshed"
Murder Collection

From a deadly island paradise to haunted castles. Three novella length tales of murder, mystery, and malicious intent.

"Castle Bloodshed" – A tour of Wesley Castle turns into a fight for survival as six stranded tourists discover the haunting secrets within the castle walls. A mystery writer teams up with an uptight butler in order stop a killer who may already be dead. Novella length paranormal murder mystery.

"Fleshies" – Is Uncle Rutger crazy? Five years ago, four business partners died within their newly purchased, fixer-upper castle. Their bodies were never found. The surviving partner, Rutger, claims a demon keeps him as its slave. Rutger's nephew schemes to save his uncle by sacrificing the lives of a group of stranded motorists and a high-profile novelist. Novella length supernatural murder mystery.

"Demon Island" – A group of strangers are invited to a remote island for the reading of a will. The guests soon discover they were brought to the island to be executed one-by-one. It's up to a private detective and a tenacious young woman to solve the murders and find a way to escape paradise. Novella length murder mystery.

"Brighton Island"

When a psychic visits a haunted island mansion, he inadvertently awakens the ghosts' tortured souls.

Something's not right with Simon. When Jacklyn brings her eccentric friend to her uncle's island mansion, she didn't expect him to slip into psychic overload. As Simon attempts to solve a decade-old, double homicide, Jacklyn is confronted with the possibility that she could be next to join the mansion ghosts. When they find themselves stranded on the secluded island, her Uncle Hyland wages his own war to save them from a flesh and blood killer. Will her uncle's "shock and awe" military tactics save them or get them killed? Can Simon bring peace to the tortured souls or unexpectedly join them?

"A.L.F. Resort"

A fantasy vacation turns into a nightmare when the resort's artificial life forms are compromised.

Welcome to A.L.F. Resort where you can live out your fantasies with safe, state-of-the-art artificial life form robots! When a young journalist and a photographer are sent to A.L.F. Resort to do a story for their magazine, Shay and Becka believe they've hit the jackpot of all work-cations. The engineers pull out all the stops to make their fantasies memorable. Unfortunately, the newly designed A.L.F., the Gen X, is smarter than his programming and creates havoc within Shay's fantasy. A computer malfunction removes their safety inhibitors and the A.L.F.s play out their own hostile fantasies. Zombies, bikers, and mobsters run amuck, turning fantasies into nightmares. Shay gets more of a story than she anticipates, but will she survive long enough to write it?

"Jungle Princess"

While stranded on a prison island, a young woman discovers a creature of "unknown" origin.

After their cruise ship sinks, Alex and two of her shipmates are stranded on a deserted, tropical island. Unfortunately, the castaways soon realize they're not alone. They discover an abandoned prison with over two dozen inmates living on the island's south side. While avoiding the prison on the far side of the island, Alex discovers a strange but loveable creature of unknown origin. When one of her fellow castaways is in trouble, Alex reluctantly seeks help from the prisoners. After the brutal murder of several inmates, their questions surrounding the abandoned prison are about to be answered. What really killed over one hundred prisoners? And is it still out there?

"Murder in Wax"

A series of brutal murders plague a quiet farming community when beautiful women audition for the same acting job.

While all the young women in town are fighting over a once-in-a-lifetime acting opportunity, Devon Vincent is excited about her new job at the local wax museum. Although supportive of her friend's acting aspirations, Devon has a hard time understanding the rivalry among the women in town. When the aspiring actresses are brutally murdered one-by-one, Devon fears her friend may be the next victim. Devon finds herself in the middle of a murderous revenge plot that leads back to the wax museum's doorstep and possibly implicates her boss as the killer. Will Devon's newly found feelings for her boss bring a killer closer to her? Or is the killer already in her circle?

"Witness Protection 6"
Alpha Dogs

An easy rescue turns into a wild ride for retired Navy SEAL team Whiskey Tango Foxtrot when everyone wants to kill their client.

It was a simple task. Rescue a young woman from her mob boss father-in-law. Little did Jackie and company realize that rescuing the young woman was the easy part. Keeping her alive would be a massive undertaking, especially when everyone wants a piece of the mafia heiress. The team fights for survival against their toughest adversaries yet. How many innocent people must die in order to save one woman? Can the team survive the ultimate battle between mercenaries and assassins?

"Midnight Requisition"

A series of brutal murders leaves a distressed young woman on a hunt for a killer.

When they were just babies, Scorpio and her twin brother, Kane, tragically lost their parents under mysterious circumstances. Refusing to accept his father was dead, Kane set off on a mission to find a man he'd never met. A home invasion gone wrong leaves Scorpio grieving the loss of those she loves. Out of the tragedy of her loss, two fallen heroes are thrust upon her. Scorpio soon realizes someone wants her dead and the killer may already be in her circle. As her entire life unravels in a web of betrayal and lies, can Scorpio trust her new, slightly questionable friends?

"Jumpers"

When a cruise ship is exposed to a deadly virus, the fate of the world rests in the hands of a lounge dancer and a conman.

An infectious outbreak threatens the passengers and crew of the "Queen Anita" and the entire world if the virus makes it back to civilization. Lounge dancer, Maxine, must find a way to prevent the destruction of the world, but in order to do that, she needs to trust a conman with unique insight into the virus.

"Until Death"

Liars, cheaters, blackmail and murder. It would be a wedding no one would forget.

Despite knowing her father's making the biggest mistake of his life, Raina Steele reluctantly attends his third wedding. What should have been a boring reception turns into a web of lies, betrayal, and murder. With no one above suspicion, Raina puts aside her feud with the arrogant yet insanely handsome butler in order to catch the killer before he finds his next victim. With a murderer waiting to strike and lives hanging in the balance, the real question remains...the bride is wearing white?

"Tainted"

What happens at the Dark Forest Hotel, stays at the Dark Forest Hotel...for all eternity.

What secrets surround Dark Forest Hotel? After her parents die under mysterious circumstances, sixteen-year-old Jeri escapes foster care and seeks refuge at a "closed for the season" hotel. Over the next six years, Jeri graduates from teenage runaway to the hotel's assistant general manager. When she learns a convention is secretly held every year in her absence, she demands answers from her boss, friends, and co-workers. After getting conflicting stories, Jeri sets out to discover the truth. She's suddenly thrown into a horrifying new world where vampires and vicious creatures are craving her virgin blood. After six years of everyone lying to her, is there anyone she can trust?

"Cemetery Stalkers"
Horror Collection

Four tales of horror from flesh eating alien monsters to blood sucking vampires.

"Night Creatures" – When a rescue party becomes stranded on an abandoned cruise ship, they discover the terrifying secret unleashed from the cargo hold. What starts out as a rescue mission rapidly deteriorates into survival as the small group is hunted by a frightening creature with a taste for human flesh. Novella horror book.

"Ravenous" – After escaping a carjacking in the back woods, a young woman seeks refuge in a mysterious mansion with a terrifying secret. Despite promises of a ride to town in the morning, she's convinced she's being held prisoner by a cult leader. Short paranormal story.

"The Feast" – Five years ago, a killer went on a murderous rampage at the church picnic. Despite eyewitness accounts of a non-human killer, the local law refused to believe the town's citizens. When a group of teenagers stumble upon the contained remains of the killer, they unwittingly set him free to continue his terror upon the small town. Novella length paranormal book.

"Cemetery Stalkers" - When 'The Reaper' stalks a cemetery, death follows. Following a series of bizarre incidents in the cemetery, a young woman fears for the safety of her friend, who lives in the middle of spook central. Short horror story.

"Midnight Requisition 2"
Amateur Night

A brother and sister duo team up to catch a potential kidnapper.

After finally reuniting with her not-so-dead brother, Scorpio and her friends are taunted into helping him with his new case. A wealthy cattle rancher believes someone wants to abduct his daughter, but the team suspects her ex-boyfriend is pulling off an elaborate scheme to win her back. What appears to be a slice of paradise in the Colorado Mountains turns out to be a venomous snake pit filled with lies, lust, betrayal, and murder. Surviving the depraved family becomes the least of the team's worries when a botched kidnapping turns into murder.

"Witness Protection 7"
Bravo Foxtrot

An Army deserter on the run brings mayhem to a retired Navy SEAL team when his teenage daughter is caught in a mercenary's cross-hairs.

A weekend of fun turns into a race for survival as Monique and Colleen's surrogate big brother, Bogart, rescues the girls from mercenaries hunting Colleen's Army deserter father. With the girls safely stashed at their Colorado hideaway, trouble brews when the team discovers Colleen's father was framed by his former commander over a stolen, high-tech weapon. In order to clear Colleen's father and bring him home, the team must fight one of their toughest advisories yet...a high-ranking military officer with countless mercenaries and the U.S. military behind him.

"Witness Protection 8"
Midnight Requisition

A brother and sister duo finds themselves on an explosive collision course with a team of retired Navy SEALs.

Obsessed with the belief that his father is still alive, Kane Wayland embarks on a foolhardy mission to confront the elusive, former Navy SEAL, Zack Kinsley. Despite heavy protests, Kane's sister, Scorpio, joins him on his quest. The disastrous "reunion" comes with a steep price that none are prepared to pay. With the haunting reality of the botched mission, Midnight Requisition, still looming over each of them, can the two teams pull together in time to prevent another tragedy?

"Midnight Requisition 3"
Circular Run

A brother and sister reopen a hotel with a tainted history only to discover its past refuses to stay dead and buried.

Scorpio and Kane Wayland finally realize their dream of reopening their grandfather's cliffside hotel in Maine. With the hotel's checkered past behind it, the relaunch is a dream come true. Unfortunately, history has a habit of repeating itself. When guests mysteriously vanish, the hotel's somewhat seedy clientele are all suspects. In order to save their hotel, Scorpio and Kane must stop a killer. When your guests are mercenaries, bounty hunters, and mobsters, who can you trust?

"Raven Force"

An inn keeper becomes involved in a game of espionage after picking up a mysterious hitchhiker.

After surviving a nightmare of a date, Maxine Croft didn't think her evening could get any worse...until she nearly hits a stranger on a dark back road. This unprecedented meeting would turn Max's world upside down as she's thrust into a world of murder, corruption, and deception within her own backyard. As she gets in deeper with an elite, special task force, Max inadvertently puts her sisters' lives in danger. Will Max and her sisters become just more "collateral damage" to facilitate the team's mission?

"Witness Protection 9"
S.N.A.F.U.

A notorious mob boss turns to a retired Navy SEAL team to keep his son alive.

They were made an offer they couldn't refuse. When his son is accused of murdering mobsters throughout Colorado, Giovanni turns to the retired Navy SEAL team of Whiskey Tango Foxtrot to keep his boy alive and prevent a war between the "families". With the mobster's son in the crosshairs of every hitman and bounty hunter on the West Coast, Jackie and the boys need to find Marco and go completely off-grid. But is the team risking their lives to protect a serial killer?

ABOUT THE AUTHOR

Holly Copella has been writing since the age of twelve when her frustration at a book's poor plot drove her to author her own story. Over the last decade, she's written a number of screenplays, some of which she's now adapting into novels. Her fascination with zombies and other darker material lends an edge to her writing, which tends to lean toward horror. As a fan of Agatha Christie, she appreciates the craft of a good plot and the importance of creating significant characters.

Hailing from Pennsylvania, Copella lives in the Endless Mountains on a farm with her rescue horses and other animals. In addition to writing and reading fiction, she enjoys riding horses and traveling to Las Vegas and Disney World.